AGE OF ORDER
By Julian North

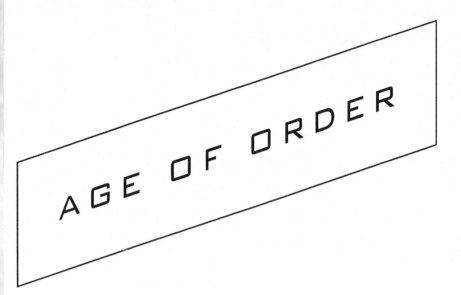

AGE OF ORDER

JULIAN NORTH

For centuries we have been building a civilization of Gold and Steel! What has it given us? Peace? Understanding? Happiness?

METROPOLIS

CHAPTER

ONE

A gunshot pierced the night.

A hollow ring echoed in its wake. The sound was familiar: the bullet had struck the impenetrable armor of an enforcement drone. The noise declared that anyone within earshot should flee the tattered streets. Most of the denizens of the barrio heeded the warning. A few did not. I joined the tide of those that ran.

The machine rolled onto the avenue like a wolf among sheep. Flashing globes scrutinized the scene beneath the drone's rotating turret, an artificial gaze seeing, recording, targeting. Caterpillar-tracked wheels dragged the metal monster's alloy chassis across the cracked asphalt, its bulk brimming with spray guns, antennas, jammers and the devil knew what else.

"YOU ARE ORDERED TO CLEAR THE STREETS AND RETURN TO YOUR HOMES," commanded a reverberating voice. "THE FIVE CITIES PROTECTION AUTHORITY HAS AUTHORIZED THE USE OF CORRECTIVE FORCE TO RESTORE CALM TO THIS AREA."

Another machine appeared behind the first, a bitter twin of its companion. A dozen rays of light flickered from the monstrosities, forming a latticework of ominous crimson. A beam grazed my back. It caused a hint of heat on my spine, but a torrent of terror in my heart. The warning was clear: *We know who you are, Daniela Machado. You are dead if we wish it.*

I ran faster, cutting in front of the ragged shell of a man galloping beside me. He was a dweller of the barrio: hopeless eyes, gaunt arms, and a torn, sleeveless undershirt. I dashed across the street, putting his body in the path of the finder beam that had glued itself to my backside. I felt guilty about it. But people needed me. That was life in my part of the Five Cities.

"*Puta*," he shouted when he realized what I'd done. He reached for my mane of ink-dark hair, its mass woven into a tight tail behind my head, but only his fingertips brushed against me. I was always fast—faster than anyone else on my school's track team. Faster even than the boys. Long legs and a lean frame helped.

I dashed towards the dilapidated collection of storefronts hugging the fringes of the worn avenue, the rusted metal gates firmly closed, lean-to homes piled on their concrete roofs. Makeshift cardboard dwellings crowded the sidewalk. I ran for one of the lightless alleys between the buildings. Lurkers lived in those narrow corridors as surely as rats lived in the sewer, but I'd rather face them than the machines. I leaped towards the darkness.

A finder beam latched onto me as I sailed through the air, the comparative safety of the alley as tantalizingly close as candy in a shop window. I imagined the tight little dot on my leg, hot and hungry. I could almost touch the alley wall. But not quite. The hulking metal slave fired.

A correction pellet sliced through the fabricated leather of my sneaker and bit into my flesh. The force of the impact was enough to screw up my balance too. I landed on one foot instead of two, falling forward. Chewed-up concrete surged towards me. I sacrificed my right palm and left elbow to protect my head, and the viser strapped to my left forearm.

I scrambled to my feet and ran down the alley, my jaw clenched, but the pain wasn't what was bothering me. I told myself that my shoe had blocked a lot of the pellet. That I probably hadn't gotten hit with a full dose. That what was coming wouldn't be that bad.

Liar.

Blood seeped from the gashes on my hands and arm, as I half-ran, half-stumbled through the narrow passage. Screams followed in my wake. Frail hands grabbed my ankles and legs. The fingers were weak, skeletal things, their owners little more than hollow shells of skin and bone. Still, they were dangerous in numbers.

I jumped like a hurdler whenever one of them came close, knowing that the pain in my foot would be nothing compared to what I would feel if I stumbled amid a nest of lurkers, inhuman and hungry. The air stank and the ground was slick from substances I didn't want to contemplate. I had run my share of track meets in horrid conditions, but nothing like this. I told myself this was still just a race. If I won, I got to stay alive.

My good foot slipped just as I reached the end of the miserable alley. I should have fallen, but somehow I didn't. My blood went icy cold, the way it does at the end of my track meets when someone is pushing hard from behind, when I call upon that place within me for extra strength. Everything slowed down, and the world came into tight focus. My injured foot planted on dry, solid ground, enabling me to keep my balance. I twirled awkwardly, feeling more like an acrobat than a runner, but it worked. I made it through.

Riverdale Jungle greeted me in all its sordid glory. The shacks, tents, shipping containers and abandoned automobiles of the sprawling squatter colony extended from the remains of Ewen Park onto the ruined asphalt of Riverdale Avenue like a tumor, covering the streets where vehicles had once roamed.

The whole place was shadows and shades of dark, except for the fires that burned in scorched metal garbage receptacles. The one nearest to me still had the words "New York City" visible on its exterior. Ancient history. People stood about, anxious and wary. They must have heard the shots and the screams, but the machines had not come here. Not yet.

I stole a quick glance at my viser, its flexible circuitry curled around my forearm like a large bracelet, the edge of its display extending into the lower part of my palm. Its fluorescent glow reassured me that my sacrificial fall had not been in vain—it still worked, although the signal was being jammed. I didn't have anyone to ping anyway. I flicked a finger at the device, my movement instructing it to go completely dark.

I waded into the labyrinthine shanty town, willing myself to walk rather than run. I tried not to show my limp. The place stank of poverty and seethed with anger. I wouldn't normally dare walk through here by myself, even with the repulse spray I had in my pocket. The calculating stares of predators followed me. My ankle felt like it was trying to escape the skin around it. Running on Sunday wasn't going to be easy, but losing my undefeated racing record would hurt worse. If my fool of a brother had been around, I'd have kicked him in the place where he did most of his thinking. Him and the other jack-A's who'd brought the Authority's metal enforcers here.

I reached the edge of the camp without being challenged. Relieved, I hurried across the narrow street just beyond its perimeter. I didn't need to turn around to know that someone was following me. Call it my spider-sense. A few people ran down the avenue ahead, fleeing the enforcers. The footsteps behind me drew closer.

I took off at my best speed.

"*Perra!*" I heard in my wake, along with a few curses that made that one seem tame. English, Barriola, and Spanish. Excellent. I preferred my muggers to be of the polyglot variety.

They gave chase. A glimpse over my shoulder revealed two guys, around my age, dressed in dark hooded sweaters. They could have been students at my high school, although I doubted they had the tax receipts for school if they lived in the Jungle. Both ran hard, but they had no form. Definitely weren't on a track team. Any other night I could've dusted them, but not tonight. I ducked around the corner onto a larger avenue. There were a few battered cars on the road, old gas models, groaning as they spewed filth into the air. A couple of people ran along the sidewalks. No one who was going to help me. Blood looked out for blood in Bronx City, and no one else.

I pushed myself hard down the avenue, its sidewalk battered but also long and clear. My foot had gone numb—early effects of the correction compound. The calm before the storm.

My pursuers were gaining on me. If I kept up this pace with no feeling in my foot, I was going to lose a lot more than my viser. I clutched the repulse spray in my front pocket, reassured by its cool, metal surface. The cylinder-shaped dispenser blended into whatever surface it touched. It was California tech—precious and illegal. My brother, Mateo, claimed that even the best Manhattan weapon scanners couldn't detect it. He had missed my sixteenth birthday party, but had woken me late that night to give it to me. It was the best gift I had gotten.

A hand reached for my back. Fingers scraped my shirt but couldn't get a hold. Decision made.

I spun around using my good leg as a pivot, spraying as I came about. I nailed them both, coating their faces in translucent liquid. The spray took only a second to work. Their hands flew to their faces, first in surprise, then in horror. I didn't get to enjoy the moment. I'd let them get too close. The shorter of the two slammed into me. He whirled in agony even as our bodies came down in a twisted pretzel onto the pavement. My satisfaction at his pain didn't make the fall hurt any less. He stank of sweat and sizzling skin and the streets. Shortie was only about five foot one—a full seven inches shorter than me—but he had a sturdier frame. Some distant corner of my mind added a scraped knee to my growing list of injuries. I scrambled to my feet as the dubious gentlemen from the Jungle squirmed. As they writhed on the ground, I stomped on Shortie's knee to repay him for the tumble. His scream sounded like justice.

I limped towards home through mostly deserted streets. Sirens and screams from nearby provided the adrenaline I needed to keep going. Sweat dripped down my face; my throat burned. After a few more blocks, my vision began to blur. Perhaps from the pain, perhaps from the correction serum in my body. I wasn't going to make it. If I collapsed outside, I wouldn't be getting up again.

Time to visit a friend.

I stumbled towards a low-rise tenement that resembled every other in the neighborhood: neglected, crumbling, depressing.

"'Jes, sista'?" came a mocking voice from behind the rusted gate pulled in front of the doorway. Pele's ugly mug of a face appeared before me. He wore a shiny-looking red beret, probably in homage to some military type he had seen on the net sims. It looked ridiculous, particularly when matched with his ratty shirt and torn jeans.

"Just open up," I said through gritted teeth.

"I'm not sure Kortilla can play right now. Enforcers out there, ya' know?" A blackened front tooth made his grin even less charming than it would have been otherwise. He made a show of tapping his viser, shaking his head in mock sadness. "The net is down. Please come back later. *Gracias.*"

I rolled my eyes. I had played this idiotic game with him countless times. No one else in the building wanted guard duty in the evening. It was hard to believe this guy was going to graduate high school next year.

"Pele, now." I hoped he caught the warning in my tone.

"What the magic word?" My fist couldn't fit through the gate. Probably a good thing.

"I'm hit," I told him, the admission more painful than my ankle.

"Corrected?" His grin vanished. The gate opened. I hurried in and Pele locked the portal behind me.

"Ya' should've told me, little Dee." He had the grace to look sheepish.

I ground my teeth. I didn't want sympathy, particularly from the likes of Pele. I tried to walk across the cracked checkerboard plastika floor to the tattered stairwell without limping, but didn't quite succeed.

"Daniela, wait!" He sounded almost desperate. I made the mistake of turning.

"I'll buzz you in," Pele proclaimed, theatrically pressing one of the rectangular buttons that had once opened an inter-com channel to the upstairs apartments, but hadn't worked in decades. That stupid black-toothed grin returned.

I shook my head and headed up the stairs. Even without lighting, I could usually navigate these steps with the same confidence I had in finding my way to the bathroom at night. But I didn't usually feel like I'd been run over by a truck. I flicked a finger to switch my viser back on, hoping for some illumination. It didn't work. I must've busted it when Short-ie knocked me down. Losing my viser was worse than being punched in the gut. Now I truly was lost in the dark. I could just make out the faint light of a stair dweller's tent on the first-floor landing. It was enough to get me up the first flight of steps. The old woman living inside, Granny Lupo we called her, peeked out at me as I passed, suspicion on her shrunken, toothless features.

I wasn't sure how long it took me to climb all three flights, hugging the railing and trying not to provoke any of the terri-torial squatters living in the stairwell. I staggered onto the third floor landing like a sick pilgrim seeking relics.

Before I could knock on the drab olive door, a whirlwind of Latina energy bounded out to greet me. Boasting a sensuous mane of midnight curls, shining round eyes and enviable curves, Kortilla Gonzales looked as different from me as the sky from the earth: all flesh and flash. Her eyes sparkled with a life that not even the best Manhattan alterator could emulate. She grabbed me in an embrace that made it feel like it had been a year since we had last seen each other, rather than twelve hours. I squeezed her back harder than usual.

Kortilla pulled back to study my eyes, but kept her hand wrapped around mine. "What happened?"

"Apart from my brother and his friends bringing the goon squad home, getting hit with a correction pellet and breaking my viser? I'm rocking." The words tasted pathetic.

"Come in, *hermana*." She slung an arm around my waist, intending to support my weight.

"I got it," I assured her. Kortilla pursed her lips, but withdrew her arm.

The Gonzales residence felt more like home than my actual home. It was three rooms, a worn couch, an old table, beds, and some rickety chairs, but that was plenty. Her parents made me imagine what it might have been like if mine were still alive. Her two surviving older brothers were enough like Mateo to give me heartburn. I might have cried more than Kortilla at her eldest brother Francis's funeral, because I could not stop imagining Mateo in that coffin. Blood protects blood, and these people could have mine if they wanted it. I forced a smile as I entered. Elena Gonzales rose from the well-worn couch to greet me with a grin so warm it made me forget how badly I hurt. Kortilla's thick-chested father raised a glass in a mock toast at my entrance, while her brothers shouted my name in greeting. For a moment, I felt safe, even as a mountain of woe teetered over me.

"Daniela! What has happened to you?" Ms. Gonzales asked while simultaneously planting two firm kisses on each of my cheeks. She smelled of too much perfume, but it had stopped bothering me years ago.

Kortilla gave her mother a firm, "*Mamá*" accompanied by a hard stare. Ms. Gonzales retreated with a concerned frown. I let Kortilla lead me away. As the only daughter, Kortilla enjoyed the privilege of her own room, window included. Her parents shared the other, while her brothers made do in the living room when they were around. Kortilla shut the door behind us.

"Sit," she commanded, pointing at the bed. She disappeared outside, reappearing with a few basic first aid necessities that she applied to my superficial wounds. The real injuries were not so easily mended.

"Where's Mateo?" Kortilla's eyes squinted with concern.

"I'm not his keeper," I said, glancing down at my busted viser.

"No, you're his little sister, and that's an even higher rank." She studied my face for a moment. "He went to Manhattan." It wasn't a question.

I nodded, my eyes downcast. "Some pastor led a march to the bridge. Maybe a thousand people from a couple of the churches came out to protest. The usual gripes: power cuts, dirty ration water, whatever. Mateo said *los richos* couldn't hear them. So he and a few dozen roving idiots—*Los Corazones* or whatever they call themselves—decided to ride some gas motorbikes into Manhattan. They must've run the toll gates." I sucked in a deep breath. "Damn that jack-A. He and the rest think they can make the highborn give a crap. They think if they yell loud enough, someone will listen. As if raw fury can change the fact that people are hungry, or that we're dying for no reason. And dying for every reason."

Kortilla placed a hand on my shoe, tracing the outline of the fabricated leather where the correction pellet had entered. "They seem to have heard him."

"Of course. You push someone, they push back. In the barrio or Manhattan. We just need to stay out of their way. Damn the Orderists, and damn the richies. I don't want anything from them. We don't need anything from them."

Kortilla shrugged. She knew I wasn't being honest with myself. I did need something from them. She kept staring at the puncture hole. "You going in to get the freedom juice?" The question hung in the air like a foul odor. "You never did anything wrong. Star student. Best natural-born runner in Bronx City. You can get the juice and be done."

I frowned. "You mean limp into an Authority sub-station, head low, tell them their metal enforcer shot me with a correction pellet by mistake on my way home, I'm a good girl, give me a shot of the blue stuff so I don't have to spend the next two days in unbearable agony? Yeah, I'll do that."

"Why go through hell if you don't have to?" Kortilla replied, her back straightening. "Your record is clean. Hell, your family even pays tax—you got a friggin' voter in there. They'll give it to you." In a whisper, she added, "No one is going to know if you go in."

I held onto my lofty speech about not humiliating myself in front of the richie stooges that I might have spouted off to almost anyone else. "I'm clean, no record. Nothing on video except me running away," I conceded. "But Mateo isn't. I've got no idea what he did in Manhattan tonight. Or where he is now. He's desperate. They all are. I won't become leverage for *los richos* if he's on the run. No Authority."

"It won't start getting bad till morning. You can stay here to wait it out. I'll speak to my mama and papa. They've been through it."

"I can't do that; they've got you and your brothers to worry about. I don't—"

Kortilla put a finger on my lip. "I hope you're not stupid enough to think you'll get through correction easier than everyone else." Her tone was cold.

I swallowed hard. "I don't want them to see me screaming, crying…" I shut my eyes, not liking any of my choices.

"I've got you covered, Dee."

I looked away, my eyes nearly wet. After a moment I turned back, rubbing my busted viser. "Is your viser working yet?"

Kortilla looked down at the device wrapped snugly around her wrist, a sleek, glittering thing that was as much fashion as function. Not that she needed it. Kortilla could make a pimple look like a gem so elegant that the rest of the girls at school would be dotting their faces with red by the following day.

"Got a signal," she declared with a grin. "I guess the Authority machines are done. You want me to red ping Mateo?"

"No," I told her. "It's too soon. The Authority will be listening after what just happened. If he's in trouble, I don't want you tied to it."

The barest hint of a smirk made it to the far end of Kortilla's lips. "I'll use Pele's viser."

"How…" I began, but Kortilla raised her brows in a "you're going to question me?" expression. I chuckled in spite of everything. It hurt my ribs, but felt nice deeper inside.

"How about Aba?" Kortilla asked, already flicking the fingers on her visered hand. Only Kortilla, Mateo, and I called my grandmother Aba.

"You up for that call?" I asked her.

Kortilla puffed up like a marching soldier. "Blood takes care of blood. Besides, it's only a ping. I'll keep away from her for a while afterwards."

I closed my eyes again, more weary than I thought. "Thank you, *hermana*."

"Rest for a bit," Kortilla urged. "I got you."

CHAPTER

THREE

P ain woke me. A knife sliced through my veins, the pulsing
agony spreading from the foot that had taken the correction pellet through the rest of my body. I twitched and turned,
trying to escape the inescapable. My teeth gritted shut, trap-
ping the howl of anguish that wanted to break out of my
mouth.

"She's awake," said a tired voice. A male voice.

I forgot about my suffering and worried about my clothes.
Luckily, the most naked part of me was my arm: I wasn't wearing my viser. The rest of me was under the covers of Kortilla's
bed, dressed in what I guessed to be her pajamas because the
arms and legs were too short, and the fabric too silky to be anything I would own. That all made me feel better. As did recognizing that the voice belonged to Kortilla's brother, Otega. He
was the younger and gentler of her surviving siblings, although
still four years older than me. His gentleness included a wicked
left hook. He leaned back in his chair, calling out to Kortilla. I
smelled the stim-chew he had in his mouth.

Kortilla strode in wearing the same clothes she had on
last night. Bleary eyes, no makeup, hair tousled, and she still
looked better than I could on my best day. She held a small
rectangular box in one hand and a glass of precious, clear water

in the other. A wave of nausea swept over me as she knelt beside the bed.

"Hang in there," Kortilla said, her voice gentle. I appreciated her skipping silly questions, like how I felt. She held the glass to my lips. "See if you can manage a sip. It's the good stuff: ration-issued, machine filtered."

I tried to drink, but ended up choking.

"How long?" I managed to croak out between spasms. My throat smoldered like charcoal.

"It's ten in the morning. We hoped you'd sleep longer, for your sake," Kortilla said. Otega hovered over her shoulder, pitch-dark hair dripping in front of his equally dark eyes, the resemblance to his sister obvious. Lucky him. They both looked worried. I hated that.

I urged myself to put the pain aside. I knew how to do that. I did it almost every race, even if this hurt was a deluge compared to the trickle I dealt with when running. I reached for that place of cold I had inside myself, where I could turn it off. That place where my strength was hidden. But the agony in my veins pushed back. My head spun; I grunted. All hope of peace disappeared as my body spasmed.

"Breathe through it," Kortilla said. "Every minute is a minute closer to it being over."

I sucked in air as if it were anesthetic. Another wave hit me. I clenched my teeth till the worst of it passed.

"Mateo...and Aba?" I managed to ask.

"I spoke to Aba last night, I told her...I did my best for you. She came over this morning, early, before she had to get to work. She didn't stay long. 'No sick days, no excuses,' she said." I groaned, and not from the pain. "It's going to be okay. She loves you, she's just—she's from a different world." Kortilla put a hand on mine. "We tried to reach Mateo. Don't worry, I was smart about it."

"I helped," Otega interrupted. "And I got you what you need."

Kortilla glared at her brother, but didn't correct him. Instead she opened the small box in her hand. It held a clear syringe filled with a liquid the color of a radioactive sapphire.

"Mateo's not answering his viser, but Otega found one of his boys, Vincent, at one of their usual haunts late last night. Claimed he crossed the bridge with your bro, and he's safe. Said he'd get him a message about you."

"Vince is a rabid pup," I said, not feeling reassured.

Kortilla held forth the syringe. "Well, he dropped this off early this morning. Said Mateo wanted you to have it."

"Is…is that the juice?" I wondered, hope rising in my voice. I didn't know if I could take two days of what I felt right now. "How'd he get it?"

"It's a fabrication. The best possible, though. Supposedly it's just like the real stuff."

"People have died using fabricated counteragent."

Kortilla pursed her lips, looking hard at the syringe. "Mateo wouldn't have sent it if he thought it would hurt you."

I thought about my brother, trying to be objective through the pain he had indirectly inflicted on me. He always meant well, at least where I was concerned. That didn't make him any less of a fool. The cold truth was that dying people made bad choices. And I didn't trust Vincent. He hung with Mateo for the action, the fighting, the thrills. He didn't care about anything Mateo cared about, he just wanted to look important and hurt people. There was no telling where the syringe had come from.

"I don't want it," I said between clenched teeth.

Kortilla and Otega's jaws dropped.

"You *loca*, Daniela?" asked Otega. "I almost got my rear beaten trying to find your bro and get this—"

Kortilla silenced him with a sharp elbow. She leaned closer to me, her voice a whisper. "It's going to get worse. Bad like you can't imagine. So bad you'll wish you were dead. And that's not even the end. After, you'll remember. At night, in your dreams, you'll remember the pain. It chases you. Every time you think about...about doing something they don't want, you remember, just for an instant. Think carefully before you decide, sister."

I managed to meet her eyes. "I'm not afraid of them. I can take whatever they want to hit me with. No shot."

Kortilla drew back. "We'll keep it handy in case you change your mind."

"Get rid of it," I told them, my voice strained. I thought of the gaunt man who had been running beside me last night, the one I had swerved in front of. "A lot of other people got hit. Give it to one of them. Shouldn't be hard to find takers."

Otega shook his head in disbelief, although there was also a bit of a sparkle in those smoldering eyes. I had said "give," but he had heard "sell."

"Anything else you need?" Kortilla asked.

I bit my lip, hoping it looked like I was thinking; I was actually fighting off a wave of burning spears dancing in my belly. "Tell your parents I'm sorry..."

Kortilla snorted. "You're the smartest girl I know, *hermana*, but you have some stupid thoughts." She left me alone, dragging Otega along with her. Kortilla knew I did my best fighting alone.

Within an hour, I regretted letting the magic syringe get away. By noon, I had to fight off the urge to scream for Otega to get it back for me. The only thing that stopped me was that I was too nauseous to get out of bed, and in too much pain to make intelligible sounds. Fire surged through my body, searing my flesh from the inside, then receding just enough to make the agony's inevitable return even more dreadful. Drool dripped from my lips, and even the faint light from the closed window forced my eyes shut. Desperate for an escape, any escape, I retreated inward, to the place that had always saved me in the past.

I found it when I was five, the night I finally accepted that my mother was never coming home. It was a place in my mind, but I felt like I was outside my body when I went there. I could see myself sometimes, as if I was a spirit watching my body from above. A sphere surrounded me, a seamless shell of shining silver, so brilliant that I could only look inward at myself. And it was cold. So very cold. That was how I found the place, by remembering the bone-chilling sensation inside. If the walls of the sphere weren't there, I would lose myself forever in that ethereal place. But the silvery shield protected me. When I was there, I could usually make myself do the things that needed to be done.

When my mom disappeared from my life, that place helped me fill the hole enough to go on living. When I raced, that place let me call on more strength, more speed. There, I could turn off the pain of an injury, or the burning sensation in my lungs and legs as I reached what I thought were my physical limits. That was why no one could beat me in a race. I had an on/off switch for strength and pain. But I'd never endured a level of physical punishment like that inflicted by the correction pellet. The burning inside made it hard to remember the cold, and I struggled to focus my thoughts with the hammering inside my head.

Waves of torment came at me as unceasingly as the ocean tide. The pain hit me high and low, with brute force and deft subtlety. I just couldn't catch my breath, couldn't get the window of peace I needed to concentrate. I had no idea how long I fought; time flowed imperceptibly, like in my nightmares. I didn't know if my eyes were open or closed, if it was day or night. Until I got angry. Suffering gave way to frustration. From frustration came hate. I hated that I didn't have parents. I hated that I worked my ass off every day for nothing. I hated that everyone I loved lived in the same bleak world. I hated that my brother was dying, and that I couldn't find a way to save him. Hate overcame pain, at least for long enough for me to get to where I needed to be. Once inside my shining sphere, I controlled the pain. I willed my body to feel peace, to free itself of the poison within. It didn't work, of course. Not completely—but enough. I ached like I'd had major surgery without pain meds, but it was an improvement. Time returned to normal; I knew who I was, and where. I made a choice not to cry or scream. I lay there for countless hours, willing the pain to end. Finally, it did.

A little more than forty-eight hours after being struck by the correction pellet, I crawled out of Kortilla's bed, her arm wrapped protectively around my waist.

"I don't believe it," she said, awe in her voice. "No one gets through a correction so easily. You got steel, girl."

"I must've gotten a partial dose. Shoe took some of it."

Kortilla grunted her skepticism.

"You sure you're okay to walk home? You could take a day to rest before, you know…"

I did know. Aba was not keen on excuses. "Another day isn't going to make it any better. Best to get it over with."

"I'll get you something to eat at least."

I was about to decline when Kortilla interrupted me. "Mama's not home. You don't have to explain anything to anyone. She left it for you. Eat it, girl. She may not have your Aba's will, but she'd have my head if I sent you home with an empty stomach."

I ate their food and drank their ration water, careful to pace myself after two days with nothing. It was tomato and beans. Fabricated, of course, but Kortilla's mom could make the humblest fare taste like heaven. Afterwards, Kortilla and Otega walked me home. Otega hung back, strolling casually behind us, although I knew he was armed. We walked past two crushed cars pushed up onto the sidewalk, their hoods torn apart by an enforcer's caterpillar tracks. The graffiti of defiance already covered the ruined hulks. The few other people on the streets looked sullen, the way a child might after a spanking. Still, I was walking, and that was something. All too quickly we arrived at the sorrowful six-story block of crumbling bricks where I lived on the nights I wasn't with Kortilla's family.

Otega gave me a fist bump and a wide smile genuine enough to make me feel guilty about the difficulty I had mustering my own. "If you can handle what you just been through, you can run with anyone, girl."

Kortilla wrapped me in a great hug. As we parted, she slipped my viser back onto my arm. "All fixed. Otega knows a guy."

Relief surged through me, guilt hard on its heels. What had it cost? I knew Kortilla wouldn't take my money. I hated debts, even to those I loved.

Kortilla read my mind. "You can be damn sure he sold that syringe for way more than it cost to fix your viser. Go home, girl. Tomorrow's Saturday, so get some sleep. Ping me when you get up."

I left them to face home.

FOUR

I walked through the door to my apartment with the courage of a mouse, my steps just slightly more than a tip-toe. The ancient wooden floorboards mocked my attempt at silence. A familiar figure, elf-like in stature, with tightly pulled iron hair and eyes stern enough to peel skin, stared at me from an upholstered armchair in the den. The sight reminded me of an aged queen sitting on a threadbare throne. A muted screen flashed on the wall behind her. She said nothing as I ventured deeper into her domain. When I stood where she wanted, Aba spoke, her voice graveled.

"Feeling better?" There was no softness in her words, but no mockery either.

"Yes, Aba," I replied, meek.

"You missed two days of school."

"Yes." I might have noted to anyone else I was being tortured during that time, but not to Aba.

"Your shoe is broken, your ankle injured," she noted without her eyes releasing their hold on my own. "Does that mean you aren't competing this weekend either?"

"I'm still running on Sunday," I declared in the face of her challenge, although for the first time since I was a kid, I didn't want to. My ankle throbbed. But I couldn't admit I would quit to Aba. I couldn't admit I wouldn't try. She raised my mother, then Mateo and me, by herself. She owned this place. She was a citizen, and proud of it. How could I quit when she never did?

"Have you seen your brother?" she asked. I saw just a hint of worry around those life-hardened eyes.

My teeth clenched. I considered not telling her what little I knew. For a fleeting instant, I considered asking her why she only worried about my older brother. But the fire faded quickly. Most folks around here had it worse than me. Way worse. I told her what Kortilla had told me, the hearsay of Mateo's safety as related by Vincent.

A huff from the old woman's throat told me she thought even less of Vincent's message than I did. "When did you see him last, with your own eyes?" she asked.

"Wednesday, the morning before the protest," I admitted, seeing her eyes go rigid as I spoke. "I told him not to do anything foolish. I tried to make him promise—"

"But you left him after that," Aba pressed. "To go wherever."

"I went to school, yes," I replied, more sharply than I had intended. "He's four years older than me, I can't control him."

Aba scowled. "He's scared, you aren't. His vision is clouded, yours isn't...usually. He can pull through this. But not if he gets himself killed. Go save him. Go succeed."

"He can take care of himself," I declared, not believing it.

Aba paused, studying me, her face as unreadable as ever. "He can ruin your future too, if you both aren't careful."

I flushed. "So what?" I regretted saying it. I sounded like a spoiled little girl.

"You wouldn't run so hard if you thought that. Stop lying to yourself, and to me." Her words slapped my face. "Get some rest if you really are going to run on Sunday." She huffed again, this time as punctuation. I knew the sound well. I retreated with relief.

My room consisted of half of the single bedroom in our home. A sliding door separated my portion from Mateo's. He had the window, but I didn't mind. I liked the quiet. Aba slept on the couch in the living room, even though this was her place. She had worked just about every day of her life to own it, earning a crap wage as a clerk at the city ration dispensary. But she had a job, and that meant we had a place to live, heat in the winter, and food to eat. She paid taxes, so we could go to school. She dutifully used her single vote allocation every election. In the eleven years I had lived with her there was not a single day where she had complained about anything.

I lay down gingerly on my bed and whispered out a message to Kortilla, letting her know I had survived my initial encounter. My body ached and Aba's words still stung. I knew she was disappointed in me, even if she never said it. I just didn't know why.

From the day that we came to live with her, after Mom died, up through today, Aba had never once told me what she expected of me. She told Mateo and me only one thing: "Go succeed." I still didn't know what that meant.

I drifted off to sleep quickly, and slept longer than I had in ages. The delicious aroma of bacon jolted my eyes open. Smelling meat cooking in our house was like seeing an elephant on the street—it just didn't happen. I dragged myself into the den to find Mateo standing in the kitchen, gaping at the stove. A small fire had broken out in the pan. I bolted into the kitchen, knocking my taller, more solid brother aside. I grabbed a dented cover from one of the wall cabinets and covered the pan. Smoke flooded out from the uneven edges of the lid.

"Get it out of there!" Mateo urged. "That's real bacon!"

I lifted the cover, sucking in acrid smoke. Quickly, I slid the rashers onto the plate that had been laid out beside the stove.

"Burned, but salvageable, I think. You can't let the real stuff get too hot. The fat catches fire. It's not like fabricants."

My brother regarded me with a guileless grin and twinkling eyes that had no business on his face, given what he had put me through.

"I got the eggs right though," he said indicating a plate full of fluffy scrambled eggs that looked like they had been taken from a net simulation.

"You rob a bank down in Manhattan?"

"When I walked in, the first thing I saw were four eggs and a heap of fresh-cut bacon on the counter, calling to me like a rooster. I guess Aba was in a good mood. I haven't seen real stuff like that around here since Christmas."

Fury at Mateo's obliviousness mixed with a wave of gratitude as I thought about those precious items. Had Aba really left them for me?

"Out of here." I pointed in the direction of our small table adjacent to the kitchen.

I grabbed the eggs and bacon, along with two more plates, and put them on the table between us. Hunger trumped conversation. We made short work of the rare feast. The real stuff satisfied—salty and greasy. Fabrications just didn't taste the same.

I had my fill before Mateo finished. I took the opportunity to watch him as he shoveled eggs into his mouth, barely chewing between bites. I understood why people liked him. He had sculpted features molded onto an open, expressive face that made it easy to believe you were seeing into his soul. The opposite of me. His eyes were just a shade lighter than mine, but far warmer. Only someone who knew him his whole life would've noticed the slight yellowing at the edge of his eyes, a frame that was not quite as hardy as it had been a few years ago, an occasional tremor in his hands that easily could have been dismissed as clumsiness. But I had lived with Mateo every day of my life, and I knew what happened to people around his age when they had that look. As sure as the sun rose in the east, it was the Waste. It would eventually claim him, unless I did something about it.

"Tell me about your evening in Manhattan," I said, impatient with the pace of his eating.

Mateo looked up with infuriating sincerity, as if he had no idea why I could be angry. He wiped some egg from his mouth with his sleeve.

"Good times," he declared with merriment that made me want to reach across the table and strangle him. "Those black boots from the Authority were so focused on that pastor and his sheep on the North Bridge that they never expected us at the Broadway crossing. Zipped by them, under the monitors, onto the streets. We split up—dozens of us, riding every old gas guzzler we could find. Hell, I don't even know where some of those boys came from. Not *Corazones* even, most of them, so the word is spreading. Surveyor drones came in from above, but not enough. Those gasoline engines haul. I got into the heart of the place. Past the Vision Quad. Right down to their private, snob-only streets on the east side. I even got to Central Park. Reminded me of when Mom used to take us there. Saw those green trees, and scared the hell out of some highborn kids with their nannies and familiars." He laughed, sounding like a child bragging about a goal in a football game instead of someone involved in a life-or-death chase.

My blood sizzled. "And what the hell good did that do anyone? Except bring the friggin' Authority's machines here, shooting at everyone who had nothing to do with your stupid, hopeless games."

Chagrin erupted on Mateo's face as he contemplated the consequences of his actions, probably for the first time since it had happened, but it faded as quickly as it came. He stuck his chin in the air. "You've heard the way the government talks about us. That Orderist Chairman's hints about 'long-term solutions' and 'prosperity through order.' We're all dead if we don't do something."

"I'm not dead! Kortilla's not dead, neither are her parents. We're living just fine. We don't need you getting us killed, or corrected. Or yourself either." My face burned as I unloaded on him.

Mateo looked away. "Sorry you got hit." Then he tacked on, "I thought I taught you to run faster than that."

I didn't laugh at his attempt at a joke. I stared in hard silence until he faced me again.

"You are living, Dee, but only as much as they let you. You and Kortilla have got people with jobs—crap ones with the gov or fixing overused clothes like Kortilla's mom, or whatever—so you've got a roof over your head and food. For now. But most don't. The highborn talk about merit, bettering yourself, democracy, but it's all crap. A rich man's got a vote allocation of a thousand, and Aba's got one, because she pays less tax. They get their own streets, their own parks, their own police, their own special net. Then they complain about the burden of the low Aptitude Tiers of society. They make the rules, and they're stacked against us. It was never supposed to be that way. You do great in school, sure, but you'll never get into one of those fancy colleges. Even if you did, you couldn't pay for it. You'll never get out of here playing by their rules."

"I'll get where I need to be," I told him, even though I wasn't sure I believed it anymore. "And I don't need a huge townhouse, three vacation homes, and ten servants to be living, Mateo. I got people. Right here in the barrio, I got 'em.

And I want to hang on to them. All of them." Emotion crept into my voice at the end, but my brother didn't notice.

"They've taken everything away from us—everything. They killed Dad, they killed Mom. One way or the other, they killed her. They take whatever they want, leave us the dregs, and tell themselves it's what we deserve. Well, I'm not going to just let them. That's what got us here—people who let it happen. Mom told me not to give in, and I'm not."

I saw the pain on his face and swallowed hard. I reached for his cheek with my hand. Principled. Intelligent. Naive. My brother. "Listen, Mateo. We'll find a way to fix you. I know I can get—"

He snapped back from my grasp with a viper's quickness. "Ain't nothing to fix. We all got fuses burning. Mine might be quicker, might not." He got up and took a quick backwards step towards the door. "I came to make sure you were okay. I should've known a little correction pellet couldn't break your stubbornness. I ain't done with those *riobos*."

Then he was gone.

CHAPTER
FIVE

I trotted onto the outdoor track located behind the Inocensio Basanova School of Bronx City, known in official nomenclature as Public School 62. Coach Darwin and several of my emerald and white-clad teammates acknowledged my presence with reticent nods in my direction, but otherwise left me alone. They knew my routine. They knew I would win my race. They didn't know I'd been whirling under the punishing influence of a correction pellet a little over twenty-four hours ago. But that didn't matter. No excuses.

The dilapidated hulk of the school building looming over the cracked asphalt track betrayed every one of its nearly hundred years of existence, the facade consisting of more fabricated patches than original brick. Inside, a withered interior of crumbling halls and dingy classrooms accommodated thousands of students, no more than two dozen of whom had bothered to bestir themselves out of bed on a clear Sunday morning to sit on the plastika bleachers and watch our team run around a big oval. I didn't care. I didn't run for them.

Most of the runners were older than me—seniors or juniors. I was also one of only two girls on the track. The gender-equality laws prohibited separate boys and girls teams. I rather liked the change. I preferred to beat people who expected to beat me.

I caught a few of our competitors from PS 155 and PS 188 checking me out, whispering to themselves. The trophies I'd earned from being the undefeated Bronx City champion for the past three years lay in some nearby landfill, but everyone who ran in BC had heard of me. People who hadn't raced against me still thought they could beat me. They were wrong, bad ankle and all.

Kortilla's silky dark eyes flashed at me from the stands. I couldn't help smiling.

You woke up on a Sunday? I asked with eyes and brows.

She gave an exaggerated yawn in reply. I continued my warm-up, suddenly feeling far less stiffness or pain. I thought back to my conversation with Mateo the day before. *Did it matter where I lived if I had people like Kortilla?* Of course, I didn't have the Waste ravaging my body. At least not yet.

A short siren burst informed everyone that the meet would begin shortly. I took my place among my teammates, each of us dressed in green with a silly gopher emblazoned on our shirts. The rodent's beady eyes and off color reminded me of a leprechaun high on Z-Pop.

I watched my teammates compete as I awaited my opportunity to run. We got smoked in the two hundred meter, with our best runner finishing fourth. We didn't do much better at four hundred meters, having a single runner come in third. I usually ran multiple distances, as well as doing cross-country, but Coach Darwin was new, and I hadn't convinced him to permit me that privilege. I hadn't pushed the issue. Spots on the team were precious; just because I was good didn't mean my teammates wouldn't knife me in the halls. As I tried to focus on the competition, my spider-sense told me someone had eyes on my back. And not friendly eyes, like Kortilla's, but the kind that made me squirm.

I jerked around to see a tall suited figure standing in the front row of the bleachers, his chrome eyes fixed on me, his hair an unnatural flaxen that might have been considered stylish among the Manhattan set. In the stands, within a sea of color ranging from coffee to charcoal, this porcelain-skinned stranger stood out like a fox in a litter of kittens. I glanced at Kortilla, who acknowledged my bafflement with her own. A sharp whistle signaled that it was time to line up for my primary event, the fifteen-hundred-meter run.

I took my place on the starting line wondering what the *gringo* wanted. I reasoned that it probably had something to do with the protest. Or Mateo. I tried to clear my mind and prepare to race. I took careful note of my competition. There was only one other girl, along with half a dozen boys of various shapes, ages and sizes. We all bolted at the sound of the starter's pistol.

The fifteen hundred was my favorite distance because it required you to excel at both speed and endurance. Races of four hundred meters or less were just sprints, with the one hundred meter too often being determined by who could get the best start. Blink and it was over. But the fifteen hundred was a metric mile—three and three-quarters laps around the track so you needed speed, but you couldn't go full throttle the whole way, or you would burn yourself out. It was about being patient, managing your energy so you were in a position to sprint at the finish. I loved coming from the second or third position during that last lap, releasing speed that no one thought I could possibly have left.

I hadn't had a chance to research the other teams. I'd missed practice in order to fulfill my dream of being tortured by highborn chemicals, so I ran this race using my usual strategy: pacing myself with the next fastest runner, who happened to be a dusky-skinned boy with long, rangy legs and a shaved head, wearing the crimson dragon of PS 188. I let him pull ahead of me on the first lap, feeling the presence of two other runners over each of my shoulders. One of them was the girl. No way she could beat me, but I was rooting for her to take second.

The PS 188 guy set an aggressive pace. He had long, gliding strides that ate up distance and saved energy. My legs didn't have his reach or power, so I was burning more reserves than I wanted to keep pace. I heard some unsteady panting from behind as we finished the first lap. I wasn't alone in pushing myself. My ankle ached, and there was some sluggishness in my legs, but I kept up. Mr. PS 188 stole a furtive glance over his shoulder. I winked.

We took the second lap faster than I expected. The other runners dropped back far enough that only Mr. PS 188, the unnamed girl, and I were in serious contention. Mr. PS 188 pushed harder, but I kept pace, dogged as a street mutt. I kept close enough to ensure he stayed concerned about what I had left in my tank.

With half a lap to go, it was just the two of us. Mr. PS 188 maintained his impressive speed, but I liked my position—just a stride behind. We were running out of track. A split second before I made my move, he took off with a burst of speed I hadn't expected. I dashed forward, feeling some panic. I was fast, but even I needed some time to make up the gap between us; the finish line loomed perilously close. I reached inside for my cold place, but couldn't find it at first. I gritted my teeth: *no way this guy beats me.* A grunt of frustration escaped my lips. I could almost feel the smile on Mr. PS 188's face. That's when I found it: my lair, my chilled control room. There was a pool of essence there—energy I could draw upon. I drank in the power until the fatigue faded, my breathing steadied, and my legs felt fresh again. This was what I lived for. This was mine.

I ran like a one-hundred-meter sprinter, my knees firing like pistons. Mr. PS 188 cried out when I drew even. The finish line beckoned no more than a dozen strides ahead. But that was all I needed to put him away. I streaked ahead. I didn't look at him or the judge as I crossed the finish line. Hearing Kortilla shout "*Vamos!*" at the top of her lungs was all I needed. The other girl in the race finished third, sweat soaking her indigo uniform. She gave me a thumbs up. I nodded back.

By the time I returned to my place among my teammates, my heart rate had returned to normal, but my foot pulsed angrily. I could temporarily turn off pain using my cold place, but that didn't mean I couldn't hurt myself. Indeed, without pain, it was easy to make an injury worse, and I had just done so.

I approached Coach Darwin. He looked like what he was: a former linebacker whose body had fallen into the perils of middle age. "I gotta get some icy stuff for my foot."

It took a few seconds before he turned to look at me. "Nice race," he said, as if I hadn't spoken. "You got pushed more than you expected at the end."

"And I pushed back," I replied, intending to sound confident. "I've got to go inside."

Coach arched a brow at me. "So you don't feel you need to practice, and you don't need to stick around to support your teammates? Track is a team sport."

I caught myself before I rolled my eyes. Coach didn't know me yet. I was afraid he was beginning to think I was someone that I didn't want to be. "I know, Coach. The explanation for both is the same. I'll tell you all about it. And I'll be here for the team, I promise. But I need to put something on this before it gets too swollen. Please?"

He sized me up as if evaluating a race horse. "Go."

I waved to Kortilla as I limped past the stands and headed for our locker room. We didn't have much, but there were some chemical cold packs in there. Coach might have bought them himself. The dark-suited man watched me walk past. I had forgotten about him. He followed me as I headed towards the school building.

"Excuse me, Ms. Machado—may I speak to you?" He pronounced my name so it sounded more like 'Munch-add-oh' but his other words were crisp Manhattan English.

I could've run away, but it didn't seem like that would help the situation. "It's Mach-a-do," I told him as I turned.

"Got it." He didn't hide his impatience. "We've been trying to contact you. You haven't been in school for the past two days. And your viser is offline."

"I had a little accident. Happens around here."

"Ah, I see." He actually had no idea what I was talking about. Kortilla was creeping up behind him. My eyes told her to back off for now. "I'm here with very exciting news for you."

I huffed at him, but inwardly I was relieved he wasn't with the Authority. My best guess, based on the clothes, creepy eyes, and modified hair, was a U-date service. They occasionally combed the high schools, looking for candidates for their high-paying customers. Best to get this over with quickly. My foot hurt. "What?"

"My name is Christopher Howards. I represent the Tuck School in Manhattan. Due to an unexpected development, we have a slot available." He hesitated for a moment, his back stiffening. "I'm pleased to extend to you an offer of admission to join this year's fall class."

I gaped. My mind raced, searching for the gimmick. I had heard of the Tuck School, of course. Everyone in the Five Cities had. It was the highest of highborn institutions. Even

the elite families of Manhattan struggled to get their little
ones in there. It cost more than Aba earned in a decade to go
there for one year, not that cost mattered to the richies who
attended.

"Bullshit," I said, trying to keep the tiny part of me that
wished this wasn't a lie from showing. "I never applied. I
couldn't get an application even if I wanted one—they don't
take tenth-grade transfers. I couldn't pay the processing fee,
much less the tuition. And it's three weeks into the school year,
even in Manhattan."

"Ah, well, the circumstances are unusual, I must agree," the
white guy admitted, shuffling his feet. "You did, however, apply to the Five Cities Gifted and Talented Program several
years ago. Your test scores were near perfect, and your athletic
achievements are quite impressive. We do strive for a well-
rounded student. And we...ah...we have access to that information. We estimate your Aptitude Tier rating is thirty-three:
the ninety-ninth percentile of the population. As to—"

"They terminated the gifted program. Budget cuts."

Howards gave me an impatient nod. "Yes, well, as I was
saying. Due to a provision in our school's charter and the unexpected vacancy, we find ourselves with a slot available that
must be filled, even at this late date. And we would like to offer
it to you, along with a financial incentive package, renewable
annually, until graduation."

"That's crap," I declared, but my voice was shaking.

He tapped his viser. "I've transmitted the offer letter and financial package to your viser. I would encourage you to review
it soon. The offer expires at midnight tomorrow."

"Tomorrow?" I parroted like an idiot.

"As I said, the circumstances are quite unusual. If you aren't
interested, well, there are plenty of others who will be. We
don't expect you to decide without seeing the school first. As

such, I've sent you a pre-paid travel pass for the subway into Manhattan for tomorrow. We'll have a volunteer parent guide available to give you and your grandmother, who I believe is your legal guardian, a tour of the school at four o'clock tomorrow afternoon. Mr. Havelock, the headmaster, will meet with you following your tour, before you make a final decision."

I looked Howards up and down, from his shoes to his artificial hair, searching for something that didn't match his story. Kortilla's mom had taught me to spot the difference between fabricated cloth and real cotton, as well as quality tailoring from the printed stuff. This guy's clothes checked out, so did his silly hair and pale face. If he had an angle, I couldn't figure it out.

"I'll read it."

"Please do," he said without much sincerity. "I hope I'll have the opportunity to see you again." He finished our conversation with an uncomfortable, Manhattan-style head bow, then strode off towards the street, to what I presumed would be a waiting car ready to whisk him back across the river.

As soon as Howards had gone ten steps, Kortilla was on me like a dog to dinner. "What the hell was that all about?"

CHAPTER

SIX

Kortilla and I boarded the subway train at the Fordman Road station, picking our way through the dubious collection of loiterers clustered around its entrance. There was no way I was bringing Aba down to Manhattan, whatever that *gringo* said. Having Aba involved would only make my life harder.

"An all-expense paid ride to the fanciest, richest school is too good to be true," Kortilla reminded me as we slipped inside the train, jostling for a pair of empty seats. "They ain't never going to offer it to a Latina girl from Bronx City who ain't even applied."

"I know."

"They want something from you. Something they can't buy with their money, so it's gotta be something big...and bad."

"I want something too," I said, my voice not much more than a whisper. "Tuck could help me get it. For Mateo."

Kortilla squeezed my shoulder.

"THE NEXT STOP IS GRAND CONCOURSE STATION," announced a garbled voice from the train's ceiling. "PLEASE BE ADVISED THAT PASSENGERS CONTINUING ON THIS TRAIN BEYOND THE NEXT STATION TO MANHATTAN WITHOUT A VALID ENTRY PERMIT OR TRAVEL PASS

WILL INCUR A CHARGE OF TWENTY-FIVE DOLLARS.
VIOLATORS WILL FACE IDENTITY INDENTURE."

I check my viser, confirming that Howards travel pass was online. Neither of us could afford the fine.

"When was your last trip to Big M?" Kortilla asked me.

"I was five. My mom used to take us." I didn't want to talk about it.

"Sorry," Kortilla said, recognizing my tone.

I gave her a better answer as penance. I'd asked her to come, after all. "I barely remember. Mateo told me about it. She worked as a maternity nurse in one of their fancy hospitals, so she had a work permit that let her travel into the city whenever she wanted. She could even go into the parks, no extra charge. So she'd take us on the days she didn't have to work."

"And now you could go there every day too," Kortilla offered. "No lurkers, or muggers. Long afternoons lying on the real grass of Central Park with your highborn friends..." She had her mocking voice in full form by the time she got to the last. I pushed my shoulder into hers, and we both laughed.

"You?" I asked.

"Never," Kortilla admitted. "Guess you'll have to show me around."

The train became more crowded as we journeyed further into Manhattan. Men and women hopped on and off at the various stops, much as I would've expected elsewhere. Manhattan passengers differed from Bronx City riders primarily in terms of clothes, which looked newer; ornamentation, which included a dizzying array of glittering jewelry, hair beads, and skin implants that would've seen you robbed within five minutes if you wore them around Bronx City; and facial features, which were overwhelmingly Caucasian or Asian.

I wore the best of my limited wardrobe, a chocolate-colored blouse and midnight slacks, conservative and proper. Both were fabricated, but of the higher quality variety. I did not intend to present myself as a beggar, even if the highborn undoubtedly thought of me as such. Kortilla took a different tack. She looked beautiful, as she always did, but she had selected a tighter and lower cut ensemble for this journey than she would have ordinarily worn on a typical school day. The denizens of Manhattan seemed to appreciate her decision. Most of the men, and no small number of women, gave her more than one glance upon entering the train.

We exited the subway at Eighty-Sixth Street. It took several moments to take it all in. Manhattan was a bigger, sleeker version of Bronx City. Except no boxes littered the streets, no illegal shacks crowded the roofs of the buildings, no beggars huddled about, and there were no lurkers in the alleys. I didn't see a single gas guzzler on the roads. The gray of Bronx City had been replaced by brighter, clearer air; the giant spires of Midtown loomed in the distance to the south, grand peaks of commerce. Northward were the bizarre architectural goliaths of the Vision Quad. Above us, at least a dozen small flying saucers danced in the breeze, silently tracking their human owners. Familiars.

My viser vibrated as I gaped at my surroundings. When I looked down at my arm, I saw a street map displaying directions that would lead us to Tuck. I wrinkled my nose. "What are the red streets?"

Kortilla leaned over to glance at my viser. "Private streets. Restricted to residents and people on official business with entry passes. They've got some near City Hall in Bronx City too."

"It's most of the neighborhood, including the street Tuck is on…"

"Yeah, sister, so don't go wandering about looking for fancy houses," Kortilla advised. "And don't get too close to any of these richies. I don't want to get zapped by some floating attack dog. Let's get moving so you're not late."

My viser illuminated its suggested route and we set off at a brisk pace, eventually turning onto Madison Avenue. Elegant shops lined the sidewalk, selling clothing, ornaments, fragrances, cosmetic enhancements of every sort as well as a variety of wares so alien I couldn't guess their purpose. It was stuff I had not even considered needing, but Kortilla looked inside the shop windows hungrily.

A woman with legs up to my chest emerged from one of the illustrious establishments. She was shaped like an hourglass, but had the shrunken face of a mummy. A tiny dog, prim and bejeweled, traveled in her substantial shadow. The creature emitted a yelp of disdain upon gazing at us. Mummy sucked in her breath at the mere sight of us. She retreated as if confronted by lurkers, conferring urgently with the distinguished shop's door minder.

I forced a laugh, but my skin crawled with each speculative glance aimed at us. I wanted to get this whole thing over with. I wanted to get back to where I belonged.

We turned onto Eighty-Ninth Street, heading towards the center of the block. Both sides of the street were lined with stately townhouses between four and five stories high, many with massive windows that pre-dated climate control. None looked like a school. My viser directed us to six rigidly carved steps guarded by twin stone tigers that stared at us with disapproval. We were strangers in a strange land. A pair of matching antique oak doors with wrought iron trim and ancient brass knockers loomed before us at the top of the stairs. They looked like something out of a Victorian-era sim show. We climbed the steps and stared at the ominous doorway. Before we could even consider how to open the giant things, they swung towards us. A swirl of glitter, hair and alterator-sculpted beauty

emerged, beaming like a child on her fifth birthday. I'd never
seen teeth so white—I think I saw my reflection as she bounded towards me.

"Oh, you must be Daniela Mach-ado!"

Smiley got the pronunciation mostly correct. I guessed
she'd been practicing in the mirror. That must've been a
strange effect, given the reflectiveness of her teeth.

"We're so pleased you could come for your tour." Smiley's
voice reminded me of a bird's chirp, its edges almost song-like.
I suspected the alterations to her hair, skin, teeth, and who
knew where else, included some voice modifications as well.
"I'm Meredith Flint-Dayish, lead parent tour guide. I want you
to know right away that both my daughters go here. One is in
middle school, the other is a junior in the high school. I know
what it's like. You can ask me anything."

Kortilla and I both gaped at her. I wasn't trying to be rude,
I'd just never met anyone like Smiley in real life. It felt like having an animated sim character jump into my bedroom. These
richies were a different species. Getting no immediate response
from me, Smiley finally noticed Kortilla. The grin vanished.

"And…you…are?" No-Longer-Smiley arched her eyebrows
as she pored over Kortilla and her inappropriate outfit.

I had a hunch Kortilla intended to give Ms. Flint-Dayish a
zinger that would make the next hour or so of my life very uncomfortable. I threw an arm around Kortilla's shoulder. "This
is my sister. My grandmother couldn't make it, unfortunately."

"She couldn't make it to a tour of Tuck?" Ms. Flint-Dayish
looked like I had just informed her that I had descended from
another planet. Whatever the alterator had done to her face, it
had made her unusually expressive. I was starting to enjoy myself more than I had anticipated. "Well, I'm sure that will be
fine." Her tone indicated that she didn't think that at all.

Smiley motioned for us to follow her inside. We passed through those ancient doors into a chamber of abrupt modernity. To our left, a pair of serious-looking men in silly lemon-citrus uniforms stood behind a duraglass shield. To our right, I saw an anteroom fitted with rotating shelves, many filled with familiars. A rectangular hatch set high in the wall opened to the outside, allowing the machines to depart without using the doorway. Directly in front of us, another set of doors stood sentinel, transparent, but thick and unmistakably tough.

"Familiars are not allowed anywhere within the school," Ms. Flint-Dayish informed us as if we cared. "Nor weapons of any kind. If your viser has protection features, they must be disabled at all times within the school. External networks are jammed within school grounds. We want our students focused."

I nodded, wondering if they had weapon scanners here. Probably. Well, I didn't have to worry about expulsion, so I might as well see how good their sensors were. Flint-Dayish took our silence as acquiescence. She nodded to the security personnel who opened the portals, allowing us to enter the infamous Tuck School. We did. No alarm went off. The sensors had failed to detect either my repulse spray or my skin color.

It smelled like old people inside.

"This whole block is the school—both sides. Underground as well. We've kept the historical facades, but it's all Tuck inside now. Classes are done for the day, but many of our students are still here, working on homework or other after-school activities. Just about everything you can imagine can be pursued here, you know."

She wasn't kidding. Flint-Dayish showed us things I never imagined seeing in a school. Tuck had four fabrication labs, some of which had equipment that could replicate liquids and gasses. It had reality simulation rooms, an observatory, and its own power plant to run it all in the event the grid failed. The classrooms were ancient, beautiful, and scary. Some were rigged with the latest screen and simulation technology; in others, I saw students hunched over desks using antique ink pens and real paper. The cafeteria was the most opulent room I had ever seen, with curtains of gold and candelabras of crystal below windows of colored glass. Plants—real ones—dotted the wood-paneled hallways. But the one thing that topped it all was the recreation facilities. These people had their own indoor track on one of the sub-levels, with environmental simulators that could mimic almost any condition.

"This is for practice," Flint-Dayish explained, probably enjoying my stupid awe. "We compete at the Armory, of course."

I got the chills hearing that. I couldn't help it. The Armory was legend. The finest track facility in the country. Olympians competed there. I'd dreamed about that place. It had been a reason to keep living.

Kortilla saw my expression, felt my resolve waver. She poked me with a sharp elbow.

"They also make you eat correction pellets," she whispered.

I bit my lip as Flint-Dayish continued the tour. She showed us everything from the kindergarten through the high school. She gave us the highlights, never lingering too long in any one place. We encountered a few students, all immaculately dressed in the navy and white colors of Tuck, but otherwise quite normal looking, except for some outrageous hair styles. They greeted Ms. Flint-Dayish politely, and unfailingly made offers to Kortilla and me to answer any questions we might have. They spoke directly to us, making eye contact, their words laced with superficial sincerity. Even the elementary school kids.

As we neared the end of the tour, I found the nerve to ask a question. "Have all the students been here since kindergarten?"

"Some even before that," Flint-Dayish said.

"They give admission tests to three-year-olds?" Kortilla asked, incredulous.

"Of course," Flint-Dayish replied. "They have their methods of determining Aptitude Tiers, even at that age. It's mostly in the genes."

"I thought the barrio was *loco*," Kortilla muttered.

Flint-Dayish sighed heavily, looking as if she was going to comment, then stopped herself. Her blazing smile abruptly reappeared. I wondered how much pain was beneath that mask. She didn't feel any more comfortable in this place than I did.

"I better get you to Mr. Havelock," Flint-Dayish informed us with artificial sweetness.

She ushered us down several flights of stairs that creaked like the floorboards in my own apartment. The tour had educated me in the difference between "traditional" and "run-down": it was determined by whether you could afford to fix the object in question or not.

We entered a suite of administrative cubicles on the school's second floor, past a collection of persons who ignored us in favor of their screens, until we came to a set of offices at the back of the area. There, an ancient lady graced by natural-looking gray hair rose from her desk to greet us with the swiftness of a far younger woman.

"Welcome, Ms. Machado," she said, sounding like a native speaker and extending a hand in greeting. "I'm Elsa Mark, Mr. Havelock's assistant."

I took her hand and noticed something that looked like genuine warmth in her eyes. She offered her hand to Kortilla as well, making a note of her name. If she felt any annoyance at my bringing a high school pal rather than my legal guardian, she hid it well. Elsa Mark looked to be in her sixties—a decade too old to be highborn.

"Ms. Machado, Mr. Havelock said to send you right in when you arrived. Ms. Gonzales can wait here." To Kortilla she added, "I'll get you a guest code for our network since your viser's external functions are blocked. Would you like something to eat or drink while you wait?"

Kortilla grinned. She would probably order a steak. I hoped she wouldn't embarrass me too much. Kortilla leaned over and whispered in my ear. "Stay strong. Do what you have to do."

I walked towards the door of Mr. Havelock's office with those words echoing in my ear, but with very different sentiments stirring in my heart. *They want something big from me.* I just couldn't imagine what that could be.

Mr. Yonas James Havelock had skin as dark as midnight, a gracious manner, and child-like delight in his eyes as he walked from behind a great mahogany desk to greet me. He wore an antique-style suit, red bow tie at his neck. If he had introduced himself as my long-dead father, I wouldn't have been any more surprised than I was at that moment. He extended his long, spidery arm towards me.

"Such a pleasure to meet you, Ms. Machado." He took my hand in his and covered it with his other palm. "Thank you for coming in on such short notice, and in such unusual circumstances."

He led us to a pair of oversized chairs arrayed about a circular coffee table. The carpet was so thick it felt like walking on pudding. The table top was a screen. Pictures of triumphant Tuck students cycled across its surface. Havelock blanked the display with a flick of his fingers.

He offered me tea, which I accepted, mostly because I wanted more time to study him. To my surprise, he prepared everything himself; in short order, he brought over a steaming

pot and a pair of tiny cups, brushstrokes visible on their exterior. The liquid was a richly toasted-amber. I'd never tasted
anything quite like it.

Seeing my reaction Mr. Havelock commented, "It's from
Japan. Grown in real soil, an original strain of leaf that goes
back a thousand years—not engineered. The cups were made
by a fifth-generation craftsman from Kyoto, by hand. It was a
gift from a former pupil, one of the rare ones I accepted." He
had a deeper, more calming, voice than his tall, lanky frame
suggested. I suspected English was not his native language.
Havelock called to mind an image of one of the native sym-
pathizers who had helped the British administer their ancient
empire, sans accent. His clothes certainly fit the picture. *A trai-
tor to his people*, I concluded, albeit an urbane one.

He sat, sampled his drink, then spoke. "What do you think
of our school?"

"An amazing place," I admitted. But it wasn't "our" anything; it was theirs: the highborn and those who wished they
were born as such. I did not belong here. I did not want to
belong here. "What you have here, it's unimaginable where I
come from."

"And you think that quite unfair, I suppose, that so few enjoy so much privilege. And they are the ones who already have
more than anyone else."

"Well…y-yes," I stammered. "You all talk about the laws of
equality, merit. But kids who grow up learning in their own
gas-fabrication labs can't be fairly measured against kids who
have to make do with whatever gas comes out their own asses."

Havelock laughed at my crassness. "I knew I was right
about you. We do need you here."

My eyes narrowed. "And what *am* I doing here?"

"Please, indulge with me in a bit of history so that I may
answer your question." He sat back, thoughtful. "The Tuck

School traces its history back almost two hundred years. It was founded by Anne Kelly Tuck in the year nineteen hundred and three, with the intent of utilizing the revolutionary teaching methods she saw being applied in the country known as Italy. The school has grown and evolved its teaching practices since then, of course, but our mission to produce men and women capable of achieving their maximum potential for the benefit of society remains the same. 'Go Forth Bravely' is our school motto."

I scowled. Havelock was throwing tinder on the fire of resentment inside me. "The highborn go forth to grab as much for themselves as possible. Then they use giant machines to silence anyone who complains."

He held up a hand, a gesture meant to urge patience. But I wanted to leave, not get a self-justifying lecture.

"I'm not highborn, Ms. Machado, in case you haven't guessed. I was born in Rwanda, the son of two teachers. The genetic manipulation of fetuses was unknown at the time of my birth; we had no 'highborn' as you call them. I came to this country when it was still a whole nation, before California broke away. Before the Equality and Fairness Act. I aced the clunky school-admission test that Tuck used back then and got in. This place made me more than I ever could have been without it. Throughout its history, it has done that for people. And we have a place for you. But you need to have the courage to take that chance."

"Why?" I asked, my voice almost a hiss. "I can't pay. The equality laws don't allow you to take people based on race, or even economic background. Why give me assistance? What do you get out of it?"

"Let us be clear that you are receiving an incentive package to entice you away from your existing position, something justified by our school's current situation. Financial assistance based on need is, of course, illegal." He looked at me to confirm that I understood his meaning. "We have a somewhat unique charter. You see, this place was established when the Five Cities were still New York City, and a good chunk of the very valuable property we occupy, amid the embassies of nations and mansions of allocators, once belonged to the government. It was sold to the school with the stipulation that we continue to serve as a place of learning for the City of New York, including accepting students from each of what were then the five boroughs of New York City. The deed upon which our property rights rely mandates that we have at least one student from Bronx City at all times. It's a geographic requirement, not a racial one. And we don't have anyone right now. Our lawyers have informed me that we are on quite solid ground in offering you this slot. Indeed, we place ourselves at risk if it remains vacant."

"So I'm here to bail you out of a mess. If I'm here you keep all your super-expensive fancy buildings?"

"There's a thousand people to fill that slot. Many would do it just for the travel pass, much less the education and opportunity that comes with it. You're here because I see potential in you." His eyes bulged outwards, "You're here because I want you here."

I thought about that magnificent track downstairs, four hundred meters of perfection. I thought about the classrooms, the fabrication labs. This place was a palace compared to my pathetic wreck of a school. I'd be far better positioned to get where I wanted to be if I accepted. But I knew I'd hate myself for it. The people that went to and supported this school treated every person I knew like dirt. They sent the enforcers to my home. These people said my mother's life was worth nothing. Mateo's life was just as useless to them. If the Waste had afflicted the rich people of Manhattan, the government would've done something about it. This school produced the captains of the highborn oppression machine. Besides, my spider-sense told me I still didn't have the whole story.

"Not interested," I declared, impressed with how certain I sounded.

Havelock's brows rose, but he did not seem the least bit deterred.

"You work hard in school. Top grades, best in your class. You run like no one else in all of Bronx City. But those aren't ends in themselves. You are working for something. Where do you hope to go next, young lady?"

I clenched my mouth shut.

He leaned closer, eyes intense, sincere. "I am not your enemy, Daniela. I am your ally. Let me help you."

I chewed on my lip. "MU."

"Ah, Manhattan University, formerly New York University. An interesting choice. Not Columbia. Not Harvard," he observed, the fingertips of each hand joined together. He looked me over, thinking of something. Scheming. Traitors always schemed.

Without warning, he stood. He was at least half a foot taller than me. "I would like to show you something, if I might."

"I've already had the tour." I didn't stand.

"Ms. Flint-Dayish is an accomplished tour guide, no doubt. But there is something I believe you will be interested in that is not on the tour."

I still hesitated.

"It will be worth your time. Please."

I crept out of my seat and followed him. Kortilla wasn't in the waiting area when I exited, but she could take care of herself. Havelock set a brisk pace, navigating the twisting maze of corridors and haphazard stairways with ease. We banged across the ancient wood. He glanced back to make sure I followed, leading me downward till I was certain we were beneath the school again. But we did not go to any of the recreational facilities that Ms. Flint-Dayish had shown me.

"This is a little-used access tunnel," Mr. Havelock told me as he led me into a poorly lit but still beautiful hallway, its ceiling adorned by angels carved into the stone facade. After we had walked a bit further, he added, "We're beyond the main campus. I'm taking you to a facility that I think you'll find of interest. More so than to any of our other students."

My spider-sense wasn't giving me any bad vibes despite the eerie journey. I fought back the urge to like the guy as he droned on about the old New York City water system. Eighteen reservoirs, dozens of great aqueducts. A new Rome. This tunnel had once been a part of it. Havelock had charisma. Like Mateo. I wanted to trust him.

He led me into a lift with a single glowing electronic eye and no floor buttons. "Tuck Facility," he told it, waving his viser. The machine moved swiftly, its doors snapping open at our destination before I had time to guess where he had taken me.

We stepped off the elevator into an immaculate chamber of scrubbed blankness and soothing lights. I'd never seen so much white. It was as if the rest of my life had been lived in mud. Soft classical music surrounded us. Teams of men and women dressed in ivory gowns worked behind translucent walls, monitoring screens, gazing at holograms of data. Giant machines of unknown purpose hummed soothingly. The air smelled like winter and disinfectant.

"Welcome to the Tuck Life Facility," he told me, motioning around him.

I struggled to keep my breathing steady as I looked around the palace of science and technology, measuring it against the few dilapidated clinics in Bronx City: diamonds versus frozen piss, I decided. The workers took it all for granted, as did their pampered patients.

"This is a…a clinic?" I asked as the image of a human brain appeared on a nearby screen, so real I could touch it.

"The complex is a part of the Lenox Life Center. Like most Manhattan lifecare institutions, its services are available to paying members only, the total number of whom are capped. The waitlist for this facility is about seven years. Tuck has its own floor, exclusively for our students, faculty, and alumni. This center is endowed by many of the greatest allocators in the country. Its capabilities exceed anything at Manhattan University, I assure you."

I looked at him with sharp eyes and tight lips. The bastard had guessed why I dreamed of getting into MU. Why I had worked my rear off to make sure I could get in, ever since I suspected Mateo was getting sick.

"How did you know?"

Havelock sighed, a breath burdened with memory. But he spoke analytically.

"MU is less prestigious than several other colleges in and around the Five Cities. It's an odd choice for purely academic achievement. But it does have the best university-affiliated hospital. Basic deductive reasoning. I did earn my way into Tuck, Ms. Machado."

"This place is available for my brother?" I asked, my voice shaking as I gazed around at the technology. Aba had saved every cent she earned so she could scrape together enough for a semester of tuition at MU. All for Mateo, so he could use my student health care membership when I got into school.

"Families may be included in the student membership for an additional fee," Havelock assured me. "A portion of your financial incentive package could be allocated to cover that charge." He extended a hand to me. "Can I congratulate you on accepting your offer to Tuck?"

Everything I had worked for was being offered to me. They just needed a bit of my soul. I let go of the breath I had been holding for almost four years, ever since I began to suspect that Mateo had the Waste. The burden drained out of me, leaving me deflated, but with a tiny spark of guilty elation. I took his hand.

"I'm in."

"Excellent, excellent," he told me, satisfied. Havelock motioned towards the elevator. "Let us return to the administration building. I'll have Ms. Mark complete the arrangements. I trust you'll handle the formalities with your grandmother?"

"I'll take care of it," I told him. For Mateo, she'd do anything.

Havelock hummed a tune as the lift brought us to the bowels of the facility. Classical. Something for a highborn. I studied him. He had gone to considerable lengths to get me here. He had done background investigative work on my family. Why go through so much trouble? What did he want from me? It seemed like too much just to fill an empty seat for his school.

As we left the lift and walked side-by-side down the subterranean corridor beneath Manhattan's streets, it occurred to me that I had failed to ask the most obvious question of all. I shivered as I considered the oversight, knowing I wasn't going to like the answer to my next question.

"What happened to the person who had the Bronx City slot before me?"

The humming stopped.

"She killed herself."

CHAPTER
SEVEN

I found Kortilla in the hallway, bantering in Spanish with a Tuck student who looked like the "after" image of an alterator advertisement, silver locks and all. He flipped his viser signature to her before we left. She pretended not to notice.

"I thought they were the enemy?" I asked, my mouth open in mock shock.

Kortilla shrugged. "I've never met a highborn. I can't complain about the face."

"Improved symmetry of physical features as a result of genetic correction in the womb," I said, reciting a sim I had seen offering the service to expectant mothers.

Kortilla rolled her eyes at me.

We walked back in silence. My stomach clenched as I thought about what I had done: I was abandoning my friend. I was joining the richies. On the subway, I confessed that I had accepted the offer to go to Tuck. I thought Kortilla would be mad at me, or at least disappointed. If so, she hid it well. She wrapped her arms around me.

"It's better than MU," I told her. "If anyone can stop the Waste, it'll be there."

Kortilla looked skeptical. "I hope so. But don't do this for him. Do it for you."

"He's my brother. This is all for him." I said it, but the words were hollow.

"Remember, they want something from you."

I thought about the BC girl who had died, opening the way for me. I hadn't seen anything on the net about it. I didn't follow Manhattan news much, but this girl was from Bronx City. There would've been something. I tapped my viser, looking for information on the net. There was nothing.

"What you lookin' for?" Kortilla asked as the train entered the tunnel beneath the Harlem River, leaving Manhattan behind.

I told her the little I knew about my predecessor.

"There's always a catch with those *bastardos.*"

We got off the train and walked home, traversing forlorn streets, their cracked asphalt leaking ugly steam. The sour air rolled into my lungs, the taste lingering in my mouth. The people around us wore hard faces. There was not a familiar to be seen. Here, I stood among men and women worried about survival, not elegance. These were my people. I promised myself I would not forget that.

Aba was waiting for me at home. She listened to my news in stony silence. As I told her about Tuck, I found myself wishing she would share something more of herself with me. But today was not the day for an eleven-year silence to come to an abrupt end. It wasn't until I got to the part about the Lenox Life Center that I was certain Aba understood a word I had said.

"Mateo must go there," she said as if I didn't already know that, as if I hadn't just told her that I had agreed to put myself among those highborn snakes so my brother could use their medical facility.

"I don't even know where he is," I admitted. "I'll red ping him."

"Go succeed," she urged, though it sounded more like a rebuke than a command.

I pushed the school consent from my viser to Aba's ancient handheld. I watched as she gave the obligatory thumbprint authorization. My wrist vibrated as a flood of digital contracts became effective. Just like that, I was a student at the most prestigious high school in the world, an ugly duckling among highborn swans. I should have felt proud, or at least scared. Instead, I felt dirty.

I flopped onto my bed and tried to contact Mateo, without any success. Then I searched the public net again, digging for something that hinted at a death at Tuck. Nothing. That scared me. Not even the highborn could control the net, not all of it. They might own the major news feeds, the data aggregators, the viser companies, but there was always some trace on the net. I suspected a crawler had been unleashed to cleanse any lingering trace that couldn't be suppressed directly. It must've been a good one, lots of capacity behind it, which meant lots of money. Mateo would know better than me, though.

I switched tactics. I looked for dead girls in Bronx City in the past three weeks. I found a lot. I narrowed the search to those between fifteen and eighteen years old. The number remained daunting. People stepped up to the front line in the gangs around that age, and casualty rates were high. Most didn't have funerals. I eliminated those. A girl who went to Tuck would've had a family behind her, someone who cared. Someone who would mourn her. That made it easier. Marie-Ann Rebello was her name, I was almost certain. She had been accepted into the Five Cities Gifted and Talented Program before it had been canceled. After that, there was no record of her in any of the Bronx City schools. Then a funeral. I guessed a crawler must've erased the rest, anything with her name and

Tuck's, but the pieces fit too well to be anything else. A bit more digging revealed she had a mother and father, both tax-payers. People who cared enough to pay the government for services and the right to vote. That had to be them. It was close to midnight. I sent them a ping with my verified identity and a short request to speak to them about their daughter.

I shut my eyes. Tomorrow I would face the highborn.

CHAPTER

EIGHT

The scene around the Tuck School reminded me of an anthill consisting entirely of the best-fed ants in the world. Students ranging from five to eighteen years old streamed towards the opposing entrances of the illustrious school—my school—in a navy and white parade of controlled chaos. The kids compensated for the monotony of their clothing with a dazzling array of hair colors: gold, platinum, silver, copper, chrome, and several I couldn't guess. You could've mined their skulls for precious metals, but not much else. Younger students clustered on the south side of the street, upper-school students stayed on the north side, while hulking vehicles, their exteriors colored in hostile shades of black, human drivers at the wheel, traversed the street to deposit their pampered cargo at Tuck's doorstep. Familiars ruled the skies like air cover for an invasion.

I turned onto the street atop humble feet, the only school-aged person not attired in a standard uniform, although I had chosen dark colors. Not that I expected to blend in. In addition to not being in uniform, I lacked the obligatory mechanized crown floating above my head. There was also the matter of my skin color. And I walked alone. Kortilla's absence ached inside me as I forced myself to proceed at a deliberate pace down that surreal street; I missed her strength.

All too quickly, people noticed me. They did it without pointing. But heads flipped, eyes spoke, whispers flew. My spider-sense felt the looks: curious, hostile, incredulous. These people had been together for years, in school as well as Manhattan society. I could no more blend in here than a highborn could've gone incognito at a Bronx City club party. I held my chin high, my breathing steady. I let them have their stares. Then a beam of pulsing light found my chest. My instinct, instilled from a lifetime of dealing with Authority's enforcement machines, was to bolt. But I caught myself in time. *That's what they want.* The light came from a familiar overhead. I just managed to keep my pace steady, my face blank. I heard a few snickers, but they faded quickly. So did the beam. I didn't smile on the outside.

I climbed the great stone steps, trying to project confidence while the rest of the student body continued to mill around on the street. At PS 62 they used a metal bell to alert everyone that classes were about to start. They probably used a live orchestra here.

The lemon-coated guards in the reception box took a careful look at me when I entered, but eventually waved me through to the musty premises beyond. I realized I had no idea where I was going. A schedule had been transmitted to me, but my viser had stopped functioning as soon as I had entered the school. I was as lost as a rat in a maze. I was about to ask for directions when a diminutive girl with hair as dark as mine came briskly towards me, her face set with the worry of a harried bureaucrat.

"Daniela?" she asked, as if some other Latina in street clothes could've gotten past the fruit patrol out front. Her eyes stretched like polished almonds, her coloring hinting at Asian ancestry.

"Yes," I replied, trying to sound pleasant.

"I'm Alissa Stein. I'm your navigator." Seeing my blank look, Alissa added, "I'll help you get acquainted with Tuck, and hopefully answer as many questions as I can. I'll try to keep you out of trouble."

"Thanks," I told her, trying not to sound too cold. I couldn't decide if she was highborn or not. Her skin was as perfect as Kortilla's, but she seemed too short—she couldn't have been more than an inch or two over five feet—to have undergone genetic correction. And she didn't have a double-barreled surname.

"First, let's get you onto Castle. That's what we call the internal Tuck network." She placed her viser-clad arm over my own and began flicking fingers like a practiced pianist. Like most experts, Alissa had no need for a virtual keyboard. Her viser looked like it had been tattooed on her arm. I couldn't tell where the circuits ended and the skin began.

"Interesting device," I said.

Alissa answered without looking at me, never taking her eyes from those fast-moving fingers. "The viser's Rose-Hart tech, latest model. All the rage this year. It's bioengineered, integrates into your skin. Apart from being practically unbreakable, it doesn't respond to anyone except you." As she leaned over my wrist, I noticed she had a silvery bead, no bigger than the end of a pin, embedded into her skull behind her ear. It wasn't cosmetic. The flicking stopped. "All ready for you. Welcome to Castle."

I looked at my now functioning, archaic viser with relief. It displayed a school map, suggested routes, as well as my class schedule. Alissa glanced at my screen along with me.

She gave a sigh of disapproval. My back stiffened.

"It's nothing," Alissa explained in a hurry. "Only…they gave you Marie-Ann's schedule. I guess everything else was full. Typical."

The name echoed in my head. "You knew her?"

"Sure, we all know each other," Alissa said. "We've got a couple of classes together." I couldn't tell if that was a good thing or not.

My viser vibrated. So did Alissa's.

"That's the bell. The flood is about to start," she told me. "Let's get going. We've got Literature together. I'll show you the way. But let's stop downstairs first. You can borrow one of my skins—that's what we all call the uniform—until you get your own."

I laughed. Our heights weren't even close.

Alissa endured my ignorance with a neutral expression. "The skins only look archaic. They're one size fits all; they adapt to all body types. Also, they can regulate their temperature." I should've known the richies couldn't just wear clothes like the rest of us.

We went to the sub-levels, into the girl's locker room. I felt that beautiful track calling to me from nearby. Alissa handed me a navy garment with white trim, which I handled as I might a snake.

She chuckled. "It won't bite."

I put it on like any other outfit, albeit slower. It oozed into the correct form, reminding me of lurker sludge coming out of a Bronx City alleyway.

"You can control the temperature and tweak the sizing with your viser. You could even make it change colors, if you hacked the Castle network's restrictive protocols. Of course, that's probably an honor code violation so I wouldn't advise it."

"What does that mean?"

"Honor code violation? Usually, you're thrown out of school. Of course, they can recommend a more lenient sentence for general mischief, but cheating, stealing, fighting, other dishonorable conduct, is an automatic expulsion. If that happens, you're doomed to walk the earth as a Tuck has-been."

"If you're like me," I said.

"Even the highest of the highborn can be kicked out," Alissa assured me, confirming that she was not one of them. "The headmaster and his masters on the Board of Trustees might set the rules, but we all have to live by them, even their little darlings. It happened a few years ago. A couple of boys hacked the network to try to steal a test. Even their elite allocator parents couldn't save them."

"They were still rich, still highborn, though," I noted. "Getting expelled wouldn't be worth killing yourself over. They'd never be really desperate. Like Marie-Ann must've been."

"Look to the future, Daniela," Alissa advised me. "The school will assign a locker to you by the end of the day. Skins, digiBook, and everything else you need will be inside. You'll get the details on your viser. The cost is deducted from your student account."

"Uh, great, I guess."

"Cheer up, I hear you've got track tryouts this afternoon," Alissa said. "They reopened the team just for you."

"How do you know?" I was starting to feel annoyed that she knew a bit too much about me.

"The whole school knows. Everyone is looking forward to getting a look at the best runner in Bronx City. I'll be there too. To cheer you on, of course."

I clenched my teeth. They were coming to see the monkey perform. I willed the anger bubbling inside me away. *All for Mateo*.

"Let's get to Lit," Alissa said. "Mr. Lynder is pretty tough. Let's not test him."

She led me upstairs with the ease of someone walking through their own home. The halls were empty. Paintings of old, dead people stared down at me from the wood paneled walls as I traipsed through the corridors, wearing clothes that weren't mine. We walked into class with the subtlety of a pair of elephants. Every student looked up to check me out; Mr. Lynder, a man as old and rundown as my apartment building in the Bronx, pretended not to notice us. Alissa directed me to one of the two empty desks in the room with a silent finger before taking her own seat. I slid into the ancient writing space gently, its surface rubbed smooth by the illustrious bottoms of hundreds of wealthy Manhattanites before me. The desk was of the double seater variety. My seatmate glanced over at me with sapphire eyes and a gaze as warm as a blizzard. He reminded me of a statue come to life, his hands enlarged like those of Michelangelo's David, his hair as golden as a crown.

Lynder held a genuine paper notepad in his hands, its cover worn to near rot. His voice reverberated with a depth possessed only by the naturally aged.

"...they had all been brought up, we suppose, to be fine boys—in the old English tradition, with proper manners. When did it all begin to go badly?" He paused, scanning the room. There were a mere twenty of us in the classroom. That was the line for the bathroom back in my public school.

"Mr. Sorell-Weaks?" the teacher said.

A narrow-shouldered boy near the front answered, his voice easy, confident. "It's not about when it went wrong, sir. They had the savagery within them the whole time. You could say it went bad the moment they fell out of the sky onto that island, with no communication. You could even say it happened at birth."

"Ah, so you think Golding is trying to say something about humanity itself?"

"Yes, that they are all savages inside. Civilization keeps them in line. Without it, they are animals."

They are all savages, not we. Not the highborn.

"And where else can we find themes like these? In reading or in life. An example, Mr. Sorell-Weaks, of the opposite view. That man is good, and civilization corrupts. Please."

A pause followed the question. I heard the ticking of an ancient clock. The tension grew thick. Sorell-Weaks squirmed in his seat. The teacher showed no sign of offering mercy.

"*Frankenstein*," came the reply at last. "The monster was good but became evil. People made the monster evil."

"And now, let's see...perhaps Ms. Machado," he said. My heart hurdled into my throat as every eye in the room focused on me. "Which of these themes have been laid out in a more compelling manner by the authors, in your opinion?"

I blinked, my mind balky. "Ah..."

"Oh, are you familiar with these titles? We are discussing *Lord of the Flies* and *Frankenstein*, of course." I hadn't read them. I doubted a single student in my old school had. We had more important things to deal with. Like staying alive in the halls.

"No."

"I see," he noted in a baritone voice thick with disapproval. "Here, we give our opinions, and support them with logic. All of us. If you are going to be in that seat, you must be ready."

My face burned. *Condescending bastard.*

He moved on to the next student. The statue next to me glanced in my direction. I imagined a snide grin crawling up his chiseled face, even though there wasn't one. Yet. My temperature rose to a boil. *Even the teachers are against me.* The remainder of the class passed in an angry haze.

Alissa hurried over when the lesson concluded.

"Mr. Lynder knows no mercy," she told me in soothing tones. "We've all gotten hit. You'll get over it. Look on the shelf under your desk."

I did, pulling out a hardcover book from beneath the desk. It had the severed head of a bleeding pig on its cover. I could sympathize. The author's name, William Golding, was emblazoned at the top left.

"You use paper books?" I asked. Ridiculously expensive and inefficient.

She placed her viser over it and did a little wiggle. "*Frankenstein*, Mary Shelley."

The book cover transformed to show a grotesque monster on its cover. I opened it. The inside pages had changed as well. Of course, the richies couldn't just use e-readers.

"This is the class digiBook. There will be one at almost every desk you sit in, and another in your pack for home. Your reading list is on your viser, along with access to the school library, which is basically infinite. Remember, Lynder shows no mercy, and he's not the only one. Get caught up quick. You got the rest of your schedule?"

I glanced at my viser and nodded.

"I'll see you in Chem," Alissa told me, getting ready to walk away. "Good luck. And hang in there."

"Who was the guy next to me?" I asked, not quite sure why.

"Alexander Foster-Rose-Hart," she told me with a frown. "Alexander the Great, he calls himself."

I huffed at the presumption of his alias. But the actual name sounded familiar. Alissa saw me make the connection. She tapped the viser on her hand, the one integrated into her skin, reminding me of the manufacturer's name: Rose-Hart. Then she walked away, shaking her head.

NINE

O nce I got over the unfamiliar tech, the Socratic teaching style and the wary stares of pretty highborns, school was still school. History seemed fascinating, economics mostly propaganda and Trigonometry downright basic. Script was a killer. I hadn't touched a pen in years and got ink all over my hands. My lab advisor, Eleanor Nest-Birditch, was a beautiful blond specimen who I would've pegged as a sim actress rather than a teacher. She gave me a week to think about my proposed area of study, but I told her then and there that I wanted to concentrate on bio-fabrication. I got a raised eyebrow in reply, but she said she'd get things prepared for me by the next day. Lunch blew me away. Real stuff, every bite. I ate two hamburgers, even knowing I had to run this afternoon. I couldn't help myself.

My last class of the day was Chemistry. My viser guided me to my assigned seat. I wondered if Marie-Ann had sat here before she died.

Alissa hadn't arrived yet, so I watched my fellow students shuffle in, easy laughter flowing from most. Natural light poured into the vintage classroom though giant rectangular windows. I perused the simulated pages of the digiBook at my desk, its contents far more advanced than anything I had previously seen, but logical enough that I knew I could catch up. The day was almost complete. I could handle the academics here. The highborn and other students were smart and quick, but so was I. Now I needed to get Mateo into the life facility.

A series of long and short vibrations on my viser interrupted my thoughts. The pattern was old Morse code. It felt so familiar I thought for a moment that it was Kortilla.

"D-a-y g-o-o-d?" the person wondered in vibration language.

I looked up and saw Alissa flash a wink in my direction. I forced the corners of my mouth upward. I appreciated the concern, but I wasn't ready to tell her anything more.

Chemistry was taught by Franklin Flinn III, a twenty-year veteran of Tuck. Unlike most other teachers, he ignored his students. He spoke to the formulas flashing across the smart boards as he lectured. By the conclusion of the lecture, I knew more about covalent bonds than I had ever before in my life—easy because my starting point was nothing. But I was focused on my appointment with Tuck track.

Alissa found me at my desk. "How did your first day go?"

"I'll tell you when it's over."

"This was our last class."

"I've got track tryouts," I reminded her.

Alissa glanced at the students milling around the classroom and adjacent hallway. "I'll walk down to the lockers with you. You want to grab something to eat first?"

"I've got two burgers in my stomach," I confessed.

"I know what you mean," she said with a hand on her belly.

I smiled in spite of myself. "I never get to eat—" I was going to say "real meat" but stopped. Even if Alissa wasn't highborn, she was still a richie, still a Manhattanite. She wasn't my friend, just my navigator, assigned by the school.

Alissa didn't press for the remainder of my thoughts. Maybe she understood enough about life outside Manhattan to get it. More likely she didn't. With a gentle touch on my shoulder, she led me along a route away from the main staircases, away from the crowds, towards a narrow side passage. When we were alone, she spoke in a voice resembling a whisper.

"About Coach Nessmier...he's...a difficult sort..." Alissa said, the words halting with unease.

The track coach was an ass. Perfect.

"He's not highborn," she assured me. "But he's...He's what we call a 'partisan.' He thinks like them."

"What does that mean? How do they think?"

The sound of ancient wood creaking warned us that some of our fellow students approached. "Just be ready for anything. Things work differently here, even in track. You're expected to know that, even if you just got here. Like with Mr. Lynder. Merit only, no special treatment is what they'd call it. It's worse than that, but..."

A quartet of navy and white approached us. Three were boys, each broad of shoulder, their features expertly sculpted, albeit from different types of clay. But there was no mistaking their leader: She rivaled the height of the tallest of the males, but was slender and as sleek as a leopard, with hair of gold and a face to distract Narcissus. Her eyes were a storm of blue.

Alissa turned towards the group, a smile tight across her face. They all held themselves like rulers, heads high. The dark centers of their eyes glittered with the knowledge that the world belonged to them. They were older than Alissa and me—seniors, I guessed.

"Alissa," said the queen among these nobles of Manhattan. "Very nice to see you. And you must be Daniela Machado, our newest student. Welcome. I am so glad to have a chance to welcome you to Tuck. I'm Kristolan Foster-Rose-Hart. But that is a lot of words to say, so please call me Kris."

A porcelain hand extended towards me. I took it as I might candy from a stranger on the streets of Bronx City. There was a small head bow too.

Her fingers pulsed with heat. "Daniela Machado," I proclaimed, letting Bronx City come through in each word. I didn't move my head. That was a highborn custom. One of the boys, an Aryan archetype, hissed at the slight. Kris brushed him with the back of her hand, and he quieted like a well-trained pet.

"We do take pride in our track team here," Kris told me, her voice honey, her smile one of welcome, despite the aversion of her entourage. My scowl was like an ice cube in the summer sun under her scrutiny. It soon left my face. "What you accomplished already is remarkable. I know my brother is anxious to see what you can do on the track, as are we all."

"Your brother?" I heard myself ask.

"Alexander. He's the team captain. Hopefully, you'll join him to bring back a championship this year."

"I'd be glad to make the team." I didn't quite understand why I kept talking to her. I should be getting ready to race.

She placed a gentle hand on my shoulder, like a concerned parent. "Tuck is about merit, despite what you may have heard. If you should be on the team, you will be. Alexander will see to that. He always does what's right. I won't keep you any longer. I'll be there rooting for you, though."

Kris glided away, her minions following in her wake.

"You've been blessed by royalty," Alissa told me, her voice so flat she might as well have been reciting Trig equations. "Now you know the Foster-Rose-Hart siblings. Beware."

I went downstairs to prepare.

Attired in a smart navy running skin emblazoned with the roaring head of the Tuck tiger, I stepped out onto the track. The largest crowd I had ever run in front of milled about in the polished metal stands surrounding the gym's glowing concentric ovals. There must have been four hundred people, including students from the elementary school and adults whom I assumed were part of the faculty. All for a tryout. And a chance to see the freak from across the river. I felt like a kidnapped gladiator entering an arena. A simulated sky of dazzling azure hovered above me, its fabrication so perfect I squinted at the artificial sun.

Eyes filled with curiosity and judgment watched me go through my warm-ups. I wished I could blame the double helping of burgers for the queasiness in my stomach. My potential teammates clustered alongside a stocky man with shoulder length crow-colored hair and a hawkish nose. He wore an oversized golden whistle around his neck; the thing was bigger than my fist. Mr. Whistle sensed my attention and strode towards me, his eyes getting smaller as the distance between us closed. I went back to my warm-ups.

He positioned himself an inch from my head as I bent my hands down to my toes. I heard an annoyed sigh as he waited for me. His squinty stare greeted me when I finished my stretch. His whistle was a finger's length from my chest. I held my ground.

"Ms. Machado, I'm Coach Nessmier, Director of Athletics here at Tuck. I'm also the upper-school track coach."

"Nice to meet you, Coach."

He frowned. "In the ten years I've been leading the track team, we've taken six Manhattan titles and four national championships. But we've never reopened tryouts during the school year. For anyone."

"Um…thanks. But it wasn't my idea."

"Mine either," he informed me. I wondered whose idea it was then. "I think you'll find the competition in Manhattan is a little different from what you're used to, as are the rules."

"I hope so," I offered back.

The edges of Nessmier's lips looked like they had been weighed down by barbells.

"We'll run the fifteen hundred meters since that's your primary event. We use two runners at that distance in meets. I already have my alternates. Which means you need to finish first or second to make the team."

"Understood," I assured him, glancing back at the navy cluster behind him.

"Do you?" he asked. "Everyone earns their place at Tuck. Alexander won the city championship in his events last year. We compete in the Manhattan Conditioned Track League here; we play by different rules, and at a higher level than elsewhere. That's why thousands of people come to watch, even at the high school level. I hope this isn't a waste of my time."

"Me too," I told him.

My Literature seatmate was doing a pogo-stick impression near the edge of the track. He caught my stare and gave me a dip of his head: the pack alpha acknowledging a challenge. Alexander the Great indeed.

Coach Nessmier placed a hand on his oversized whistle. He fingered a few buttons on the back. The track lanes lit up a bright yellow, the starting line pulsed red. The gym walls disappeared. We now stood inside the Coliseum of ancient Rome. Arcades of empty seating soared around me, magnificent arches of polished stone framing the perimeter. A chorus of trumpets called out from beyond the faux stadium, shrilling with self-importance.

"Better take your place," the coach said to me. He waved to the crowd as he walked away, a little emperor with his whistle.

The other seven runners had already lined up by the time I made my way over. I got the middle lane, with half the runners slightly ahead of me, the other half slightly behind. I felt my blood heating as I placed my foot on the line. A digital apparition of the number "1,500" appeared ahead of each of the runners.

"Get that out of my face," I told the omnipresent machine projecting holograms at me. The numbers vanished.

"Later, little nope," the mop-haired boy next to me said, his legs dauntingly long.

A pistol shot rang out. I hurled myself forward. Charged with anger, I streaked at my best speed, cutting towards the inside lane. I found Alexander already there, right on the edge of the line, a turd in my favorite spot. He flew like shot through a gun, his rhythm perfect, his feet barely touching the ground. I let him lead, hovering on his right wing, further outside than I wanted. I moved in behind him for the turn, keeping my track no longer than his. Our feet pounded the ground, quick and steady. I ran the fastest first lap in my life; sweat poured down my cheeks. No other runner in BC could've kept this pace and finished a respectable race. But I didn't need to look behind to know that six other runners were still clumped around Alexander and me.

Damn, these kids could run.

A girl, taller and longer-legged than I, crowded me on the inside as we took the first turn of the second lap. Her neck leaned forward like a giraffe's, her strides resembled a gallop, her shoulders were as wide as Alexander's. Behind me, thick breath, hot and hostile like a dragon's, blew onto my shoulder.

Giraffe matched my strides, keeping me from cutting to the inside lane.

"Back to your dirty hole," she hissed, not sounding winded at all.

Runners surrounded me on three sides, our legs churning in near unison. Which left me behind Alexander. The only place for me to go was outside. Trying to win a race from outside the first lane was stupid. I tried anyway. As we reached the third lap, I hit the gas. A mistake.

Alexander was ready.

I moved right, then jammed on the speed, pushing with everything I had. He equaled me, not a bead of sweat on his face. I let up, just a bit, to cut inside him. He matched my maneuver, keeping me outside. My heart pounded in my chest. But it wasn't because I was tired.

I reached for the reservoir of strength inside me. Anger guided me there. I saw myself from above, running, surrounded by highborn, desperate. Ice flowed around me, through me. I drank it and used it. All my strength, no pain. Just go. My legs pumped, my feet moved like they had fire beneath them. But Alexander still hugged my left side. Dragon-breath had dropped back, but not too far. He had legs like tree trunks and good position in the inside lane. The turn approached. I would be running a longer track against the best runner I had ever faced if I stayed pinned outside. I reached within for even more. No one could sprint faster than me. Wrong.

I took the turn in the third lane, Alexander like a devoted groom next to me. Dragon-breath pulled even with us using the shorter track inside. I knew a tie wouldn't go my way.

We went flat out down the straightaway, Alexander, Dragon-breath and me. No one else on the track had what we had. Alexander edged closer to the inside lane as the next turn approached. Beating Dragon-breath mattered to him also. I crept into the second lane.

"You gonna lose, nope," someone proclaimed from behind me. The highborn didn't get irony.

We took the next turn like a cluster of rockets, but I emerged behind the other two. The ice in my limbs began to thaw. Pain clawed at the edge of my perception. My feet danced on knives. The prospect of losing to these mutants ate at me. I remembered the sneering mummy-faced richie on Madison Avenue from yesterday, her pampered dog, her sneer. Anger was my nitro. I pushed harder. I was ice again. I could fly; a blizzard with legs. I pulled even, then ahead, just a nose. Third lap done. Three hundred meters left.

I felt the others behind me, like an inferno outside my locked door. They grew hotter behind me, but I had the lead now, and the inside. The finish line was a dancing rope of fluorescent violet ahead. There was nothing between me and another victory. *Alexander the Not So Great.*

As I hit the last stretch of track, a gusting wind whipped at me as unexpectedly as lightning appearing in a clear sky. Sand, minute but sharp, stung my eyes. A hundred needles grazed my face, my arms, my legs. A tiny cry escaped my lips. My rhythm faltered, ever so slightly. Alexander and Dragon-breath were on me, even with me, ahead of me. My body numbed and I commanded my legs to fly forth. Too late. We hurled through the finish line, Alexander, Dragon-breath, then me.

A wicked red image informing me of my third-place finish flashed in front of me. I sucked hard for air, my fingers locked behind my head. I was drenched. Fire smoldered beneath my feet, in my lungs. The crowd's roar penetrated the fog around me. Boys and girls hooted, fists pumped the air. Chants broke out.

"Tuck! Tuck! Tuck!"

Near the finish line, Coach Nessmier fingered his golden whistle, a smile on the edges of his lips. I felt something foreign in my throat, pressure behind my eyes. Someone handed me a towel, which I snatched to my face, sinking my aching teeth into the terrycloth.

When I was strong enough to look at the world again, I caught sight of a tall, slender man with dark skin slipping out of the gym. I realized then who had pushed Coach Nessmier to hold another round of tryouts. The door closed silently behind Headmaster Havelock.

TEN

I tried to walk to the locker room; I might have run. I don't remember.

I stripped off my clothes, rubbed the stink off my body as best as I could with a towel and jumped back into the clothes I had worn this morning. I grabbed my bag with the digiBook. No time to shower. Giraffe and the others would be here soon, and I intended to be gone before that.

I shut my locker, resting my head against the cool metal for a guilty moment, my eyes squeezed shut. I remembered the last time I lost a race: I was five. Mateo had beaten me, on a clear morning in Central Park, with my mother watching. I had been so mad, I'd attacked him afterward, tiny arms flailing.

"You've got strength enough inside you to never lose if you don't want to," my mom had whispered to me on the subway going home.

I had found my cold place not long after that, but only after I'd lost her. Bad trade.

Something wet dribbled down my cheek. I wiped it away, walking fast out of the locker room. I took the stairs two at time, maneuvering through the halls with my head down. A few students stared at me as I passed. I was only vaguely aware of where I was headed, but certain of where I wanted to be: outside this place.

I got lost, but with a little help from the increasingly familiar portraits on the walls, managed to find my way to the exit. Security watched me walk out with eyes usually reserved for the janitorial staff. Alissa was waiting for me on the great steps. A brooding September sky cast a gloom over her face as she watched me descend. I didn't stop to chat.

"Daniela…wait," she said as I blew past her, my head still focused on the ground. I noticed how nice the sidewalks were here; the surface some kind of high-traction polymer that resisted blemish. Alissa chased after me, jogging to match my pace. I was faster than her at least.

"Come on," Alissa urged. "You did fine."

I looked up from the ground at her, my eye screaming for her to leave me alone. She kept walking.

"Damn it, don't let them get you. Don't let them win." Alissa put her hand on my shoulder. She probably meant it as comfort. I turned on her the way I would've if someone had challenged me in the barrio, fist clenched, body tense for a fight.

"They won—didn't you see?" I near yelled the words.

"I saw you push Alexander Foster-Rose-Hart to the limit. I saw you pass him on the final lap. *No one* has ever done that. I saw you dust Mona Lisa Reves-Wyatt, and the rest of the team, except Drake Pillis-Smith, and everyone knows he takes supplementation to try to keep up with Alexander. Damn girl, I saw you run your tail off. We all did."

"And you all just love that I lost," I said. "I heard the crowd."

"People cheered because that's what we do here. We support Tuck. Don't be so sure everyone was chanting *against* you. I sure wasn't."

I realized the spectators might not have seen the wind. Or the sand. Or they were used to it and thought it fair game. Coach had told me there were different rules. I just hadn't been ready. Even though Alissa had tried to warn me. *No excuses*, I reminded myself.

"Sure sounded like they were against me, the foreign barbarian. Right down to the Roman backdrop. Coach all but told me he wanted me to lose. And I didn't disappoint."

"He's a partisan jack-A, and everyone knows it. Even the highborn don't respect him. But you need to understand that Alexander and his sister, Kris, they win at everything. People love to be a part of that…glow."

"But not you?"

"What do you think?" she replied, her eyes locking onto mine.

"I think you're rich like the rest of them."

Alissa snorted. "I'm not at all like them. My parents work for a living—for a salary. I'm not saying we aren't lucky. We are. I am. I'm at Tuck, after all. But those highborn kids," she indicated towards the school. "Their parents are *allocators*. They're *officials*. Their parents own companies with government service contracts from the perpetual President himself. Some of them are second-generation highborn, the elite of the elite."

I shrugged. "I don't get the difference in rich. You all eat real meat, real fruit. You have heat, water, clothes, medicine, and no one knifes you on the street for your fancy viser."

"Fine, Daniela. Hate us, if that is all you can see. Play the martyr, if that's all you can do," Alissa declared. "But you have a chance here. You're a fool not to take it."

Her stare lingered on me. Disappointment melted onto her face. She turned away.

After she took a step, I muttered, "*Soy una tonta.*" I said it to her back, just loud enough that she might hear. I wasn't sure if I wanted her to or not.

Alissa whipped around, hints of a grin on her lips. "I'm a fool too. People like you and me, we know what we are. The highborn can't imagine that they have flaws. That's their weakness. That's why we can beat them." She whispered the last as if sharing a great secret.

"Why do you want to beat them?"

"You noticed these?" She indicated the tiny silver beads protruding from behind her ears. "Hearing aids. Bypasses my bum auditory nerve and feeds directly to my brain. They're mostly organic material, so I don't have to worry about setting off weapon detectors every time I walk through. And I can hear better than anyone at school."

I hoped I looked less surprised than I felt. "B-but, why? Manhattan docs…That Tuck center…they can grow whatever organs you need…You can pay…can't you?"

"My mom and dad weren't born rich. They earned their jobs. Yup, it happens, Daniela. Meritocracy is not all crap. I'm not a lifer here. I got in for fifth grade, once my parents could afford it. Took the test: Aptitude Tier thirty-one. They could get me a Tuck education or get me new ears. They chose Tuck. I'm too old to have my head chopped open. And I wouldn't let them do it even if they could."

"Why not?"

She took a step towards me, eyes as serious as any I'd ever seen. "So I'll never try to be like them, no matter where I get to in life."

I smiled. "It's good to meet another fool."

I pinged Kortilla on my way back to BC. She met me at the station exit. She looked anxious, as if she was returning from her first day at school.

The girlish grin on her face disappeared as soon as she saw me. "What happened?"

I told her about it all. Except for Alissa. I wasn't ready to share about her yet.

Kortilla threw her arm around my shoulders when I told her about the race. "You didn't lose. They cheated," she assured me, disbelief in her voice. I was glad I wasn't the only one surprised that I'd been beaten.

"No excuses." I sounded like Aba.

"Who gives a deuce? They don't deserve you. You're still getting a free ride. Mateo's still going to get cured in their fancy hospital, right?"

"He's not answering my pings," I said glancing in vain at my viser. "I red pinged that I needed to speak to him. When I tell him that he always finds a way to get back to me. But nothing yet."

"I know you worry, Dee. But he'll be all right. He's not a babe."

I grunted rather than agree. We headed for home.

We crossed a busy intersection onto One Hundred and Eighty-Eighth Street, dodging filth-spewing diesel lift trucks and early model electrics that jockeyed in vain for position amid the street traffic. Repetitive slabs of concrete marred in their monotony by a few scattered windows lined both sides of the road. Men and women of all colors and creeds teemed around us on the crumbling sidewalk, their clothes shabby, their eyes wary. Even the adults were shorter than many of the boys at Tuck, their shoulders slumped forward rather than being drawn back. I never knew enough about the world of Manhattan to notice the difference before now.

On our way, we came upon a girl, no more than a couple of years older than me, spinning aimlessly around the middle of the sidewalk, her mouth belching out "ring around the rosie" in a near-drunken slur. She wore a threadbare shirt of bright pink that extended down to her knees. Her bare feet were filthy, the skin of her face pulled to her cheekbones, her body gaunt though not yet starved. People gave her as wide a berth as the sidewalk allowed, but otherwise ignored her.

"Z-Pop," Kortilla muttered as we made our way around the girl.

Like Kortilla, I'd been trained that the best way to deal with crazies was to ignore them while creating as much distance between you and them as possible. But this girl caught my eye, and I didn't look away. Her body moved with an uncomfortable cadence. The pallor of her skin was a shade of rotten apricot, more like something out of a net cartoon than real-life. Scabs and rashes encrusted swaths of her limbs; she reminded me of a caterpillar forming its cocoon, her body forced into metamorphosis by the drug in her system. I stopped to study her. Kortilla put her hand on my shoulder to hurry me along. That was when I noticed it. The tawny creases on her lips, around her eyes: the Waste.

"What you doin'? Let's go," Kortilla urged.

I broke out of my trance, falling back in beside my friend. "She's got the Waste..."

Kortilla didn't look back. "Least of her problems. She's an addict and on her way to worse. Half lurker already. You see those scabs? And her eyes? Better the Waste than become one of the friggin' Z-Pop zombies..."

"It starts around the same age...We're not too far away."

"We ain't getting the Waste. You're in the best shape of any person I know, and neither of us touch the Pop," Kortilla assured me.

"Neither did Mateo. People have been dying for five years, and nobody knows anything. People barely talk about it."

"Everyone is dying around here, Daniela. Gangs, or Z-Pop, or Resister-H, cancer, or whatever. The Waste is just another item on the list."

"But it kills people our age. No one else. Just us. Teenagers, and maybe a bit older."

"So live for now," Kortilla said, a touch of defiance in her voice. "Enjoy the days we have, before the Orderists decide that the low AT classes are too much of a burden on society."

ELEVEN

I couldn't sleep, so I set off for school early.

A wave of my viser and twenty minutes on the subway took me to Wonderland: doormen tidied the area in front of their buildings, sanitation workers collected refuse, servants walked overweight dogs with shining fur, dutifully cleaning up after their charges. Real flowers and trees grew in planters along the sidewalks of Park Avenue. Hints of dawn tantalized on the warming horizon just barely visible through the corridors of elegant towers. The great doors of Tuck opened at the silent beckoning of my viser; security waved me through the protective portal as if I belonged here.

I headed to my locker, gliding through halls and down stairways that had been alien to me just yesterday. I showered in their unlimited water supply and swapped my street clothes for the strange techno-skin, completing my outward transformation into a native of Tuck. I placed a hand over my heart, just to be sure it was the same one as yesterday. My viser told me I had over twenty minutes left before the official start of classes.

There was no sign of my humiliating defeat in the locker room, no banners marked the occasion of another highborn victory. But the image of Alexander crossing the finish line half a step ahead lingered. I gazed at the heavy metal door that led to the track that I would never run on again. I left the locker room the way I came in, my blood simmering.

Mona Lisa Reves-Wyatt and Drake Pillis-Smith stood in the hallway, blocking my way to the stairs. Their eyes widened, then narrowed.

Mona Lisa stood an inch taller than me, with wider shoulders and a sloping face. Her hair flowed Irish red, ending at her neck. Drake was taller still, with hair of gold and black. His nostrils flared, his brows as sharp as a cliff. Something reptilian and dangerous lurked in that face. They slithered towards me, unhurried; their grins held no warmth.

"You ran off without congratulating me," Drake said, his eyes gleaming with sadistic pleasure. "Bad sportsmanship."

"Forget it, Drake. She doesn't get advanced human concepts," Mona Lisa added.

"And what would the two of you know about being human?"

Mona Lisa stepped into my personal space. "Oh, little girl, you are going down fast. With an uppity mouth like that, you're going to end up jumping onto the sidewalk like Marie-Ann. Such a mess. And our Mr. Havelock will have to find yet another token who doesn't belong here."

My repulse spray was tucked into the pocket of my uniform. I wanted to use it. My finger ached to use it. I imagined the justice in their screams. But I also remembered Alissa's warning about the honor code. These two wanted me gone; I wasn't going to do anything. Not until Mateo had gotten what he needed. I tried to duck around Mona Lisa, but Drake's arm flashed across my path, his hand grabbing my shoulder. I cocked a fist, checking the blow at the last instant.

"Whoa there, girl," Mona Lisa taunted. "Drake's big brother is on the honor council, so I wouldn't go trying to mark him up."

"What's your honor code say about being a couple of jack-A's?"

"We're just trying to be help you find your way around here," Drake told me.

"Yeah, you were lost. I heard Drake offer to show you to class, when you started in on him. Bitter about losing, making all sorts of accusations. Unbecoming for a Tuck student," Mona Lisa added, a satisfied smirk on her face.

Drake shot his elbow at my face; it was a feint that came up short. He'd hoped I'd react, maybe throw a punch that would get me expelled.

"Come on, nope. Afraid you'll be too slow again?" He took a step forward, putting his face close enough that I felt the heat of his breath.

A new voice joined the conversation, low-pitched but powerful. "Not unless Coach Nessmier is around to blow sand in her face again."

Kristolan strode into the hallway from the main stairway, her eyes appraising each of us. Her frown reminded me of a mother bird returning to find her nest is in disarray.

"The little half-breed thinks she entitled because she's Havelock's pet," Drake protested. "Just giving her an education."

I used the distraction to step through the wall of idiocy blocking my path. Drake went to grab my shoulder, his other hand balled tight.

"Hold there," Kris commanded in a general's voice. Her eyes were like the fire spoken of in Revelation. The bigger man froze. "We are all Tuck. All owners of its history and its future. There is a place here for all people of merit." She glided over to us, stopping beside Drake. Kris rested a hand on his hulking shoulder. The blaze I had witnessed in him was gone. "He gets carried away sometimes. But don't let that fool you. He is among the best of us." Reptilian fury softened before my eyes. Kris's voice was music for the savage beast.

"I'll take your word for it."

"You ran as a champion yesterday," she assured me. "I think you would have beaten my brother. Even Coach Nessmier may come around to seeing that. And you'll see that this place is special. You'll find your spot here, I know. And we'll all be better for it. Drake and Mona Lisa included."

"Uh…sure," I mumbled, staring at Drake's frown.

"Come on, I'll walk you to class."

I fell in beside a scion of one of the richest families in the world, allowing her to guide me to Mr. Lynder's Literature class. The first bell approached, and students infested the hallways. Every one of them stared at us. Kris somehow managed to smile, wink or acknowledge each of them while speaking with me as if we were long-lost friends reunited.

"I hope you won't judge this place, or the people here, by your experience with Drake Pillis-Smith," Kris half-whispered to me. "He's still finding his path."

I grunted my skepticism.

"You know that we call the network that runs this place Castle, right?"

"Yeah."

"Well, there is a reason for that, apart from the obvious. We have a fortress here. A place where the rules outside don't have to matter. We come here to learn. To do better. To *be* better. We emerge from Tuck stronger, united. It is my hope that everyone can find their place."

"'To Go Forth Bravely.'" My tone mocked, and I sensed Kris's disapproval.

She shifted her attention to a fawning passerby, then back to me. "Tell me, why did you start running track?"

"I've always wanted to run fast," I told her. "Since I was five." *When my mom vanished, never to return.*

"Early to the game then. It did something for you, running. And it still does."

Those luminous eyes saw through me. My spine prickled. "How would you know?"

"Contrary to what you may have heard, highborn does not mean no feelings, Daniela. Wealth does not mean that I don't know about struggle. The people at this school may not know you, but you don't know us either. Don't imagine that you are the only person in this world who has had trouble finding peace."

She didn't say anything more until we reached the threshold of my classroom. Kris's eyes scanned the room. She nodded in Alexander's direction, but I saw no warmth in their exchange. Indeed, Alexander looked wary.

"It was so nice to meet you, Daniela. Please don't give up on this place so quickly. Come to me if you need anything."

She said it with casual sincerity, like a queen reassuring a subject. She smiled a beautiful smile as she waved goodbye, yet I shivered. Then she was gone.

Alissa was staring at me, head tilted with a question. I shrugged. My viser shook, telling me it was time to find my seat. I slid in beside he who had vanquished me. Alexander kept his eyes fixed forward, his body so still he could have been the statue he resembled.

Mr. Lynder took the stage. His aged eyes lingered on me for just a moment. He tapped a hand against his aged notepad.

"The first of your three-essay examinations will be forthcoming the Friday after next," he announced. "Topic…a surprise, of course. Don't bother trying to memorize reams of analysis on the net. I assure you, the questions will force you to think for yourselves. Just make sure you've read the books, and come ready to have original thoughts. I hope we can all manage that."

Nervous laughter followed, but Mr. Lynder didn't smile.

"Let's get on with class," he proclaimed.

He called on me first, asking me if I knew a place like Golding's island in *Lord of the Flies*. I could feel the highborn smirks. I knew what they thought of my home.

"Tuck," I told them, defiant. The advantage of not being able to sleep was plenty of time to read and think. I rather liked *Lord of the Flies*. I could relate to it.

Murmurs of surprise, laughter, outrage.

"Do explain yourself, Ms. Machado."

"Everyone wears their manners in this place, draped in uniforms, your honor code, your head bows. You even have a special name for the computers here—Castle. That's like the island." My voice shook at first, but soon steadied. "Except that when the collective shame of society isn't watching, you compete, you strive to be on top, you follow the leader that promises the kill, like vultures trailing a lion. You seek to push others down so you may rise. In short, things are no different in this place than they are anywhere else. It's no different from the island, it's just not as isolated."

I heard snaps echo from other students. Not everyone, but enough to be heard by everyone. A few huffed in outrage.

"It seems you have some fans, Ms. Machado. As well as some detractors." Lynder wore a thoughtful look. "I remember my days here, as long ago as that was. Your analogy isn't perfect, but it had some truth then. It might still today. Better answer than yesterday, in any case. At least you read the book."

Lynder moved on. Paulis Horce-Jilly was the next victim. I permitted myself the luxury of sitting back in my seat, tuning out the discussion. Alexander maintained his razor focus on Mr. Lynder. I stole a look at him out of the corner of my eye.

He had the same aristocratic beauty as his sister, though without Kris's softening curves and inner light. She was a deity and he a mere statue of one. He wasn't even that big, except for his hands. Looking at him, I wouldn't have guessed he possessed such speed or endurance. He might have beaten me even without the sand and wind.

A message from my lab advisor came through just as class ended. My requested equipment had been procured, and I had a new room to report to for my third-period lab. When I looked up, Alexander stood beside me, posing above my seat like Colossus.

"I didn't know Coach would do that in the race. I did not need him to. He was not honorable."

Such an odd choice of words. He spoke with strange formality. "Excuses don't matter where I come from. For anyone."

Alexander looked taken aback. An odd pose for a statue. "Listen, I'm telling you that you're fast...girl," he stumbled a bit at the end.

I stood up. He was taller than me, but not by much. Our eyes were almost level. "I know I'm fast."

Alexander nodded with gravitas. "I'm going speak to the coach about what happened. We can use you on the team."

My heart kicked into a high gear, but I kept my face blank. "I don't need favors. I don't want favors."

"I will speak to him because you run well," he told me, his face resembling hard stone. "I offer no favors." He turned and left.

TWELVE

The next three hours passed in a blur. I sat in classes and pretended to listen, but my mind was thinking about the track team. I kept trying to pull myself away from that hope. I should've been worried about Mateo, about getting him into the life center. But the track was like a siren's song. Mom's words from when I was five, about the strength inside me, still echoed. I wanted the richies to admit I was a good as *them*. Maybe better.

Fifth period was lunch for the upper school. I didn't even have both feet inside the cafeteria before Alissa was on me.

"I already got your lunch," she told me. "It's at our table. You–come–now."

She ushered me through the massive dining hall; we walked alongside long antique tables of darkened wood, under the illustrious light of crystal chandeliers that hovered beneath the arched ceilings, watching those below like ancient vultures. External light entered the chamber from soaring glass windows stained with scenes from forgotten Scriptures. The hall was big enough to accommodate the entire school; the upper school students filled only a third. But they all snatched at least a quick glance in my direction as I crossed the room. Their judgment felt like ants crawling on my skin. My jaw clenched.

Alissa led me to the end of one of the long dining tables, urging me into a seat between two students I didn't know: a petite Korean girl with a wide, cold face and a snow-haired boy with alabaster skin and eyes nearly as white as his cheeks, except for a faint blue tint circling the edges. Alissa zipped around to take an empty seat opposite me. No one else sat at our table. A steaming plate of pasta covered with chunky tomato sauce and fist-sized meatballs dazzled in front of me.

"Okay, Daniela, to your left is Lara Rae, the first girl who dared to speak to me when I started here, and her companion is the illustrious Nythan Royce."

"She means notorious, not illustrious," Nythan informed me.

"He's a black sheep here. Ironic considering how white he is everywhere else," Alissa said. Lara rolled her eyes.

"Just explain already," Lara commanded, her bored voice a bit more than a whisper.

Alissa cleared her throat. "May I present the only person at Tuck who has managed to piss off the highborn, the nopes and the administration in a single swoop."

I took a hard look at the pale boy—and he did look like a boy compared to the highborn of his age; my Bronx eyes saw an easy mark in those soft features and quick eyes. Drake's neck wasn't much smaller than Nythan's torso.

"A nope?" I asked. "I keep hearing that."

"Normally Produced Embryo," Alissa informed me. "Those of us who haven't been genetically altered in the womb. Otherwise known as normal people."

"The term 'nope' is highborn crap," Nythan said. "I prefer pure."

"Pure?"

"It's a joke," Nythan added. "But no else gets it. Story of my life. The name comes from a twentieth-century role-playing game called Gamma World. The pure-strain humans were the only characters who hadn't mutated into monsters after the nuclear war. I'm trying to convince these miscreants that it's better than letting those bastards call us nopes. But it's an up-hill battle with this generation of net-raised zombie kids. They fail to appreciate the elegant strategy of ancient gaming."

"Spare us the conceited history trivia," Lara urged.

"What'd you do to everyone?" I asked Nythan.

"I won the Manhattan Math League Championship last year," he proclaimed with mocking pride.

"And the highborn hate you for that?"

"The Tuck team won, not Nythan-the-modest," Alissa corrected. "But Nythan scored the most points on the team. And yeah, that ruffled some genetically enhanced feathers. Nythan's the only nope—sorry—pure on the team."

"Good for you," I told him.

"Yeah, good for him. Our boy Nythan leads Tuck's glorious mathletes to victory last year and leaves his highborn team-mates—a bunch of whom are upperclassmen by the way—steaming with jealousy," Alissa said. "Then he turns around this year and proclaims he won't be participating, much to the consternation of the faculty, and probably the rest of the student body. The highborn on the team are furious they won't have a chance to top him, but at the same time they are terrified of looking foolish if they fail to win without him."

Nythan crossed his arms, a satisfied look on his face.

"It's nice to meet you, Nythan," I said.

That got me a pasty smile.

"On to new business," Lara announced. "What did the Fos-ter-Rose-Harts want with you? On only your second day, and you a mere nope."

I frowned, studying the eager faces of the near strangers around me. I was certain none of them were highborn—too

short, too thin, too pale, too foreign, too imperfect. But that
didn't make them my friends. They were richies. They weren't
blood.

Alissa saw my expression. "These are the good ones,
Daniela. Lara's not much of a smiler, but she's had my back
since fifth grade. My hearing implants might just as well have
been a Resister-H virus to everyone else here. And we're the
only two girls at Tuck that would even talk to Nythan, much
less share lunch with him." Nythan scoffed at that. Alissa ignored him, her eyes fixed on me. "All of us have had our moments with the highborn. We stick together."

My eyes drifted over each of my neighbors. "So this is what
a blood gang looks like in Manhattan?"

"You bet," Alissa assured me. "What do you think?"

"Stay in Manhattan."

The other three laughed. I didn't.

"Well?" Alissa asked again.

I dug into my spaghetti, the sauce thick and rich with gar-
lic. These kids had no idea. They stared at me. I swallowed
too much and told them what happened. "Your precious hon-
or code isn't quite as iron-clad as you made out, Alissa."

She rubbed her chin, thoughtful. "Drake's brother is a
council prefect. He likes to throw that around. But it's crap.
They'd still throw him out if he gets too far out of line. Havelock has a vote as well."

I sucked in more of my lunch. "Anyway, Kris happened
along."

"Oh, *Kris*, is it?" Nythan interjected. "Ain't you girls been
buds since your early days at her daddy's company?"

"She saved you from her fellow highborn goons?" Alissa
shook her head. "The empress never misses a chance to extend
her domain."

I felt my face harden. "She didn't save me from anything. I could've handled them. But she has a way…of calming things down. For everyone."

Nythan coughed in derision. Lara's face was a twist of scowls. That expression wasn't dislike—it was hatred. But Alissa nodded sagely.

"She urged me to give this place a chance."

"She and I agree on that, at least," Alissa told me, her tone soft.

"And you took her advice and decided to make friends with her brother?" Nythan asked. "I'm not even sure those two like each other, although they hide it well. What did the self-proclaimed future ruler of the world have to say?"

"He wants to race me again."

Three chins dropped. I went back to my lunch.

Alissa and Lara switched the topic to some big allocator event I didn't know or care about while I cleaned my plate. I didn't linger. They were still talking when I left.

Script was my first class after lunch. I walked swiftly and arrived early. The room was still empty. Unlike my other classes, Script had no assigned seats, so I chose a heavy wooden table near the back. I slipped inside, drowsy from carbohydrates. Nythan startled me awake moments later, nearly jumping into the desk beside me.

"This whole notion of handwriting with ink is barbaric," he said to me.

I looked around the room. "The money these antique materials cost…for what? A rich person's vanity."

Nythan's face told me the words bit more than I intended. Still, I didn't apologize for the truth.

"It matters to the alumni who donate money. Tradition is very important at Tuck."

I didn't answer. I didn't know what to say.

Students streamed into the room. They came in all shapes and hair colors, but my gaze locked on one in particular: Drake Pillis-Smith. He'd been just another face to me yesterday. Today, he flashed his jackal's teeth before taking the seat directly in front of me.

Muscles that had no place on a boy his age bulged beneath his uniform. Mr. Yadlow entered the room, his thick leathery hair dripping onto a once-handsome face that had yielded to time.

"We'll be doing Jefferson's Declaration of Independence today," he announced. "Dip pen and ink are to be used. And I want to see precise script. We're learning patience and precision here, ladies and gentlemen. Form orderly lines for the supplies, please. Conduct yourselves appropriately."

I was the last person to fetch the ink and pen. The instrument was a garish silvery thing with a golden nib that probably cost more than it would've to get Mateo in to see a real doctor. I eyed the ink pot as I might a witch's cauldron. The ancient document displayed on my digiBook was daunting. I had heard of the Declaration of Independence but had never read it. I did so now, initially to procrastinate, but then with interest. When I had finished reading, I looked to see if anyone else had noticed the hypocrisy of the document—a paper revered for its history, its sentiments against oppression forgotten. Everyone else had their head down, focused on penmanship.

I dipped my pen and began to scrawl. The instrument felt like a lead weight. The ink flowed unevenly, worsening my already challenged script. I concentrated on one flowing letter at a time, trying to emulate the elegant penmanship of the author, paying no mind to the intended meaning. Deep into the second passage, my desktop jerked. I scrawled down the page, lines of ink ruining the past half-hour of work. I looked up in time to catch Drake twisting back into his regular position. Fire ignited within me. I put aside my ruined work and stood, the silver pen clutched in my right hand like a knife. Drake kept his back to me even though I was sure he knew I stood behind him.

A violent coughing fit erupted to my right. Several pasty fingers wrapped themselves around my arm.

"I'm so sorry, Daniela," Nythan stammered between huffs. "I think I bumped your desk. I just needed some water. It's completely my fault."

"What the hell are you doing?" I hissed.

"Just not feeling well." Nythan let off another rattling fit.

Mr. Yadlow ambled over, hands tucked behind his back as if out for a country stroll. "A problem, pupils?"

"No problem, sir," Nythan assured him. "I may have accidently bumped Daniela's desk." He punctuated his faux confession with a sharp hack.

"Ah, well, no great loss," Mr. Yadlow declared, glancing over at my scribbles. "Plenty of time to finish tomorrow. Collect your water, then return to work as you are able, Mr. Royce. In fact, you might want to start over as well." Yadlow strolled away with the same easy gait. I glanced at Nythan's writing; even without ink stains, it was worse than mine.

Nythan returned with a glass of fresh water from the hall dispenser and new sheets of paper for both of us. "Go gently," he told me. I took a hard, unhappy breath, looking everywhere but at Nythan. My viser vibrated soon afterwards, signaling the end of class.

Drake didn't turn around as he got up to leave, but I could feel the smug look on his face. I stayed at my seat as the class filed out. Nythan bent down beside me.

"We fight differently here," he whispered. "Know the difference between a battle and a war."

I flushed, nodding reluctantly as I got up to leave. I whispered Mateo's name to myself several times as I walked away.

I had History next, then Chemistry. I didn't pay attention in either.

Alissa hooked her arm into mine immediately after the final signal, guiding me into the hall. Eager students flowed around us like we were giant rocks in rapids.

"We're headed to the park," she informed me. "Won't be many more days as nice as this. Come with us."

"Can't," I said, looking at her as I might a dancing cobra.

"Thursday then," she said.

"Listen, Alissa…you may mean well, but—"

She pretended not to hear me. "And come to my place for dinner after."

Something caught in my throat. "What?"

"People do eat in Manhattan. Knives, forks, the usual. I've seen that you know how to use them, based on what you did to your lunch. I'm sure you'll manage to get the hang of eating with us. No excuses."

I felt my palms grow moist. I shook my head violently.

Alissa waited for me to stop squirming. Her eyes found mine. "Don't try to do this on your own, Daniela." I held her stare. "Think about it."

She left me alone after that. I wrestled with my feelings about Alissa's invitation all the way back to Bronx City. Kortilla met me at the station again, and I told her about it—all of it. The confession reminded me of the last time I went to church, back when I was seven. I had told the pale priest that I hated my father for never knowing me, and my mother for being gone. Telling him didn't change anything. I never went to church again.

"You remember Guapo John?" Kortilla asked.

"Dung-eating psycho," I spat the words, remembering the blood, the tears, the grave. "After what he did to Francis, I'll never forget him."

"Remember how quick he moved? How strong he was? Even his loose temper served him well—nobody messed with Guapo John. He was the most dangerous dealer in southern Bronx City, and everyone knew it."

"Yeah, but his parts are floating in the Harlem River somewhere, none of them attached to each other," I pointed out.

"Because he was alone, an independent; because no one else could stand him. As big and as mean a bastard as he was, he couldn't handle the *Corazones* by himself. He put Francis down, but what my brother's blood did to him was worse."

"I'm not Guapo John."

"Even you need people, Dee. Or you *will* end up like Guapo John."

Kortilla's advice stung. It usually did. She slung an arm around me.

I pinged Alissa on my way home: SEE YOU AT DINNER TOMORROW.

CHAPTER

THIRTEEN

T he next day started off ordinary, which was rather extra-
ordinary. I went through each of my morning classes
without incident. The lessons ranged from fascinating to dull.
There were students who knew more than me, but plenty who
knew less. I even had people to talk to, if I had wanted to talk.

I received a gracious nod from Kris as I passed her in the
hall, one among countless others. For a few precious moments
during the day, I almost forgot where I was. Then came Script.
Nythan sat next to me again. Drake relocated to a safer distance, huddled among cronies, people of beauty and spite. I resumed my work transcribing the Declaration of Independence,
trying to improve on the work Mr. Yadlow had deemed un-
worthy yesterday. It wasn't shaping up any better.

About halfway through class, a delicious curse cut through
the silence. Drake Pillis-Smith stood over his desk, his hands
and uniform drenched in runny black ink. I judged his tirade
worthy of a Bronx City street corner brawl, even if I didn't
know what a "pendelnut-jack-A" was.

"Decorum, Mr. Pillis-Smith," Mr. Yadlow reminded him,
his voice stern. "Your clumsiness and some spilled ink is no
reason to act like a savage."

Drake turned hard on his heels, his arms held stiffly in front as if the ink had frozen his hands. He glowered with rage as he looked at me. I smiled innocently.

"You," he mouthed.

Nythan emitted something between a cough and a laugh that was neither. It was a claim. Nythan had done it, somehow, without leaving his desk. And he wanted Drake to know it. The burly highborn turned his glare towards Nythan. I had seen looks like the one Drake wore in the barrio. It never ended well.

"You're excused to change uniforms and clean up," Mr. Yadlow told Drake. "Please return in a better condition."

He stomped out of the class, the door slamming hard behind him. I got back to my scribbling. My writing was still lousy, but my mood had improved.

———⧓———

We met on the great steps of Tuck after school, Alissa, Lara, Nythan, and I. These, if not my friends, then my allies.

Only Nythan and Lara had familiars. The machines hovered above us as we walked toward Central Park, like children's balloons without the string. I glanced upward, uneasy. I wasn't sure Nythan or Lara remembered the drones were there, watching us all. But they had never been chased by the Authority's metal monsters.

It was one of those fall days in the Five Cities when the wind was just cool enough to refresh beneath a not-too-hot sun. The pampered trees lining Eighty-Ninth Street shed their leaves as we strolled along. I thought about the people with so much money they could buy clean water for growing ornaments rather than having to rely on ration cards. People like those I walked beside.

We passed beneath the awnings of buildings that sheltered the rich and powerful of Manhattan. We all looked like we belonged in our Tuck uniforms, accompanied by familiars; a few of the doormen smiled, even at me. They wouldn't have if they knew where I lived.

We crossed Fifth Avenue. I stared over the low brick wall into the unimaginable lushness of Central Park. Pathways traveled up hills and across green fields. Leaves, some with the barest hints of yellow, adorned the branches that peeked over the park's boundary. I thought of my mother, our trips here. I had clearer images of this place in my head than I did of her. The memories were precious, dream-like. My legs faltered. They didn't want me to go any further.

"It's even better inside," Nythan promised, misreading my hesitation.

"I've been here before," I said, my words sharp.

"Then what's the issue?"

His eyes, clear and genuine, made me bite back a dismissive reply. "Nothing," I told him, forcing one foot in front of the other.

We crossed the threshold of the park at Eighty-Fourth Street, merging into a steady trickle of people, many wearing the uniforms of Manhattan's elite private schools, all seeking the greenery.

"How did you do it?" I asked Nythan.

"Do what?" He reeked of satisfaction.

"Fine. I guess Drake is a clumsy oaf then."

Nythan held out for about ten seconds. "Fabricated polytetrafluoroethylene, with a little twist of my own design."

"Huh?"

"You just need to know that it's one of the slipperiest substances in existence, especially when adapted by yours truly so it could be rubbed on an ink pot by some handsome genius."

I thought about the prank, chewing my bottom lip. "Yad-low will notice you did something to the ink pot. They'll have evidence."

"It turns back into a gas in less than an hour. Gave me something to do in one of my labs today."

"How many labs do you have?"

"Two."

"I thought we only could have one."

"I've got special permission from Havelock to foster my creative mind," Nythan informed me, his teeth as white as his skin. "One at Tuck, I do the other at Lenox in a research lab."

We reached the great lawn. Hundreds of people, many of them students, hunkered down in groups across the grassy meadow. Some threw flying disks at each other, others sat in circles, stroking their visers like pets. More familiars than I cared to count clogged the airspace above them. All that was missing were slaves to feed them grapes.

"Did you do that to Drake because of what he did to me?" I asked Nythan, not sure if I wanted the answer.

"I don't like Drake Pillis-Smith."

"Him in particular? Or all highborn?"

Hints of a smile tickled the corners of Nythan's mouth. "It's refreshing to meet someone who hasn't been raised in this cesspool, who doesn't come in knowing everyone's backstory."

"Why should I care?"

"You're one of us now, Bronx girl," he proclaimed. "Did you not know that Drake Pillis-Smith's father is Atkin Pillis-Smith, Mayor of Manhattan?"

"Can't say I did. Or that I care now that I do." I nibbled at my lip again. "What does that matter to you?"

"My father was the mayor of New York City, a long time ago. Back when there was still a New York City," Nythan said.

"Drake's dad ran against him in elections, twice. Old Atkin lost both times."

"There hasn't been a New York City in over a decade. Seems a long time to hold a grudge."

Nythan shook his head. "It was just yesterday in Manhattan. Families hold grudges for generations. Some misguided notion of family honor. But this one is a bit fresher. Atkin is an Orderist, same as our dear President. He, along with Landrew Foster-Rose-Hart, got the Taxation for Representation Amendment through, under questionable circumstances. That's when California broke off. As part of the payback for Atkin's help in bringing much of the Northeast into line, New York City was broken into five legally distinct cities. Manhattan became the new capital of the remaining forty-nine states. President Ryan-Hayes got his amendment, won the next election, and every one since. Our perpetual President."

I stifled a yawn. "Richie politics. The allocators and the government found more ways to screw with us, and each other, making themselves even richer. But they were doing that long before Cali broke away, long before the Five Cities. Nothing new."

Nythan's jaw grew taut. "My dad didn't give up as easily as *you*. He didn't accept what they had done. He organized the unions, the workers, anyone he could. In the outer boroughs—Staten Island, Queen, the Bronx, Brooklyn, a lot of city employees backed him, including most of the old police. He organized marches, sit-ins, strikes…and other things."

The moisture emptied from my mouth and throat. I was breathing, but it felt like I wasn't getting any air. "When was this?"

"About fifteen years ago, around the time we were born," Nythan said.

The words knocked the breath out of me. "My dad died in those marches. For your father's lost cause. Richie fighting richie. But it's the regular folks who paid." I bit off the last words.

Nythan looked away from me. "Your father wasn't the only person who paid. My dad spent ten years in prison, on crap charges. He got stabbed in the back by another prisoner. Paralyzed from the waist down. They let him out a few years ago." He said it into the wind, but I heard the bitterness clearly.

"The Mayor did that?"

Nythan's face shone red when he turned back to me. "The Mayor, the Orderists, it's all the same. They said they would be the party that governed, restored an orderly nation. Success through merit alone. Economic rationalism. Prosperity through order.'" He snickered. "Finally, a party that kept their campaign promises. Judges, politicians, leaders of any kind were jailed, intimidated, or paid off. Just about every major news service was bought out by Orderist supporters. What was left was mostly drowned out."

I sensed a kinship of hate with Nythan. "So you have a blood feud with Drake and his family? With all the Orderists?"

"It sounds like you might as well. The Orderists fight among themselves now. Over the spoils of government. Over California, the embargo. Economic rationalism or simple self-interest. For example, Rose-Hart does defense work. Not surprisingly, they're big advocates of a military solution. Their allies would prosper from conflict. The President is more patient."

Alissa and Lara chose that moment to join us.

"You two look way too serious for a day like this," Alissa declared.

We all took a moment to absorb the near-perfect azure of
the sky, the delicate breeze, the juxtaposition of nature and the
city. Sounds of laughter and satisfaction were thick in the air.

"Even you must admit it's beautiful, Daniela," Alissa said.
"There's no place else quite like this. Not London, not
Shanghai."

"I see why you think it's beautiful," I replied. "Because it's
yours."

She didn't answer me.

"This place is packed with highborn," Lara said. "Let's head
to the back trails. Maybe our big rock."

"Good idea," Alissa said. "I've got snacks."

Her pronouncement elicited several grunts of knowing
laughter. I didn't get it.

We headed south from the sprawling lawn, taking dirt
paths into less manicured sections of the park. Birds that had
no business living in proximity to masses of humanity danced
among the trees. Squirrels scurried about, gathering nuts, looking cute. They would've been someone's dinner back in BC.
Something close to quiet surrounded us. We saw no one else as
we walked deeper into the woods, although I knew we weren't
really alone. The real world lurked a mere stone's throw away,
beyond the thicket of strategically planted trees. Alissa led us
off the paths entirely, dodging low branches across sloping
ground, into areas that resembled the wilderness of my imagination. Something close to the forests that existed mostly in
images now. I kept to the rear of the group, absorbing sights
and sounds the rest ignored as ordinary. This place wasn't ordinary, not for people like me.

After a couple of minutes of walking, we arrived at a great
slab of stone jutting upwards from the ground like a beached
ship. Veins of polluted crystal streaked through the drab gray
of the rock. Great sycamores, rich with emerald-teethed leaves,

encircled us, leaving a grand circular space directly above, like a private viewport to heaven.

"Let's divvy up the booty," Alissa announced, withdrawing a thin metal case from the bag slung at her shoulder. She clicked it open, revealing half a dozen thin, precisely rolled cylinders. A powerful odor, something akin to burnt syrup, wafted over to me.

"Are those cigarettes? Like on the net?" I asked.

"Updated, of course," Alissa informed me. "It's a tobacco-cannabis engineered hybrid. They're safe. Buzz, but not fuzz."

Everyone grabbed one, except me. Alissa offered the case to me. She had a flame lighter in her other hand. I shook my head.

"Bronx girl doesn't touch benders?" Lara asked. "The air up there is worse for you than these things."

My spine tingled. *As if you would know*, I thought, but I held back. I could've told her about the Z-Pop dealers who would do almost anything to get you to take that first dose. I could've told her about what I thought of richie ignorance. But I didn't do any of those things. I needed allies.

"Not my thing," I said.

The rest of them began to scale the rock, puffing as they climbed. I didn't follow. My spider-sense held me back. There were eyes of menace on me. I peered into the woods, looking in every direction. Nothing but trees and leaves. But the feeling of ill remained, and I trusted my unnamed sense more than conventional sight.

"Hold up," I called out to the group.

They ignored me, absorbed in their own hijinks. I scrambled up the rock-face after them. My head tingled, pinpricks of danger putting me on edge. Branches rustled in the thicket around us. Danger stalked us. I stopped, closed my eyes, and tried to imagine the threat. In an instant, I knew.

I dove forward. My shoulder slammed into Nythan, pushing him to the ground as a small drone buzzed through the airspace his head had occupied a split second earlier. The familiar's rotor engine hissed with heat as it whizzed past. Pulsing sparks of white lightning flashed on its belly as it climbed into the sky. A sour burning smell clogged my nostrils. It smelled like the barrio, when stolen electricity contacted cheap, fabricated plastika.

"Son of a bitch," Nythan exclaimed, his hands frantically patting his singed scalp.

Another familiar, this one presumably slaved to Nythan, dove at him like a hungry hawk, pulling up just out of arm's reach above us. The lights along its circumference flashed a panicked shade of red as its turret rotated back and forth. A klaxon sounded, similar to an Authority siren.

"Where is it?" Nythan demanded, getting back to his feet, gazing up at the sky.

Lara alternated between looking at her viser and the azure above, her movement repetitive and manic. I didn't fare much better. The tall, thick trees made our viewing angle near impossible.

"The operator is close," Alissa proclaimed, scrambling down from the rock, towards a section of wood to our right. I followed her. But the immediate danger had passed. The message had been sent.

Nythan's familiar turned off its alarm and flew towards the trees not far from me, its rotors kicking up dirt and leaves as it hovered at eye-level. The machine looked like a wicked, mutated Frisbee up close, its rotating eyes glowing with the malevolence of an Authority enforcement machine.

"Keep away from it," Nythan shouted from the rock. "I'm going to send a directional EMP blast. I don't need to know where it is for that. I'll fry that thing's brain."

"Don't—you'll wipe everyone's visers," Alissa yelled back at him. "And you'll get into trouble. The Authority is going to go nuts if they detect an EMP pulse."

Nythan's face bubbled with rage. His head still smoldered. I laughed at the sight. I couldn't help it.

"It's funny to you?" he snapped.

I shrugged, banishing the vestiges of my grin. "You look like one of your fancy cigarettes."

"But he smells like burning dog poop," Lara added.

Nythan's scowl deepened. His hand remained poised above his viser, his eyes longing to send out the wrecking pulse.

"Score one for Drake," Alissa commented, placing her hand over Nythan's wrist. "But there will be another time to pay him back."

Nythan let himself appear mollified as Alissa pulled his hand away. But a razor's edge glinted in his irises. I knew the look well enough; his anger had cooled, not dissipated.

We returned to the rock, where the others scrounged for the remains of their precious cigarettes. Nythan sucked on his as if solace for some grave misfortune could be found at the end of the burning weed. Such were the problems of the rich.

"I thought familiars weren't allowed to carry anything except stun weapons," I ventured.

Lara rolled her eyes. Alissa answered me.

"The list of banned payloads is quite lengthy, but it's just a list. It can't include everything. Just major things."

"And how do you explain an electro-magnetic pulse?" I asked Nythan.

"My familiar isn't some off-the-shelf model like Drake and Lara have. It's one of a kind. No dealer would dare sell something like that. I make my familiars myself." I heard the pride again.

"You built an EMP yourself?"

Nythan took a last, satisfied drag, then tossed the smoldering butt away with grating nonchalance.

"Directional EMP—the wave knocks out what I point it at."

"What happens if the Authority finds out?"

"I've taken measures," he assured me. "If anyone but me tries to crack my baby open, they won't find anything but melted alloy."

"You belong in California."

He flushed red but didn't reply.

The topic turned away from dangerous highborn pranks, eventually turning to unflattering discussions of teachers, then evolving into a rigorous analysis of the previous summer's best parties. The banter flowed like a twisting river's current. I said little but found myself relaxing. I could almost imagine having a similar conversation with Kortilla. I reminded myself this place was a means to an end. I shouldn't be enjoying myself.

"Okay, kids, time for Daniela and me to depart for an evening of glamor," Alissa announced. I glanced at my viser to see it was past six o'clock. I felt my back stiffen. I willed myself to take a deep breath as I stood up.

Alissa led us down. At the bottom of the rock, I turned to find Nythan's eyes on me. He gave me a deep nod, as if acknowledging something that I should have known. I gave a curt wave before hurrying off to catch Alissa.

Alissa lived in a towering rectangle of concrete and glass two avenues east of Park Avenue. The trees were fewer and smaller on her street, but they still had them. Uniformed doormen minded the building's entranceway with fastidious care. We took a viser-enabled elevator to the thirty-sixth floor, riding up with an old lady and her small, barking dog. It was the highest I'd ever been in my life. A wave of dizziness assaulted me as I stepped out of the elevator.

The door to Alissa's apartment clicked open as we approached. I followed her inside, rubbing the clumsy viser on my arm.

"Mom, we're home," Alissa announced, slinging her bag on an iron trimmed entrance table to emphasize the point. I placed my backpack next to hers with less drama.

A woman of stature stepped gracefully into the alcove, her shining dark hair flowing as if there was a breeze in the apartment. Her legs were like stilts. She looked like a runner, with toned muscles and a lean, flat face. A pair of almond-shaped eyes that looked like the fabrication design mold for Alissa's regarded me.

"You must be Daniela," she said. "I'm Sung, Alissa's mom." She gave me a feathery hug, the way the *gringos* did it, kissing the air beside my right cheek before withdrawing.

"It's nice to meet you, Ms. Stein," I replied.

"Sung, please."

I managed an uncertain smile for her, this richie who welcomed me with hugs and hadn't surrendered her obviously foreign first name despite her place in Manhattan society.

"Why don't you girls wash up? We're going to eat in about fifteen minutes."

Alissa flipped off her shoes at the doorway and bid me to do the same before leading me to her room, which was about twice the size of the space Mateo and I shared. But the starkest difference from my own bedroom was that Alissa kept her space scrupulously tidy, her bed made, and not a dirty sock or scrap of dirt to be found anywhere. The dark wood floor reflected my features back at me. I spied a similar chamber next door, arranged as an office space with a terminal and a fabrication machine.

"You can clean up in there," Alissa told me, pointing at the door just outside her bedroom.

As she changed, I entered the bathroom, another pristine, angular space, adorned with gleaming ivory tiles and sleek metal. The faucets spit out cool crystal water, deliciously lacking the pungent odor of Bronx City's recycled swill. It looked like you could drink it from the tap. I felt a pang of guilt as I splashed my face and rubbed my arms, the excess escaping down a silvery drain.

"I'd send the enforcement drones out for anyone who tried to take this away from me too," I whispered.

"What's that you're saying?" Alissa called out as she stomped out of her room to check on me. "Want to change into something of mine? I've got some clothes that'll adjust to fit you."

"I'm good."

"You're almost as pale as Nythan," Alissa grinned. "Relax. It's just dinner—noodles, I believe. My parents are okay. They haven't forgotten where they came from. That's why I wanted you to meet them."

I clenched my teeth. I didn't like the sound of that. Alissa walked away. Not seeing any other choice, I followed her.

The Stein dining room was a magnificent space: a rectangular table of finely polished acacia wood that still showed its natural grain stretched through the center of the room. Six high-backed chairs of the same material were evenly spaced around the table. China, bone white with a gold trim, sat in front of four of the seats, sparkling expectantly. A magnificent turquoise vase sat on a smaller table nearby. An open kitchen, as much a cathedral as a place to cook, occupied the space adjacent to the dining room, with a whitewashed marble counter separating the areas. Amid the stainless metal appliances, Alissa's mother spun about, as harried as a chicken in a slaughterhouse, smoke rising around her.

"Your mom cooks?" I realized too late that the surprise in my voice might not be appreciated. But Alissa just laughed.

"She tries. Once a week she sneaks out of work early to make us a Korean meal. And tonight's the night. Lucky you."

Sung noticed us, even while dashing around the kitchen. "Four minutes," she declared before turning her attention back to the cacophony of pots, pans, fire, and smoke. The activity seemed too frantic to be concluded in the time she suggested. But whatever she was cooking smelled delicious. Rich and salty and exotic.

"Where's Dad?" Alissa asked.

"Late," her mom replied. "He'll be here. He knows the rules. He's still got a few minutes."

"Everyone's got to be at the table at seven sharp for Korean night," Alissa explained. "Or face the consequences."

"Which are?"

"The dishes!" Sung called to us. "And there are a lot of them. He's got about three minutes left. Take your seats. We'll be on time, even if he isn't."

Alissa placed herself in one of the high-back chairs, motioning me to the seat beside hers. Its weight surprised me. I hadn't spent much time around solid wood furniture before.

"Sorry if it's rude, but, well, don't you have a housekeeper or a cook? I thought all…well, that is…I thought many families in Manhattan, you know…" I struggled to complete my sentence without giving offense.

"You figured everyone in Manhattan has armies of servants at their beck and call, oppressing them while paying slave wages, right?" Alissa asked, mocking rather than angry.

"Don't they?"

"I'm not sure about *everyone*. I suppose the Foster-Rose-Harts have armies of servants, and I can't speak to their compensation. We have Irena, who practically raised me. She doesn't work on cooking days. And she's more like family than a servant."

"Where is she? Surely, she doesn't live in Manhattan."

"She lives in Queens City," Alissa told me, a grin of fond memories on her face. "A nice apartment not far from the river. I used to love going there as a kid. Before..." Her smile faded.

"Before?"

Alissa looked uneasily at her mother, her face contorted as if she had been struck. "Before the red bus attack."

"But wasn't that staged by the Orderists to—" Alissa's face drained of color, making her look like a bleached sheet, with dark, angry eyes. "Sorry, my brother...He's into politics."

Alissa glared at me. The air seemed to have been drained of oxygen.

Sung watched us from the kitchen, her eyes hovering on her daughter. "Finito!" she exclaimed, a bit louder than she should have. Still, it was a mercy to be pulled out of whatever pit I'd stumbled into.

"You're late, Mom!" Alissa shot a last glare at me then turned to her mother. "It's past seven. And Dad's worse."

"I got this, I got it," Sung assured us, a forced smile on her face.

I had my doubts about her declaration of completion, but within moments, the chaotic din from the kitchen fell silent. Giant serving bowls made of perfect azure ceramic appeared before us on the table. Heaps of steam poured from the top of a massive collection of noodles, meat, vegetables, and rice. I'd never seen so much real food in one place in my life.

"It looks amazing, Ms. Stein."

"Japchae and bulgogi," Alissa's mom explained, pointing to the noodles and meat, in that order. "The vegetable is bok choy with soybean paste. It's my mom's recipe, from Korea."

The door clicked open.

"Dad, you're late," Alissa proclaimed. "You're doing the cleaning tonight."

A handsome Caucasian man attired in the dark stretched waistcoat popular among the corporate elite stepped sheepishly into the dining room. His salt and pepper hair hung like a lopsided mop off the side of his head.

"Sorry everyone," he declared. "I'll be there in a minute. Please get started."

He returned in just a few moments, sliding into the seat next to his wife and opposite Alissa.

"I'm Harren," Alissa's dad said, offering a hand across the table. "You must be Daniela. Alissa has told us a lot about you."

I took his hand, but before I had a chance to reply, Alissa interrupted. "Why so late, Dad?"

Harren shifted in his seat. The edge of his mouth twitched. "Work's busy. Big project."

"Because of the Robin Hood meeting?" Alissa asked. To me she said, "The Allocators' Ball is coming up. That's when the biggest money managers in the country gather together in Manhattan. They throw themselves a fabulously expensive party, supposedly to raise money for the less fortunate. But mostly it's to show off to each other."

Sung began heaping food onto my plate. An intimidating mountain of steaming, slightly pink noodles, chunks of meat—*real meat*—and half a plate of the shining emerald bok choy.

"Robin Hood, like the fable?" I wondered, feeling a bit foolish.

"It's what the allocators call their big charity," Alissa explained. "It funds special schools, work programs, clinics, social services all around the country, using donated money from the corporate and financial community. Robin Hood—rob from the rich, give to the poor, get it? They named it decades ago, before votes were determined by tax payments, and allocators didn't actually run much of the country. Back when they didn't take themselves quite so seriously. But the name stuck."

"I've never heard of it. Not in Bronx City, at least."

"The company Dad works for programs drones," Alissa informed me. "A lot of them are used to provide security for big events, like the Allocators' Ball."

"You work for the Authority?" I croaked.

"No, no, RocketDyn, a private contractor. Like most contractors, we deliver a certain voting quota to the Orderist government and get a proportional amount of government-funded work in return. We do everything from heavy construction to network design. The division I work for does the software and related coding that runs various drones. Some do surveillance and security work, of course. But I'm just a coder."

It sounded like he worked for the Authority, but I figured I'd said enough stupid things to people who were trying to be nice, so I kept my mouth shut. I concentrated on eating instead, which was what I should've been doing all along.

"This is amazing," I said. "I've never tasted anything like it." I thought of what people were eating back in BC. Nothing like this. I didn't belong here.

"You can't get Korean like this anymore. Reminds me of when I was growing up," Harren told me.

"Why not?" I asked. "I thought Manhattan had everything."

"Ah, it's not like home though," Harren told me. "They have the best Korean places there."

"Dad grew up in Cali," Alissa said. Harren winced.

"Why leave?" I asked, even though I knew he didn't want me asking about it. Californians were traitors to the Orderists. Mateo talked about the place like it was paradise—one of the last democracies of one person, one vote, like the United States before the Orderists. The government net channels said it was a cesspool of chaos. I'd never met anyone who'd actually lived there.

Harren shook his head, slow and with regret. "Things fell apart, after the split."

"Because of the embargo?"

Alissa's parents exchanged looks. I was asking questions I shouldn't. But I had the feeling I wasn't going to get another chance at this topic.

Harren sighed. "Things were bad even before the embargo. It wasn't the place I grew up in anymore," he told me. Mateo wouldn't like hearing that. "And Alissa needed things that we couldn't get there." He didn't mention her hearing aids, but I suspected it was something like that. Although California supposedly had some of the best tech in the world, even now. My repulse spray was proof of that.

"And there's nothing like Tuck there—no private schools allowed. You both have such tremendous opportunities here," Sung said, smiling at Alissa, then me. "Your family must be so proud, Daniela."

I looked around the table at this family, each one of them beautiful in their own way, well-fed, prosperous, and so naive. But being wealthy didn't make them bad people. I decided to stop saying stupid things.

"Yeah, proud," I agreed, and got back to the meat.

FOURTEEN

I t was dark by the time dinner ended. The Steins offered to get me a car. Actually, they insisted on it. It was only after Alissa told them to back off that her mom relented. I had to practically dodge her dad to get out the door. No way I was showing up in BC in some chauffeured richie car. I'd be toast.

I walked through the streets of Manhattan towards the subway more worried about the groans of my overfilled stomach than being mugged. Indeed, the place was thick with Authority patrols suited in night-colored body armor and surveillance helmets. Drones buzzed in the sky—way more than during the day. What were they afraid of?

Richies still filled the streets, some walking and laughing, others eating and drinking at sidewalk cafés along Third Avenue. No one gave me a second glance, dressed in Tuck clothes, travel pass electronically embedded in my viser. Those dark-suited Authority police would probably rush to protect me if something happened, thinking I was one of the Manhattan elite.

A black sedan, bulky like a tank, with tinted windows and flashing blue lights, sped past. It was moving so fast that it unleashed a vortex of wind onto the sidewalk. There was no other traffic on the street. It must have been cleared for someone important.

Three other sedans, each identical to the lead vehicle except for the lack of lights, appeared in the distance, closing fast. Above them, a pair of wing-shaped drones kept pace. They were far larger than the surveillance models that patrolled Bronx City. I shivered, danger approached.

I spun around, intending to run down the street behind me. Three drones, shaped like fat spheres, turned the corner into my line of sight. They flew low, no higher than my chest. They had a quartet of undersized rotors for lift, the engines unusually quiet. *Low and silent enough to evade aerial scanning.*

I dove towards the café on my right, leaping over a sidewalk table where a pretty couple was enjoying their dinner. Glass shattered somewhere nearby as I hit concrete, the skin of my elbow tearing as I scraped the rough ground. A woman screamed. The ugly percussion of projectile fire erupted in reply.

"Get down," I yelled at the pair beside me, even as I grabbed their table and flung it onto its side, creating a barrier between us and the street. I crouched behind it. The man, chiseled and stern, grabbed his companion by the arm and yanked her to the ground beside me.

Just in front of us, one of the spherical drones exploded into a brilliant cascade of fire. It resembled a fireworks display, with blazing particles flying in every direction. Several pieces struck the glass wall of the café, sending shards flying and unleashing pandemonium inside. People flooded out onto the street, yelling and screaming at each other and their visers in equal measure.

"Let's go," the chiseled man said to the platinum-haired woman with him. I met his eyes for a moment, then turned my attention back to the street.

The two remaining drones retreated backwards and upwards in different directions; one of the wing-shaped machines approached them, the muzzle of its gun flashing in the night. A second sphere detonated into a fountain of white light. The last drone moved farther from the approaching convoy of cars; the winged drone continued to pursue. *Decoys*, I realized, turning my attention back to the street.

A blast erupted beneath the first of the black vehicles. The force lifted the car off the ground by at least a foot before it came crashing down. Fire burst out from beneath the vehicle. The front tires exploded in a deafening bang and the sound of metal grating on asphalt echoed in my ears. The second car slammed into the rear bumper of the first, speed and proximity overwhelming its anti-collision system. Then the real attack began.

Three men appeared on the roof of the building across from me. They had the perfect vantage point. Black masks obscured their faces. Long tubes of metal rested upon each of their shoulders, poised like wide-mouthed serpents.

The first missile slammed into the winged drone that had remained sentinel over the convoy. The impact flipped the machine over, cracking its fuselage into two pieces. One fragment crashed into the building just north of me, the twisting hunk of metal striking the facade with enough force to shake the street. A hail of fabricated bricks and other debris rained onto the sidewalk. Blood appeared beside me, flowing from the body lying on the ground inside the otherwise empty café.

Another missile hit the second vehicle. Fire engulfed the car like a giant hand of judgment. The flames soared three stories into the air. The heat pulsed, finding me even behind my table. Yet when the smoke cleared the vehicle remained intact. Its roof had plunged inward, but its reinforced windows were holding.

As the third man aimed his weapon at the vehicle below, his head jerked violently to the side. Then his skull disappeared, shattering into a constellation of gore. The returning wing-drone raked the building's roof with gunfire as it hurled itself back towards the true assault. The other two attackers disappeared. I thought I saw at least one of them take a hit.

Sirens shrieked toward me from every direction. Teams of dark, armored men clutching hulking force rifles dashed towards the attackers' building from multiple directions. The air smelled of acrid smoke and lingering fear. I ran, intending to get as far away from this mess as possible. I got as far as the corner. A wall of black booted Authority officers stood in my way.

"That's far enough, ma'am," one told me. "This area has been sealed."

I looked at the officer, dead-eyed behind his helmet, weapon in hand. "I just want to get home."

"Once you've been verified," he assured me, far more patient that he would've been if he knew I was from BC. "Your permit please."

I sighed and held out my visered arm. It was going to be a long night.

A pock-marked Authority officer led me towards a black police van. It had wheels taller than my waist and a gun turret with a wicked-looking muzzle mounted on its roof. I'd seen vehicles like this in BC. People who went into them didn't always come out.

The rear door swung open to reveal two narrow rows of metal benches where prisoners would sit facing each other. The officer who escorted me bid me to sit. There was no one else inside. There were manacles attached to the benches.

"I'd rather stand," I told him, fighting to keep the quiver out of my voice.

The officer looked me over, wary. His eye lingered on the Tuck insignia over my breast. He glanced at his viser, then back at me. Uncertainty clouded his craggy features. I was both a miscreant and an elite.

"Suit yourself," he said. "You live in Bronx City?"

"Yes."

"Is your brother Mateo Machado?"

"Yes."

"Someone will come to speak to you."

He prodded me inside with a gentle push on my back, then went to close the door. My mouth went dry.

"I'm not a criminal. You had best leave that open. It's bad enough you're detaining me without cause."

He shut the door.

Fluorescent lights illuminated the windowless interior. I had to bend over to avoid hitting the ceiling, but I preferred that to sitting in the torture seats. I wondered if this vehicle had been used to detain people I knew, if anyone I knew had died in here. Probably.

I flicked my viser, but its external communications were jammed, of course. The whole area would've been blacked out the instant after the attack. I didn't know who I could ping anyway. This was the Authority.

An hour passed. The interior got hot and stuffy. I compensated with the climate controls of my Tuck uniform. When I got tired of standing, I sat on the metal floor. I wondered who was in the convoy. Someone rich if the Authority had closed the street and allowed armed drones into Manhattan to protect him. Even more important was who had carried out the attack. No one from BC. Not with drones and missiles. But this would send the Authority into a frenzy. I pictured the machines rolling down the streets of Manhattan's four tributary cities even now. Precautionary measures, they would call it.

The rear door startled me when it reopened. I jerked to my feet, almost hitting my head on the low ceiling. The same ugly-faced officer stood in the entryway. Another black boot, older, with wrinkled eyes and four ruby-red bars on the shoulders of his midnight uniform, stood beside him. Behind them was Headmaster Havelock, dressed impeccably in his colonial-style three-piece suit and red bow tie.

"Please escort the lady out," the older officer told his pockmarked subordinate. The black boot stepped into the vehicle and offered his gloved hand as if he were my escort to a ball. I didn't take it.

"I can manage," I said, pushing past him.

The night air had the sweet scent of liberation.

"Ms. Machado, I'm Captain Taylor, FCPA. I would like to extend the department's apologies for detaining you this evening. I hope you understand that it's been a terrible night."

I looked at him, trying to put on the kind of face that Kris Foster-Rose-Hart would have if she had been locked in an Authority detention van for an hour.

"I've had a rather terrible night also, Captain," I said. "Your men should conduct themselves more professionally."

The captain's face flashed annoyance, quickly banished. "Yes, well, you're free to go now. We may have some routine follow-up questions."

"Oh? What kind of routine questions?" I asked, hoping he could feel the ice of my words.

Captain Taylor's face soured again. Havelock spoke into the gap. "Captain, Ms. Machado, and the entire school appreciates your quick action to rectify an unfortunate situation. I'm sure you and your men have done a tremendous job tonight, as you always do."

The captain nodded. "We value our relationship with the community greatly, Headmaster. You can always count on that."

"I trust there is no need for there to be a formal record of this incident, which I think we both agree should never have happened."

"Ah, yes, of course," the captain said with his eyes locked on his subordinate.

"It's getting quite late, and tomorrow is a school day. If there is nothing else, I think Ms. Machado and I will take our leave now. Good night, gentlemen. I'm sure this affront to order will be dealt with using your customary efficiency."

Havelock's long, thin, fingers wrapped around my arm and guided me away from the van, the Authority officers, and the smoldering wreck of machines.

"How did you know I was in there?" I asked as soon as we were comfortable a distance from battle scene.

Havelock pulled me around the corner onto Eighty-Seventh Street. Huddled beneath the awning of a building's service door stood Alissa, and her mother and father. Alissa grabbed me in a tight embrace. Her mother extended her arms around us both. Richies or not, it made me feel better.

"We heard the explosions right after you left," Alissa said, releasing me. "I knew you had to have been caught up in it. It's just so, so...you."

I gave a half smile at that.

"The net was down, but your friend came to my home to let me know you might be in some trouble," Havelock told me.

"And you got the Authority to release me, even though I'm from BC, even though my brother must be on their watch list or something?"

Havelock shrugged. "The Board, our alumni—they are important people. That means that I have influence with the Authority. And it's not as if you had done anything wrong." He pulled his lips into an expression that wasn't quite a smile. "Remember, we look after each other at Tuck."

"It seems so," I replied, my voice just above a whisper. "Thank you, sir. And thank you Alissa, and you Ms. Ste...Sung, and Mr. Stein. I do appreciate it."

"It is late, Ms. Machado, and you have had a rather interesting night," Havelock said. "I suggest we all go home and get some sleep. Ms. Stein, I trust you'll take it from here?" The headmaster tilted his head towards Alissa, locking his eyes with hers.

"I've got her, sir," she assured him.

Havelock tipped his head at the Steins, then began a leisurely stroll down the street. I shook my head, not quite having absorbed all that had happened. Still, I knew that the headmaster had saved my rear. He and Alissa both. A debt now existed. I didn't like that, but at least I was out of the van.

"Let's get home," Alissa said. "I've got everything you'll need there."

"Not necessary," I declared. "I'm grateful, really, but I need to get back to BC. Aba will be worried. I'll be fine. I can take care of myself, really."

"All the trains are stopped, all bridges and tunnels into Manhattan are closed. There is no way out of the city, dear," Sung told me. "Don't worry, Daniela, we don't bite. You can contact your family as soon as the net is back up. It won't be much longer. The Authority can't disrupt electronic traffic in Manhattan too long without incurring the wrath of some very powerful people."

"What happened anyway?" I asked. "Who was in that car?"

Alissa looked at me in shock. "You don't know?"

"How would I?"

"It was Landrew Foster-Rose-Hart himself."

FIFTEEN

They didn't get him.

Whoever they were, they hadn't accounted for the modifications to the car. According to net reports, a standard factory-produced armored vehicle of the make and model carrying Landrew should have been destroyed by the missile. But Landrew's hadn't. So everyone speculated that the car had been customized after delivery, perhaps with reinforced armor, perhaps with other defensive features. That part was being kept secret, as was the exact origins of the missiles used. But word had it that the projectiles used were twenty-year-old military Stingers. California had a substantial stockpile when it seceded from the union.

Landrew was supposedly recovering at an undisclosed location, but had issued a statement to declare that he would not be intimidated by terrorists or secessionists, and would be returning to his duties both at Rose-Hart Industries, and as the Orderist Party Chairman, shortly. Landrew's stock photo flashed across multiple net feeds as his words were broadcast. He was a thin man, his hair gray like ash, his face chillingly lifeless despite its veneer of dignified beauty. He had neither Alexander's stature nor Kris's charisma. His image reeked of the severe. His transcribed words informed everyone that he had no doubt the perpetrators would be punished swiftly. The statement concluded: prosperity through order.

School buzzed with the excitement of calamity. I could sense it in the air as Alissa and I walked onto Eighty-Ninth Street, into the din of the swarming elite outside. Too many conversations swirled in the ether to make out the particulars of any single one, but I caught enough to confirm that the attempted assassination of Alexander and Kris's father was the topic of all of them.

"Think they'll be in school today?" Alissa asked me.

"Couldn't begin to guess."

I had showered in clear Manhattan water last night and wore one of Alissa's freshly pressed uniforms, but the biting odor of explosives still lingered in my memory. I wondered if these kids would have been so anxious to discuss the attack if they'd been there. I preferred to forget it.

"There's Nythan and Lara," Alissa said, preparing to wade into the crowd. I put a hand on her shoulder.

"Not a word to anyone that I was there, about the van or the headmaster—not even to Nythan and Lara," I told her in a harsh whisper.

"But they're our friends," Alissa protested. "You should trust them."

"It's not about trust. It's about my privacy, and me being me," I said. In a softer voice, I added, "Please, Alissa."

She nodded with reluctance. "Let's go speak to Nythan. He always knows interesting tidbits. I think he unscrambles Authority encryption for fun."

I shook my head. "Not interested. I'm going in. Too crowded out here."

"You're no fun. See you in Lit."

The Authority was waiting inside. Two hulking guys in the standard uniform with their helmets' optic screens down. They stood beside the translucent security door like statues, force pistols at their waist. Even without the massive rifles of BC troops, the officers looked ominous. The black boots were in addition to the usual team of lemon-coated school security cops in the observation room. One of the Authority officers took a scanning wand from a holster at his side when he saw me. I thought about the repulse spray in my pocket as my jaw locked.

"Please approach, arms out," he ordered as he raised his helmet shield to expose a pair of tiny, suspicious eyes.

"Extra precautions today, I guess."

The darkly attired officer began at my feet, working his way up, looking at the data feed on his viser more than me. The device was silent, which I took to be a good sign. Gradually, the scanner moved upwards, towards my pocket, towards the repulse spray. I tried to relax. *California tech. The best*, I told myself. If the Authority discovered the spray, even Havelock wouldn't be able to bail me out.

The scanning wand reached my faux lipstick. It went past, moving upwards. Just as I relaxed, the officer's arm paused. He squinted at his viser. His eyes met mine. I could have run fifteen hundred meters in the time gap between my last heartbeat and the one that followed. The wand resumed its journey upwards.

"All done here," he announced.

Not completely trusting my knees, I walked inside, focusing on putting one foot in front of the other without falling. I traversed the near-empty halls with quick steps. The Lit classroom looked empty, and I found my seat, my thoughts on exploding missiles and my missing brother. I was sitting right next to Alexander before I noticed him. I jerked in surprise.

"I'm the one that's supposed to be jumpy," he commented in a dry, tired voice.

"Sorry, I wasn't expecting you to be here...I mean, I wasn't expecting...you know...in school...Or in that seat, I guess."

"We don't give in to terrorists in my family," he said stiffly.

"I saw what happened. It was awful, terrifying."

"You saw a net recording. It won't hurt you." He sounded annoyed, condescending.

"No, I was there actually, big boy. I almost got roasted."

This time Alexander jumped. "What were you doing there?"

I wouldn't have answered him on most mornings, but I decided to cut him a bit of slack given his father's ordeal.

"Trying to get back to the subway. Almost walked smack into one of those strange fat drones..."

His brows came down like a collapsing tunnel. "What drones?"

Students flooded into the room before I could answer, drawn to Alexander like moths to a flame. He turned his attention to his worthier supplicants. I heard outrage, expressions of support, and vows of solidarity. At first I thought it sounded ridiculous; these kids were talking like the politicos on the net, as if they wielded real power. But on reflection, I supposed it wasn't much different than the banter of gang members like Mateo or Otega or Vincent. These highborn kids would lead the country one day. I didn't want to think about what Alexander might be in charge of one day.

Mr. Lynder's arrival ended all conversation. He had merely to sweep the room with those aged, hawkish eyes to drive the last straggler into his desk. The last student to conform with the silent directive fell under questioning worthy of an Authority interrogator, even if the topic related to the previous evening's assigned reading rather than disorderly activities.

As the unfortunate Darin Sorell-Weaks squirmed under questioning, I caught Alexander glancing over at me. I pretended not to notice. He continued to do so throughout class, his hands fidgety. I tried putting myself in his place, imagining what it might be like to have a father, imagining how I would feel if someone tried to kill him. The closest I could come was thinking about how I felt about Mateo's struggle, although I doubted my brother's life, or death, would merit a minute of net time. Still, I would've hated coming to school and have people talk to me about it, pretending to understand.

After Mr. Lynder finished terrifying us, he reminded the class about the forthcoming essay examination in his ominous voice. I had a mountain to read in the next two weeks. As soon as class ended, Alexander was swarmed by classmates. I left him trapped amid the circle of fawning sycophants.

I spotted Headmaster Havelock in the hall ahead of me, his head bobbing above the shorter masses around him. I followed him rather than go directly to class, hurrying to close the distance between us. When I got near, he noticed me, but pretended not to. Instead, he ducked into a classroom and engaged in a discussion with a teacher I didn't recognize. *Not anxious to see me*, it seemed. Perhaps I had exhausted my quota of goodwill. Blowing my track tryout and getting myself detained by the Authority could have that effect.

I retraced my path, heading towards my next class against a tide of students. I turned onto a gloomy, truncated corridor that led to the battered amphitheater-like room that was perfect for lectures on economic theory. As I walked, warm vise-like fingers reached out from one of the corridor's dark alcoves. They wrapped themselves around my arm. My hands balled into fists. When he tugged at me, I turned on the perpetrator, a right hook leading the way.

I didn't pull the punch, even when I saw who the hand belonged to. Bastard deserved it for grabbing me. But somehow, Alexander caught my fist in his huge palm. Damn, he was quick. I'd thrown dozens of punches in the barrio over the years, and no one had ever managed to duck, much less grab my hand.

"Easy, I mean you no ill," he said, his speech stiff. "This is Tuck. Not...elsewhere."

"What the hell do you think you're doing, laying hands on another student?"

He looked stung. "I just want to talk in private. You did not seem the type to startle easily. I was mistaken, it seems."

My knee itched with the urge to show him how mistaken he was, but the tiny bit of softness in those sapphire eyes stopped me. It was like seeing a baby turtle crossing the street. Odds were that it wasn't going to make it, but I didn't want to be the one that did the deed.

"What's so important?" I asked.

"You mentioned running into drones last night. Were you serious?"

"Of course," I told him. "Three of them. Large and sphere-shaped. Way slower than the wing-shaped ones guarding your father's convoy."

His eyes scoured my face so intensely I could feel his skepticism. "There was no mention of attacking drones on the net. No footage of anything like that, not even on the deepnet sites playing personal videos."

I pursed my lips. Alissa had been more interested in the net reports than I had been last night. But she hadn't asked me about any drones, and she'd questioned me rather intently about everything else.

"I saw what I saw. I don't have any reason to lie to you."

"You said they looked like spheres?" He was glancing at his viser as he spoke, a dazzling device forged of gold so thin it was translucent.

"Yes, with four small rotors for power. Decoys, I think. Those winged military type machines made quick work of them."

He held his viser up in front of my face, closer than it needed to be. It displayed a picture of a machine that closely resembled the trio I had seen yesterday, except this image was embedded into what looked like a design schematic pulled from one of the books in Castle's directory. "That's them. And my eyesight is just fine, even if I am a nope." I pushed the viser away.

"Doesn't make sense," he said more to himself than to me. "No one controls the entire net. There would've been something." He looked at me again, daring me to prove myself correct.

"There are ways of scrubbing the net. I've seen it done." As soon as I said it, I wondered why I'd offered anything additional to a boy with the manners of a barrio beggar.

"When?" It sounded like a challenge.

I gritted my teeth. "I need to get to class. Out of my way."

"Daniela, wait. I do not mean to accuse you of dishonesty. Please, I'm trying to figure this out. It...it is important to me. And I could use your help, as the only witness I have access to. When have you seen something edited from the net?"

"Out of my way."

He stood aside. But I caught a glimpse of the turtle again. I sighed. "Once you're out of Castle's domain, do a search for Marie-Ann and Tuck. You won't find anything, not even on the darkest parts of the net. So it can be done. But I've no idea how."

I left him staring dumbly in the hallway. I hoped the turtle would be okay.

CHAPTER

SIXTEEN

A short buzz of excitement from my viser signaled that my first week at Tuck was over. I walked out of those imposing doors, marveling at how much my life had changed in just a few short days. The streets of Manhattan had become familiar, but I lived uneasily in this second world. I just had to hang on until Mateo came to his senses.

Alissa met me on the stone steps outside of school. I hadn't asked her to be there, but I was surprised to find that I was glad to see her. The sun was shining, and the towering trees of Eighty-Ninth Street swayed in the gentle breeze. A tiny cardinal, its feathers luxuriously red, stared at me from a nearby branch, blissfully unaware of its nest's privileged location.

"You made it through a week at Tuck," Alissa proclaimed. "After tryouts on Tuesday, I wasn't sure you would."

A dark cloud passed in front of the sun, or it could have just been my mood changing at the passing memory. I wondered if Alexander had spoken to Coach Nessmier about me. Was that why I had cut him so much slack?

"Last night, I expected to spend the rest of the term in an Authority cell."

"Well, you made it to the weekend, at least," Alissa said. "Lara and Nythan are going to meet us around the corner."

I fell into stride beside her, this girl who I'd just met, but to whom I already owed at least one great debt. Were four days long enough to make a friend?

"How you doing with Lynder's reading list?" she asked me.

"I'm through Shelley, Golding, and Orwell. I've still got Huxley, Atwood and Vonnegut to go. I haven't even thought about how they fit together."

"Pay attention to Huxley," Alissa advised, her voice sage. "Doomsday will be here before you know it."

"Is it really that bad? It's just an exam."

Alissa looked at me, her gaze sharp. "Colleges look at this stuff. Not to mention the egos around here. Lynder has quite a reputation on grades. He fails students every year. Make sure you know every last bit of what those authors wrote, and not just the stories. Mr. Lynder's tests are always zingers, which is why he makes everyone so nervous. He writes the damn questions out by hand, delivered to us on paper in class on the day of the test. No real way to prepare in advance."

"Great," I said, feeling much worse than I had a minute ago.

Alissa led us onto Madison Avenue, past the store where Kortilla and I had nearly been mistaken for lurkers. Now, I wore a Tuck uniform. When people noticed me, it was with respect, approval, or envy. That felt better than it should have.

Alissa stopped outside a café with round, marble-topped tables scattered around its interior as well as on the adjacent side-walk. A looming grass-colored awning kept the outside seats shady. A glass counter filled with pastries, more art than food, sat just inside the transparent doorway. Dark-suited waiters scampered between the tables.

"There they are." Alissa headed towards a half-occupied table next to the window.

"Wait," I told her. "I'm not going."

Alissa spun at me. "What?"

She spoke loud enough that a few heads turned toward us. I stepped closer. "Alissa, this place...what does it cost to even sit at one of these tables? I don't have money to waste on this cr—well, on this sort of thing." My face flushed when I admitted it. I dug my nails into my palm as penance for my idiocy.

Alissa waved her hand at a non-existent fly. Her dismissiveness made my blood heat. "We're talking coffee. I'm happy to treat on this one, Daniela. It's not a big—"

"I don't take charity."

Eye roll. "You're being ridiculous. This is just the way people—"

I was pretty sure I knew how the sentence ended, but given the distance I had put between us, and the anger ringing in my ears, I didn't actually hear her. Not that it mattered. *Los richos.*

I stormed toward the subway, fire flaring through my eyes. Familiars hovered above, watching me as I sped along the sidewalk, coming almost too close to their precious cubs below. At least one finder beam clicked on me. I ignored it.

My viser vibrated with a ping as I reached the Eighty-Sixth Street station, but I didn't look at it. I took the steps two at a time. A train pulled out of the platform as I arrived, leaving me to cool my heels for another eight aggravating minutes. My curiosity bested me during the wait. It was a text message from Nythan: "WE WILL HARVEST HER ORGANS TO PAY BILL IF YOU RETURN -N."

The note garnered a half smile, but not a return trip to the richie café. I wanted to go home, to be with my blood. I wasn't ready to sit in a Manhattan café sipping a day's wage worth of coffee picked by a chipped slave in Colombia, discussing things fashionable and fancy. I hoped I would never be ready for that.

Kortilla was there for me when I got back, as always. We had dinner at her house with her parents and Otega—*tortilla de patatas* and a rich tomato soup, thick and filling. We laughed about Pele's outfit, Otega's lame attempt at a beard, the carrot-shaped holes in Mr. Gonzales' shoes, and a dozen other things I wouldn't be able to remember tomorrow. The knots in my legs and back came undone over the course of dinner. I missed the savory taste of Sung's bulgogi, but otherwise managed to forget about my other life for a few precious hours. Otega and Kortilla walked me home afterwards, through streets lined with vagrants instead of trees, repair shops instead of cafés.

"I checked in at a few of Mateo's haunts. He's still in the wind," Kortilla told me. "He'll be okay, wherever he is. He always is."

I nodded, but without conviction. "It's different this time. He's not even letting his friends know what he's up to or where he is. Something about him feels desperate."

"You're making too much of it, Dee," Kortilla assured me. "You worry about him too much."

"He's someplace dangerous," I said, my voice a husky whisper. "I can feel it."

The look my friend gave me had fear in it. Kortilla knew about my special sense—my spider-sense. She used to laugh about it when we were younger. She didn't anymore. It had saved our rears too many times—keeping us a step ahead of muggers, and worse. Kortilla said it was a spirit, my mom probably, looking over me. That was a nice fantasy.

Rather than offer words, she took my hand and kept it until I felt a bit better.

"I'm going to try to find Marie-Ann's parents tomorrow," I told her. "They never answered my ping. But they've got a bodega on Melrose."

"I'll meet you," Kortilla declared without hesitation. "Not crazy early though, okay?"

———✦✦✦———

Aba was dozing in her chair when I walked in. She saw me with a half of a groggy eye, but didn't say anything. I didn't either. We both knew how the conversation would've gone. We were both worried about Mateo, in our own ways. Talking about it wasn't going to help. If I had anything to tell her, I would have. I fell asleep quickly. When I awoke, Aba had left for work, even though the sun still hid itself. Early genes were in my family.

I headed out to the old PS 62 track rather than trying to rouse Kortilla. The only people awake and on the street were dealers and addicts. I attracted looks from both groups in my running clothes, bag slung around my shoulder, but I kept a brisk enough pace that it wasn't worth bothering me. I didn't run hard—just enough to stretch, to think, to pass the time.

I met Kortilla in front of her building afterwards.

"You smell," were her first words. My dear sister.

"I had a run this morning, so *you* could sleep in," I told her. "Deal with it."

"Hah. It's friggin' eight-thirty in the morning, *hermana*. You have no idea what 'sleep in' means, do you?"

I guess I didn't. I should've run a few more laps.

Pedro and Anita Rebello's store sat mid-block on Melrose Street. The sign above the steel-gated doorway read "*La Bodega*." I didn't have a picture of either of them, but tax records had the couple listed as joint owners of the property as of this year. They were on the tax rolls for the past sixteen years, which fit together with the year of Marie-Ann's birth: They started paying into the system when they needed it.

We entered the store accompanied by the chiming of simulated bells. The whole place consisted of three long, battered plastika shelves filled with necessities like private label water, bags of fabricated rice, beans and flour, as well as mouth spray, med cleansers and the like. Vacuum pouches of pre-fabricated meals, along with the usual selection of stim-chews, adorned one wall. Closer to the front were the real items, all located behind a rusted metal gate: eggs, field-grown rice, milk, and a few aging carrots and potatoes. Glum and typical. There was nothing like this place in Manhattan.

The proprietor watched us from behind a duraglass booth at the front of the store. He was an older man, worn down in the slow-grind way people usually were around here. His leathery eyes were open, but they looked like they'd rather be closed. He wore a sour frown and several days' worth of a salt-and-pepper beard.

Kortilla and I approached the front of the store, keeping our hands in easy view. The man behind the duraglass shield watched warily. We couldn't see under the counter, but I was certain he had a weapon of some kind.

"Mr. Rebello?" I asked.

A bit of light flickered in those eyes, then extinguished itself. "You buying anything?"

"Please, you're Pedro Rebello, right? Your daughter was Marie-Ann?"

He searched my face, trying to place me. He couldn't, of course. "I need you girls to leave. *Am'screy o urchach.*" The last being Barriola for get the hell out.

I stepped up to his shielding, the material scratched and smudged, much like the man behind it. My breath fogged the glass I was so close. I wanted him to see my face, my eyes.

He rattled something beneath the counter. He meant it to sound threatening. Kortilla put a hand on my shoulder to urge me away, but I didn't budge. I trusted my senses. He wouldn't hurt me. He didn't have it in him. Not anymore.

"My name, sir, is Daniela Machado. I go to the Tuck School, the same as your daughter did, yes?"

Surprise registered on his face as he looked at me anew—a Latina girl from BC, saying she went to a highborn school. I read him easily: He didn't understand why his daughter would never have mentioned me. He wanted to ask me, but something held him back. He couldn't. He was scared, I realized. Not of me, but of something else.

"They gave me her spot," I whispered. "What happened to her?"

Now there was pain in Pedro Rebello's eyes. A weary pain, the agony of a man beyond tears.

"You're mistaken. I have a son, his name is Amillo, that's all," he said finally, his voice like dry sand. He placed a small bottle of horchata on the counter. "This is on sale today. Fifty cents. Buy it or not, but either way, leave now or I'll call the black boots."

I studied the milky white container, noticing the brand mark and the seal. According to the package, the rice and sugar used to make it were the real thing—it should've cost twenty times the quoted price. I held out my viser. He scanned it with his own, then handed me the bottle through an open slit in his booth. It was cool to the touch. Something he had kept in refrigeration. Rarer still. Kortilla and I left without another word.

When we had turned the corner onto the street, Kortilla grabbed the horchata from my hand. "*Amigos* is a real brand—this is sealed, and chilled. It's worth ten bucks. He practically gave it to you. Or he's trying to poison you."

I glanced at my flashing viser. A data transfer had accompanied the transaction receipt. I opened the attachment, holding my arm out for Kortilla to see. An image appeared, of a young girl, about my age, with plump cheeks and a crooked smile, her hair flowing in dark waves. She stood someplace elegant, with expensive-looking decorations in the background. But it was her clothes that drew my attention: she wore a navy skin, the Tuck tiger emblazoned on her chest.

"That her?" Kortilla asked.

I nodded. "I've only seen an old picture from the net, but it's her."

"So that's her dad. But why wouldn't he talk to us? He was scared of us, it seemed."

I thought about that. I recalled the torment in his eyes, and each word he had said.

"He mentioned a son," I said, thinking aloud.

"Yeah, what does that matter? Does he think he's going to get that kid into Tuck or something? Or that we'll cause trouble for him?"

I looked at my viser again, calling up the tax records I had used to find the Rebellos' store. "He and his wife only became the owners of that place a few weeks ago. Before that they were just taxpayers in good standing. Her mom worked in Manhattan, paid some city tax there, according to the records. Probably a maid or something. Her dad ran the store. He was a tenant until after his daughter died."

"So those highborn bought them the store—a better life. Money to give their other kid a better shot at whatever," Kortilla said. "Why would the richies do that?"

I chewed on my lip. "Havelock is a good man, I think. He looks out for the students. Like he did for me, when the Authority goons had me. He might have arranged it. A death benefit—something for the family. Perhaps he felt responsible."

"Then why wouldn't Mr. Rebello speak to us?" Kortilla asked. "Why was he so afraid that all he could do was ping you a picture?"

I struggled with her question. "Confidentiality, maybe. Quid pro quo for the payment is silence. That's what Tuck would've wanted."

Kortilla snapped open the horchata and took a long, deep swallow. "That's good stuff. Do you really believe the school gave them that store because they felt bad for some barrio parents' losing their daughter? C'mon."

We walked another block without speaking. Kortilla had finished the horchata by the time we got to the corner. Never even offered me a sip. I tasted a bit of blood from where my teeth had bored too deeply into my lip as I thought about her last question. "No," I said softly. "Highborn don't give things away. There must be something else."

I pulled the picture up on my viser again. This time I didn't look at the girl. Instead, I looked at the background. At the turquoise vase. At the dragons on it, hand painted. Expensive. I'd seen it before. When I was at Alissa's house.

"They were friends," I said. "Better friends than Alissa let on."

CHAPTER

SEVENTEEN

M onday came too soon. Just as I began to remember what my life was supposed to be like, I had to get back onto the subway and return to that other world. I did so with more questions than answers. I didn't know what had happened to Marie-Ann, and I still had no word from Mateo. I hadn't heard from Alissa or her gang all weekend either.

There had been even more violence in Manhattan on Sunday. In the wake of Friday's attack on the Chairman of the Orderist Party, the Authority had been raiding apartments all over the city, leading to a shootout with unknown perpetrators, several of whom had somehow escaped the Authority's dragnet. There was no word on whether it was the same men who had attacked Landrew's car. Depending on which net channel you scanned, California was either behind it all or had nothing to do with it. Invasion was either required or foolhardy. Always there was the same reminder: prosperity through order.

Authority officers greeted me and my fellow commuters on the subway platform, checking travel passes and conducting random scans as we waited for the train. I had my repulse spray in my pocket, but I didn't panic; I'd become a believer in the organic camouflage of California tech. The device had latched itself onto my skin, mimicking itself to the material.

I needn't have worried. My travel permit and Tuck uniform
got me off easy: I was waved onto the next train, while the
women on either side of me—domestic help by the look of
their outfits—got more intensive scrutiny. I watched them being searched outside the train window when I pulled away,
their faces masks of fortitude. The image stayed with me until
I left the train.

I arrived on Eighty-Ninth Street before most of the crowd
had gathered outside the school, as had become my custom. I
slipped past a few kids I didn't recognize, then endured another
screen by the Authority supervised school security squad before
entering the hallowed halls. I found Nythan leaning against the
wall of the first corridor I turned down, fabrifoam cup in one
hand, a lame attempt at a satisfied grin on his face. The pose
just didn't work for someone with such a pale face and barely
any eye color.

"You didn't answer my ping," Nythan said.

"I was busy. I have a life outside of Tuck. Anyway, I wasn't
aware your jokes required a response."

"Hey, I'm a peacemaker here. Can't you see how white I am?
I'm a walking flag of truce."

I unclenched my jaw a bit. "What's so important?"

He sighed heavily, shaking his head. "Miss Alissa is dis-
pleased. You are stubborn. Lara loves to egg on a good fight.
So, alas, it falls to me to keep the Beatles together. Call me
un-Yoko."

"Now I'm a bug?" I asked, brow arched. "And what is Alissa
so upset about?"

"Ugh, look up 'Beatles' under twentieth-century pop cul-
ture." He hit himself on the forehead. "Let me explain about
Alissa. She's no less a queen bee than Miss Kris Fart, just a different kind—the kind that doesn't like to think of herself that
way. The way she sees it, she has graciously offered to take you

into her protective embrace, and she does not deal well with rejection. And Ms. Lara is usually happy to think the worst of anyone, so you see, it falls on my ivory shoulders to keep this garden blossoming."

It never occurred to me that Alissa could be mad at *me*. If that were the case, she was beyond oblivious. The only thing I wanted to speak to Alissa about was her true relationship with Marie-Ann. "What makes you think I care? I don't need to drink coffee in cafés."

"Ah…Well, if you had tried great coffee, you might feel differently. And don't go getting all high and mighty on me. Drinking coffee doesn't make me a bad person. Drinking Colombian coffee might, but that particular establishment serves Rwandan beans, not the best taste, but no chip slaves. It's all freeholder grown, so relax."

I fixed my best exasperated gaze at him. "What do you want me to do here, Nythan?"

"Climb off the holier-than-thou horse, Bronx girl. I like you. So does Alissa. And Lara tolerates you, and that's all you can really hope for with her. Make it easier on Alissa, okay? Take deep breaths, don't storm off when people try to do something nice for you. We're the best there is at this place. Trust me."

He was right. I didn't know how long it would take to treat Mateo. I hoped to spend four years here. Still, I hadn't done anything wrong. "I'll see what I can do."

Nythan tented his fingertips, then strummed each of them in quick succession. "Excellent," he declared in a strange voice.

"Another twentieth-century parody?"

He nodded. "Montgomery Burns. Oh, do look *him* up. You'll love him. As highborn as they came back then."

I nodded, not intending to do any such thing. "By the way, did you call Kris Foster-Rose-Hart Kris Fart?"

He turned away, strumming his fingers as he walked, laughing a mocking, evil-ish laugh. "Excellent!" echoed down the hall.

I had a faint smile on my lips by the time I got to Lit. Alexander wasn't in his seat yet, but I spied the back of Alissa's head several rows in front of me. With Nythan's advice and his stupid twentieth-century impressions ringing in my head, I started to flick out a Morse code ping. An incoming administrative message popped up on the screen before I could finish it. I stared at the words. It was Coach Nessmier. A simple message, but enough to stop my heart beating:

"REPORT TO TRACK TODAY AND EVERY WEEKDAY FOR PRACTICE."

I didn't clear the message; I didn't take my eyes off it for fear it might vanish, like the fleeting pleasure of a fading dream. A bead of sweat dripped down my face. Only the unmistakable presence of Alexander sliding in next to me pulled me from my conflicted trance. He looked over at me, his face hard, blank.

"Did you do this?" I said, finding my voice.

"I did what I said I would. I told you why." If Michelangelo had imagined his creation's voice, I'm sure it would have sounded like Alexander Foster-Rose-Hart at that moment.

I heard Mr. Lynder enter, ruffling the pages of his scruffy notebook.

"Thank you," I whispered.

Most of the day was a blur. I kept thinking about that track. They had held a tryout for me, and I had failed, in front of the whole school. Now I got a spot anyway? Why? It certainly wasn't because Coach Nessmier wanted me. Would the coach change his mind because Alexander asked him? The team captain didn't usually make those decisions.

I didn't go to lunch. Instead, I went down to the track. I was the only one there, the stands empty, the screens looking like plain walls. I jogged along the length of the stretched circle in the inside lane—no more than a light trot that didn't even wind me. I had to save myself for practice. After two circuits, I glided into an easy walk, soaking in the immaculate facilities, the purity of the filtered air. I wanted to run here. I wanted to go against the best and beat them. The idea of owing my chance to Alexander the Great rankled though. Did he help me because he thought I'd earned it? Or did he want something? I couldn't imagine anything I had that he could possibly want.

Nythan gave me evil looks in Script. Not his mocking evil look that almost made me laugh, but actual evil, annoyed looks. I realized I hadn't spoken to Alissa all day. I was sure I hadn't even looked at her in Lit once I got the message about the track team. She had probably taken it the wrong way.

After class, Nythan ambled over. His face was as serious as I had seen it. "You blew her off in Lit and all of us at lunch?"

"I didn't mean to, it's just..." I noticed Drake lingering a row ahead of us, listening. "I'll take care of it."

"Very wise. Whoever told you that is a smart fellow." He lifted his milky brows and left.

I intended to reach out to Alissa in Chemistry. Only she wasn't in class. I could've pinged her, but I wanted to speak in person. Anyway, I had no idea what kept her out of Chem. It might be something serious. I resolved to check in with Nythan later. After which I spent the rest of class thinking about tracks, pacing, form, and about the Armory. It had multiple tracks, including the National Stadium on top. The best runners in the country proved themselves there: Moko Die, Vincent Anton Freeman, Thomas Glader. I had never dared to believe I'd race in the same place as such legends before. I did now. It was way more interesting than Chemistry.

EIGHTEEN

I stepped into the den of wolves.

They, who just a short time ago had done their best to defeat and humiliate me, now milled before me, near docile—talking, laughing, stretching. Drake's hulking form was easy to spot among them, as was Mona Lisa Reves-Wyatt, with her great height and mannishly wide shoulders. The rest of the team milled about. My arrival was like that of an objector at a wedding, an event imagined but never expected. Every eye fixed upon me.

"Nope to the damn nope," came a mutter from the pack.

Unease rippled through the team. They looked at each other, unsure how to react. For that they looked to the alphas. Those who took their cues from Drake or Mona Lisa saw disdain, and took up the silent directive. If it had been only those two, I think the scene would've turned ugly. But Alexander's presence kept the team in check. He fixed his eyes on the heckler, a gaze that warned a wayward pup he had erred. Most kept their silence as I walked towards the center of the track. I struggled to keep my pace measured, my knees steady. *Of course, Nessmier didn't make it easy for me by telling them...*

Only Drake continued to defy Alexander. "You're lost, nope. No do-overs. Crawl back to the slums."

I stared back at him, not breaking stride. My throat felt dry, but I had to answer. I didn't need to be liked to be part of the team, but I needed respect. I needed to answer without becoming the person that tore the team apart. I searched for the words. A high-pitched whistle intervened.

"That's quite enough, Mr. Pillis-Smith," said Coach Nessmier. "We are all a team here."

Surprise on most faces. Resentment on a few.

"Really, Coach?" Drake challenged, his words every bit highborn, in tone and attitude. This was their school, their world, said that voice. It was the first time I heard a student speak to an elder of this place with such arrogance.

"I asked the coach to give her a chance," declared Alexander, putting himself between the rest of the team and me. Drake looked as though he had been punched in the gut. "We're about merit here. Not timing. It is not her fault she was not here for the initial trials. When she got her chance, she earned a spot. We all know it. On a different day, she might have done even better."

I noted the diplomacy. Don't insult the coach, don't antagonize Drake by saying I would've won, don't admit to anyone that I could've beaten *you*. He was good.

"Daniela has earned a spot on this team," Alexander continued. It was the first time he had ever said my name. I felt a chill ascend through my spine. He extended a giant hand to me. I took it. "Is there anyone who would like to race her? Winner gets a place on the team, loser walks." The gaze of a blue storm swept across the team. No one met the challenge. Then Alexander stared at Drake, who flushed a shade of crimson. Oh, if only Nythan could see that face—they'd hear his laugh in BC.

The silence that followed felt like a warm embrace.

"Welcome to the team," Alexander said.

A roar of approval followed the pronouncement, then chants of "Tuck! Tuck!" as if Alexander had delivered to them what they had always wanted. I, who moments ago had been prey, was welcomed into the pack. I felt hands upon my shoulders, squeezes of approval, acknowledgments of my speed. Who the hell were these people? But then I realized it wasn't them; it was Alexander. I looked through the crowd of new teammates to find him, standing next to Coach Nessmier. I kept my gaze on him until he noticed it. He finally acknowledged me with a slow tilt of his head, a gesture that told me: *now hold up your end of the deal.*

I did, at least that day. It was only practice, but I ran my tail off. When it was not my turn on the track, I was an attentive spectator. I forced myself to acknowledge their efforts, wringing a "great" or "blazing" out of my reluctant jaw. That I spoke the truth made the words come easier. These boys and girls were the fastest and most coordinated collection of runners I had ever beheld. Highborn—every one of them.

At the end of an hour and a half of practice, my body ached from my efforts. But a smile had curled onto my lips: My first day as part of the Tuck track team had gone far better than I would've dared hope. Mona Lisa jostled me from behind as I stepped into the locker room, but even that I let pass. At least this time. She and Drake might fume, but I was a member of this pack now. And I intended to show every one of these highborn that I could help the team win. I think Mom would've been proud, but this was for me.

I remembered Nythan's admonishment on stubbornness and neglect after I slid into my seat in Lit class the next day. Alexander gave me a curt chin nod. It was practically a hug, coming from him.

"T-R-U-C-E" I messaged to Alissa. I didn't get a response. The back of her head didn't budge. Alissa didn't stick around after class either. I gritted my teeth. It wasn't like I had done anything to her. Nythan be damned; I didn't want to deal with crap like this. So I didn't. I grabbed a roasted turkey sandwich from the kitchen and took it to lab to eat. Practice was going to cut into my study time, and I had plenty to do. The infamous Literature examination loomed like a well-forecast storm. But it was hard to focus on anything academic. I kept thinking about my first meet as part of the Tuck team.

Nythan shook his head when saw me in Script, the gesture of a disappointed mentor. That pale head kept moving like a bleached metronome as I walked over.

"I pinged her," I protested. "She ignored me. I'm not going to play silly games. You might barely know me, but you should know me well enough to get that."

"Just come to lunch tomorrow, okay?" Nythan asked. "Pretty please."

I paused, bottom lip trapped in my teeth like a snared rabbit. "Okay."

"You can be sure Lara will have a jab or two for you. With your joining forces with our pal Drake on the track team, it's going to be hard to resist. Try to be icy tomorrow—don't storm off."

My face had gone to a dangerous blank as soon as I heard the bit about the track team. "Why do you care what team I run on? Or any of this for that matter?"

Something I hadn't seen before flashed onto Nythan's face. Maybe anger. Maybe annoyance. It was an emotion that was ill-suited to those milky, mocking features. Then it was gone.

The Nythan I knew gave me an exaggerated eye roll, as if he could stare at the top of the inside of his skull.

"I'm trying to do good, for all the peoples of this fair land. Shall we not all go forth bravely together?"

"Wrong us, shall we not revenge?" I shot back.

"Ha, I know that line too. Did you read the play? Or did you watch *Star Trek* VI like me?"

I had gotten that line from Mateo. Mom used to say it, supposedly. "Huh?"

Eye roll again. "Try not to storm off again. We just need to get through this."

⸻

Wednesday afternoon soon arrived. After I finished up in Trig, after taking my time cleaning my workspace and after doing a full power down of my digiBook, I trudged to the dining hall. For once, I wasn't hungry. I had poured just about everything I had into track practice, and my remaining time and energy went to my studies. I hadn't focused on whatever was bothering Alissa, and I didn't want to do so now. But I'd told Nythan I'd be here, and that I'd keep cool. I was going to do it.

I put one heavy foot in front of the other and they carried me up to the third floor, into the controlled chaos of the dining hall. Students maneuvered with reckless abandon through alternating traffic flows; people jockeyed for position at the food counter while others searched for seats. Still another group wandered about making social rounds at various tables. I felt like a rock in navy blue rapids as students walked, ran, and jumped around me, their voices combining in a chorus of babble. Alissa sat with Lara in their usual spot. I considered getting this over with immediately, but I wanted Nythan there. So I got in line for food. I figured a sandwich would make it

easy to walk away without abandoning my lunch if that became necessary. Once I had my food in hand, I steeled myself
and headed over.

Nythan had arrived, but I didn't have a clear view of his
face. Alissa was staring at him and not speaking, so I suspected
he was telling her something similar to what he had told me.
She nodded, the way I did when Aba reminded me about
truths I already knew.

I had thought of several things to say when I arrived, phras-
es tinged with my version of humor, or maybe just a simple
"hi." I chose none of those. I just sat. Nythan was to my left,
Alissa and Lara across from me. I fixed my attention on Alissa.
She stared back. For a long moment, I thought things would
go badly. Nythan must've felt it also.

"'Everything was beautiful and nothing hurt...'" Nythan
announced with understated drama.

"*Slaughterhouse-Five*," Alissa and I both replied
simultaneously.

"Shall we all again live in that beautiful time?" Nythan
asked. "Let us all unite, my silly high-Aptitude-Tier friends."

"Vonnegut meant it ironically," I started.

Nythan flapped his eyelids like a butterfly. "Did he?"

I realized I had fallen into his trap. Reluctant hints of a
smile appeared on Alissa's face. The ice had been broken.

"I'm dying slogging through Vonnegut's stuff," Alissa declared. "He's so unfocused."

An easier conversation followed, and I joined in. It was always easy to complain about school-work. Nothing like a common enemy to unite people. Nythan kept a close eye on us all.
I wanted to question Alissa about Marie-Ann, but the place
and time was wrong.

"Do you even have time to study, Daniela?" Lara asked in her cutting voice. "It must be hard with all the time you spend with the track team now they let you on as a special favor?"

Nythan's forewarning made it easier for me not to rise to the provocation. Instead, I forced a grin I didn't feel and hurled it at her. "You should've seen Drake's face on that first day. It'd be worth failing Lit, just to have seen that."

Nythan laughed at the image, and Alissa smiled wide enough that I could see white.

"I'm glad you got what you wanted, Daniela," she said, low and cautious. I knew the "but" was coming. "But, look, it may seem they have included you. That you can belong with the highborn. Just be careful."

"Aren't you the people who keep telling me to give this place a chance?"

"Tuck can help you. But the track team—that's for them. Or at least that's the way the highborn see it."

Nythan's leg tapped mine under the table. I got the message.

"I just want to run."

Lara went to speak, but Alissa put her hand on her friend's shoulder. "Then we'll be there to see it. Race on Saturday, right?"

"Yes," I confirmed.

"Why don't you stay over at my place afterwards?" Alissa suggested. "My parents are out of town at some conference. We'll have the place to ourselves. We can get ready for next Friday's Lit test together."

I opened my mouth to decline. I didn't want to spend any more time in the world where I didn't belong than I had to. I didn't want to get used to Manhattan water and farm-raised meat. I searched for the right excuse. Nythan's knee found mine again: This was a peace offering. Slapping it away would be like walking away from the café. At least that was what Nythan was trying to tell me. I tried not to grind my teeth.

"Sure, thanks."

CHAPTER

NINETEEN

The team was supposed to meet at school at nine o'clock in the morning to go over to the Armory together, as one unit. I arrived so early I wasn't even sure anyone would be there, but Tuck security was bright-eyed and waiting for me, wand scanner and everything. No Authority backup on the weekends, though. After a cursory scan, the guard waved me through.

"Good luck at the meet," he said. "I-It's nice to see you getting a chance. Good luck."

I bowed my head, highborn style, then stopped. I looked at the rent-a-cop whom I recognized but hadn't paid much attention to before. He had a doughy face, with thick leathery brows. He was not old by any means—no more than thirty, I guessed. But deep creases crossed his face and his hands looked worn, as if scraped by sandpaper.

"Thank you," I said, not knowing why I whispered.

The school was dark, quiet. I went downstairs to the locker room. Before I made it through the heavy door leading inside, I heard voices, muffled but agitated. I stopped, considering. It was none of my business, except who else would be here at this hour? I crept down the hall, my shoes squeaking on the buffed floor. The noise was coming from just around the corner. I got closer, close enough to discover where the conversation was coming from: Coach Nessmier's office. One of the voices filtered through the closed door. The agitated one. Apparently, the coach's voice got even more nasal when he was upset.

The other speaker didn't yell; I couldn't make out any of the words spoken by that voice. But I could hear Coach Nessmier.

"I thought you'd be pleased...now...gave...wanted," Nessmier declared, exasperated.

More talking, the deeper voice, under control.

"You don't have that right!" the coach yelled. "I can't do anything about it!"

The other man replied. Nessmier answered. Calmer. Mollified. Or perhaps beaten.

My spider-sense told me to get away from there. But I didn't. I wanted to know the identity of the other speaker. Someone who could threaten Coach Nessmier. Someone who'd come down here early to berate him, or to order him to do something, or not do something. It had to be someone from the school, or they wouldn't have been able to get inside.

The urge to run grew. It was a tugging at my legs, a voice yelling inside my head. I willed myself to stay put. Just a few more seconds. The door moved, ever so slightly. *Go now!* The ringing was so loud it ached. My feet felt like I had ants crawling over them. The door opened slowly. I saw an arm. I bolted, opting for speed over stealth.

I was inside the girl's locker room in seconds, panting behind the metal door. I pressed my ear to its cold surface. The throbbing in my head had stopped, but I could only hear the beating of my heart. I wasn't sure I would've been able to hear footsteps over the thumping. It didn't matter. I was pretty certain he wouldn't come in here, even if he had heard me.

My throat was dry, my breathing unsteady. It had only been an arm, but that was enough. With the other pieces—the deep, steady voice, and the person being able to access the school—seeing that arm was enough to know. It probably would've been enough without hearing the voice. The other man in Coach Nessmier's office was Headmaster Havelock.

———✂———

I sat on a bench in the locker room in lonely silence. Each word I had overheard replayed in my head. They had been arguing about what the headmaster wanted, about the extent of his authority. I didn't want that conversation to be about me. I didn't want anyone discussing what I could and could not do. I had wanted to *earn* a spot on the team and run. But I was certain it had been about me.

When I started at Tuck, Havelock had forced Coach Nessmier to reopen tryouts for me. But Nessmier had found a way to keep me off the team. I could see why that would've led to conflict between them. But the coach had taken me on now. He had given me a slot running the fifteen hundred meters. I thought that had been Alexander's doing, although he had never really said one way or the other. Perhaps Havelock had a hand in it as well? But why the fight now, when I was on the team, preparing for my first meet? I didn't get it. I definitely didn't like it. I was good enough to run with any of them, highborn or not. I just wanted a fair chance to prove it.

I took a Tuck athletic skin from my locker, looking down upon its almost glassy surface. It was a single piece of cloth, no seams, no threads. I yanked at the manufactured fabric, silky light but strong. I couldn't rip it, no matter how I tried. I hurled the skin into the row of lockers facing me and kicked the nearest door. The thud was dull and unsatisfying.

The team began to arrive in a trickle, then a stream. There were twenty-one students on the Tuck team; I was one of four

girls. My luck being what it was, Mona Lisa was the first of my
teammates to enter the girl's locker room.

"You look green, nope girl," she said, looming with contempt. "There's nothing to it, even for the likes of you. Just
follow Alexander until he tells you to stop. Same as always."

I should have gotten angry, but I had used up a lot of emotion already that morning, on top of a nearly sleepless night.
Instead, I cast a pair of weary eyes upon her.

"Why do you hate me so much?"

Her eyes narrowed. "There is an *order* to things, girl. A way
the world is supposed to be, needs to be. For everyone. Or else
there is chaos. And you don't fit into that order. You think the
world should make exceptions for you, that you can do whatever you want. I believe in prosperity through order."

"I can help you win meets. Even you must know that."

"If we need a nope to win, we've won nothing," she hissed
back.

I grabbed my bag and stormed off. The rest of the team was
gathering on the front steps of the school. A minibus painted
in Tuck colors with our logo on the side was parked on the
street outside the school entrance. Alexander stood next to it,
speaking with Anise Titan-Wind, a wiry chestnut-haired girl
who seem to float rather than run along the track. Her limbs
reminded me of chopsticks, thin and pointy, but she could fly
like a hawk. She specialized in sprints—the two hundred meter
was her primary event, but she was effective in the four hundred meter. If I had developed anything close to a friend on the
team over the past week, it would be Anise. She occasionally
spoke to me and I hadn't heard her insult me yet.

I maneuvered my way through the crowd to them. Alexander looked, if not happy to see me, at least not unhappy. Anise
graced me with half a smirk. From a couple of highborn, it was
like a welcome parade.

"Ready?" Alexander inquired without preamble. "Proper nutrition loading?"

I didn't know what that was, but I had forgotten about breakfast. My stomach hadn't been up to it. Rookie mistake, to say the least. Alexander saw my chagrin.

"These aren't a bunch of Bronx City kids," he said. "Redwell won last year's championship—as a team. Not my event, of course."

Of course, I wanted to echo, but I bit it back. I didn't want any more battles today. I didn't want Alexander as my enemy.

He reached into his bag, withdrawing a crispy silver package that he placed in my hand. The label said "CUSTOMIZED NUTRITION FOR ALEXANDER FOSTER-ROSE-HART" in dark, bold letters.

"Will this turn me into you? Please?" I just couldn't resist.

Not even a blink. "Don't take your competition lightly. Not in this league. These will be the best runners you've ever faced. Anise and I were just discussing the Redwell team; they might be as good as us since we don't have Augie anymore. Their two-hundred-meter champ beat Anise last year. The other school, Legacy Academy, isn't quite in Redwell's class, but their fifteen-hundred runners are good, their sprinters are even better. One of them placed second in the city last year."

"Daniela, there's never been anyone who joined the team like you did," Anise said, not unkindly. "Alexander, he took a risk—"

"I won't let you down," I promised. "I won't let the team down."

Coach Nessmier's golden whistle sounded. "On the bus. Everyone on the bus. It's time for business." He herded everyone towards the vehicle's open door. I turned to board as well. I took two steps then I felt a hand on my arm. Clawish, icky. I spun, alarmed.

"Change of plan, Machado," Coach Nessmier said, looking at the bus, not me. "You'll run the conditioned fifteen hundred meter today. Anise will take your spot in the standard fifteen hundred. And I'm pulling you from the five thousand meter. Alexander will switch places with you. Just one event for you today. We'll see how you manage it."

"A conditioned event, in my first meet?" I asked, dumbfounded. I'd never run a conditioned event, and hadn't practiced them all week. We were stacked with talent there. They didn't need me.

"You run in the events I tell you, or not at all. You want to be on this team or not?"

I swallowed pain and outrage in equal measures.

"The conditioned fifteen hundred meter. Got it. No problem."

I hoped the Alexander the Great nutrition bar tasted better than this crap.

chapter TWENTY

C oach wanted me off the team. Something had gone on between Havelock and Coach Nessmier; the result was that I was now slated in the conditioned fifteen hundred meter against Drake, as well as a clutch of great athletes from competing schools—I was being set up to fail. Nessmier intended to show that I didn't belong on the team, or get me to quit. Neither was going to happen. I tore into Alexander's bar wishing it was Coach's throat.

I seethed on the bus ride from Tuck. If anyone noticed my silent rage or wondered at Coach's decision, they didn't care enough to walk a few rows back to find out more. It was the sight of the Armory that finally yanked me from my stupor. I'd first seen it on the net, during the Olympic Trials that took place in the massive, glass-topped, John Masterman National Track Stadium. The arching silver dome looked like some kind of alien spaceship that had descended on the far smaller, red brick castle-style building that had given the original structure its name, back from the time it had served as headquarters for the New York militia. The soaring coliseum on top held fifty thousand souls and could simulate any condition or obstacle. The proving ground of champions.

Those men and women fighting for spots on the United States Olympic team had seemed like giants to me, years ago, every movement one of discipline and strength. Crowds screamed at the conclusion of each race, as if the winner of the race would somehow change the plight of the people watching. But it was the eyes of one woman, Moko Die, that stuck with me long after the netcast ended. She had won the traditional and conditioned fifteen hundred, setting national records in each. Fans cheered, flowers rained down on her after each victory, but the look in her eyes never changed. I wasn't sure she heard or even saw the mayhem that erupted in her honor. She just wanted to race. Her gaze held no sign of triumph or satisfaction. Instead, there was peace that could only come when racing. I dragged Mateo to the elementary school track the next day.

Our meet would be held in an annex to the old castle, but I intended to get into the real stadium one day. I had come too far, endured too much, to not claim that satisfaction.

"You coming?" Alexander called back to me before he left the bus.

I scrambled down the aisle, past the rows of plush leather seats, crossing the stone archway into the Armory. Coach led us to the locker rooms, which in turn had tunnels leading out to the secondary track. I counted fewer than ten girls among the four teams sharing the massive locker room. I was the first onto the track from Tuck.

The stadium was about twice the size of our practice facility back at school. Most of the extra space was utilized for seating, which stretched upwards for twenty rows. A retractable dome soared above us. A dozen translucent tubes resembling upside down glass lighthouses hung from the ceiling. These, I knew, would be used in the conditioned events to simulate rain, snow, sand—whatever the gamekeepers decided. I walked along the length of track where the conditioned events would be run.

"Focus on what is ahead, not on what you are doing," said a rumbling voice behind me. I turned to find Alexander. "It's different from the standard event in that way."

"Got it," I said. "Focus on what's going to jump out at me. No problem." I sounded robotic, numb. I couldn't help it.

"You haven't had a chance to practice conditioned events. But you've got the skills. I've seen you on the hurdles. You're quick. The conditions impact everyone equally. Just don't get surprised—like in tryouts."

"I've run in tough conditions before," I told him. "But I haven't had conditions change from lap to lap in a single race."

Alexander's mouth twitched, his uncertainty nagging like an itchy sweater. "I don't know why Coach Nessmier made such a sudden switch. And such an ill-advised one."

"I'll try not to ruin everything for everyone."

"It won't matter," Alexander told me, as plain as if he were relating today's weather. "I've run against you enough to know you can win any of these events. You're faster than Drake, or anyone else here, except me...perhaps. Unless you make a mistake. With the conditioned events, your drive, your endurance, it matters less."

"I know," I assured him. "But thank you."

"The conditioned events are at the end. Try to stay focused. Forget why, just run."

I watched the stands fill out of the corner of my eyes as I stretched and bent and ran through my drills: high-knees, skips, swings, strides. I finished up with mock starts. I felt Kortilla enter the stadium before I saw her. I got the sense of someone watching over me. The filtered air of the stadium tasted a bit fresher. I had to scan the rows of stands several times before I found her eyes watching me from the sixth row of the

eastern stands. My knees buckled ever so slightly, feeling warm
on the inside. The cost to come into Manhattan was high for
her. Too high. Even for her family, if they had helped, it was
too much. She was alone. There was no one else in the world
that would make such a sacrifice, just to see me run. I stopped
everything, turning straight towards her, my arms locked at my
sides. The mask I put up for the world fell away, for my sister
in all but birth staring back at me. I let her know that I hurt,
that I would fight, and that nothing meant more to me than
her being here. After several minutes I dipped my head, just a
fraction.

"What the hell are you doing, Daniela?" Anise asked me.

I didn't answer.

An announcer's voice filled the restless stadium. Events were
to begin in five minutes. Coach Nessmier called us over. He
spoke about strategy for each of the meets. Reminded us each
of our opponents, their strengths and weaknesses, and of our
own. He reviewed the possible weather scenarios and lighting
possibilities for the conditioned meets, and how to adjust for
each. He didn't mention my name. I was already gone to him.

I watched the one hundred meter in stony silence, standing
at the edge of the rest of the team. Our runners placed second
and third. I knew their names, perhaps they knew mine. But
we meant nothing to each other. I realized that now.

Anise paced along the edge of my vision wearing a deep
frown. Drake looked over several times as well. I didn't need to
see his face to know the scorn it registered. Events came and
went. Alexander won the traditional fifteen hundred meters, as
well as the five thousand in my stead.

Finally, it was my turn. Until now, I had only seen conditioned racing on the net. These were spectator competi-
tions—trials that couldn't be fully appreciated except live and
in person. People came to the stadium for the conditioned

races. There were three events at our meet. Alexander and
Drake were our usual champions in the conditioned fifteen
hundred meter. They were strong runners, but the elements of
the conditioned races required a supplemental skill set.

Lane assignments were randomly determined before the
event, and I'd drawn lane five. Not great, but better than being
on the extreme outside. Drake had drawn lane two, which was
where I would've wanted to be if I'd had a choice. Redwell's
ace, Flavius Elias-Hammer, was just inside him. Flavius resembled a bullet, his buffed silver hair shaved to stubs on his tapered head, which in turn seemed to slide into his low-hang-
ing, sloped shoulders.

"Runners, take your marks," shouted the starter, his voice
echoing through the stadium. The din quieted. I placed the
fingers of each of my hands on the enhanced traction ground. I
sucked in a deep breath and looked inside myself. Coach Ness-
micr was in my mind, that rat-like face, his squinting eyes.
Slowly, I released my grip on the anger inside me, at my coach,
at Drake, at everyone. Rage coursed through my veins, powerful and intoxicating.

"Get set!"

I reached for the cold. It came easily, the chill a comfortable
embrace. My blood was liquid ice. The gun sounded. I pushed
myself forward, firing out low, drawing upon the reserves I
usually saved for the end of a race. My legs responded with
such power that I had to lessen my effort at the last moment
for fear of losing control.

My feet snapped forward. The artificial stalactites above
hummed; the temperature dropped as if I had walked into a
freezer. My joints stiffened. I eased my pace, wary of injury in
the rapidly changing conditions. The steamy breath of other
runners surrounded me. Drake hugged my right shoulder. My
feet pounded the ground, my arms keeping precise cadence

with each stride. I paced myself with Flavius-the-Bullet, who ran a stride ahead of me. I kept waiting for the hurdles to rise. But they didn't. It felt like racing around the outside track at my old school in winter. No problem. One lap gone.

Wind blew hard into my face as I took the curve into the second lap. Drake raced ahead of me like a lion after its prey. I kept my eyes focused down the track, on what would come next. The first hurdle appeared, less than five feet ahead of me, its height gyrating. Timing was critical. Drake and Flavius took the obstacle easily, adjusting their strides without disruption to their rhythm. I had to slow to avoid hitting the hurdle. *Deuces.* Three more obstacles rose ahead of me. I mistimed my strides again and stutter-stepped to get my jump correct for the last two. I fell into fourth place, then fifth. Drake led at the end of the second lap, Flavius just behind him.

Sand and twilight descended on the third lap. My outline was illuminated as royal purple for the benefit of the crowd. Drake dashed ahead of us all in a green blur. I pressed for more speed, calling upon my inner will. My legs crossed faster. I moved back to third place, trailing Drake and Flavius by two strides. I remained wary of more hurdles, but the track was getting shorter. I couldn't let Coach Nessmier have an excuse to throw me off the team. I couldn't let anyone else win.

I sucked at the cold within me, demanding more from myself. The other runners had experience, but I wanted this more. My legs thundered so hard that I struggled to keep my balance as we hit the curve. I couldn't see the ground. If I stumbled I was done. If I missed a hurdle I was done. Coach would love that. Each foot had to plant at a slightly modified angle. I had the geometry in my head; my legs knew just where to go. I remained disciplined. I ached to let loose, but control was more important for now. I took a sudden hurdle without breaking stride. But so did Drake and Flavius. One stride behind. The third lap was over.

The cold surrounding me became heat. We were running through the desert, a blazing sun above. I tried to stay with them through the curve. The muscles in my legs loosened. I was ready. I grinned as the last turn ended. The straightway to the finish began, with only Drake and Flavius-the-Bullet ahead of me. Drake had me by about two strides, while the Bullet ran almost even with me. Tiny sand particles flew at my face. I barely felt it. I was fresh, powerful. No more curve to worry about. Just open space. I turned it on, everything I had.

Fire hurled from my feet, but it was the cold inside that propelled me. The ice of my will, of my rage. I knew each foot-fall before it happened. And I foresaw each of my competitors' strides. Only Drake was with me now. He ran with desperation too. I felt his urge to win, and his contempt. I realized then just how much he hated me, far more than I did him. As I pulled ahead, he began to fear. He too drew on something extra. His feet moved faster. He pulled even with me. For a second, then two, we were dead even. It was eternity; less than one hundred meters remained. He was taller than me. His lean at the finish would edge me if we stayed like this. I needed more.

I sucked at that icy pool within, my life's essence, far more deeply than I thought possible before that moment. I stole more than I should have. Images of my mother, clearer than anything I could consciously conjure, flashed before me. I saw Mateo too, and Kortilla. Then it went black. I was above my-self, watching the race, watching my legs churn in a tornado-like blur. It was more than Drake could match, more than any of them could match.

I crossed first. There could be no question about it, no way to manipulate the result. My eyes found Coach Nessmier. He was looking at the replay board, a frown as sour as rotten eggs etched on his face. I followed his gaze: three minutes and forty-one seconds. A new city high school record, I knew. Drake stormed off.

My teammates greeted me with unease, their congratulations sparse and hesitant. I sensed Mona Lisa's words in their thoughts: *There's an order to things, girl.* To hell with their order. Let Coach Nessmier try to cut me after that race.

Anise made a point of coming up to me afterwards, in front of everyone. She placed a hand on my arm. "That was the most amazing run I've ever seen. Congratulations."

She walked off before I had a chance to answer. The words were harder for her to speak than she had expected, but that made me appreciate them more.

Alexander congratulated me too, in his own way. He betrayed no emotion of course; he displayed neither respect nor resentment.

"You kept control, that was the key," he critiqued. "But you won it with that burst at the end. It comes from deep inside, that kind of intensity. But there is a cost, as we both know. A true champion is willing to pay."

I set my eyes upon his carved face, hunting for the intent behind those words. Did he know about my cold place? Our teammates stood within an arm's length. Now was not the time to ask, even if I had dared to. He was the highest of the highborn, a product of two generations of genetic perfection. Not someone with whom I would share secrets.

I climbed into the stands to find Kortilla as soon as I could, even before returning to the locker room to shower. Several of my teammates did the same. Even Drake set off, presumably looking for parents or friends, his face grim. The aisles were crowded with supportive students, parents looking for their favored offspring, college scouts, and aficionados of the competition. I ducked and dodged till I reached Kortilla, we two humble creatures of the barrio. I reached out towards her. She threw both arms around me.

"You stink," she told me. "But you showed those *richos* about haulin'. It's not even your event, *hermana*, and you took them. The lady next to me was asking everyone what family you were from. I told her you were from the *Corazones* of Bronx City."

I smiled weakly. "Was she impressed with my pedigree?"

"She didn't say. She left soon after. Didn't see her again. Kept muttering something about xs drugs, or some other stim."

I shook my head, unsure how much Kortilla was exaggerating, if at all.

She grabbed the back of my neck and pulled me closer. "I'm proud of you. We all are. Your mom would be too. Keep up the fight."

In reply, I slumped before her, my true friend, letting the toll of the day show. I was exhausted, and I let it show on my face. Kortilla saw into me, her eyes heavy, waiting for me to speak. I raised both my hands, rubbing the inside corners of my eyes as I contemplated what to say here, and what to save for later. When I brought my hands down, Alissa and Nythan were standing beside Kortilla.

"*That* was some fine running," Alissa proclaimed.

I had forgotten about her—and forgotten about my promise to stay over.

Kortilla arched a skeptical brow at what must have seemed a picture of Manhattan urban beauty, this girl who had pushed in beside us without a word of apology. Alissa wore a form-fitting navy-and-silver slip that shimmered when she moved. Golden stars twinkled in her midnight hair. The platinum cord around her neck was probably worth more than the Gonzales family earned in a year. On the other hand, Nythan

looked like he could've come from BC, with fabricated navy
slacks and a faded shirt with the words "Make It So" emblazoned across the front. But Kortilla's attention was fixed on
Alissa.

My face morphed into its usual mask. "Thanks," I managed. "Alissa and Nythan, this is my oldest friend—my sister
really—Kortilla Gonzales."

"No hyphen necessary," Kortilla quipped, her lips tight.

Alissa flashed a wide smile, the one Tuck students generated
for school visitors, and gave a small head bow. Kortilla was
unimpressed with either gesture, but she played along. In con-
trast to Alissa's manufactured pleasantries, I had no doubt
about Nythan's genuine delight at meeting Kortilla. He practically knocked Alissa over reaching across her body to introduce
himself. I believe he considered kissing her hand, but lost his
nerve at the last minute. Bad call. Kortilla would've liked it.

"So you're the person who's gotten Daniela this far? And
you came all the way into Manhattan to watch her run?" Alissa
asked. I knew she meant well, but she didn't know Kortilla.

"Blood takes care of blood where we come from," Kortilla
said, her words a hard whisper.

"Maids take care of spilled milk where we come from,"
Nythan interjected into the tension. "And we all loved watching Daniela wipe the track with the rest of them today."

"Hell, yes," Alissa enthused. "Drake was probably pumped
full of XS, and you *still* whipped him."

She said it too loud. Remembering that I had seen Drake in
the stands earlier, I twisted my head about, searching, expecting the worst. His height made him easy to locate. He stood
several rows above us, surrounded by a clutch of adults and
students, none of whom I recognized. I thought for a moment
that he was far enough away not to have heard, even with the
acute senses of the highborn. But he turned as my gaze be-

gan to leave him. Those deep tunneled eyes lingered on me for just a moment, then moved to Alissa. Hate rose off Drake like smoke from a chimney.

Kortilla followed my gaze. She didn't know Drake, not by sight anyway, but she knew danger the same as I did, the way no Manhattan kid could. On the streets of BC, we answered to no honor council. Kortilla saw the hate; the eyes of a person pushed, and ready to strike.

"It's been a pleasure, Alissa and Nythan," Kortilla said. "But Daniela and I should be crawling back to where we belong. Smelling like she does, she'll fit right in again."

Alissa made an awkward sound, looking at me expectantly. *Deuces.*

I wanted to go with Kortilla. I wanted to blow Alissa off. Kortilla had come so far, at such cost. Nythan and Alissa didn't understand how much it meant to me. And I wanted to go home. Nythan shot bullets at me from both eyes, guessing my thoughts. I cursed myself for not mentioning my evening plans to Kortilla.

"*Lo siento mucho.*" I knew Alissa and Nythan understood the apology too, but I wanted it to be more personal. "I need to stay."

The surprise in Kortilla's eyes was like a slap; the hurt that followed, however quickly she hid it, was like a knife sliding into my gut.

Kortilla shrugged. "I need to get going then. Stores to rob before dark."

I snatched her hand before she turned, slinging an arm over her shoulder, as much to keep her from getting away as to hold her close.

"I need you, *hermana*," I whispered into her ear.

"Do you?" Kortilla huffed. "What color is your blood?"

"I need a gang here too," I tried to explain. "I need someone. Even if they aren't you."

Kortilla gave me a curt nod. "I need to go."

I let her.

TWENTY-ONE

I wanted a shower, a bed, and to be left alone. I got Alissa, Nythan, and Lara instead.

We gathered at Alissa's place after I had cleaned up from the meet. My unwillingness to expend precious dollars in overpriced Manhattan establishments may have played a part in the choice of location, but I think the absence of Alissa's parents was the real determinant. Although we weren't exactly alone. Alissa's housekeeper, Irena, was there.

Alissa's childhood nanny and servant wasn't quite Alissa's height, but she made up for it in width. By the look of her, she could've eaten the lot of us and had room for dessert. Irena had rounded features, a head of dirty gray hair and sausage-like fingers that looked well used. She spoke with a slight Polish accent. Whenever Alissa spoke to her, Irena displayed the barest hint of a smile at the corner of her lips.

Alissa's family had a sprawling sofa in their living room that hugged two intersecting walls. It was upholstered in a luxurious hazel fabric that felt like nothing I had sat on before—fur, silk, and leather wrapped in one beautiful mess. It melted around my body. We all could've slept comfortably there. I tried, but the racket of the others foiled my efforts.

My companions were playing v-Smack on their visers, swinging their arms at a non-existent ball, shouting at action that was invisible to me. No way was my body going to let me participate in *virtual* sports.

Irena brought us tea in an earthy ceramic pot and four white minimalist cups devoid of handles. She poured the chestnut-colored liquid with a practiced hand. Silky steam rose from my cup.

"Uh-oh, Alissa. Who grew these tea leaves?" Nythan mocked, switching off his viser with a flick of his finger.

"Why, Nythan, I'm glad you asked," Alissa replied. "These leaves were grown in Korea. As you know, they don't allow migrants, or child labor, much less chipped slaves, so it's safe for even Daniela to drink. It was given to my mom as a gift—therefore, you will not be receiving an invoice when you leave today. We Manhattanites call this hospitality."

"You joke and mock," I said to them. "It's easy to make light of things when you're looking down from the top. When you are closer to being a slave, you might appreciate their plight a bit more." I might have sounded more convincing if I hadn't been ensconced on Alissa's comfy sofa.

"There aren't any slaves in this country," Alissa said, almost flippant.

Lara's face transformed from its usual glumness into a mask dominated by tight lines of anger. "And you know about slavery, Alissa?"

Lara's icy tone took Alissa by surprise. She gaped at her friend.

Nythan interjected, his voice quiet, but no less thoughtful for it. "You mean there will never be slaves in this country *again*, right, Alissa? You need to pay attention in History."

"Oh, come on, Nythan. I'm no Orderist, but even the most hardcore of them, like Landrew Foster-Rose-Hart, who openly advocate using force to deal with the ten percent problem, wouldn't go that far. No chipping allowed here. Land of the free, right?" Alissa said, a wary eye on Lara whose jaw still pulsed with tension. I didn't know what to make of it.

The conversation forced me out of the plush sinkhole of cushions. I'd heard Mateo talk about some of these things. But it was different hearing it from this group. These people were from the part of society that made the decisions. There was one term I had not heard before.

"Sorry, what is the 'ten percent problem?'"

Nythan smiled the way a teacher does when a student asks a question that he wants to answer.

"It's the same problem Huxley dealt with so eloquently in his book: the hard truth is that the world does not *need* the number of people it has. At least, not if you're an economic rationalist like our leader. The economies of the world need brilliant people—super alphas, people with high ATs to design things and discover new ideas, and it needs some regular alphas to run things, a few betas to carry out orders, perhaps some deltas for…well…" he lowered his voice so Irena wouldn't hear, "…to help with mundane tasks. Like raising spoiled little girls." He jerked his head at Alissa. She hit him with a pillow.

"So in your world, only ten percent of the population is needed?" I asked.

Nythan shrugged. "Not my world. We're talking economics here. But the world as seen by men like Landrew Fart, yes. We're not there yet, but it's coming. So, the question becomes: What do we about it? Do you think they should put the rest under the iceberg, so to speak? I'm guessing not."

"Is that all the people who don't measure high enough on some stupid AT scale are? A problem to be solved? Should we just chip everyone who fails a test, so they can be 'productive,' like the slave countries? Just economics, nothing personal?" I hadn't intended it to come out so intense, but there it was.

He lifted his arms as if fending off an attack. "Whoa there. I'm not saying I'm for anything. I might be off the AT scale of genius, yes, but I don't have the answer. No one does. It isn't a question with a solution."

"Huh?"

Again with the teacher's smile. "It's a question of philosophy. What do you value? Which is why you see so many different countries trying different solutions. In the past we had communism, or socialism, which essentially tried to redistribute the value created by the super alphas among everyone—each person got a job and a piece of the output, even if they just stood around. That didn't work, of course. People are too greedy, particularly those who ended up running the system. Some of the northern European countries are still trying it in different forms—socialism, direct subsistence payments to their people, localism. We've got chipped slaves in parts of Central and South America, and a subtle version of slavery in the so-called "Harmonious Societies" of the east, where the government merely watches every aspect of your life, rather than using direct control. Until you step out of line. Korea is ruled by a corporate council, while other places have no government at all. Canada tried to value their people rather than money—until Alberta split off and winter came. None of it seems to work particularly well if you happen to be in the bottom ninety percent. So pick your poison."

"What about California? People are free, they have Silicon Valley."

"Ah yes, the California dream. While the Orderist propaganda about chaos in the streets of San Francisco is exaggerated, it's becoming increasingly true. Cali has a democracy problem—the people vote for whoever promises more and screams against the rich the loudest. Even their once mighty thought giants are failing. The embargo isn't helping, of course. It's not like Asia is particularly anxious to see them succeed either. I doubt they'll last. We'll have unification eventually, even if Landrew Fart and his faction don't force the President to invade. One year or ten, but not much more."

My blood began to heat. "So this is the best there is? Correction for the masses, tea for the high ATs. Their so-called prosperity through order. I should be satisfied with that? Be glad I'm not chipped? People won't stand for it." I sounded like Mateo.

Nythan shrugged. "Scary, I know. I'm not excusing the Orderists, but there is a certain elegance to some of their theories: By tying voting rights to tax revenue they solved several problems at once. First, the government is controlled by those that contribute the greatest amount to economic output, so policy should be conducive to economic expansion—such as establishing the Vision Quad so our own thought giants can thrive. Next, they pretty much ended all material tax evasion, and saved a bundle in the process. Corporations line up to pay, because they want the votes. Individual rights—"

"Crap," Alissa declared. "This country is riddled with corruption. They created a thriving patronage network. My parents see it every day at work. The government controls people through the corporations that own the echo stations on the net. No chips, but the net is another form of the same garbage."

"The Orderist theory is better than the reality," Nythan admitted.

"What happens to Bronx City, and everywhere else that isn't Manhattan, Buckhead, Wilmet, Palm Beach...what happens to those of us that aren't highborn or AT stars?"

Silence reigned in the room, unease on the faces of my wealthy companions. Even Lara's eyes were downcast. The gravity among these people surprised me. I thought we were just talking, or at least Nythan was talking. I sat among the winners in Nythan's theory—the elite above the water on Huxley's iceberg. No one wanted to meet my eyes. I realized they weren't worried about themselves. It was something else. Something worse.

Irena stepped in the room, shattering the prophetic atmosphere, if that's what it had been.

"It's past five, Ms. Alissa," she said. "I need to be getting home if you don't need anything else?"

There was no resentment in the housekeeper's voice even though she was speaking to a sixteen-year-old. If anything, those eyes looked worried—the way a parent or grandmother was supposed to feel when leaving their offspring.

"We're fine, Irena, thank you for coming in on a weekend," Alissa told her, sounding gracious, but not like any sixteen-year-old I knew. "Please take anything from the fridge you'd like."

I clenched my teeth as Irena gathered up the empty teapot and cups, carrying them away without another word. No one else paid attention to her, or the exchange with Alissa. All eyes were focused on visers.

Lara left soon after Irena. She had a dinner to go to, at Blah-Blah-Rich's house, or something like that. Sounded fabulous to me. My shoulders unclenched as Alissa walked her out the door. Whatever had provoked Lara's earlier flash of anger had faded.

"Think your friend Kortilla would come to a Manhattan party, if we could solve the travel pass issue?" Nythan asked me when we were alone.

"She's not a U-date, or whatever those Manhattan 'intro-duction' services call it," I replied, an edge in my voice.

Nythan gave me a smirk. "I haven't seen that look before. Even when you're furious."

"That's my really dangerous face."

"Why? Does Kortilla need protecting?"

I rolled the question around in my head. "She gave me a family when I had none. Not something most kids would do, or even understand to do. And she never stopped sharing." I dared to allow myself a memory of that curly-haired girl, her arm around my shoulder as I cried, an eternity ago. I pushed it away before it grabbed hold of me. "She doesn't need protec-tion. But she has it just the same."

The three of us had just settled back on the sofa when Alissa got a ping. She walked to the door, returning a short time later with a pizza box. The most amazing, delicious aroma sur-rounded her. My mouth was like a river.

"You could say 'no' to eating this, Daniela," Alissa said to me. "But you'd regret it. Call it a victory prize from your ador-ing fans. Besides, you'll need fuel for the study session we're starting after dinner, when Nythan finally leaves."

I caved. It was worth it.

After my third slice, I knew the elite of Manhattan would never accept wealth redistribution in any form. No way they would switch to fabricated pizza after eating the real thing.

TWENTY-TWO

Alissa owned three digiBooks, each capable of multiple screen displays. She could also take notes on her viser's virtual keyboard while simultaneously reading and speaking. She remembered every word she looked at. I suspected she had an eidetic memory, or something close to it. She had also covered way more material for the Lit exam than I had.

"What do you mean, you haven't read it?" Alissa asked as if I had told her I never showered.

"It's not on Lynder's reading list. Why should I read things he isn't going to test us on?"

She rolled her eyes. "He *probably* won't ask a direct question on a book not on the list, but you can be sure he'll be asking questions where *you* can mention the author's other works. It's not just about the answers. You've got to show off a little to stand out at Tuck. Vonnegut wrote thirteen novels that weren't *Slaughterhouse-Five*."

"I don't have time to read thirteen novels that I might be able to mention, but aren't really on the test, Alissa. I need to read the words, not just glance at them like you."

"You've got to be strategic," she said, flipping through one of her screens.

I looked down as my viser vibrated with an incoming ping. I blinked several times at the message. My heart raced as I considered the implication of what I saw. None of my thoughts were good. A cold hand gripped my heart.

"What's wrong?" Alissa asked, her fingers still.

"It's from Kortilla—I think," I said, still trying to puzzle out what was going on. "And I think something bad has happened." *Please let me be wrong.*

"What do you mean, you think?"

"The message is in Barriola. It's been sent from the viser of Pele Ostevez."

"None of those things mean anything to me. Why do you think it's from Kortilla if it's from someone else?"

"It says 'your cat caught a bad thorn.' I sometimes call my brother my cat because he comes to our room to piss and do his business, but is out hunting trouble the rest of the time. Pele is a punk kid, works the door in Kortilla's building. He's got a thing for her."

Alissa shook her head. "I still don't get it. If your brother is hurt, why wouldn't Kortilla red ping you herself?"

I chewed my bottom lip as I stared at Alissa. She had bailed me out of trouble once already. I couldn't think of anything I had that she wanted, yet she stood with me. Against that, she hadn't told me everything about Marie-Ann. But I needed help.

"My brother—he's political, you might say. If his troubles involved the Authority, Kortilla would be cautious. She never uses Barriola. She calls it toilet talk. But the Authority has trouble with it. No standard spellings or grammar and it changes all the time, so their computers can't track it. They might be monitoring my viser, hers as well. Her brothers run in the same circle as Mateo."

Alissa didn't hesitate. She stripped off her viser and handed it to me. "No way anyone associates me with your brother. Ping this Pele."

I did, before Alissa came to her senses. My fingers shook as I input Pele's information. I set the ping for audio only.

"Ms. Gatto?" asked Pele's voice.

"*Jes*, Pele."

Kortilla's voice came on. "Cat's hurt. My big bro' got a message. Your pet's on wheels, on the money island." I wondered what the hell he was doing in Manhattan, then remembered the netcasts about the raids the Authority had been conducting for so-called terrorists. If he was mixed up in that, it would explain why I hadn't heard back from him.

"How bad?" I tried to keep my voice steady. I wasn't breathing.

"*Hermana*, cat needs a vet bad. I'm sorry. But if he goes to one on money island...You know..."

I did know. If he turned up at a hospital, any hospital, they would be legally bound to report any suspicious injury to the Authority. In BC, I could've managed to find someone. But in Manhattan, I didn't know anyone. It was too risky trying to cross one of the bridges—inspection points and sensors were everywhere.

"I can help," Alissa told me.

I gaped. "How?"

"Tell them to get him to the southeast corner of Eighty-Seventh Street and Lexington."

"How soon?" I didn't understand how she was going to get a doctor, but I didn't have any other choice, and she seemed certain.

"Stay here," Alissa said. "I'll be right back."

"Nothing about this over the open net," I urged her. "The Authority could be listening."

"Don't worry. I'll use the Tuck network—it's encrypted. And they wouldn't dare spy on it anyway." Alissa ran out of the room, towards the back of the apartment. Maybe to her room. Maybe to the office with its terminals. As a Tuck student, she'd have direct access to the Castle private network at home—a system isolated from the rest of the net by design. But that was only good to contact students. Or teachers.

"I'm working on it," I told Kortilla. "Can you get a message to bring kitty to Eighty-Seventh and Lexington, southeast corner?"

There was a pause, an uncomfortable one. "I'll get them the message," Kortilla told me finally.

Alissa ran back into the room, quicker than I would've dared hope. "Get them there. We'll have a doctor ready. Have the vehicle with your brother stop at the corner and flash its headlights three times."

I relayed the signal information to Kortilla. "Thank you, *hermana*. There are no words."

The connection ended.

"Alissa, what doctor did you get? This sounds serious. If the Authority finds out—"

"Havelock is arranging it."

"Why would he do that?"

Alissa grimaced, her eyes glazed. That agile mind that could handle three simultaneous tasks was making a judgment about how much to tell me. "He takes care of us. People like you, and me."

"You mean students that aren't highborn?"

"Something like that. You can trust him with this. He knows what he's doing. He'll get someone to help your brother."

"Why would he take this kind of risk for a student? Not even a student—my brother. Pulling some strings to get me out of an Authority van, I get that. But this is facilitating illegal medical care—he could lose his job, end up in detention, or worse."

Alissa shook her head. "It's his story to tell, not mine. Ask him when you can." I went to protest, but she held up her hand to let me know it would be futile. "I'll get you a coat to wear over your clothes. You look too BC. Something dark. One of my mom's should work. Bring it back, though."

Alissa fetched me an elegant black pea coat that hung past my knees. Jade buttons adorned its front, genuine silk lined its interior. I would've been paranoid about ruining it on any other night. But tonight there was only Mateo.

She walked me to the door. There was no way I would've let her come along, and she didn't try. This was my fight. She had already done too much. I hugged Alissa as I left. Whatever the cost for this, I'd find a way to pay.

I tried not to run the three blocks to the meeting point. There wasn't any reason to rush. I doubted the car would be there yet. Certainly, Havelock and the doctor wouldn't be so quick. But I found my legs moving faster than they should have been. Sweat clung to my skin. The coat Alissa had given me was too warm for the early fall air, but that wasn't the reason. I rubbed my fingers against my palms, trying to banish the numbness.

Finely dressed couples wandered the streets and filled the restaurants and pleasure parlors, their concerns a world away from mine. They strolled while I rushed. Every time a group blocked my path on the sidewalk I gritted my teeth, struggling to maintain my outward appearance of belonging. I forced myself not to look up at the surveillance drones buzzing overhead. I arrived at the designated corner and stood next to a towering woman in a silky black dress and impossibly high heels. She crossed the street when the light changed. I stayed, focused on the traffic around me.

A steady stream of vehicles passed, going west to east and north to south, but not so many as to clog the streets. Their low humming motors sounded like bees' song, rather than the chaotic rumble of gasoline engines I was used to in Bronx City. U-cabs continuously picked up and deposited passengers on both sides of the street. Pedestrians flowed to and from the subway station one block south on Eighty-Sixth Street. I hid in that constant stream of people and machines. My feet shuffled of their own volition. I glanced at my viser every twenty seconds. I stared down the headlights of every vehicle that slowed near my corner.

A dark U-cab approached the intersection, the soft puff of its engine dissipating as it slowed. It was one of the Austin FX3 replicas—the twentieth-century London taxis that had become popular rent-a-rides over the past few years in Manhattan. The windows were tinted, but the "L" on the curb side window was illuminated, indicating it was awaiting a fare. I cursed under my breath. If it was picking up, the vehicle might stay here for five minutes or more, waiting for the passenger who had summoned it with their viser. I didn't need a clogged corner or additional witnesses arriving at a bad moment.

My heart jumped into my throat when the U-cab's headlights flashed at me. I blinked, not trusting myself. U-cabs don't have drivers. They are summoned, they pick up, they drop off. The passenger controls did not include the ability to switch the vehicle's headlights on and off. It flashed a second time. Then a third. I moved to the curb. The door opened as I got close, the way it would have had I summoned it. I held my breath as I slid inside. The door shut behind me.

I swallowed the gasp that tried to escape my lips the moment the darkened interior of the car became visible. My brother lay across the rear seat, bare-chested, an ugly mess of crimson expanding through the bandage pressed to the left side of his ribs. His eyes were shut, his face haggard. His friend Chris-Chris knelt on the floor beside him, holding the slap-dash dressing in place. Panic reigned in Chris-Chris's wide eyes; his hands shook. Chris-Chris had been at Mateo's side for as long as I could remember, an enforcer and trusted lieu-tenant. On the streets, he projected steady maturity. Right now, he looked like a kid, even if he was a few years older than me.

"Kortilla told me we were getting a doc, not M's little sis-ter," he near screamed. The car was soundproof, but I still didn't like the yelling. I felt the numbness in my hands spread-ing as I looked at Mateo and the frightened boy trying to nurse him.

I forced certainty that I didn't feel into my voice. "Doc's coming. We can't stay here without attracting attention. U-cabs don't sit around. What's the deal with this thing? How did you control the lights?" I looked around the interior. The vehicle had been modified. A portable terminal had been set up on the floor. A row of seats had been removed, creating a roomy interior space. One big enough to hold…well, almost anything.

"Cab's command node has been hacked," Chris-Chris in-formed me. "I can set any destination. It's reportin' whatever we want back to its central dispatch. Everyplace we go shows up as a requested ride from some dummy viser. Internal cam-eras are on a loop. We got fake passenger pictures and every-thing. Totally pro."

He sounded stupidly proud of the set-up. My heart sank. It was way more than Chris-Chris could have managed by him-self. Or even Mateo. *Oh, big brother, how deep in the deuce are you this time?*

"Take us somewhere, then. A place a normal richie customer would go. Then back here. Let's hope the doc is ready by then." The more I spoke, the steadier my voice became. I stopped shaking. My blood turned cold.

"Hold the bandage, and keep pressin'. I gotta check the terminal."

I put my hand on the bloody cloth, the sticky warmth of my brother's blood leaking onto my fingers. I placed my other hand on Mateo's forehead. His skin felt like a low-burning fire. I watched his chest straining to rise and fall. Chris-Chris tapped a virtual keyboard with his visered hand, looking at the screen as he worked.

"DESTINATION IS ELEVEN SIXTY-SEVEN MADISON AVENUE, M-PASTA CUCINA," said the too-sweet-to-be-real female voice of the U-cab. We sped into traffic.

I leaned in close to my brother. "I got you, Mateo. You'll be fine. Just like always. Just like always."

One of Mateo's eyes cracked open, just a fraction. I saw a sliver of white polluted with veins of blood. The lid closed. His mouth jerked. He started coughing, a foul sound. Mateo's body convulsed.

"Don't speak," I urged him, amazed at how calm I sounded. I stroked his hair, remembering the day he carried me home on his shoulders after I won my first track meet. I watched his breathing, matching my rhythm to his. "You can do it, *hermano*." I said it, but I felt his life slipping through my hands.

"DESTINATION IS ON YOUR LEFT," said the artificial U-cab lady. "PLEASE USE CAUTION WHEN EXITING THE VEHICLE. DOORS WILL OPEN AND CLOSE AUTOMATICALLY."

A U-cab opening and closing its doors without anyone getting in or out got a few glances, but nothing serious. The machines were far from perfect, and phantom rides were common enough.

"Take us back to the corner," I told Chris-Chris. "The doctor should be there."

I muttered a quick prayer that Alissa and Havelock would come through for me. I didn't address my pleas to anyone in particular. I just hoped someone was listening—and wasn't too pissed at me for never having spoken to them before.

As the U-cab made its way to the designated drop-off location along the most efficient possible route, a large twin rotor drone flashed past the window.

"That's not a regular surveyor," I said, trying not to sound alarmed.

Chris-Chris craned his neck to get a look at the imposing machine, its belly wide and circular like a plate, a pair of massive rotating engines perched above. It was twice the size of a standard Authority surveillance drone.

"Damn, I think it's a bluekent."

"A what?"

"It can see through walls and the carbon fiber of a U-cab." I heard the tremble in his voice.

"It can see us?"

"I think it can see heat: people or force weapons. Energy. I think."

Mateo groaned.

"Is it looking for us?" I asked.

"Maybe," Chris-Chris said. "Mateo got hit while we were running away. Maybe the blood…" He stared at the terminal as if it had the answer. "We're not carrying weapons, though."

The U-cab stopped at the corner of Eighty-Seventh and Lexington. I wasn't worried about people noticing us. U-cabs in Manhattan were like cockroaches in Bronx City. But the drones were another matter. They downloaded their data to a central node at regular intervals. The Authority had computers that collected information from every possible source, sifted it, analyzed it, found patterns. "Technology to maintain order," went the slogan.

The bluekent lingered over a building several blocks to the south while Chris-Chris blinked the U-cab's headlights. People on the street were watching the strange drone, alarmed. Not surprising, given the dire warnings on the net lately.

I counted my heartbeats as the vehicle idled. One. Two. Three. How many more times could we circle? Four. Five. Maybe Havelock couldn't find a doctor. Six. Maybe...

The door swung open. A waifish body ducked inside, her short-hair glittering a precious copper. Beneath her bangs were eyes like twin moons, glowing softly in the half-light of the cab's interior. She carried a small black handbag in her right hand. Her luminous eyes fixated on Mateo, barely sparing a glance for Chris-Chris or me.

"Take your hand away from that bloody rag, back away, and get this thing moving," she commanded. There was nothing slight about her voice. This woman expected people to listen to her.

She took something from her bag—a delicate combination of metal and glass that resembled twentieth-century reading spectacles. The lenses changed color as she flicked her fingers. Data splashed across her viser screen.

"A little more light in here."

"Are you the doctor?" I asked.

She didn't look at me. "No, I'm the Tooth Fairy. I heard you were smart, Daniela. Please do the smart thing: Be quiet, and let me save your brother's life."

I shut up and watched Tooth-Fairy-Doc do her stuff. Her hands matched the confidence of her voice, each movement steady and precise. Mateo's wound got a spray of something that smelled like a lurker alleyway, then more peering through the special glasses. I alternated between watching the gore and the windows. The bluekent had disappeared, for now.

"Take us on the highway, someplace without stops," Doc ordered.

She gave Mateo a shot of something clear. He became still, his breathing steady. The U-cab had entered the highway on-ramp when I saw the drone sailing in the sky again. It was headed east. Just like us.

"Chris-Chris, is that the same drone?" I asked, tapping the window.

He looked up. "Can't tell. Don't matter, anyhow. They link their data."

"You said they scan for heat, that they can detect weapons. What about medical equipment? Those glasses?"

Chris-Chris shrugged. "Dunno."

"Deuces," I commented as we pulled onto the highway. The drone was about seven hundred yards ahead of us, hovering over the traffic, its sensor array examining every vehicle passing beneath it.

"Doc, can you turn those glasses off?" I asked. "And anything else with an unusual power signature."

She held a translucent rod in one hand, its circumference no larger than a straw. Its tip was long and sharp like a needle. "I need to implant some nanites to stop the bleeding, internal and external. Both are critical right now. He's lost a lot of blood. The procedure is quick, but it does use power, several quick surges as the nanites power up, and I need the glasses too."

"Can it wait?"

"If you wanted me to wait, you should've told me before I prepped the machines in my syringe. The implant needs to be deposited inside a human host within five minutes of exposure to air or the nanites go bad. I don't have another group with me. These things aren't cheap or easy to come by. His best chance to live is if I do it now."

A shiver ran up my spine.

"We've got another choice," Chris-Chris said. "They gave us something—a J-Pulse they called it. Something like that. It confuses the Authority drones, supposedly sends them into hibernation mode. It's like a system error. They can fly but they're effectively blind. We could try it on that thing up there."

"Who's 'they?'" I asked.

"Do you want me to hit it or not?" Chris-Chris flicked his fingers, priming the device or whatever it was. "Or you going to let Mateo bleed to death?"

I glanced at my brother. He was ghost pale. I reached over and placed a hand on his forehead again. That boyish face from days long ago flashed in my head. He had worn an imp-ish grin back then, so full of spark, energy. Some of that was still inside him. Mateo was strong then, and now.

"We can wait four minutes and fifty-eight seconds, doc," I told her. "Jamming that machine is going to send the Author-ity into a frenzy. Chris-Chris, whatever you were about to do, power it down."

"You goin' to play dice with Mateo's life? Girl, you—"

There was enough anger in me to birth an inferno. Some of it must've shown on my face, because Chris-Chris cut his ill-considered rebuke short. He looked out the window instead.

Doc put on an unhappy frown but said nothing. Instead, she held her viser screen out to where I could see it. It displayed various data—medical information about Mateo, I presumed. But in the middle was a countdown. Just over three minutes were left. Tick, tick, tick. So went the life of the nanites, and my brother.

Our U-cab sped towards the drone, pacing itself with the vehicles around us. Steady, efficient, normal. Nothing to see here. The Authority's machine hovered low, no more than ten feet above the traffic. The drone disappeared from my view as we passed directly beneath its sensors. I imagined the information being collected above me, an unfathomable collection of binary data to be analyzed by the networked machines that served the Authority. What did it see inside our U-cab? Just a rent-a-ride, like thousands of others? Or did it know more?

I held my breath until the bluekent reappeared outside the rear window. It hadn't moved; its engines kept it unnaturally steady as it continued to search for the supposed enemies of order. People like my brother. The distance between our U-cab and the drone grew ever longer, the machine's outline shrinking behind us gradually. Doc still held out her arm, her viser still counted down. A little under two minutes remained before the nanites expired.

"Any idea of the range of that thing's sensors?" I asked Chris-Chris.

"No idea, state secret, all that Authority slag."

I looked at Doc's countdown, then at Mateo. "Steady as she goes, Doc. Let's take no chances."

Doc ground her teeth. "You've got guts. Or you don't give a damn. And I wouldn't be here if it was the second one, would I?"

I kept my eye on the timer, the speedometer and the drone. One minute and thirty seconds left.

"Go do your thing, Doc. Save him," My voice didn't betray the relief I felt at letting the words out.

She already had the glasses on. They powered up immediately. Hands, poised and confident, went to work. Glass and metal went into my brother's chest. Mateo didn't even twitch. Fingers flicked, the rod got a small twist. More flicking. The instrument came out coated in my brother's blood. But Doc's face was less unhappy.

She stared at her viser, the light of the screen illuminating her eyes in the twilight of the car's interior. Reams of data scrolled in the reflection. More flicking. She worked for several minutes. Finally, the corners of Doc's mouth relaxed.

"It's done," she announced. "It's working."

My heart beat again. "Thank you."

"Why four minutes and fifty-*eight* seconds?" she asked me.

"I like to keep some margin for error."

TWENTY-THREE

"Where to now, *locas*?" Chris-Chris asked.

Doc told him an address: Arden Street. Upper Manhattan.

"That up in the Vision Quad. What the hell you wanna' go there for?" Chris-Chris asked. "Just a bunch of fancy techie campuses around there, bunches of AT busters wishing they wus' in Cali."

Doc flashed him an annoyed grimace. "This is on the edge of the research parks, where they are still developing land. It's a safe place. And drone flights are heavily restricted in that area. The thought giant corps don't trust anyone snooping—not even the Authority."

"Why can't I just take him home?" I asked.

"The nanites are repairing the cellular damage of the force gun blast, but he's not safe yet. It'd be a shame to have gone through all this trouble and have him die from an infection, don't you think?"

"How do you know about this place we're going to? How do you know it's safe?"

"Because I'm a doctor." Her voice told me to drop it.

"I can ping a few of the boys for protection. You know, just in case," Chris-Chris offered.

Doc turned on him. "If you reveal our location, if you contact anyone, if you don't do exactly what I tell you, I'm gone. That goes for both of you. And your boy can go live or die on his own. Clear?"

The U-cab fell silent. Doc took that for acquiescence. She busied herself with the data on her viser. She had a smooth face, no wrinkles. Her eyes were hard, but not worn. The doctor was younger than I had thought initially. Her demeanor masked her youth. I guessed she was in her early twenties, maybe.

We drove northwest, past the tip of Central Park, away from the luxury high rises and stately townhomes of the Manhattan elite. Traffic was lighter up here, the night deeper. The grid pattern of Manhattan broke down as the look and feel of the city transformed. Gone was the block-by-block menagerie of distinct stores, parlors, restaurants, and homes that I associated with Manhattan. Instead, immense edifices, each consuming a square block or more, arose from the newly paved streets as unexpected as a waterfall in the desert. The constructions dazzled in their defiance of architectural norms. We passed twin intersecting arches standing next to a geodesic dome, then a soaring obelisk rising among a sea of greenhouses. But each of those constructions were dwarfed by the soaring glass ziggurat that emerged amid a field of seemingly wild greenery, its base consuming three square city blocks. Bright, multi-colored lights shone upon each of the buildings like proud parents. Some structures bore the names of companies or products I recognized, others meant nothing to me. None were illuminated brighter than the rose helix of Rose-Hart Industries.

"Ay, why build such stupid-looking places? Why can't the richies work in buildings like everyone else?" Chris-Chris muttered as the U-cab wove its way through the increasingly empty streets.

"Almost everything here has been newly built in the last fifteen years or so. This area used to be government housing, a lot of it anyway. Lots of poor folks, lots of working people," I said, remembering Mateo's stories. "After Cali split off, the government razed it to create a new home for the great innovators the country supposedly needs: the so-called thought giants."

"A lot of the corps came from California rather than face the embargo. Even more were started by Silicon Valley refugees with stolen tech, anxious to get rich off someone else's work. The rest of the US doesn't recognize Cali's patent protections," Doc added.

I stared at it all. The net images couldn't capture the true presence of these constructions. Their scale, their ability to make fantasy real. At least on the outside. A new Rome. I heard Nythan's voice echo in my head: Here is the tip of the iceberg. What are the rest of you planning to do?

We made quick time through the streets. We passed the occasional surface patrol vehicle, but that was it. There weren't many people around either. The AT elite who populated these monstrosities mostly lived elsewhere in Manhattan—Soho, Downtown, Chelsea. Doc was right about the drones. The skies were clear.

"Can you take this car off the grid? Show that we stopped somewhere else?" she asked Chris-Chris.

"I'll try. Should be able to show a stop. Then some kind of transmission error, going out of service. Fine so long as there are no drones around to cross-check the data."

The U-cab turned a corner onto a street that was darker than the others. There were no architectural monuments near this road, just lots filled with hills of rubble where older, less amazing, buildings had once stood. Cranes, excavators, fabricators, and other equipment sat parked on several of the lots. We crossed an intersection. More rubble and half-constructed structures. A bore machine, larger than my apartment building in Bronx City, was parked just off the side of the road. I stared at its massive corkscrew-like drill, my mouth involuntarily open.

"What do they build with those?" I asked. "Another subway?"

Doc shook her head, a gesture mostly lost in the dark interior of the vehicle. "Magnetic Transportation System. The MTS will link many of the campuses together, along with some of the production facilities further north—so the tech babes don't have to mix with the rabble on the subway. This system will replace the subway eventually. No more direct train links with the rest of the Five Cities. The new system is more secure, and it can move material. Built under government contract by RocketDyn, a key voting supporter of the Orderists, of course. The new extension will link up with the new dormitories they are building out here, as well as some new housing developments up north."

"Of course, they don't want the subway links between BC and Manhattan," I said mostly to myself.

We passed more excavation, great mounds of dirt, concrete and steel accompanied by even greater-sized machinery, including two more bore machines of different configurations.

"They could rebuild Bronx City for what this must be costing," I observed.

"Not a good investment," Doc replied.

We finally slowed at the end of a dark, dead-end street. The U-cab's headlights provided the only external illumination. The burning light of the high beams revealed a collection of squat brick facade towers, perhaps ten stories in height. They were encased in some sort of blue-tinted plastika film, like the kind used to seal up partially eaten food scraps. Portions of one of the structures had collapsed. The windows were either open holes or had been boarded up with fabricated wood.

"Stop here," Doc told Chris-Chris.

She climbed into the front row of seats, fiddling with the wheel and the manual controls.

"What is this place?" I asked.

"Used to be rent controlled housing. Way back. When the city went to tear it down, they found it was loaded with asbestos."

"Ab...what?"

"Ancient stuff they used to insulate buildings with. Except it kills you if you inhale it. The corps nearby freaked when they found out, demanded a proper clean-up. The thing is, there's hardly anyone left alive who knows how to handle the stuff, much less dispose of it. They sealed the buildings up in plastika till they figure it all out. RocketDyn still dug their transit tunnels, right up to where these buildings are. The bore machines are rather expensive to rent, and they don't want to have to come back and dig later."

"And that's where you want to take us? Into a building made of stuff that kills us."

Doc waved my concerns away. "Relax. Don't touch the walls or ceilings, or anything that looks like cotton candy. Don't bother the asbestos, it won't bother you. Besides, the place we're going to has been swept clean."

I didn't relax, but I stopped protesting.

"Switch it to manual," she ordered Chris-Chris.

"Really?" Chris-Chris wondered. "I thought you richies didn't bother learning to drive anymore."

"Just do it."

Chris-Chris flicked a few commands. The U-cab jerked forward awkwardly. I grabbed Mateo just before he rolled off the seat onto the floor.

"Be careful!" I scolded.

Doc got the hang of it after that. We glided forward, then off the street, onto uneven, rocky ground. The U-cab bumped up and down. So did Mateo. I held him tight. He stirred, but only a bit. The fresh dressing Doc had put on looked clean.

Doc drove us to the back of one of the wrapped buildings, then down a ramp into what I supposed was an underground parking garage of some kind. Pitch-dark surrounded the area except for the area illuminated by the U-cab's headlights. A mixture of ruined concrete, food wrapping, and unidentifiable detritus littered the slice of ground that was visible. Beyond the rubble was a battered, dented but otherwise intact metal door.

"Okay, we are on foot from here," Doc told us. "Since I'm the only one who knows the way, you two should carry the patient. Carefully please. Once he's settled, Chris-Chris, you are going to go take this car someplace very far from here. Can you handle that?"

We both nodded.

"Let's finish saving your brother."

TWENTY-FOUR

The building's elevators hadn't functioned in half a century, so Chris-Chris and I carried Mateo upstairs to Doc's second floor hideaway. Our visers provided enough light to reveal portions of the building's apocalyptic interior. The concrete walls had turned partially to dust and the ceilings dropped downward at random intervals, occasionally bending so low that I had to duck to pass through. Sections of the stairs had collapsed, with fabricated traction boards put in to act as ramps. The rats, cockroaches and other creatures made little attempt to conceal their presence. It made Kortilla's squatter-clogged stairway seem downright cozy.

Entering the safe house was like waking from a nightmare. Behind boarded-up windows and a false front door was a tidy two-bedroom apartment. It was furnished with expensive-looking machinery: terminals, a portable generator, what looked like an elaborate fabricator, and two other refrigerator-sized machines I couldn't identify. Another device that looked like a telescope was pressed up against a slit of one of the boarded windows. There were beds in each of the other rooms, a kitchen table, four badly fabricated chairs, and a couple of dim desk lights to keep the darkness at bay. We laid Mateo on one of the beds. Doc took his vitals, examined the wound, and changed his dressing.

"Let him rest," she said, leading us out of the room to the kitchen table and its rickety chairs.

She told Chris-Chris to get rid of the car, carefully, and not to come back. To forget he'd ever been here. "Go back to Bronx City, stay low."

"You think I'm just goin' ta' leave Mateo here, with some bleached-skinned richie?"

Doc stared at him as she might an ignorant, pestering child. "If you come stumbling back here and get seen by the corp security, what do you think will happen to him?"

"You think you know more about lurkin' and snoopin' than me, lady?"

I placed a hand on his shoulder. "I'm not leaving Mateo until he's better," I assured Chris-Chris. "We need to get rid of that car, or someone is going to come looking. Only you know the deal with that thing, and what you and Mateo have been up to. So unless you want to take us into your confidence, you've got to get rid of it. I'll red ping you when Mateo is out of here."

"On your blood, princess?"

"On the heart."

He took another lingering look at Doc, then nodded.

After Chris-Chris left, she asked me, "Can he really drive?"

"I think so. Mateo said they drove a bunch of vehicles into Manhattan a few weeks ago, so he's had some kind of practice."

Doc stepped over to one of the terminals, waving her viser till the devices linked up with each other. A picture of the U-cab driving away appeared after a few moments. Another car, a two-seater, followed a short time later. It didn't have any head-lights on.

"Is someone following him?"

"To make sure he doesn't screw up," Doc told me after a moment. I didn't like the sound of that.

"You've got surveillance around here," I observed.

"Sort of. It's ancient optical stuff. The corporate counter-measures don't bother screening for primitive devices."

"Why? What are you doing here?"

She pursed her lips. "Headmaster Havelock must trust you to risk sending me out like this, and letting me bring you here, but that's need to know only. And for now, you don't need to know."

I studied her face. The apartment was better lit than the U-cab. I'd been right about her age. She was young. Barely old enough to be done with her medical residency. Tough, confident, but not necessarily experienced. Then there was the matter of her words. They told me something as well.

"You said 'Headmaster Havelock'…you were a Tuck student, weren't you?"

She thought about denying it, then shrugged. "The good old days."

"And Havelock helped you, in some way? He does that for people like you, me, Alissa…"

"Need to know," Doc told me.

"How many people like you and Alissa are there?" I already knew she wouldn't answer. I chewed my lip as I considered the question I had been asking myself since Havelock's man had shown up at my track meet at PS 62: What did he want from me?

"Done asking questions I'm not going to answer?" Doc asked.

"For now," I said. "How's Mateo?"

She stared at her viser. "Okay," she pronounced. But her reply took too long. "Force weapons are nasty. But those Lenox nanites are the best available. If he's strong, he'll make it."

Lenox nanites. That meant she worked near Tuck, at the Lenox Life Center. That was why she was able to get to the corner so quickly. I bit harder on my lip. "What if he isn't strong?"

Doc put a hand under her chin. It made her look very doctorly. I wondered if they taught that in medical school. "What do you mean?"

"You know the Waste? Have you heard of it in Manhattan?"

"I've heard of it," Doc said, each word slow, wary.

"He's got it. I can see it around the edges of his eyes. His skin. I've seen it coming for years." I cursed the emotion in my voice. "It kills everyone who gets it. No one with the Waste makes it much past twenty. No one knows what it is. The doctors in Bronx City are useless. Just pill pushers. They always blame something else. Drugs, or Resister-H...but never the Waste."

She kept the hand under her chin, but looked less doctorly now, less certain. "I'll take some samples. I don't have the equipment I need here. But I can run some tests at work. Then I can tell you more. Perhaps."

"Can you cure it? Those richie medical places, they can cure anything, can't they?"

Doc looked uncomfortable. No more hand on her chin. She was standing. She wanted to get away.

"Let me get those samples, then I need to go. I'll come back tomorrow if I can. If not me, then someone else. There's some packaged food in the kitchen, and a jug of clean water. Don't use the fabricator unless you have to. Keep energy use low. The corps spend most of their time spying on each other, but we don't want to attract attention."

"How do I get in touch if I need you?"

Doc looked me up and down. "Your friend Nythan. Tell him you need a handshake from Doctor Willis. He'll know how to get in touch with me."

"Nythan?"

"I do some lab work with him. Bright kid, that one."

"So they are all a part of this," I said, mostly to myself. Dr. Willis had gone into Mateo's room to get whatever blood and tissue she needed from him.

We are all part of Headmaster Havelock's scheme. Whatever it is.

It didn't take Dr. Willis long to get her samples. She stood at the doorway, facing me, her expression focused. "He's going to be fine," she said, though there was no feeling in her tone. It was just something she was supposed to say. "I'll be back, hopefully with some more answers."

As soon as the door shut, I searched the place. There wasn't much to see beyond what I had already found. I couldn't figure out what the other machines did without switching them on and experimenting, and I wasn't willing to risk that. Not till Dr. Willis had done all she could for Mateo. There were four strange charcoal uniforms with unusually high collars stored in the closet of the other bedroom. On the back of the neck of each of the outfits was writing, but not in English. I ran the image through my viser. The writing was Korean: *Daehan*. But the word had no proper meaning according to the net.

Finding nothing else, I went to sit next to my brother, dragging one of the flimsy chairs with me. I stayed there until a few intrepid strands of light slipped through the fabricated sheeting covering the bedroom window. The soft illumination brought me back from the half-sleep I had lingered in through the night. My eyes opened to find the worrying pallor of my brother's face had gone. His breathing was steady. I tried to stretch the stiffness in my back away. Mateo let out a loud snore that brought a smile to my face. Like old times.

I went to the kitchen to get a glass of water. When I returned, Mateo was staring at me, his hands rubbing the bandage clinging to his ribs.

"Didn't think those jack-A's could shoot that well."

I took a sip of the water then sat next to him again. "Sit up and drink this."

Mateo pulled himself up, wincing as he did. He took the glass and finished it in three long, deep swallows.

"How did you get here?" he asked. "And where are we?"

"I get to go first. How did you get yourself roasted by a force rifle blast?"

He stroked his bandage, as if proud. "The Authority raided the building we were holed up in. We got onto the roof, ran across a couple of buildings, got down into an alley. We were haulin' it to the garage where we had our U-cab parked. Thought we got clear of them. Guess not. One of 'em must've snagged me from the roof or something. Chris-Chris got me the rest of the way, then I blacked out. Where is he?"

"Went to ditch the car. It's still my turn to ask questions," I said curtly. "Why were you holed up in Manhattan, in a building the Authority was raiding?"

Mateo closed his eyes, as if in pain. But that wasn't it. He was stalling.

"I'm sick of people not telling me the whole damn story," I said, fire in every word. "People put their lives on the line to bail you out. Including me, and Kortilla. So if you don't 'fess up, I'm going to reopen that gash, and give you a matching one on the other side."

"Dee, it's…You got a good thing…I don't want you involved. It's to protect you."

"Look where you are, genius. This ain't a hospital. You're in a safe house near the Vision Quad, and those nanites that healed your injury didn't come out of some back-alley fabricator. I'm in it too now. You helped put me here. Worse, you put Kortilla and some of my other friends in it as well. Start talking big brother, or blood or not, I'll see you finished."

"Your temper always scared the hell out of me," he said, trying to lighten my mood.

I put my hand on his wound.

"What the hell..."

I pressed my thumb inward. Not too hard, but enough.

Mateo screamed.

"Finally getting to feel some of the pain you cause others?" My hand was poised.

"You're *loca*," he accused. "I always knew it—"

"I already know you're involved with some heavy crap. The equipment in that car, the hacking, it took serious hardware. Way beyond what Chris-Chris, you, or any of your little *Corazones* could manage. And I don't believe it's a coincidence that you're holed up in Manhattan at the same time there's an attack on Landrew Foster-Rose-Hart, which also used some serious hardware. So I've already guessed a lot of it."

He stared at me: Mateo, my brother, a reflection of my soul.

"Deuces," he muttered, surrendering.

"Talk. Did you try to kill Landrew Fart?"

"Fart? I like that. No, I had nothing to do with it."

I was surprised by how much relief I felt. My brother hadn't tried to kill Alexander's dad. That was something.

"But you know about it? It has something to do with you?"

"The people who did that...They were...misled, I think." He shook his head. "Gatta, Kally, a couple of others...I don't know..."

"What?" I stood, knocking over the chair. "Kally was on that roof? With drones and rocket launchers? That boy can barely get his shoes on without someone helping him. What the hell is going on, Mateo? Why were you in Manhattan?"

"The allocator thing, their party," he confessed, finally. "We were going to hit it, hard."

"You mean kill people?" I couldn't believe this was my brother. Mateo, a terrorist.

"Richies," he declared, as if speaking of insects. "They don't consider us people, Dee. We're nothing to them…We're—"

"Below the iceberg," I whispered.

"Huh?"

"Never mind. Keep talking. What was the plan?"

"This guy, Kelvin, was our contact. Got us the equipment, schematics of the event space. Knew their defenses. Everything."

My eyes narrowed. "Where did you meet him?"

"One of my boys, Nacho, set up a meet. Says there's a guy, a Californian, that needed help. Had some big dollars. That I should meet him."

I could picture it. Greedy little Nacho, who Mateo trusted, but never should have. Introducing my brother to a man with cash, a man with promises and stories. Mateo always did love a good story.

"And this Kelvin, who is he?"

"A patriot," Mateo declared. I felt the hairs on my brother's back rising without seeing them. "Someone who believes that America should be one country again. But people need to do something to make it happen. He told us California had a plan, but they needed help."

I shook my head, more resigned than upset.

"He's right, Dee. The Orderist ideas aren't working. Things are getting worse. But the highborn, they crush any dissent. Nothing can happen as long as they have a stranglehold on power. And who are the richest of the highborn? The most powerful?"

"The allocators."

"Right. So if we dent their power, their influence…If we could show everyone they aren't invincible—"

"People would rise up? The Orderists would change their mind, say all is forgiven, California? We were wrong, you were right, let's reunite, bring back the old Constitution and the old USA?" I rolled my eyes the way Nythan would have.

"Yes!" Mateo yelled, hard enough that he was clutching his side in pain the next moment. "Someone has to do something."

"Got it," I said, my voice cold. "What were you going to do?"

"They beef up security on the bridges and tunnels starting a few weeks before the event. We needed to be inside before that, with our stuff, then lay low. Otherwise we wouldn't get past the perimeter. So we got to where we needed to be. Kelvin arranged it. Got us everything we needed, places to stay. Great equipment. We just had to sit tight."

"Why didn't you?"

Mateo rubbed his forehead. "This girl. She shows up one night, like a ghost. Just walks in. She's got a key, got the password. She's…she's gorgeous. Decked out in a black jumper like nothing you ever saw. She's young, but the way she spoke…her eyes flashed lightning—"

"I got it. What did she say?"

Mateo looked troubled for the first time. Plotting to kill dozens of people didn't seem to bother him, but somehow this girl did. "She talked like no one I've ever heard. About a special chance, one in a million, to do more than we ever could blowing up a few allocators. A chance to change the world, and we only need to get to one guy."

"Landrew Foster-Rose-Hart."

"The way she explained it sounded…great. So easy. The first domino to change the world. Kally and some of the others went with her. Right then and there. Took some of our best equipment with them. Drones, stealth suits…"

Alexander had wanted to know about drones. "Why didn't you go?"

"I wanted to," Mateo confessed, sounding miserable. "But there was something wrong about her. Wrong about what she was saying. Not that I disagreed. It was more a feeling than a decision."

"I don't understand."

"Her words—they were like Z-Pop. They made you soar. A high like no person is ever meant to experience, because nothing in real-life can feel that good. That girl spoke something primal, something chemical, but artificial. Like Z-Pop. It's a lie. It creates feelings that aren't there. I touched that crap once—never again. So I said 'no.' Yanked Chris-Chris back. Literally had to hold the kid down for a couple of minutes. But the rest went."

I nodded as if I got it. I didn't, though. Not yet. But I was on the edge of understanding. And I knew it was big, and bad.

"Then what?"

"Nothing. We got in touch with some of the other *Corazones*. We switched hidey holes. But once those idiots botched the attack, the Authority was everywhere. They went house-to-house, searching everywhere. Systematic and relentless. They finally caught up with us."

I took a deep breath, leaned forward, and took Mateo's hand into mine. I looked into the dark of his eyes and saw my reflection.

"You're an idiot."

Dr. Willis returned before lunch. Dark circles lingered under her eyes. She brought Mateo a protein shake to drink, and nothing for me. She ordered him to sit up and finish it while she reviewed the data and did a lot of other doctor finger flicking.

"What are you doing, exactly?" I inquired, standing in the doorway.

"Making a few command adjustments to the nanites to take care of infection and other residual issues." She sounded annoyed. "It's a bad idea to distract me while I'm working. I'll speak with you when I'm done."

I sat down at the table, stewing and impatient. Dr. Willis took her time coming out. I had a hunch she did it on purpose. She closed the door of Mateo's bedroom after she left.

"There was a sedative in the drink," she told me. "He'll be asleep for a couple of hours, at least. It'll help him heal."

"How's he doing?" I asked.

"A lot better. He should be able to get up tomorrow. I've got the nanites working on closing that wound. It'll be gone without a trace in the next two days."

"Thanks, great. He'll be able to leave and that will be it?"

Doc placed her hands on the table. "That's what I want to discuss. There is no easy way to say this so I just will: He's got a progressive genetic degeneration condition—what you call the Waste."

I knew it. I had expected it. I still wanted to puke.

"What was that you called it?" I managed, my voice weak.

"Progressive genetic degeneration. Without burdening you with a lot of unnecessary terminology, his cells are degrading. Slow but steady. Each time a cell replaces itself, its successor is weaker."

I shook my head, numb. "Again, please."

"Our bodies are made up of trillions and trillions of cells: white cells, red cells, liver cells, brain cells. Almost all of them, except those in our brain and a few others, continuously die off and are replaced. Something is happening every time one of his cells gets replaced. The successor is…less…then the cell that preceded it. The damage varies by cell type, but the degradation is universal and constant."

"Can you cure it?" I asked, but I already knew the answer. It was written on her face.

"We're pretty certain the cause is genetic. That means it is written into who he is. This isn't some virus to be killed, a cancer to be removed or attacked. His genes are doing this to him. To change it now, even if it were possible, would mean re-writing portions of his genetic code."

"So you can't cure him?" Blackness was closing in at the edge of my vision. Everything I had worked for, everything I had done—useless. I saw myself riding on his shoulders again, beginning to fall, as he did.

"I didn't say that. I've told you the problem is…well, daunting. But I'm not saying nothing can be done. We have treatments for genetic issues. Good ones. We have treatments that can repair cells. And, more importantly, something caused this. That is what we need to understand, if we are to beat this Waste, as you call it. And no one is better at genetics than Lenox."

The doctor offered a ray of hope in a soot-choked sky. I willed my mind to focus—to be cold and smart. I forced myself to take several deep breaths before I said anything more. "You know all this after a night and a morning?"

She blinked off rhythm. Twice. "This isn't the first case I've seen."

"Why isn't anyone talking about it? Doing something about it? The net is silent on this too."

"*I'm* trying to do something about it," Doctor Willis declared. "I think you can guess why no one else is focused on it."

"It doesn't affect the highborn."

She nodded.

"Now what?" I asked.

"Get him to me at Lenox. I can do more for him there than I can here. We've got equipment, drugs, treatments…"

"He's wanted…The black boots monitor hospital admissions. They'll catch him, and you."

"No outstanding warrants, I checked," Doctor Willis assured me. "Whoever shot him didn't know who they were shooting at. Must've had a mask on, because even the street monitors didn't record his face. He's got some minor offenses from Bronx City, but nothing that would attract the Authority—not right now, certainly. And they don't march into a private facility like Lenox lightly."

"How do you know all that?" I wondered. "Do you have sources in the Authority? Another Havelock pupil?"

She gave me a smile that said "need to know."

"I'll try to get him to go," I told her. It wouldn't be easy convincing Mateo to get help at a richie facility. I couldn't even promise they could cure him. Still, doing nothing was a death sentence. Doctor Willis had confirmed it.

"Do that," she urged me. "Soon."

The darkness returned. "Why?"

"You said it yourself. No one with this condition makes it much past twenty. How old is he?"

"Nineteen."

"Exactly. It's accelerating. Get him to me. And keep to your normal routine. That means school tomorrow. If there is one Tuck student most likely to draw unwanted attention to herself, to her brother and to us, it's you, young lady. So for everyone's sake, go to school and act normal. All our lives depend on it."

CHAPTER
TWENTY-FIVE

Doctor Willis arranged for a car to pick me up in the underground garage before the crack of dawn. It was one of the countless automated corporate sedans that zipped around Manhattan most mornings and evenings, and I had no clue as to its origins. The car dropped me off close to the Eighty-Sixth Street subway station. Doc told me it would pick me up at the same corner, at a designated time, to bring me back to Mateo. She'd pumped him full of meds that morning and promised she'd be back to check on him later in the day. I didn't like it. But I also knew I couldn't do anything for him in that apartment, and there were people at Tuck I needed to speak to.

I sought out the headmaster first, hovering outside the administrative offices until someone arrived. It turned out to be his assistant, Elsa Mark. She smiled when she saw me, despite the hour and the expression on my face.

"I am glad you ended up joining us here, Ms. Machado," she said to me, unperturbed at finding me waiting outside her office suite an hour before classes started. "I wasn't sure you would that first day you came in. You looked a tad angry."

"How do I look now?"

"Worried," she said, her tone unfailingly cheerful. "What can I help you with?"

I want to find your boss so I can grab him and hold him down till he's answered every question I have. "I'd like to make an appointment to see Headmaster Havelock."

Elsa Mark frowned. "He doesn't generally meet one-on-one with students. What is this concerning?"

I stammered. "I-I need his help. Something urgent."

She sighed, shaking her head. "I'm afraid he isn't in today. A bit of an unexpected matter." She glanced down at her viser. "I'm not quite sure about his availability tomorrow, either, I'm afraid."

"Please, is there any way I might contact him?"

Ms. Mark looked at me, then her viser. "I will get a message to him. I'll be in touch with his answer."

I didn't move.

"That's all I can do, Ms. Machado. Do try to have a good day."

I was grinding my teeth as I left.

I hurried downstairs to Lit. The room was empty. I stood in that silent place, gazing at the oil portraits, pictures of light-skinned men who had probably made a lot of money in their day and given a portion of it to Tuck, so the school might educate their sons and daughters to be just like them. Now here I was. I had come for Mateo; or at least, that was what I had convinced myself. But I was no closer to saving him than I had been on the first day. It felt like trying to cross a river with weights strapped to my back. The boy just didn't want to get to the other side.

I lifted my viser, searching the Castle directory for a name I had never pinged before. I stared at it, my fingers hesitating. I told myself I needed answers for Mateo.

It was the second time this month I had lied to myself.

I tapped out a message to Alexander Foster-Rose-Hart. "CAN YOU MEET ME BEFORE CLASS? IMPORTANT."

I waited, wondering where he was. Swimming in an enormous golden bathtub? Flying into Manhattan from his country estate? Visiting his father? I forced myself to stop staring at my viser, pulling my hand to my side. I took a seat in the nearest desk. The weight on my shoulders didn't lessen. Did I really think Alexander was going to jump to attention because I asked? He was probably trying to remember who I was.

My viser shook. "DOWNSTAIRS. JUST FINISHED AT THE TRACK. MEET YOU IN TEAM ROOM IN 5 MINS."

The golden bathtub scenario was more interesting, but this satisfied my impatience. Two minutes later, I swung open the door to the windowless, bland, rectangle of a room that we used for team meetings. Alexander was already there, seated on the backrest of one of the many scattered chairs. Tuck banners and trophies surrounded him. The fluorescent lights flickered to full potency. Alexander's face seemed to change as the light brightened around him. For a moment, I imagined a ray of pleasure in his eyes, around his mouth. But when I looked again, a blank face stared back at me.

I walked across the room to stand in front of him. The height of the chair was such that our eyes were level with each other. He neither moved nor spoke as I approached. People said I was no fun at parties. They should try making small talk with Alexander.

"Thanks for meeting me," I said.

"I was practicing at the track anyway. It helps me think."

I wanted to ask what Alexander spent his time pondering, if he, too, had things to run from. But Mateo came before idle curiosity.

"The other day you wanted to know about the drones." My tongue was heavier than it should have been.

"Yes."

I exhaled my displeasure at his curt response. "When I told you about them you said 'it didn't make sense.' You didn't believe that I saw what I saw." He nodded. "What was it about the drones that didn't make sense?"

Alexander's eyes moved to the door, then back at me. "Why are you asking?"

I held in the cry of frustration budding in my throat. "I just need..." I stopped. I met his gaze. "Someone very important to me is in trouble. I'm trying to figure it out. I'm trying to help him."

Alexander kept those cold sapphires fixed on me. Being caught in his gaze felt like swimming on a cold day: it was uncomfortable staying in, but worse getting out.

"Someone who has something to do with those drones?" he asked, his tone tinged with a hint of suspicion.

Damn. He'd know if I lied. Those eyes saw everything. "He wasn't involved in the attack on your father. But I'm afraid someone is trying to use him. Please. Can you trust me, and just tell me?"

I felt my heart beating in my toes as I waited for Alexander to make up his mind.

"The drones you described are called Jammer-K's."

My heart beat faster. "What is the significance of these Jammer-K's?"

"Everyone is accusing California of being involved in the attack on Landr...my father. There's nothing on the net about Jammer-K's being used. Cali doesn't have those types of drones. You called them decoys, but they are a lot more than that. The nighthawks protecting my father's caravan are smart. They wouldn't attack a regular decoy drone. Jammer-K's make themselves appear more threatening than they are to another drone's sensors, even sophisticated ones like the nighthawk model. They are designed to draw away the best fighting drones, like what happened when my father was attacked."

"How do you know California doesn't have them? Even if they aren't made there, they could've bought them, stolen them."

"Jammer-K's are manufactured by our family's company. They are sophisticated, and new. Sale controls are tight and they are all accounted for. No way Jammer-K's found their way to California." He sounded grave. "And you were right about the net scrubbing. It's been erased. By someone very good, with expertise and resources."

"So you believe me?"

"Yes, I believe you. I did not want to. The truth can be hard. Doing what is right even harder."

"What do you mean?"

He shook his head. "Does what I told you help?"

I wasn't sure if it would. My brother was stubborn. "It might. Either way, I appreciate you telling me."

My mind switched gears to Mateo. I was already rehearsing what I would say to him when I got back to the safe house, what I could do to convince him to get off the road he was on. How could I get him into Lenox with Dr. Willis? My brother never made anything easy.

Without any conscious thought, I placed a light hand on Alexander's shoulder. I might have done the same with Kortilla. Maybe even with Alissa. But never Alexander. It was like touching artwork in a museum. I realized what I had done after a split second and yanked my hand back, my face flushed.

"Anyway, thanks again." I backed up, then spun out of the room.

I tripped getting back upstairs. I couldn't remember the last time I'd tripped.

Alissa was standing just inside the doorway of our Lit classroom waiting for me. "It's good to see you," was all she said, but I got the meaning. If I was here, it meant Mateo was okay. I wondered how much she knew about what was going on. But we couldn't speak here. Students started to file into the room. They jostled, and joked. A few stared at me and hissed ill whispers, but no more than usual for a Monday.

Alexander sauntered into class right before the bell, but he didn't look at me. It might have been my imagination, but I think he sat a bit farther from me than usual. He may have feared further nope contamination, I suppose. I did my best to ignore him. It was like trying not to take one last peek at a traffic accident.

Lunch was almost as painful as Lit class. Alissa sat opposite me as usual, looking everywhere but at me. She had helped me and Mateo, and I owed her. But I now knew she had been deceiving me since the day I met her: about Marie-Ann, about Havelock, and probably other things. Even if she thought she had some reason for doing that, some cause that was important to her, I couldn't forget that she had been showing me a false face. I didn't want to forget it.

Nythan was prattling on about some ancient film—something about apes and buried statues. His lips moved and made sounds, but I focused on his face, his expression, his eyes. Nythan didn't seem to have any guile in him. Or he was so full of it he could hide it better. *Did he know about Mateo also?*

"What do you do in your other lab?" I asked. "You mentioned that you had two."

Alissa finally looked at me, her gaze as sharp as a knife. Lara watched everyone, her countenance brooding.

"Where did that come from?" Nythan asked.

"J-Just curious," I stammered. "I was thinking if I could squeeze in another lab. I want to do genetics."

Nythan's eyes flipped towards Alissa, just for a moment. But that was all I needed. He might not know what had happened with Mateo, but he was part of this. At least in some way. Alissa's frown turned deep enough that she might need an alterator to get it off her face.

"You've got to have a reason for a second lab," Nythan explained. "A good reason. Like humanity is wasting precious resources by putting you in ridiculous classes like Script, when you could be changing the world."

"You still have Script," Lara noted.

"Like I said, you need a really good reason to get extra labs."

They kept talking, but I barely heard the rest. I wanted to get back to the safe house. Dr. Willis had arranged for my car to depart at six fifteen. The day passed at an agonizing pace. I forced myself to go to practice afterwards.

My spider-sense prickled as soon as I left the locker room to join the team on the track. The underground cavern that held our practice track felt cold and sterile, despite the false azure above us. With all that had happened since Saturday, I had forgotten about beating Drake at the meet. I had forgotten about Alissa's comments afterward. Drake hadn't forgotten, though. The memory was etched into his face, his features smoldering with hate. That kind of loathing did not dissipate on its own. One did not work through hate that reached into your soul. People like Drake would strike out, or be consumed by their own darkness.

Coach strode onto the track fingering his whistle; such an aggrieved little man. His eyes swept over the team onto me. I wondered what he'd try next. Alexander jogged out to meet the coach before he reached us. Alexander spoke quietly to Nessmier; the coach's frown soured as he looked over at Drake, then his viser. Alexander jogged back to rejoin the team, standing as far away from me as the cluster of runners allowed.

"Ladies and gentlemen, let me first congratulate you on a fine meet on Saturday. We took six out of eight events, including the conditioned events," the coach announced to a round of cheers. "Due to forthcoming festivities for the Allocators' Ball and security considerations, no meet is scheduled for next week. But that doesn't mean we can relax if we want to qualify for the City Championship. Therefore, after everyone has run their eight hundred meters of warm-ups, we're going to break up into event teams for practice and drills, with team leaders taking their assignees through the exercises."

My stomach clenched. The bastard better not put me into a drill team with Drake.

He started reading names. "Reves-Wyatt team leader. With her: Titan-Wind, Hester-Jobs, Killian-Red…" I kept waiting, expecting the worst. My fists were balls, my palms white.

"You're with me today," Alexander said over my shoulder. I convulsed in surprise. For a big guy, he could be terribly quiet.

"How do you know?"

"I asked for you. I hope that's okay."

I didn't answer, but it was okay.

Whatever he might have thought of me off the track, we pushed each other hard on it. There were four of us on his mini-team, and we all ran hard, but really it was only Alexander and me competing. I beat him off the starting block on two fifty-meter sprints. He took me on the third. We ran hidden hurdles against the wind along the east side of the track. Alexander beat me all four times, but my reaction time was faster and more efficient over the hurdles than his—he just had better acceleration after the jumps. I saw him watching my stats on the board after every run. Not that I wasn't watching his as well. We pushed each other on a one-hundred-meter sprint. I'm not sure who won, since the electronic tracking system wasn't active for that one. He might've had me with his lean in. His eyes met mine as we both doubled over catching our breath. There was approval there, where I would've expected resentment from anyone else on the team.

I felt an ugly chill as I pulled myself back up. I turned to find Drake looking across the track at me.

"Keep away from him," Alexander warned.

"Why?"

"He is like the rest of his family, an opportunist. One without boundaries…and for other reasons."

"Your sister told me he was among the best of us," I huffed.

"His kind is drawn to Kris like a moth to flame. His family seeks to be close to ours. There are debts to pay." Alexander's jaw clenched. "Nor is Kris one to waste an opportunity. Drake is best avoided."

"I can take care of myself. You just worry about trying to keep up with me."

We kept up the frantic pace throughout the rest of practice: incline runs, heel kicks, burst and reflex drills. Coach walked over a few times, shouting about form, angle, and positioning. At least for the other runners. He never spoke to me.

When Coach called an end to practice, Alexander and I both knew what had to come next. We went through our usual cool down routine, just much slower. Once everyone else had slogged off to the locker rooms we took our positions on the starting line. When he turned his head towards me, I saw a grin that reflected my own.

"You call it," he told me.

"Go," I said instantly, taking off at a sprint.

Usually I hold back just a bit at the start, saving something extra for later. But this wasn't an official practice, and I just wanted to run. I hauled flat out, as if I were doing a hundred-meter sprint. I wanted to dust him, to show that I could. I was drenched, exhausted and hurting, but still I pushed. My legs churned in a blur. I pulled away. But not for long.

Right around one hundred meters, Alexander's footfalls echoed to my right. I pushed harder, urging myself forward. My arms and legs pumped with frenzied speed. It didn't do any good. Alexander didn't move an inch back or forward. I took it down a gear, slowing almost imperceptibly. He did the same. *Bastard was toying with me.*

I reached for the cold, my store of power, my secret weapon. I drank it in—not too much, but enough to show Alexander that I could still take the fight to him. I felt the weight I had been dragging lift, my legs surged. He fell back, but only for a few seconds. No matter how hard I pushed, he kept on my shoulder. My lungs began to burn. He drew even. We turned onto a straightaway. We never agreed on the distance of our impromptu race, but we both knew this was the final stretch. I drew on more of my inner self than I should have, particularly for a practice run. Cold pulsed through my veins, banishing pain and bestowing strength. My feet flew, my arms raced. I put on enough speed to beat any other person in the Five Cities. Except Alexander. He pulled ahead of me ten meters before the finish line. Not by a lot, but enough that we both knew he won. *Deuces.*

I sucked hard for air once I finally stopped moving. My feet burned, my calves were furious. I forced myself to walk, letting my lungs take in as much oxygen as they wanted. Alexander looked harried for once; his hair hung like a wet mop down to his eyes, his face was flushed red, his chest heaved. I'd barely seen him break a sweat before. It was small consolation for losing, but it was something.

"How do you do it?" he asked.

"One foot in front of the other. You seem to know how as well."

No grin for that. Serious Alexander had returned. "You know what I mean. There aren't many people who can keep up with me. Only Drake, and, well…" Alexander shrugged. I got the impression that accusing a competitor of cheating without direct evidence wasn't his style. It wouldn't have been honorable.

"How do you do it then? Why can't anyone else keep up with you?" I asked him.

"It's who I am. How I was made."

"Alexander the Great," I said, regretting it.

He flushed, and it wasn't from the race. "Contrary to myth, I didn't make that up. Kris did. For reasons quite her own. A complicated person, my sister." His eyes turned dark.

"I shouldn't have said it."

"It's your turn to answer the question."

I shifted my weight from foot to foot before steadying myself before Alexander's too serious face. "I get…angry. When I run. Other times too, but especially when I run. And when I do, there's something inside me. It gives me something extra, something no one else can match." I swallowed. "Until now. Until you."

His eyes were like tunnels leading up to a clear sky, intense as the mid-day sun. They revealed nothing of what was behind them though.

"Anyway, thank you," I said. "For speaking to me this morning, and for what you did today."

"What did I do?" Alexander asked. "We both ran hard."

"You spoke to the coach. Again."

Alexander bowed his head, ever so slightly. Even soaked with sweat, his hair gleamed gold. I could see over him just for a moment as he bent down, to the time display on the wall. My car would be there in ten minutes. I'd forgotten all about Mateo, and my ride. *Selfish. Stupid.*

"Listen, Daniela, would you…"

"Alexander, sorry…" I was already backing away. Just like this morning. "I have to be somewhere…"

I ran into the locker room, grabbed my bag, viser and a skin, then dashed up the stairs, taking them two at a time. I race-walked through the halls, twisting and turning through the corridors to the security vestibule. We don't run at Tuck, even when the school is empty. I jumped down the front stairs, then jogged through the streets of Manhattan. The requisite black sedan was waiting at the designated corner. I slid inside, my damp rear squeaking against the fabricated leather interior of the vehicle. Nothing for the drones above to take notice of. Just another rich girl headed somewhere glamorous. If they only knew.

Manhattan passed me on the other side of the tinted windows. I tried to focus on Mateo. I needed to convince him to go to Lenox. But I'd never persuade him without leverage. What did my brother need or fear that I could use? My mind balked. I couldn't get the picture of Alexander Foster-Rose-Hart out of my head. Specifically, his shocked expression as I dashed away from him, mid-sentence, for the second time in a day. After he had gotten me on the track team, after bailing me out of a torture session with Drake that might've gotten me kicked off the team, and after treating me better than anyone else at this place. He hadn't tried to hide who he was. Better than Alissa and Nythan could claim. Alexander might be cold, but he had treated me far better than I had him.

The vehicle passed into the Vision Quad, bringing me back among the monuments of innovative commerce, of economic disruption. Light had almost faded from the sky. Soon great machines and greater mountains of rock and dirt appeared around me. Almost there. I wondered what Mateo had been doing all day. It wasn't like him to sit around, even if he was hurt, even if Dr. Willis had pumped him full of meds. That seemed obvious now. So when I saw the dark outline of a person hugging the roadside, I knew who it was even before the sedan's headlights flashed on his surprised face and disheveled black hair. Damn my brother.

"Stop here," I commanded, already wiggling the door handle. It didn't budge.

"WE HAVE NOT REACHED THE DESTINATION. FOR YOUR OWN SAFETY, PLEASE REMAIN—"

"Safety override, *puta*," I yelled at it, banging on the window.

"I AM SORRY. I DO NOT UNDERSTAND YOUR REQUEST."

I jumped into the front seat, yanking the steering wheel to the left as I slammed on the brakes. Once, twice I pounded on the pedal. The car kept humming along.

"Engage manual control," I yelled.

"I AM SORRY. I DO NOT UNDERSTAND YOUR REQUEST."

I reached for my bag on the back seat, grabbing the digi-Book from inside. I slammed the electronic device into the sedan's front dashboard. No effect. I hammered with the digiBook again. It crunched and crackled in a manner unintended by the manufacturer, but so did the sedan's control display. Lights flickered. The speed and distance indicators turned black.

"INITIATING EMERGENCY PROCEDURES. PLEASE ENSURE YOUR SEAT BELT IS SECURELY FASTENED."

The sedan slowed to crawl. The hum of the engine faded. All four doors clicked. The headlights remained on. I shoved my door open and raced towards my brother as he hobbled along the darkened road like a vagabond begging to be picked up by an Authority patrol. I didn't see how he was going to manage to get to the end of the street, much less the nearest transport station.

"Where do you think you're going?" I demanded. His body appeared damaged and weary, but there was nothing tired in his eyes.

"Back to where I belong," Mateo said.

"To throw away your life trying to kill a few highborn?"

"To fight for people like us."

I put myself in his path. "They're using you. Your contact, Kelvin, whoever he is, is lying to you. He isn't with California."

"How would you know?"

"The Jammer-K's you told me about. They're special—new. California doesn't have them."

Mateo snarled. "How would you know? Your richie school teach you about drone exports? Or did one of your highborn pals tell you?"

His words stung. My anger boiled. I sucked in as much wind as my lungs would hold. "Use your head. Or look it up on the net. Anyway, forget the drones. What about that car you and Chris-Chris had? Hacking U-cab's network? Drone jammers? You think California turned that kind of hardware over to the likes of you based on some connection they made through a minor Bronx City thug?"

Uncertainty flashed across my brother's face. I laid my hand on his shoulder.

"You're caught up in some highborn feud. Think about the girl who arranged the attack on Landrew Foster-Rose-Hart. They are using you."

More hesitation. I thought I had him.

"Even if Kelvin isn't who he says, better to die fighting. Doing some good," Mateo said.

"Nothing good is going to come from killing," I lowered my voice. "Let me help you. I know people who can do something about what you've got. That's why I went to Tuck. There's a place where—"

Headlights approached. I muttered another silent plea to whoever might be listening that it wasn't the Authority. No one was going to save us if we got picked up here.

"You think you're in any different position from me?" Mateo scoffed, not even glancing at the oncoming vehicle. "You think that doctor and whoever is behind her aren't using you? You think a bunch of richies helped me because they are good people? What do they want, huh?"

"I don't know."

The car stopped beside us and switched off its headlights. I smelled gasoline and heard the churning of a turbine engine.

"*Vamos, amigo*," called a barrio voice from the dark window. It might have been Inky. The vehicle's back door opened.

Mateo limped away from me and towards his crew, his blood.

"Don't go," I told him, my voice barely carrying over the soft rumble of the engine.

Mateo turned back to me. His eyes were soft, like the brother I remembered taking care of me growing up. "Forget about me, Daniela."

"Never."

"Don't trust those *gringos*," he said. "That doctor. Whoever she works for. From us, *los richos* always take, they do not give."

Mateo got into the back seat of the car, disappearing into the darkness of its interior. The engine became louder, but the door didn't close. Mateo's face reappeared. "Come with me, Daniela."

I shook my head. My throat was so stiff it was hard to speak. "I'm not giving up."

Mateo's eyes locked on mine. "No one has heard from Chris-Chris since he left this place. He might've gone to ground with Kelvin and his people. Or something else might have happened to him. Remember what I said: Don't trust these people."

The door shut. My brother was gone.

CHAPTER

TWENTY-SIX

M y crippled sedan must have signaled someone. Less than five minutes after Mateo pulled away, while I was fiddling with my viser and wondering if I should ping Nythan, an electrocycle showed up. The bike was lit in an orange and blue trim, with an unfamiliar corporate insignia on the side. The thing looked like a clown face. The rider wore a technician's outfit emblazoned with the same markings. He had a smooth face, tightly combed silver hair, and eyes shaped like eggs tipped onto their sides. His tone became hard once he saw the damage to the sedan.

"Get the hell back to where you should've gone, and wait for someone to collect you, little girl."

I didn't have much choice. I had no idea how to reach a transit station from here, nor did I have any plausible explanation as to what I was doing in the Vision Quad if an Authority patrol stopped to question me. My legs were heavy as I walked. The memory of Mateo's gentle eyes as he got into that car lingered. His words echoed. *Forget about me.* But I couldn't do that.

I recalled an old memory on my walk back to the safe house. It was from the time before I had Kortilla, those first days when we realized my mother would never be coming home again. I lived in the darkness then. Pain was my companion, and I had no intention of giving up its company. I remembered the corner in Aba's apartment, with its little red table. My face was to the wall, my back to the world. I stopped talking so I could be alone with my hurt and emptiness. Aba had told me to come out to face the world, because it would not come to me. But Mateo came. I didn't speak to him. When he tried to touch me, I clawed at him. I drew blood twice. But he kept coming. "Come outside with me, Daniela," he said.

I had no clock or sense of time as I sulked with my gloom. Perhaps Mateo came every hour. Perhaps every ten minutes. "Come outside with me, Daniela."

My sorrow didn't end. Always, he came. He brought me food I wouldn't eat, then hid it for later, so Aba wouldn't know. I didn't know how long it went on for. Days. My throat was so dry by the end that I couldn't have spoken if I wanted to. I certainly couldn't have stood up.

"Come outside with me, Daniela." Then he added, "I'm never giving up."

It was the "never" that did it. That was what I needed to hear, what I needed to believe. That night, I found a place inside me that was cold. It gave me the strength to go on living.

I meant it when I told Mateo "never."

Dr. Willis arrived at the safe house an hour or so later, her knuckles white with rage. "What the hell were you thinking?"

"I wasn't—he's my brother."

"Damn it, Daniela, I can help him. But he's got to come in."

Don't trust these people, Mateo had said.

"Why are you willing to do this for me? For him?" I asked, low and even.

"I'm a doctor," she said. "But I need the patient if I'm going to do any actual doctor stuff. What was the point in healing the force rifle blast if he's going to go off and die anyway? A waste of good nanites." She paced while I sat at the kitchen table.

My eyes watched her move, the agitation in her fisted hands. I didn't believe her answer. She wanted something more than to help Mateo.

"Can you get a message to him?" Doctor Willis asked.

Don't trust these people.

"It might take a while, given the method I have to use."

"It's important. He needs to reconsider."

"Nothing is more important to me than Mateo. But I need to go back to Bronx City to get in touch with him."

"Right," she nodded, looking around as if realizing where we were for the first time. "I'll arrange something."

Dr. Willis disappeared into the other bedroom. Ten minutes later, a nondescript corporate car picked me up at a corner a couple of blocks away.

Aba was asleep by the time I got home. As far as she knew, I had been studying with a friend in Manhattan. If she had been worried about me, there was no sign of it. I imagined my mom would've known something was wrong, if she'd been alive. A nice thought, a nice illusion. I wanted to ping Kortilla, but it was past midnight.

I crawled into bed. My bones ached to their core, my head spun, but sleep didn't come. Instead, I stared into the same corner I had retreated to a decade ago. The wobbly red table was faded but still hanging on. Just like Mateo. Minutes became hours as I lay there, the air stiff and warm. I told myself there was still hope for my brother. Doctor Willis might not be telling me the whole truth, but she did know about the Waste. She had studied it. I tried to piece together how I fit into all of this. The answers had to be at Tuck. Havelock had them. I wanted to get back to school and talk to the man. There were only a few hours left before sunrise when sleep finally took me.

As soon as I arrived at school the next morning, I went down to the track. Alexander wasn't there today. It was still early, and I'd gotten home late, so I showered in the locker room, letting gallons of warm, clean water wash over me, enjoying the decadence of it. Towards the end of washing, I remembered I was going to need a new digiBook. I'd have to head over to administration at lunch. I didn't see how that conversation was going to be anything except awful. I didn't even have the wrecked remains of the thing to show them. They'd probably assume I sold it.

Alexander was at his seat by the time I got myself to Lit class. He was twiddling with his digiBook. He turned to me, his face typically unreadable.

"Sorry I ran off yesterday," I said.

"What happened? If it is something you wish to talk about, of course."

"Family emergency."

"I understand," he said. His tone was so flat I would've thought he was mocking me if this had been anyone except Alexander. "Family is not easy."

I let a slight grin crawl onto the edge of my lips. "Maybe we can stretch our legs downstairs at lunch?"

No smile, but I got a full nod.

"I've gotta get a new digiBook first," I told him right as class started. "Might be a few minutes late."

It took split-second reflexes to be the first student out of my Trig class, combined with cat-like agility to maneuver around the other hungry competitors in the hallways, then sheer will to overtake my final adversaries climbing the stairs up to the dining hall, but I did it: third in line for food. I loaded up on bananas and sliced carrots, then headed down a flight of stairs to the administration floor. Castle's directory informed me that I was looking for the Office of School Services. I'd only been on this floor twice, both times to see the headmaster. Its layout was even more maze-like than the rest of the school. My viser displayed a map and suggested route, but I was having trouble distinguishing between the dark warren-like corridors that twisted, intersected, and abruptly ended without logical purpose. I made a couple of turns that my map didn't think existed. Based on the plaques on the doors around me, I had stumbled into the teachers' office area. I thought about Alexander waiting for me downstairs and walked faster. I stopped looking at the map as I turned repeatedly, then doubled back. I covered a fair amount of ground, but seemed to get nowhere new. There wasn't even a teacher around to ask. They took their lunch at the same time we did.

As I crossed an intersection of two hallways, I caught a glimpse of two students just outside a doorway down one of the smaller passages. I didn't stop. I didn't have time. I turned another corner. But the image of the students lingered, gradually coming into focus in my mind. I slowed. It couldn't be. It made no sense and I didn't have time to chase the imaginary and the impossible. I glanced at my viser. I'd been searching for ten minutes already. There was no telling how much time I'd have to waste talking to the people in school services. But I turned around anyway. This time I ran, rules be damned.

I slowed before the intersection where I might have seen the impossible. I peeked my head around, telling myself I was wrong. But there they were. The air flooded out of my lungs as I tried to understand what I was seeing: Alissa, standing not more than six inches from Drake Pillis-Smith. I was perhaps forty feet away, but there was no mistaking those two people. Alissa had a blank, almost confused look on her face as she gazed at Drake. I would've guessed they were about to kiss, except for the look on Drake's face. There was an intensity there, an expression more appropriate for the starting line of a one-hundred-meter sprint than casual conversation. He might have even been sweating.

Just as I was about to leave, Alissa gave a grave nod of her head and turned abruptly. She walked away from me, her expression hidden. Drake watched her for a few seconds, then walked in the same direction. With a reluctant sigh, I followed as quietly as I could. Alexander was going to hate me.

Alissa disappeared into one of the teachers' offices. The doors were unlocked, of course. Tuck didn't bother with locks; we had the honor code. Drake stood a few steps behind her, as if keeping watch. His lips curled in a look of wicked satisfaction. He moved closer to the office door. The fingers on his visered hand twitched. His head jerked. I slid behind the corner that concealed me a moment before he stole a quick glance over his shoulder. When I judged it safe to stick my head out again, Drake was just outside the open door, his visered hand inside. I tried to see what he was doing, but the door and Drake's hulking body blocked my view. Ten seconds later he backed away, walking quickly down the hall away from me. A shiver ran up my back. Alissa exited a few moments later. She walked towards me. I ducked into the office of Ms. Marisa Jones-Mailer, whom I had never met. She had a messy desk and a dusty terminal in her small cubicle. Blood pumped in my ears as Alissa walked past. Once the sound of her feet had disappeared, I ran back to the office she and Drake had entered. The inscription on the door plaque made my heart skip: George Lynder, Literature. I checked to make sure no one else was around, then opened the door a crack. I knew what I'd find even before I saw it lying on the small mahogany desk: Mr. Lynder's notebook.

"Why, Alissa?" I whispered as I shut the door and hurried away.

I dashed up the stairs to the dining hall, dodging throngs of students with food trays to where Nythan and Lara sat. Lara gave me a cold stare as I approached. I grabbed Nythan's arm.

"I need you to come with me, right now."

He spun in surprise, his mouth open, some mockery at the tip of his tongue. Then he absorbed the look on my face. His mouth snapped shut. I dragged, he followed. I heard Lara asking what the hell was going on.

"Where are we going?"

I didn't answer. My mind was too consumed by the implications of what I had just seen. It shouldn't have been possible. Alissa loathed Drake. I'd seen it. I couldn't have been that wrong about her. He was highborn, she a malformed nope. It made no sense. But that didn't matter. She was in trouble, and I owed her twice over.

I led Nythan up the stairs, four flights to the top. Then down a corridor and up another flight of stairs marked "Roof Access."

"Daniela, you're starting to freak me out."

I shoved the heavy door that led to the top of Tuck, yanking Nythan into a gloomy afternoon haze. We had a magnificent view of Central Park, and the great edifices of Manhattan encircled us in the distance. This was where Marie-Ann took the leap that ended her life.

"Why-are-we-here?" Nythan demanded. "Not that I don't enjoy being manhandled but—"

"There aren't any cameras out here."

His mocking grin vanished. "Why are you worried about being overheard?"

"Because I just watched Alissa sneak into Mr. Lynder's office and steal a look at the exam questions."

I wanted to punch the center of the arrogant grimace that appeared on Nythan's face. "No way, my friend. Alissa ain't wired that way. I've known her forever. She's a devoted follower, not a cheater. You saw wrong. Just talk—"

"Shut up and listen to me. She did it, but that's not the worst part. The really screwed up part is that I saw her talking to Drake right before. So up close and personal I thought they might've decided to be a couple. Then our crazy girl walks off without a care, waltzes into Lynder's office, and doesn't seem to notice the huge troll with his viser just outside, recording the whole thing."

I didn't think it was possible for Nythan to get any whiter, but I was wrong. He'd gone so pale I could see the veins in his face.

"Were they talking? Could you hear the words?"

"No, too far away. And I didn't see Alissa speak. Only Drake, I think. He had a strange look—like whatever he was saying was the most important thing in the world."

Nythan rubbed his forehead. "It can't be."

"I saw it, Nythan. I don't make mistakes about things like this."

He waved an absent hand at me. "I believe you."

"Why would she do it? I thought she and Drake hated each other. How could Alissa be so stupid?"

"They do hate each other. And Alissa hates the highborn—maybe more than you. She just hides it better. What she said about Drake at the track meet...it must've pushed that hulky psycho over some edge. That chemically engineered swill he takes to compete with Alexander probably didn't help. But I can't believe he'd dare this. Or that Kris would be so stupid, even if his family is in debt to them."

"Kris Foster-Rose-Hart? You're not making any sense. And if Alissa hates Drake that much, why would she speak to him, much less put herself in that position? He's going to get her expelled. That recording, it's the end for her."

Nythan stared into the distance as I spoke. I wasn't sure he heard me. Then he blinked, as if suddenly returning to the real world.

"The recording...yes, you're right. We need to deal with the recording first. Then the rest."

"Yeah, but how? He's got it on his viser."

Nythan looked at me, his eyes intense. "This is decision time, Daniela. We can save her, but we're going to have to put our futures on the line. If we fail, we get expelled with her."

I pursed my lips. A few weeks ago, walking away from this place would've been easy, except for Mateo. Now I wasn't sure my being at Tuck would do my brother any good, but the prospect of losing this place weighed on me. I didn't want to give up what I had here: the place, the track meets, and the people too. Some of them, anyway. But I knew what had to be done.

"Alissa saved me, and she helped saved my brother. Blood pays its debts."

"Here we go then."

Nythan's fingers flicked and pointed. His viser screen flashed data faster than I thought possible, his eyes danced in a frenzied tango with the code displayed on his palm and arm. He looked more machine than human as he worked, his body seemingly frozen, except for his eyes and fingers. I tried to make out the flood of numbers scrolling across the screen on Nythan's wrist. It was mostly beyond me. Except that he was downloading something big. After several minutes, Nythan's fingers slowed and his eyes became still. The data stopped flashing. He shut his eyes, as if in a trance.

"You in there, Nythan?"

His eyes opened. He was looking right past me, at some point on the horizon.

"Gort, Klaatu Barada Nikto," he pronounced, stifling a grin.

Even I got that one. Over one hundred years old, but so classic it had been remade as a VR simulation on the net. I punched him on the arm, not as hard as I could have, but hard enough. He winced.

"This isn't *The Day the Earth Stood Still*. There's nothing to shut off."

"Oh, yeah? Look at your viser," Nythan replied. Smug.

I looked at the device wrapped around my arm: "NO CONNECTION AVAILABLE."

"You crashed the network?"

Nythan bowed. "Not just crashed. It's jamming itself, and everyone else's visers too. No one can use Castle, and no one can transmit viser-to-viser either."

"You carry computer viruses around with you?"

He squirmed. "It was for something else. But easily adaptable for a man like me."

"What does crashing Castle get us?"

"You've got an AT above thirty and you need to ask? If you're on Tuck grounds, your viser cannot link with the real net. The school blocks everything else. Hardwire connections are the only way for data to get out of this place. Castle is a closed environment. Therefore, if you have data on your viser, say an illicit recording of a girl we all love, you can only do three things with it: upload it to Castle, transfer it to someone else on Tuck property or keep it stored on your viser. I've just eliminated the first two options."

"But he's still got it on his viser. As soon as he walks out of school, he can transfer it onto the net. It could go anywhere."

"You've got the problem now, young padawan," Nythan said.

"He could just leave, walk beyond Eighty-Ninth Street and upload it to the net."

"Policy violation. Students can't leave the grounds during the school day without consent. And he'd miss classes. But I'll send a little virus to the front door locks just in case."

I huffed. "That's fine for now. But how do we get Drake's viser? He's a little big for you to tackle."

"He's gotta take it off for track practice, no? It'll be in his locker. No locks at this school." Nythan smiled at me, eyes big and expectant.

Deuces.

CHAPTER
TWENTY-SEVEN

The school was in viser withdrawal. Nythan's smile broadened every time he saw a distraught student flicking their fingers in disgust. Most class lectures had been disrupted by the failure of Castle as well, forcing some ad-hoc lessons.

Nythan explained the next part of his plan to me in Script, his demeanor giddy. It sounded simple. The boys' locker room had two doors. One led inside from the main corridor, the other led to the track. Drake would go to track practice, leaving his viser in his locker. At ten minutes past four o'clock, after practice had been going on for a few minutes, Nythan would slip into the locker room, find the viser, use his programming magic to delete the recording, and get out. Lara would keep watch on the external door, I'd monitor the door on the track side and keep an eye on Drake.

I watched the brute throughout Script. He couldn't sit still. I caught him looking at Nythan several times, who played it cool for once.

When classes finally ended, a huge line formed at the main exit as the door-locking mechanism switched on and off at random intervals. To top it all off, the vestibule holding the students' precious familiars was malfunctioning. Nythan knew his business.

I met him and Lara just before practice was set to start.

"Has anyone seen or spoken to Alissa?" I asked.

"I have. She denied everything," Nythan told me. "She might even believe that."

"Maybe Daniela imagined all this," Lara suggested.

"She didn't make it up," Nythan said. "Alissa's acting strange. If I had any doubts about what I think happened, I don't anymore. Her memory is messed up."

"What the hell you are talking about? How does any of this make sense?"

"Let's just focus on saving Alissa," Nythan said.

I gritted my teeth. "I owe Alissa, so I'm in. But this is it, do you understand? I know you're part of whatever the hell is going on around here. Havelock won't speak to me. And I want to know the truth about what you people want from me."

Nythan and Lara shared a look. Wariness? It was hard to tell. Lara's eyes had the passion of a bored cat.

"If I don't get an explanation, I'm gone," I told them. "From this place, and from whatever it is you are trying to get out of me."

"I'll make the arrangements, Daniela," Nythan said. "After we've saved Alissa. You've got my word."

He still looked like a boy at a gaming console. But I didn't think he was lying. "Right, then, let's go get Alissa out of this mess."

I stepped out onto the track looking for Drake, but my eyes found Alexander first. I got a stony statue stare from him. I winced and bowed my head. The bigger problem was that Drake wasn't there.

I paced around the edge of the team. Definitely not there. I looked at the clock. Five minutes past four. If Drake was waiting in the locker room when Nythan walked in, the game was up. If he had gone out one of the school side exits, it was even worse. Another minute passed. I watched the locker room door, willing it to spring open. It didn't. My feet were antsy. Should I run out and stop Nythan from going in?

I slid up next to Alexander. He was talking to Anise about ideal hurdle speeds. He knew I was beside him, but kept his attention on his conversation.

"Sorry to interrupt. Can I borrow Alexander for a minute?"

Anise flashed an annoyed look. Mona Lisa craned her long neck towards me.

"What's going on?" Alexander asked.

"Sorry, in private?" I felt the heat on my face. Another minute lost.

Anise had both eyebrows up, looking more than merely annoyed. But Alexander walked away with me.

"You want to play hide-and-go-seek again?"

"I'll explain that. You can hate me later. But please, this is important: Have you seen Drake?"

"Drake? Yes, he was in the locker room." Alexander did a scan of the team. His lips pressed together. "Why isn't he here?"

"You said to stay away from him. You were right." I glanced at the clock again. "Listen, please. I need your help again. I know I don't have a right to ask for it, and there's no reason for you to keep helping me, but...it's for my brother. He—"

Alexander held up a hand. "Tell me. But do it slow enough that I can understand what you are saying."

"Just go into the locker room and get Drake out here. Now. Please."

Questions flashed in Alexander's eyes. He studied my face. He must've seen something he approved of, because he nodded. "Coach will want to see him out here. I'm the captain. I'll tell him."

"Please, hurry." Two minutes left.

Alexander trotted off in the direction of the outer door. My gaze lingered on him until he disappeared inside the locker room. Mona Lisa was watching me now, her long neck peeking above the crowd. I concentrated on keeping my breathing normal—in and out, in and out. Another minute ticked away. Then two. It was ten minutes after four. Nythan would be going in. *Be a little late, Nythan. Listen to the door.*

Anise came up beside me. She looked where I was looking. "What are you up to, Daniela?"

"It's for a friend."

"A noble cause. But integrity often makes sensible people into fools. So be careful who you involve in your messes, please." She walked away.

Coach Nessmier strode onto the track, a mesh bag containing what looked like half a dozen smooth silver balls slung over his shoulder. I looked back towards the locker room just as the door opened. Drake stepped through, Alexander at his back. Air flooded out of my lungs.

"Can I see some hustle, gentlemen?" the coach called over at them. Alexander broke into a jog. Drake hesitated, then did the same.

"Well, since our vaunted computer network is acting like a sprinter with a twisted ankle, we're going to try something different today." Coach pulled out one of the silver balls. "These are propelled by compressed air, random internal settings, no network. Fast and elusive." He rolled one of the spheres onto the track. It went about five feet, then jerked into the air. After several seconds, it jumped to eye-level, switching lanes as it did so. Then it fell to the ground, propelling itself at race-car speed, before skipping back into the air. "Everyone see what they can do?"

There was a murmur of acknowledgment. I had my eyes on Drake. He was looking at the locker room. *Hurry, Nythan.*

"Then let's get going. Same groups as yesterday."

Almost there. Just a bit more time.

Drake kept his gaze fixed on the locker room door as everyone sorted themselves into groups. I felt my heart beating in my chest. He started running back to the door. *No!* Alexander looked at me. The ground between Drake and the door disappeared rapidly. My heart was pounding. *Had Nythan had enough time to wipe the viser?* Unlikely. It had only been a few minutes.

"How about we see if Drake can manage against me?" I called out.

Drake stopped dead, mid-step. The locker room door was no more than ten feet away from him. His head came around, dark eyes locking on me like the scope of a force rifle.

"He might do better chasing a ball than he could in the conditioned fifteen hundred," I added, sealing my own fate.

Silence engulfed the gym. Every eye bored into me. I looked at Alexander, begging forgiveness.

Coach took a single metal sphere from his bag, dropping the rest. The thud echoed in the silence of the giant room. He held up the ball in his hand, high above his head, as if proposing a wedding toast.

"Runners on the line," he ordered.

I jogged to the starting line. Drake snarled as he ran over to me, taking the inside.

"You're going to be sorry, nope. I promise," he hissed more than spoke.

"I like some healthy competition," Coach said. "But I don't care for arrogance. And if you can't back up your arrogance, you're a fool. No space for fools on this team. So if Drake gets the ball first, Ms. Machado, you're off the team. If you win, you're merely arrogant. In that case, you can spend the rest of practice running laps."

I hadn't expected any mercy. Not from Coach Nessmier, not from Drake, not from Alexander. So be it.

Nessmier hurled the sphere down the track directly ahead of us. Drake and I took off, chasing the flashing ball like a couple of stupid, desperate mutts. Drake shoved me two strides off the starting line, before I could get ahead of him. I stumbled as the force of his blow knocked me across my lane into the next one over, but I stayed on my feet. Barely. My shoulder ached. Coach didn't say a word. This wasn't a race. It was a street brawl.

I clenched my teeth and dashed after him. I fixed my gaze on the center of his back. The dancing silver ball was a quarter track length ahead of him. I needed to make up about thirty meters to catch Drake. I reached for the cold inside me. It was right there. I sucked at the raw power like a pig at the trough. I took more than I needed. I wanted the extra juice, just in case.

I came at him from the outside, running flat out with all I had. I stayed just behind him as we took a turn, the elusive sphere taunting us. It flew level with my head, then dropped to the ground. Drake put on a burst to try to snatch it. He thought he could close the gap before I reached him, but the ball skipped towards my lane just as he reached his hand towards it. I made a dash for the shiny thing as it passed in front of me. Drake turned his shoulder towards me again. I knew he would. I stutter-stepped at the last moment, falling a stride behind him just as he moved. He had expected me to be there, and I wasn't. He lost his balance, crossing much faster than he intended. I swept his feet from behind, the hard tip of my running sneaker smacking into his ankles as he switched lanes.

I overtook him as his legs flared and he fought to keep his balance. I heard him call out as I sped past.

"You little bitch."

I ran for the ball soaring above me. I poured on the speed, cold coursing through my veins. I almost had it. Winning the privilege of running laps wasn't a glorious prize, but it was better than getting kicked off the team—which was probably what I deserved. I reached for the sphere. A powerful pulse of air shot out from behind it as my fingers grazed its metal surface. The little thing whipped to the left, rising too high for me to catch even if I jumped. I followed it, waiting for my next opportunity. But by matching the sphere's pace, I was giving Drake a chance to catch up. His heavy steps echoed behind me. There were only seconds left before he reached me. The ball began to drop. I jumped. My hands clawed for it. Its shining surface was half a finger out of reach. Almost there. My spider-sense went crazy. I yanked my hands back and tried to spin. Too late. I felt a heavy hand on my shoulder, then another. A crushing weight loaded itself onto my back. I was like a bird trying to haul a brick. Drake yanked me to the ground. I folded both arms underneath my chest to protect myself as best I could. I smashed into the ground, and Drake smashed into me. A searing pain coursed through my back then spread into my limbs. Tears of pain escaped as I tried to roll him off me, but Drake didn't budge.

I heard the coach's whistle. The pain surged again. Drake was digging an elbow into my back. I tried to jab backwards, but I had no leverage. He was heavy, and strong, and on top of me. More whistles, but the agony kept coming.

"Enough," Alexander yelled.

Drake's elbow stopped gutting me; his weight lifted. I still hurt like hell. I rolled onto my back, my eyes clamped shut as I struggled to get control of the misery racking my body. I called on the cold, needing it this time. I looked down at my body from above, the ice sphere surrounding me, whispering that I should stop feeling pain, that it was just a nerve impulse—an illusion created by my brain as an evolutionary warning system. Just turn it off. The burning cries from inside me faded. I opened my eyes to see Alexander kneeling next to me. Drake was on his feet looming over us both, his teeth bared like a wolf. Anise stood between him and Alexander's unprotected back. The whole team was watching us now. He wouldn't dare do anything more. This was still Tuck, I assured myself.

"Mr. Pillis-Smith, laps now. Along the stands, hugging the edge. Marathon pace. Don't even think about stopping until I tell you," Nessmier ordered.

Drake didn't move. I'm not sure if he heard. He was staring down at me. Raw, animalistic anger radiated off him. If Nythan hadn't wiped the data, Alissa was going down. And that would just be the start.

"The wall or you can find a new team," Coach shouted.

That brought Drake out of it. He turned with the reluctance of a lion abandoning its supper.

"Nurse or the track, Ms. Machado?" Coach asked.

"Track," I told him through gritted teeth. "Just need a minute."

Coach nodded, approving of me for once. "Take five, then get moving. Outer lane of the track, marathon pace, until I say stop."

"Got it, Coach. Be there in five."

That meant I was still on the team. I had gotten Nythan the time he needed, and I was still on the team. Not bad at all.

"Get up, slowly," Alexander urged, his arm wrapped around my waist as I began to lift myself off the ground.

"I'm fine."

"You say you are. You might even feel okay, but we both know you're hurt. You're doing what you do in races."

I looked at him again. How much did he know about me? I wanted to ask him. Yet I didn't dare. Not here, not yet.

"Sit on the bench for a bit. You have still got four minutes. Use them."

He walked to the stands surrounding the track with me. We climbed halfway to the top to keep ourselves clear of Drake's route as he looped around the perimeter. Alexander sat down next to me.

"Thank you, again," I told him. "For everything. And I'm sorry I flaked out on you at lunch. I know this is sounding ridiculous, but I had another emergency."

He was quiet for a few seconds. "Family can be difficult. I understand that. Your life doesn't sound easy."

"It's not. I owe you."

He shook his head. "Debt is a transaction. A thing for business, for people like my father or my sister. Or for strangers. Between friends, there are no debts."

I didn't know what to say to that, so I said nothing.

"We've got less than two minutes before you run off again. Will you answer one question before that, on your honor?"

I wasn't quite sure what he meant by honor. It wasn't a word we used in the barrio. But I knew how to keep my word. For a friend, or whatever we were.

"Ask."

"There is an...event, at my father's house on Saturday. An annual event. Kris organizes it. It is quite something to see, and I must be there." My heart was running faster than my feet ever had. "Would you like to come with me?"

I tried to open my mouth to speak, but it didn't seem to be working. I heard the team running around. Dozens of feet, pounding into the floor. Shout and groans echoed around me as people dove for the silver spheres.

"Let's go, Machado. Break is over. On the track," Coach yelled.

I didn't move. I looked at Alexander.

"Yes."

I made sure he had a smile on his face, then I got up to run my laps.

TWENTY-EIGHT

My back felt like I'd been stabbed, my shoes might as well have been made of concrete and my head throbbed. But somehow none of it mattered. I showered in peace, luxuriating in warm Manhattan water. I hadn't forgotten Nythan's promise. I felt ready for whatever would be revealed. Wrong.

Nythan was waiting for me outside the locker room. He leaned against the wall, examining his fingernails. The pose was too cocky to be genuine. It was either something from one of his old movies, or he was trying too hard. I didn't care which.

I followed him to the stairs. Once we were alone I asked, "You get it?"

He winked at me. "Done and done. Drake will never know."

"He knows, trust me."

Nythan shrugged. "He's got no evidence now. He won't go to the honor council. He wouldn't be able to explain how he saw her. Only an anonymous video drop would've worked. Alissa's in the clear on this one."

"What about your promise?"

Nythan grinned. "I'm here to deliver on that as well. We need to take a short walk. Now."

"What?"

"In light of recent events, Headmaster Havelock has been so kind as to invite us all to his home for a talk. It will afford us a bit more privacy than school property."

"Why there?"

"For the same reason you dragged me onto the roof today. Just follow me down the rabbit hole."

Nythan took off down the stairs, moving with far more spring in his step than I could manage. I limped along behind him. He was tapping his foot anxiously as he waited for me outside the main entrance.

"You have to pee or something?" I asked him.

He frowned. "I thought you'd be more fire and brimstone. All your questions are soon to be answered."

"I've had a long day."

"It hasn't started yet," Nythan assured me as we started to walk.

The sun hadn't set, but clouds as thick as smog clogged the sky. We made our way by street light. Cool blasts of wind whipsawed around buildings, blowing the city's dust into our eyes at random intervals. Nythan's familiar trailed us as we walked. He was humming.

"Is this a game to you?" I asked him. "My brother almost died. He still might. Alissa almost got expelled."

We walked several blocks without speaking after that, the wind gusting around us. I thought I might have offended him. It was hard to tell with Nythan. But as we came to an empty corner, he said, "I know it's not a game. But we've been looking for someone for a while. Time is running out. I think it's you we need. I want to get on with it. You deserve some answers. And I do like to win."

"Then tell me what the hell is going on."

"That's coming. Two more blocks."

We moved faster. Nythan led me onto a street of stately townhomes, their exteriors made of varying types of pristine stone, all a century or more old. Great windows, each taller than me, lined the upper floors, looming out over the street. Wrought iron gates surrounded each residence. The houses ranged in height from three to six stories, mere dwarfs surrounded by the towering modern condominiums further to the east. Several had dark-suited attendants standing out front.

Nythan stopped near the end of the street, in front of a black metal gate. The bars were forged of interconnected tigers. Beyond the gate, steps led up to the arched doorway of a four-story house, its facade made of a whitewashed brick that managed to look both modern and aged at the same time. There was an intercom on the street, but no human security. At least none that I could see.

"This house belongs to Tuck. It's the residence of the headmaster. Perk of the job. Of course, you lose your job, you lose your home."

"So Havelock has been here for what, fifteen years?"

"Thirteen, actually. But that's still quite a while, isn't it?"

Plenty of time to recruit the people he wanted…for whatever it was he was doing.

"What are we waiting for?"

Nythan held out his hands, each balled into a fist. "There's a red pill in my left hand, and a blue pill in my right. Choose the blue pill, and I'll take you inside to learn the secrets of the universe from a man named Morpheus. Red, you go home."

"You eat them."

"Crap, Daniela. It's from *The Matrix*. I've always wanted to do the red pill, blue pill thing." Nythan shook his head and pressed the intercom. "We're here."

The gate buzzed open. Nythan walked through and held it open for me.

"You're the strangest person I know," I told him.

Havelock greeted us at the door. Despite the evening hour and the fact that we were at his home, he still wore the same old fashionable suit and bow tie. He held the door open till we came inside, then shut it behind us. His long, gaunt arms made me feel a bit like I was walking into a spider's den. The click of the door lock echoed louder than it should have.

"Welcome, welcome, my friends. Please leave your shoes and drones at the door," he said. "Then follow me into the study."

Nythan and I walked through the house behind him. Where Alissa's home was sharp angles and stark colors, Havelock's residence reeked of history. The wood-paneled walls could have been lifted from Tuck. The furniture echoed nineteenth-century England. Stiff-backed sofas and chairs, upholstered in red, gray, and black patterns, adorned the living room. The floors were covered with thick rugs that smothered the sound of our footsteps. Antique crystal chandeliers hung from the ceiling. It wasn't a place I cared to sit in, much less live in.

Havelock led us up a creaking spiral staircase with a wooden railing worn as smooth as glass.

"Here we are," he announced as he stepped through a doorway just off the second-floor landing.

Entering Havelock's study was like stepping through a portal into a different world. Three massive floor-to-ceiling panels, each four feet across, dominated one side of the rectangular space. The trio of images depicted a single scene: a snapshot of an undulating verdant hillside, with half an inch separating each panel for aesthetic effect. Men and women with brightly hued bandanas around their heads, woven baskets on their backs, and richly colored skin worked amid the dense greenery, the colors so vibrant that the pictures transported me to that place. A sprawling double-flue fireplace topped by a white marble mantle took up much of the opposite wall. The narrowest section of the rectangular room had two great arching windows that overlooked the street below. In the center of the study was a matching pair of deep couches in chocolate leather. Between them sat a long, silver-legged table with a surface screen. Alissa stood next to one of the windows, still wearing her Tuck uniform, her forehead scrunched with lines of worry. Lara lounged on one of the couches, idly gazing at her viser.

"Please, sit," Havelock offered. "Would you like some tea?"

I stepped tentatively into the room, this nest of nameless disquiet. Nythan bounded onto the couch opposite Lara, easing back with his feet up, as if this was his living room.

"I'll stand for now," I said. "Alissa, are you all right?"

She looked at me, her eyelids heavy. She nodded lamely. "Yes, I'm fine. Thanks to you and Nythan."

"You all acted with determination, intelligence and compassion for each other," Havelock declared, looking in turn at Nythan, Lara, and me. "You are to be commended for your efforts."

"But can you tell me what happened? Alissa, why did you do it?" I asked.

Her face sank towards her feet, before rising again to look at me. "I don't remember it. I believe what Nythan has told me—he even showed me the video you stole from Drake. But I can't believe that was me. I was on the administration floor, yes. I went there to ask Mr. Lynder a question. He wasn't in his office, so I left."

I turned towards Havelock, the man who had brought me to this school. The man who could explain all of this. "How can that be?"

"Are you sure about not wanting any tea?" he asked.

My nostrils flared. "No."

"Ah, well, I'm going to brew a pot. Anyone else?"

Nythan raised his hand in the affirmative. My jaw clenched tighter.

Havelock strolled to a bookshelf in the corner of the room, about three feet from where I was standing. A wave of his hand revealed a sliding panel, behind which was a water dispenser, a blue-and-white porcelain teapot, several cups, and a variety of jars containing dried leaves.

"Please excuse me, as I tell a little personal history while this steeps," Havelock began, his voice rumbling. "You noticed the pictures on my wall, no doubt. Can you take a guess as to where they are from, Daniela?"

The images were beautiful, but they weren't why I was here. "Bronx City."

"Ah, you are impatient. You think I am wasting your time. I am not. I assure you there is relevance. Perhaps you might take one more look."

I looked. "Rwanda."

"Yes, of course. It is of my homeland. More precisely, it's the farm my parents once owned, and where I was born. They sold it to raise money to pay our citizenship fee and come to this country, before any of you were born. A beautiful country, my old home…But do you know what it was like several decades ago?"

"No." I didn't bother to conceal my impatience.

"It was knee deep in blood, as one ethnic group wiped out another. They had fought before, but this time it was to create a final solution. My mother's people killed my father's. Two years of slaughter and ethnic cleansing. Seven million people dead—not that the rest of the world noticed. When it was over, a new Rwanda rose from the fields of slaughter. A country with the veneer of peace upon it, working towards a single purpose. A land that has become the envy of Africa—the most prosperous nation on the continent." Havelock held up a long, crooked finger. "But all of it was built on genocide. Don't forget that. When we're speaking this evening, do not doubt the horrors mankind is capable of committing, or the indifference of your neighbors to such crimes."

The only sounds that followed were those of the headmaster pouring steaming tea from the pot into cups. He placed one on the table in front of Nythan, then seated himself beside Lara, the other cup held delicately between his two hands.

"Daniela, I understand that you and Alissa have come to know each other well?"

"Yes." *Except for her secrets.*

"Knowing her as you do, as we all do, can you think of any reason why she would do something so dishonest as to steal a teacher's examination? Or be so reckless as to allow Drake Pillis-Smith to record her doing so?"

"No."

"Then what can explain what happened today?"

"That's what I'm here to find out—among other things. Start telling me."

"I shall give you what you want." He placed the untouched cup of tea in front of him. "You are an unintended witness to an audacious endeavor, a secret conspiracy to do what was nearly unimaginable. For years, men labored in secret to bring it about. Except that the project failed. Billions of dollars, years of toil—and it didn't work. Or so its progenitors think. But they are wrong. The seemingly impossible has come to fruition. But, until very recently, only a handful of people in this world knew."

"I'm not Nythan. I need to have things explained to me. What the hell is the secret you're keeping from me?"

Havelock's stared at me like a patient teacher. "You already know. You saw it yourself: A highly intelligent girl, whom you know well, took an action that she never otherwise would have contemplated. And she did it merely because someone instructed her to do so."

"So Drake is the key to some secret conspiracy to…What?…Help people cheat at Tuck?"

Lara barked her derision, while Nythan let loose a simultaneous snort of similar sentiment. They didn't improve my mood.

"Mr. Pillis-Smith's actions are an indication that time is running short, and a confirmation of our suspicions," Havelock told me. "He is but a pawn in this game, yet he unintentionally revealed a truth to you that we would otherwise have had a hard time convincing you of—the power of trilling."

"The power of what?"

"Trilling, that's what we call it, but the name does not quite capture the terrible genius of the trait. In nature, many animals trill—that is, make rapid, repetitive noises that aren't speech. The sounds reverberate at different frequencies, which affect the range of the sound, among other things. It can be a signal, a warning, a beacon. But what the designers of the human trill attempted was far more profound. They wanted a sound that would result in communication at the most primal level, one not processed by our brain's auditory cortex, as regular speech is. They wanted to create a form of communication that acts as a direct line to the human mind, unfiltered and unedited by the regions of the frontal lobe that would normally control our actions. When this trilling is combined with the human trait of extreme charisma—the ability to inspire—the overall effect is like an override command that can make people do whatever the triller chooses."

I stood in silence, blinking, breathing, but not much else. I thought about walking out the way I came in. I mulled jumping onto the couch and attempting to put the bottom of my foot to Havelock's throat, or bloodying Nythan's white teeth. I didn't consider accepting what I had heard as the truth.

"I've seen that face before, Daniela," Alissa said, her voice steadier than it had been a few minutes ago. "It's a hard thing to accept. But you saw what trilling can do. As much as I hate Drake, we owe him a debt for his spiteful recklessness. You're too stubborn for words alone to have convinced you."

Nythan brought himself to the edge of the sofa, assuming a rare look of gravity. "It's not such a great leap from what we take as normal, is it? The highborn have been genetically manipulated to be physically and mentally superior to the majority of conventionally conceived people—us pures, or nopes if you prefer; I'm sure that seemed fanciful when it started as a rich man's fad, decades ago. The scientists describe the procedure of birthing a highborn as 'optimization to eliminate undesirable traits or defects,' but it's simply genetic manipulation to bring out the best of the parents' DNA. Is it so great a leap to begin adding traits to the mix?"

"That's illegal," I insisted, knowing I sounded naive. Since when had the law mattered to the rich? To the highborn?

"Ah, yes, the International Treaty on the Sanctity of Human Life," Havelock said. "It outlaws research or procedures that would result in the introduction of non-indigenous genetic material or traits to the human genome. Our country is a founding signatory to the Treaty. President Ryan-Hayes himself quotes it with approval. A nice piece of work, but one totally unpersuasive to the people of whom we speak."

"Of course, the Humanity Tribunal declared that chipped slave zombies are perfectly fine, because that's not an upgrade," Nythan interjected.

"But they developed this…trilling anyway…The highborn, I assume," I said. "That's who did it, right?"

"At least one company tried it," Havelock confirmed. "But it's subtler than that. You see, we refer to the genetically manipulated as 'highborn,' as if they are the same. But there are thousands of birthing clinics offering 'corrective gene therapy' for mothers; what these places are really selling is a branded product, like toothpaste or detergent."

"You mean there are different brands of highborn?" I asked. The notion would've been funny if it wasn't so plausible. Of course, making children was just another business for the corps.

Havelock took a sip of his tea. "Genetic birthing clinics offer one or another of five strands of highly specialized bacterial DNA that, when introduced to an unfertilized human egg or a newly conceived child, result in a reordering of the DNA. The helix is sliced, diced, reordered, and manipulated to get the best possible result—as measured by the AT scale, of course. The proprietary bacterial DNA colonies, known as controlColonies, took decades and countless amounts of research to develop. They are organic things, closely guarded, and are constantly being improved. Every treatment utilized in a birthing clinic was grown from one of those controlColonies. Each company claims their product produces the best offspring, of course. Rose-Hart and Tyrell Ventures are the industry leaders."

"And one company decided to do even better, I suppose." I imagined it all too easily. "Let's not just make people with a high AT. Let's make them all generals, each one a Caesar, a Katniss, a Darrow."

Havelock dipped his head in acknowledgment, looking at me expectantly. I realized they were all looking at me that way.

"And what is that company?" I had already guessed, of course.

"Rose-Hart Industries."

It hurt somewhere inside me, hearing it. It shouldn't have, but it did. "But why does the world need a million generals?"

The hint of a smile crept onto Havelock's lips. I was thinking the way he wanted me to.

Don't trust these people.

"Indeed, why?" Havelock stood, walking over to the window. Drops of rain-water clung to the exterior of the glass. He glanced to the street before turning back to me. "First, I should say, that although our information is not perfect, we speculate that not every highborn would have been given access to that strain of the controlColonies—cycle DN10-191. It wasn't intended as a money-making product. Although I'm sure families would've laid down millions and billions to have it for their children. No, it was developed as a social tool, not an economic one."

I shivered as the words sank in.

"You are from Bronx City, Daniela. You already know what it would've been used for, don't you?"

"To control us," I whispered. "To control the people with lower AT classifications. To control those with less, who dared to want more." To control people like Mateo.

The horror of it gripped me. My skin prickled; my heart pumped cold blood. I imagined the announcement, a voice from a drone, or on the net, telling us how wonderful life was. To be calm. To live in peace. To not pee in the alley, or to scrub behind our ears. Or to eat less. To buy only this brand of soap. Worse than being a chipped slave—maybe.

"Prosperity through order," Havelock told me, sounding pleased. "Luckily for all of us, doing this thing—this audacious, horrible thing—is not easy. As they do with all control-

Colony changes before general use, the new strand was tested in controlled trials. We don't know how many subjects, but we believe it was less than one hundred over a three-year period. In all cases, the desired trait failed to materialize, and there was no trace of its genetic marker in any of the samples taken from the test subjects. Rose-Hart's very expensive gene appeared to have vanished. Eventually, they tired of pouring money into what they thought was a black hole. Our belief is that Rose-Hart abandoned research into trilling several years ago."

"But Drake can trill," I said.

"Welcome to the Planet of the Apes," Nythan declared.

I didn't get the reference, but I got the sentiment.

"Nythan, why piss off a guy who can screw with your mind?" I asked.

Havelock turned sharply towards Nythan. It was the first time I'd seen true emotion in his dark eyes. It reassured me: Havelock didn't know everything. He could be surprised.

"Who'd have thunk it?" Nythan admitted. "We had no idea."

"I don't understand," I said.

Havelock sighed. "Everyone in the world believed DN10-191 was a failure. Except for the one person who developed the ability to trill."

"Kris Foster-Rose-Hart," I reasoned.

Havelock clapped his hands together in a single gesture of compliment. "You continue to exceed even my expectations. How did you know?"

I willed myself not to bite into my lip as my mind raced.
Don't trust these people.

They didn't know about my conversation with Mateo. They didn't know a mysterious girl fitting her description had walked into a safe house and using only words, commandeered both men and equipment to try to kill Landrew Foster-Rose-

Hart. Everyone in this room had secrets. It was best to keep some of my own.

"It had to be a student here—that's how you know about it. Her dad's company developed the technology. And when I first started here, the way she handled Drake, and Mona Lisa Reves-Wyatt was...remarkable. Plus, she has an unnatural charisma. Even on me, she had an effect. People here near worship her, even utter jack-A's like Drake."

"Correct on all accounts," Havelock told me. "I noticed it about four years ago. I keep close tabs on all my students, of course, but Kris's transformation was remarkable. She went from a rich girl with a clique to...something else. An object of admiration, even among the faculty. She's something special. But it wasn't until she tried to use a trill on me that I knew for sure."

"On you?"

Havelock chuckled with memory, but not warmth. "She tried to sway the vote of the honor council to help a few cheaters. Sons of allocators."

"I mentioned them to you on your first day," Alissa added.

"But it didn't work?" I asked.

"Oh it did, after a fashion. I voted to acquit the kids, just as she wanted. But I was outvoted by the rest of the council. Kris thought I had more power than I did. It was an out-of-character action for me, that decision. They were guilty. I based my choice, or so I thought, on the good work their families had done, and would do, for the school. Another uncharacteristic position for me. Over the weeks that followed, my vote continued to nag at me. Then months later, quite out of the nowhere, I remembered a conversation in my office just a day before the honor council hearing that I had previously forgotten. A meeting with Kris Foster-Rose-Hart, where she had made that exact argument to me. I thought it strange that I should have forgotten that meeting. I went on to learn the truth, which I now share with you. After years of covertly observing her, we still don't fully understand how trilling works. We know some people are more resistant than others, and it doesn't work on highborn at all. Kris has become much more cautious over the years—she never uses her power in school anymore. What you and others experience around her is a residue of her charisma and the trilling trait, but not the full power—it's something special Kris has, an aura of charm. Something to do with her unique combination of genes. We don't know exactly. But that's all she shows us. Until today with Drake, we weren't certain she'd revealed her abilities to any other person, even her father."

"Can Alexander trill?" I asked, my voice unsteady.

From the corner of my eye, I saw an uneasy look pass between Alissa and Lara.

"We don't think so, but we cannot be certain," Havelock told me. "It may be he is just cautious. We have limited access to their activities beyond school. That family values their privacy."

I studied Havelock's face, then the faces of Nythan, Alissa, and Lara. Havelock showed me nothing—a master poker player. Alissa was hopeful, Nythan amused, and Lara, skeptical of me, as always. But none of them displayed any doubt about the veracity of this account. There was no surprise in the room, except my own. This was a tale they knew well, and had lived with for long enough for it to be part of them. Yet my spider-sense nagged at me. A low throb, not of immediate peril, but of budding danger.

Finally, I asked the question for which I had to have an answer. I forced myself to stare at Havelock, to look into his dark eyes and face the terrible truth. "Why did you bring me to Tuck?"

Havelock strode away from the windows, towards the wall displaying the memory of his family farm, the emerald hills of plenty built on top of blood-tainted soil. "I brought you in because even though Landrew Foster-Rose-Hart gave up on DN10-191, he never gave up the dream—the nightmare—it was intended to bring about. Prosperity through order…more precisely, the control of one group of people over another. That never went away. Indeed, it is coming closer." Havelock's eyes widened. "He, and those like him, have another way, a more dreadful way for the highborn to be the demigods they feel they are destined to be"—he pounded a fist against the middle picture frame—"genocide."

CHAPTER

TWENTY-NINE

It should have surprised me more than it did. But I grew up in Bronx City. In my world, people lined up for food and water rations, clawing for position like cocks in an arena. Giant machines fired correction pellets into crowds, cowing people with days of chemically induced agony the way wooden rods had once enforced discipline among children. Life was cheap, and people were angry. Once people had nothing left to lose, even emperors trembled. We were the people under the iceberg. The Waste was the answer the highborn sought.

"It is another incredible piece of engineering," Havelock said. "A creation worthy of Eichmann for the modern age. What you call the Waste is a genetic mutation. We don't understand how it is introduced. Perhaps by injection or a specialized virus. Its development began in parallel with DN10-191, but it reached the testing phase several years earlier. Like any good industrialist, Landrew hedged his bets; he recognized trilling might not work. Once introduced into the population the Waste spreads itself by corrupting certain indigenous genes related to stamina and aging. The mutated genes are dormant in most carriers, allowing a large population to spread the trait. I'll bet there are scientists at Rose-Hart who call it merciful: It targets people who possess the specific traits its creators wanted to extinguish. The Culling, they call it."

I fought my nausea. Standing became difficult as my head spun. I sat down, placing myself on the edge of the couch beside Nythan, my head heavy. "What traits?"

"Leadership and charisma, primarily," Havelock told me, his rage now switched off. He sounded like a teacher again. I wanted to hit him. "People are pre-disposed to these things through a complicated series of genes, but those markers have become increasingly well mapped over the years. Other characteristics leading to a high AT, such as intelligence, are similarly targeted, according to Doctor Willis's research."

"They're killing the leadership," I realized, my voice unsteady, my hands trembling with both rage and terror. "People like my brother."

"They want only deltas and gammas to serve," Nythan said.

I turned my head towards him, the strange genius who didn't quite seem to fit into this world. Yet, he seemed to understand it all too well.

"That still doesn't explain why you need me," I said, looking around the room. "You have brilliance around you—people like Dr. Willis and Nythan. Others will take Headmaster Havelock seriously if he speaks out. You are all rich. Why do you need me? Why-am-I-here?"

Havelock placed his hands together. "You are here because we need your help if we are to have any chance of fixing this. A war has been declared upon us, but it is a secret war. Each of us have our reasons for fighting the highborn, but the tools the rest of us have are not enough to win that war. Nythan and Doctor Willis can study the mutation, but they have perilously few samples to work from—only what they could obtain from the handful of people willing to come to Lenox in secret. Their evidence and research is fine for us, but it could be questioned. I could take it public, and perhaps some among the elite might care; maybe even some of the Orderists. But the highborn have far more control over the country and the net than anyone imagines. A more likely scenario is that Dr. Willis would be discovered, her work destroyed, and my voice silenced by thousands of other screams. The uproar among the masses would be suppressed, then the information discredited and forgotten. Meanwhile, the men who would fight—people like your brother—would be dying. The time may come to go public, but not yet. Not until we can undo the damage they have done to people like your brother. We need you to do that."

"You know I'd do anything for Mateo. You knew it before you sent Howards to fetch me out of Bronx City. Those people killed my father, they've made life hell for every person I've ever cared about. Now they want to make the world worse—forever. But what can I do that all of you cannot?"

Havelock gestured to the others in his study. "None of us are highborn. None of us have the trilling gene...except you."

It felt like one of Nythan's jokes. Only he wasn't laughing. None of them were. "Me? I'm from Bronx City. Ain't a drop of highborn in me."

Havelock lifted a brow. "Your mother was a nurse in a maternity ward, was she not? In a hospital, in Manhattan. Where you were born. Not Bronx City. We checked the records."

I was short of breath. "My mother?"

"Mt. Sinai, the hospital where she worked, was a center for the DN10-191 program," Havelock explained. "As a nurse in the maternity ward, she might have noticed any unusual activity. She might have been in a position to procure a treatment for her unborn daughter, perhaps not knowing exactly what it was. Maybe she swapped the dose with an unsuspecting patient, so no one ever knew. It might even be the reason she disappeared one day."

Both of my hands squeezed my knees as I leaned over. It couldn't be true. I didn't want it to be true. I wanted to be me, the daughter of my parents. Not some Frankenstein product of richie science, an experiment that never should have been. It had to be a mistake. Yet, I knew it wasn't. The truth had always been inside me. I just didn't know it. My cold place, my running. What if I could beat the highborn because I was one? Nythan laid a comforting hand on my back.

"Easy, easy," he said. "Being highborn doesn't mean you have to be a total jack-A. Only that you'll *probably* be one."

I croaked out a chuckle. A small fit of coughing followed. The tension in the room eased.

"I can't control anyone," I said when my head stopped spinning. "I couldn't even convince Mateo to go to Lenox so Doc Willis could look at him."

"True," Havelock conceded. "We think the trilling gene is a chameleon—it somehow disguises itself as other genes. It's there, but dormant and hidden, which is why the Rose-Hart scientists thought they'd failed. It has to be triggered. Certain types of brain activity seem to do it. We developed a process that can activate your abilities."

My eyes narrowed in on that angular, patrician face. He said it so casually, as if a mental switch could be flipped. "A process?"

Havelock looked at Nythan, who answered. "It's a combination of chemicals and virtual-reality simulation. The drug stimulates areas of the brain to a degree not replicable in everyday life, except perhaps by the most traumatic of events. The VR program augments and guides the effect." He took a deep breath. "It's not pleasant, but it seems to work."

"You've done it before?"

Nythan nodded, although I saw something in his eyes. A rare flash of doubt.

"Marie-Ann," I hissed.

Another nod.

"But she wasn't highborn either."

Havelock shrugged, a gesture somewhere between indifference and sheepishness. "Her mother was a servant in the house of a prominent highborn family, years ago. A very beautiful woman, Mrs. Rebello, if the images can be believed. Her daughter, Marie-Ann, was also born at Mt. Sinai, the same year as you. The fee was generously paid for by her highborn employer. We can speculate as to the rest. But Marie-Ann had the gene as well. Dr. Willis was able to activate it, although Marie-Ann never learned to fully control her power. She wasn't the person that you are. You'll be stronger. I've seen you on the track. You are a fighter."

"What happened to Marie-Ann, really? Did she jump?"

I heard raindrops striking the window, but nothing else.

"I was on the roof with her," Alissa said into the quiet. "Lara and I."

My back arched. "What happened?"

Alissa looked over at Lara, then back at me. She shook her head. "She was acting…strange. I can't explain it." She dropped her head towards her feet.

"The girl lost it," Lara declared. "Ranting. It started in class, before lunch. Paranoid stuff, about being watched. We managed to get her to the roof before it got out of control. Before she destroyed everything. We tried to talk to her. It didn't work. Alissa pinged for help. But it didn't come fast enough. She took off running. Didn't look back, not a moment of hesitation. Just leaped off the damn roof."

Alissa was still staring at the floor, as if the answer to what had happened was written on her shoes.

"Did your *process* drive her mad, Nythan?" I asked.

"I don't think so," he replied, so mild, so calm. "It happened many weeks later. She was under a lot of stress."

"What you should be asking, Daniela, is did Kris Foster-Rose-Hart get to her?" Lara told me. "Did Kris discover there was another triller, and decide to end any competition."

"Is that what happened?" I challenged.

"No one knows why it happened," Havelock pronounced, calming the storm.

"Weren't there any surveillance drones around?"

"Yes, but you've seen we're not without influence at the Authority," Alissa said. "Recordings disappear. It's hard to see what happened on them anyway, from so far away."

I let out a long breath, as if recovering from a race. "So you want me to take Nythan's magic treatment that might or might not have driven Marie-Ann insane...What about Kris? Why can she can trill? And Drake? I assume you didn't help them acquire the ability."

"We don't know," Nythan said, his lips curled in frustration. "We're pretty sure Kris was first. Something unique must've happened to trigger it. Our guess is that she can use her power to activate it in others, help the trait break out, as we call it. That would explain Drake. As to why she would bestow such power on an oaf like him...she must need him for something. The attempt on her father's life might be unrelated to this. Or it might not. I'm skeptical of coincidence, though."

Why would Kris want her father dead? I didn't know enough to guess. But she might've needed help making that happen. She recruited one group. There might be others.

"Even if I did this, even if I decided to risk my sanity and my life for you to turn me into something..." I struggled for the right words. "You've gone to such lengths. Recruiting me.

This process you've developed. Why do you need someone who can trill so badly?"

"Because we don't just want to stop this genocide—this Culling—we need to be able to cure it," Havelock pronounced. "With the help of a triller, I think we can succeed."

My heart skipped. I was on my feet. "Cure it? How?"

"Inside the bowels of Rose-Hart Industries. Inside their inner sanctum, under the ground, is a place—a secret place. It is where the controlColonies are kept. It is where the trilling research was conducted, and where the Waste was developed. They built it, they can stop it. Inside their internal network, in a file called Project Wool, are the answers we seek."

"Nythan can hack anything. So I get why he is here. What do you need me for?"

"They use a closed network," Nythan said. "Not even hard-lines going in and out. We aren't even sure who works down there."

"And you think I can help you get in? If I can trill?"

"You've seen the Ziggurat from the safe house nearby," Havelock said. "Their Advanced Development Complex is under there. We've got a plan to get in. But even with all the work we've done, security is too tight inside. We need things only a triller can do to have any chance. They've taken precautions against everything else. Only the unimaginable can circumvent their security."

Deuces.

"There is a cure inside that building?"

"The solution is inside," Havelock assured me.

No choice. "What do you need?"

"As Nythan mentioned, we have a plan to enter the complex that we have had in process for a length of time. But there are human guards inside. Few are trusted to guard the controlColonies, but they must be handled. They are protected in ways that only a triller can circumvent," Havelock told me.

"What's the other thing we need?"

"Genetic material. The doors and sensors use retinal scans and fingertip DNA identification. We don't even know who is authorized for access to the ADC. So there is only one person's DNA we can be sure will get us in: Landrew Foster-Rose-Hart himself."

"How do we get that?" I asked. "He was injured."

"We don't know where he is, but it doesn't matter for the DNA. A hair sample will work," Nythan assured me. "Or a toothbrush. Things that will be in his house, on the family floors."

"We don't have much time either," Havelock said. "If Landrew is in a different part of the Ziggurat when we use his DNA for access, an alarm will be triggered. We don't know his schedule. We don't know his true medical condition. But there is one day we know he won't be at work: the night of the Allocators' Ball. It's perfect. But we need the DNA first." He raised a long finger. "We've never been able to get anyone close to the Foster-Rose-Harts. Kris must be able to sense any deception. And their family staff has been with them for generations. They are incorruptible by outsiders. We need a triller to get in there."

"Everything we need is in the Foster-Rose-Hart house? Just sitting around upstairs?"

"Yeah," Nythan said. "We just need to get in somehow. You'll have to trill the servants. But it's risky. First, it is such an unusual request against such loyal people. Just like the mistake Kris made with the headmaster. The more unnatural the action, the harder it will be to persuade someone and make it stick. Worse, if any of the family is inside, you're in trouble. Like Headmaster Havelock said, trilling doesn't work on highborn, at least not the control part. Kris has that strange aura, but even she can't trill a highborn. Landrew didn't want to start a war among his own kind. But there isn't any other way to get the material we need."

I looked down at my hands, thinking about Mateo. He had told me to forget him. I wouldn't. But this wasn't about him anymore. Or not just him. The highborn planned to neuter an entire portion of the population to create a permanent servant class. I thought about Kortilla, her brothers, her family. They were also my family. These highborn wanted to create a world worse than anything I could've imagined before today. Worse than anything even Mateo feared. And no one would know they did it, until it was far too late. It might be too late even now. How many people already had the Waste? A cure was the only way.

If my mother had done what they said, if she had tried to make me something better than normal, it hadn't been so I could live in a luxurious condo off the park, and it certainly hadn't been so I could help make our people into slaves. She wanted me to fight. My anger was cold, powerful. I was ready.

"I have a way into the house," I told everyone.

CHAPTER THIRTY

The meeting ended past ten o'clock. Rain pounded the old house like a room full of schoolchildren with drumsticks. Havelock offered me a car home, or to the subway station. I refused both. I'd had enough of the headmaster's so-called generosity.

"I'll get you to the station with my familiar. It's got an extendable canopy," Nythan suggested.

It was better than the alternative. I walked out the front door, stopping under the awning, without a farewell to my fellow conspirators. A damp chill greeted me outside. I turned up the heat in my skin. We walked into the elements, Nythan's flying machine above us. The engines whined against the gusts of the storm.

The rain, dark and ugly, fell with a relentless fury. But my skin kept me warm and we had the sidewalks to ourselves. Traffic was sparse. If I couldn't take a little rain, I didn't have much chance against the highborn.

Keeping under the protective cover of Nythan's familiar meant walking slower and closer than I would've on a typical evening. My body was numb from all I'd heard tonight. Just walking or talking or doing any mundane thing felt wrong, given what I now knew. I shouldn't be doing anything but trying to fix this: trying to warn people. Fighting. Instead, I was just walking in the rain.

"I should have made the canopy bigger," Nythan observed. If anything Nythan had heard tonight troubled him, he gave no sign of it.

"Why didn't you just tell me?" I asked as we turned the corner. "I would've helped you. Any sane person would've helped you. You didn't need to put me through all this. You didn't need to lie to me."

"We didn't exactly lie—and you weren't ready. We didn't really know you either. Think about it. Would you have believed us? We were just a bunch of richies. Even if Havelock had told you about the Culling, would you have thought such a thing possible if you hadn't spent time among the highborn? Not to mention the trilling. You wouldn't have accepted a place at school if you had got all this that first day. Marie-Ann had been here for years, and she still thought it was a joke when we told her."

"How did you convince her?"

Nythan didn't answer for half of a block. "I'm not sure we did, not until the end. She went through the process of breaking out, but never seemed to quite get it. She could make someone pick a particular food, but that was about the extent of her power. Maybe she never fully believed, even knowing the highborn."

"Do you hate them all? Or just Drake?"

"I'm not sure I even hate Drake, not the way the rest of you do. He's a jack-A, and his dad is capable of great evil. But I don't burn inside the way the rest of you do."

"Then why are you part of this?" I asked. "You're risking a lot. Being on the wrong side of a fight with the Foster-Rose-Harts and the Pillis-Smiths is a dangerous thing, by the standard of your world, at least."

We heard the deep groaning of a large drone engine over
the sounds of the storm. The wind must've been giving it a
hard time. The dark and Nythan's canopy made it hard to see
anything.

"It's your world too. And this 'war,' as Havelock calls it,
makes us alive. We're inside the great machine, seeing the levers
working, shaping the future of humanity. What more could
you want?"

I knew that answer. "Live a quiet life, surrounded by people
who care about me. Plenty to eat, good health."

Nythan laughed, as if I'd made a joke. "Be honest with
yourself. Could you really go back to Bronx City now? To your
public school, to the much smaller world you lived in? All the
while living on borrowed time, while your fate is being shaped
elsewhere? We are not meant for such small things. We are
giants."

"You sound like them," I accused.

"Except that I'm mother nature's very own mutation," He
tapped his head. "No bacteria manufactured what's up here,
girl."

"Or else your parents would've asked for their money back."

I felt his smile, even in the dark. "Not bad, Daniela. Now
tell me, how does a nice girl like you end up being Alexander
Foster-Rose-Hart's date to the grandest Tuck social event of the
year? Do you like that chunk of rock?"

The muscles in my arms twitched. I forced myself to suck
in the damp air rather than let loose the first, rather crude answer which came to mind. "It gets me inside the house."

"Evasive. You said 'yes' to him before you knew anything
about stealing the organic samples we need."

"Why the hell are you concerned if some guy wants to
spend time with me?" I barked, drawing far enough away from
Nythan to get myself soaked. "The reaction of everyone in

that room when I told you...even Havelock...it was like I had Resister-H."

"Relax, relax," he said quickly. "You're getting drenched."

The cool rain water crawled into my hair and leaked onto my face. The drips pooled around my lips. It tasted sweeter than it should have. This was being alive. I didn't need a war for that. I just needed to do what had to be done, then get back to the life I wanted.

"You tell me some things," I said.

"Deal. Come back under the canopy."

I did and we resumed walking. "Could I be sick too?"

"What?"

"The Waste...my brother has it. Does that mean I have it too?"

I could almost hear the gears in Nythan's mind turning, processing. Something tickled my mind, but I was too anxious to hear his answer to give the sensation its due. "I doubt your parents were carriers. Too old. We aren't sure how the Waste was introduced. Maybe at birth, without your mom knowing. And I think DN10-191 would've corrected any mal—"

My spider-sense surged like an electric current. I dove to the ground, grabbing Nythan as I did so.

An explosion ripped through the sky above us: a brilliant flash of fire accompanied by the deafening roar of metal being ripped apart. The air became hot. Searing fire cut into my arm. Fragments fell around me like tiny meteors, sizzling as the rain struck them. I realized the sky above us was clear. Nythan's familiar was gone. Incinerated.

"Run!" I shouted, pulling us both up, and yanking him with me. We were only one avenue away from the subway.

The predator appeared in front of me, a giant hawk forged of black composite alloy, propelled by the spinning blades at its sides. Its gaze was invisible waves of infrared, its talons were projectiles fired by the ominous barrel on its nose. We ran towards it. Its engine continued to grumble as the storm yanked at its wings. My blood was ice, my limbs nimble. I bathed in the power within me. I could've outrun a car at that moment. But Nythan couldn't.

I sensed the hunger of the mechanical beast above. Each time its position shifted, each time its engines groaned with the effort of keeping its fuselage stable, I saw it, I felt it. I had a hand wrapped around Nythan's arm, my fingers locked on him like a metal vise.

"When I say move, you go," I shouted.

There wasn't time for an answer.

A gust of wind rippled through the sky, the breath of angry gods. Trees swayed and the drone veered, its engines not constructed for conditions such as these.

"Now!"

We ran towards the road, into traffic. Floating phantoms of brightness—the headlights of oncoming cars—sped towards us. The drone closed in, its mechanical mind straining for a shot that passed its safety parameters. Not easy in the storm; even harder in the middle of a sea of traffic. Brakes screeched and tires skidded as our presence triggered the vehicles' autonomous safety features. A black U-cab came to a halt two feet from my knees. In Bronx City, Nythan and I would've been plowed, but in Manhattan we'd created a corridor of parked cars up and down the street.

I yanked Nythan around the nearest vehicle, pulling him to the ground. "Under, as far as you can."

We crawled as far beneath the vehicle as we could. The sickening roar above drew closer, then passed over our heads. Its microchip brain wouldn't allow the drone to fire into Manhattan traffic.

"Up, follow me," I said, rolling out from beneath the car. I tried the vehicle door. Locked. A frightened-looking man cowered in the corner. "Run, and stay down."

We dashed down the road between two lanes of halted cars. Horns blared. The sickly-sweet voice of the U-cab lady requested we clear the road. No chance of that. I heard the angry drone behind me.

"Keep going till I say 'down.' But when I say it, you do it."

I took off again, Nythan beside me. We ran to the next lane, then back again. I heard the beast. Straining, wanting, the projectile in its barrel trained on my back, but it wasn't steady enough to fire. The emerald globe of the subway station entrance was ahead, just off the road to my right. That was my finish line. The wind pushed at me, the rain bit into my arms. The machine's hungry growl came, pushing and fighting against the elements.

"Down," I yelled over my shoulder.

"Jack me," I heard Nythan shout as we slid onto the slick roadway.

A slug of death shot past my head, not more than three inches from the base of my skull. I felt a rush of air, the heat of the projectile's passage. The shot that almost ended my life slammed into the asphalt ahead with a single spark and a dull thud. The drone passed above, whining hard, its prey still alive. For now.

"The subway station. Run."

Water flew up around us as we galloped across the street. I leaped over the hood of a fancy sedan, jumping from its surface onto the sidewalk. A screeching car siren bawled at me. Nythan lagged behind, his eyes fixed on the drone preparing for yet another pass.

"Let's go, mutation boy," I called back to him, keeping a close eye on the drone's progress. The subway station steps were less than ten feet from me. I could dive inside if necessary.

Nythan finally cleared the cars, running onto the sidewalk as the dark machine completed its circuit. Its barrel faced us again, a direct shot. I shoved Nythan at the staircase, watching him stumble to safety. I took one step, then jumped as if I was diving into a pool on some Manhattan rooftop. Except there was only concrete below. My spider-sense jolted me and I twisted in mid-flight. The drone's shot whizzed under my belly, buzzing like an angry hornet. My body burned like ice. I luxuriated in the surge of magnificent energy; I had control of every muscle, my balance perfect. Time slowed. I shifted my weight forward, somersaulting as I flew towards the stairs. Only when my feet were back under me and my arms extended for balance did the world return to normal speed. I came down like a gymnast from a triple axel, my knees bending as I stuck the landing.

"Holy hot damn," Nythan exclaimed.

"Inside," I said, pulling him into the safety of the subterranean warren.

"Not bad, not bad," Nythan babbled as we walked towards the deserted platform. He looked like a wet sheepdog. "I hope you still don't have any doubts about your gifts."

"I don't have any doubt that we've gotten the attention of some dangerous people. Are subway stations monitored?"

Nythan looked around. "Video definitely. Probably not audio. It would be illegal. But you never know. We haven't done anything wrong. Nothing to worry about."

"A drone just tried to perforate us."

"It wasn't the Authority. They would have sent officers with a warrant. It was a renegade of some kind."

"So who the hell sent that thing?" I asked.

Nythan tapped his foot on the ground several times. "A corp, I would think. They have drone licenses. You can guess the most likely candidate."

"If Rose-Hart knows, then everything is lost." I shook my head. "But that doesn't make sense. A corp has better ways, more resources. Hired thugs. This was public, sloppy."

"Maybe. They might blame it on the terrorists the Authority has been hunting."

"Or it wasn't a corp. It was a person, someone who only has a few blunt tools…" *Like stolen drones.*

A number four train glided into the station.

"Who?"

I shrugged, not willing to share my knowledge and suspicions.

The doors slid open.

"CHARGES WILL BE INCURRED UPON ENTRY TO THE TRAIN. STAND CLEAR OF THE CLOSING DOORS."

"Looks like you're going to get a chance to see Bronx City," I said, urging Nythan onto the train with a gentle push to the back. "I've got a pill in each of my hands. You're screwed whichever one you pick."

THIRTY-ONE

I called in the troops to meet us at the station. It was approaching midnight by the time our train pulled into Bronx City. Not the best time to be strolling about.

Kortilla was waiting at the exit. Her brothers, Otega and Matias, loitered a few steps away, slapping at a dancing coin projected from their visers. They looked like giant babies trying to hit the mobile above their crib.

I squeezed Kortilla tight; I hoped it was enough to thank her for Mateo, and beg her forgiveness for hurting her after the track meet. "Thank you for meeting us, *hermana*." To Otega and Matias, I called, "*Mis hermanos, qué pasa?*"

The pair sauntered over, arms hanging and swinging. Their clothes were torn, held together with fabricated stitches of faux gold, barrio style. Same for their teeth. Ink and scars—real ones—covered their arms. These two street boys were blood to me, but I understood the chagrin on Nythan's face. They didn't look friendly.

I hugged them both, one with each arm. It was good to be among those who wanted nothing from me. I felt far safer on these mean streets in the dead of night than I did any place in Manhattan.

Matias leered at Nythan, shoulders jerking in a barrio challenge. He spoke Barriola. "*Nani blancmeutro, Dee?*" Who is the white corpse?

Nythan took a step back, then another, his face contorted in indignation and horror. I slid myself between those two, each of them a prince in their own world, both lost in the other's domain.

"This is Nythan, he's my friend from school. My new school. He's here to help me."

Otega came up beside his larger, older brother. Together, the Gonzales kids had the width of four or five Nythan Royces.

"What can dis' skinny little cake kid do 'fer you, Dee? He's practically peeing his pants."

"Enough, Matias," I said.

But he wasn't ready to quit. It wasn't every day he got a real, live richie to play with. Matias threw a shadow punch. It was slow, soft, and deliberately short of its mark. Nythan still flinched. Another jab flew, this one closer.

Nythan's face hardened, his lips grew taut. "Quit trying to hit me and hit me," he said in a voice that wasn't quite his own.

Matias froze mid-punch. His eyes bore into Nythan. "Say it again."

"Come on, Neo. Quit trying to hit me and just hit me," Nythan repeated in the same off tone.

Matias's jaw dropped. "Jack-A, you seen *The Matrix*? No way. That flick is older than my mama," He dropped his fist and did a little circle dance. "Okay, skin on skin, corpse-man." He held up a fist for Nythan to tap.

I started to explain it. "You're supposed to—"

Nythan got it. He was a quick study, whatever the subject.

"Lame-ism spans race, income, and city boundaries," Kortilla muttered. "Let's get going."

Matias walked beside Nythan. "What else you seen, corpse-man?"

Nythan was talking to him, but his eyes and mind were elsewhere. Initially, he watched Kortilla. But after a block or so, he focused on what was around him: hulks of buildings, fabricated box homes, the hum of fuel-powered generators, the stink of trash, men, and desperation. Nythan held his hand over his face as we passed a lurker alley. Matias motioned Nythan excitedly toward the dark, foul-smelling passage.

"It's like friggin' *Alien*—after the babies hatch. You never seen nothin' like it. I swear, corpse-man, I've seen things you people wouldn't believe...attack ships on fire off the shoulder of Orion..."

Nythan shook his head. I pinged Aba that I'd be at Kortilla's tonight. No way I was taking Nythan home.

Even without seeing his face, I felt Nythan's disgust as we walked up the squatter-infested stairs to Kortilla's place. He looked like a man rescued from a week stranded at sea by the time we got to Kortilla's living room. I glanced at my viser to find a text ping from Nythan. He must've flicked it out on the way over.

"IF YOU TELL HER ABOUT TONIGHT, YOU ARE PUTTING HER IN DANGER."

Kortilla's mom popped out of her room when we entered, even though we'd tried to be quiet. She looked Nythan up and down.

"Ay, just bones on that one," she commented on the way to the kitchen.

Mrs. Gonzales put a big bowl of rice and black beans, with bits of spicy chorizo mixed in, on the table for us. She planted a kiss on the top of my head before trudging back to her room.

I didn't realize I was starving till I saw food. Nythan took a seat beside me. He had to be as hungry as I was. He took the food like a person not wanting to offend, but not wanting to eat it either. He chewed as if tasting something foreign.

"You don't like my mama's cooking, Nythan?" Kortilla asked, part in challenge, part in surprise.

"No, no, it's not that," Nythan said hastily. "It is rather tasty—just different."

"Fabricated," I said. "You get used to it. Especially if that's all there is."

"Better than anything manufactured in Manhattan. Better than some grown stuff I've had."

Kortilla patted him on the shoulder as she walked away. "Good boy."

"I should get a U-cab home," Nythan said once we were alone. "It's probably safe now."

I looked at my viser's newsfeed, scanning headlines. I frowned. "They're calling this a drone malfunction during storm conditions. A U-cab booking is direct from your personal credit account. You could be tracked."

"That's true any time," Nythan pointed out.

"A U-cab in the middle of the night is making it easy for them. But it's up to you, Nythan. I'm not your keeper."

Kortilla came out of her room holding a thick blanket and a pillow. She thumped them down on the floor. Otega was already asleep on the couch. "Bed's ready, Nythan."

"Guess I'll stay," he said, and went back to his food.

I took another bite. As I chewed, I studied him. Nythan was absorbed in whatever was flashing on his viser. He shoveled the rice in with his free hand.

"Nythan?"

"Yeah?" He didn't look up.

"You said earlier that you didn't hate the highborn the way the rest of us do."

Now he looked at me. "I did."

"What about the rest? Alissa and Lara?"

Nythan put his fork down and wiped his mouth with his napkin. He let go of a heavy sigh. "Alissa had an older sister. Until the red bus attack."

"She was killed in the attacks?"

Nythan shook his head. "One of the suicide bombers. Someone got to her, maybe gave her something. I don't know."

I was silent. "I mentioned at her house that the attack might have been staged by the Orderists. She stared a spear into my heart."

"She knows it was staged—to provoke sympathy, outrage. To garner the votes they needed. But if *your* sister rammed a car into a bus full of kids…"

"And Lara? She's always had an issue with me. Her family's rich, and she wasn't even born in this country. She nearly cut out Alissa's heart when she mentioned slaves. Why would she be involved? She doesn't seem to care about anyone."

"Nobody does hate like Lara. I don't know exactly what happened to her. Something in Korea. Her family lost some kind of power struggle in the Corporate Council. I've been over at her house a few times, but neither of her parents speak a word of English. They are hardcore intensive types. Might be where Lara gets it from. She may not love you, but I don't doubt her hate for highborn, and most especially for corps. And she's got a special place in her black heart for your boy Alexander and his sister. If there's a chance to go after Rose-Hart Industries, you can count on her."

"And Havelock?"

Nythan shrugged. "He started all this, brought us together. But he doesn't show us any more of the game board than he has to. He's been headmaster a long time. He's seen what the world is becoming. Maybe it's got something to do with what happened in Rwanda. Or maybe he's doing what he thinks is right because he doesn't want to see any more slaughter."

I blew a snort of skepticism.

"You don't agree? After all, he got you to where you are."

"To serve his own ends. I don't believe in altruism. I believe in blood. I trust the people in this house. No one else."

"Including me?"

"Can I trust you?"

He blinked. "Yes."

"Then tell me the truth. This process of yours…breaking out, as you call it. Is it safe?"

"I believe so, Daniela. You have my word on that. But the only person I've used it on is dead. Keep that in mind. I'm brilliant, but not perfect."

"Great."

I got up to leave.

"Remember what I said about Kortilla. It's too risky for us, and her."

"I got your message, Nythan. You're probably correct. But Kortilla's my sister, my family. The other half of me. And you can't protect someone by keeping secrets from them. You should think about that."

I left him alone.

CHAPTER THIRTY-TWO

N ythan and I rode the subway to Manhattan in silence. We rubbed shoulders with the serving class, the men and women that cleaned Manhattan homes, waited tables, tended to privileged children, and cooked field-grown food that they could never afford for their own families.

"Relieved to be home?" I asked as we walked past the still-dark shops on Madison Avenue. I kept a careful watch on the sky. "It must feel strange walking around without a tin pot over your head."

"I've got extra tin pots at home. And I'm glad to be back, but grateful to get a chance to see your world from the inside, if briefly."

"Why?"

"Because no new experience is bad. But more because it's comforting to know that you are surrounded by people who have your back. You're lucky." He sounded lonely as he said it.

Nythan led me into the warrens of Tuck, down a staircase I hadn't noticed before, onto a sub-level below the gym. I recognized the passage that I had walked with Havelock on the day of my tour. We traversed the underground passage to the Lenox Life Center, then entered the same elevator that I had ridden with Havelock.

Nythan took me to a different floor. We stepped off the lift
onto an octagon-shaped lobby area, a circular desk at its center. Corridors branched off in five directions. The milky void
of the walls was interrupted by a single pink stripe circling the
room at chest level and five ruby-red signs that indicated the
lab numbers to be found down each hallway. A stern-faced lady nearly as old as Aba, clad in a uniform that matched the
walls' paleness, sat behind the counter.

"The usual lab for me, Ilsa," Nythan said as we approached.

The attendant's face didn't warm. She wore a deep red lipstick that highlighted her age. "Early today, Nythan."

"I've got a couple of things to finish up." He passed his viser
over an obsidian square on the desk then turned to go.

"You know the rules, Nythan. Need to scan your visitor too.
Don't think I've seen her before."

"She's a Tuck student also. Special lab observation," Nythan
explained. "Doctor Willis arranged it."

"Scan, please," she said to me.

I waved my viser over the scanning square, expecting some
kind of alarm. But the machine kept quiet.

"Machado?" the lady asked, not hiding her surprise as she
reviewed my data.

I gave her a tight smile. "They ran out of lab rats. Had to
settle for me."

Nythan grabbed my arm and pulled me down one of the
hallways. Each laboratory was a glass rectangle. A few had tinted panels on the outside that concealed the interior. The rest
were slumbering rooms of gentle darkness filled with terminals, scopes, fabricators, and sinister-looking machines of unknown purpose. Only one of the labs was lit. Nythan led me
inside, flicking a privacy control as the door shut behind us.
The glass walls turned opaque.

Dr. Willis sat on a high, twirling stool, surrounded on three sides by floor-to-ceiling screens displaying data and images in an array of colors. Expensive looking silver plated equipment lined the walls. I recognized a cell analyzer and a fabricator—the biggest one I'd ever seen. A padded lounge-style chair, upholstered in maroon leather, sat just off the center of the room. Scanning machines dangled overhead. An array of ominous-looking instruments waited on a tray table next to the chair.

"Welcome to my second period classroom," Nythan told me. "The room has countermeasures, good ones. Lenox thinks we're working on artificial skin. You can speak freely so long as the door is shut."

"Does that thing have restraints?" I asked, pointing at the chair.

Doc Willis rolled her seat away from the cave of screens around her and came toward me. "Why don't you sit on one of these stools so we can talk for a bit. Nythan has a fine mind, but what comes out of his mouth can use a bit of polish."

I forced myself to sit on one of the wheeled seats. The lab was cold, even with my skin's temperature controls set higher than normal. Dr. Willis wore a long lab coat with her name above a pocket. She looked much more doctorly in the uniform, but no friendlier.

"First, Daniela, you can relax. Even if you agree to let us proceed, the only thing we are going to do today is run scans and tests."

I didn't relax at all. "What are the scanning and testing for, exactly?"

"Two very different things. Most of what we need to do is get you ready for the break-out process. To do that, we need to get to know you better, your biology and DNA. We need to verify the presence of the DN10-191 gene, as well as several associated genes that we believe enable its functioning. We need a scan of your brain, so we can see how its regions re-act to different stimuli. I'll also give you a medical check-up, to screen for any health issues that could make the breaking out…problematic."

"How long does all that take? I've got Lit in an hour and a half."

Doc flashed one of her cold doctor smiles. "An hour at most. It's crunching the data and running the tests that take time. Then we need to modify the breaking out sequence based on that information."

"When will you be ready for me to…break-out?"

"A week, if we're working around the clock. Then several more weeks to make sure it's been effective. After that, we are in the area of the unknown. We don't know how quickly you'll be able to use the ability, or how."

I looked over at Nythan, uncertain. "The event, with Alexander, is on Saturday. And the Allocators' Ball is the fol-lowing weekend. Even if we miss that, after last night, we don't have months. I'm not sure Mateo has months."

"Doctor Willis doesn't know you the way I do," Nythan said. "All we have to go on is Marie-Ann's progress. I suspect you'll be in a different league. Headmaster Havelock agrees. You'll be ready in two weeks. We'll never get a better op-portunity to get someone into Landrew's house. As for your date with the younger Mr. Fart, we've got a more mundane solution."

My teeth clenched. "What mundane solution?"

"While you'll have access to the house's lower levels and common areas for the party, my best guess is that the family levels will be guarded by additional security, including restrict-ed access doors," Dr. Willis told me. "We'll get you blueprints, or something close."

"How do I get up there?"

"If I were you, I'd get your date to take you," Dr. Willis told me stone-faced.

My back straightened. "Ask for the tour? Or am I a U-date now?"

"I would think a whisper in his ear would get the boy to take you someplace quiet. After that, Nythan's cooked up a little something to help you."

Nythan wore a sloppy grin. "We're going to give you a fake tooth. We just need to take some scans and imprints. Just like Leto Atreides from *Dune*. Hopefully, this turns out better. Anyway, you bite down on the tooth, then exhale, or plant a juicy smooch on Alexander Fart's lips, and he'll be out cold, giving you the run of the place."

"Won't there be weapon scanners there? Especially after the attempt on Landrew's life?"

Nythan's self-satisfied smile widened. "That's the genius of it. They scan for metal and energy. This is going to be solidified clorodrine encased in an enamel shell. You break the shell, the solid inside reacts to the air in your mouth and converts to gas, but slowly. It'll feel like something lighter than water for just a few moments. With a strong exhale, you should be able to blow it out without catching any of the effect. We'll give you a counter-stim before the party, just in case."

"What happens when Alexander wakes up?"

Nythan shrugged. "Maybe a headache. The chemical causes disorientation. He might be upset or suspicious. Or you can tell him he had a great time. Whatever. We'll have what we need."

I frowned.

"You're worried about no second date?" Nythan asked, annoyed. "His family is killing and enslaving millions. You'll get over it."

Nythan was right, but that didn't make me feel any better about this. I didn't know that Alexander was involved. I didn't believe that he was.

"What about Kris? If she had something to do with the drone attack yesterday, going to her house isn't exactly wise."

Nythan waved away that concern. "She'd never do anything to spoil her party. Particularly if you're her brother's date. Probably the safest place you could be. If it even was Kris, which we don't know. I'd bet on Drake myself."

"Who else will be upstairs?"

"Landrew is separated from his wife. He has various mistresses, but they aren't going to be around during Kris's big gala. It's only Landrew that's a potential issue," Dr. Willis told me.

"What do you mean?"

Dr. Willis rubbed her hands together. "Since the attack, he's been even more secretive about his whereabouts. We don't know the extent of his injuries. He might be in the private wing of some hospital. Or recovering in one of their other homes. Or it's possible he's got his own set-up in the house. In which case, there would be nurses or doctors as well."

"Great."

"Tell them Alexander sent you for something," Nythan suggested. "You're smart. You'll find a way, Daniela."

Time was ticking away. I would rather be in Lit class than here.

"Let's get started."

THIRTY-THREE

I made my way back to Tuck on my own. Nythan walked me to the elevator, and I found my way from there. Their scans hadn't hurt, but I still felt ill as I traveled down the strangely beautiful underground passage back to school. I didn't like the idea of two strangers knowing more about me than I did. I didn't like the sound of Nythan's breaking-out process. And I didn't like betraying Alexander. Not necessarily in that order.

I thought about Nythan. He'd almost died yesterday. This morning, he was as giddy as a boy in a toy shop. He didn't care if he was late to class; I doubted he cared about Tuck at all anymore. He was focused on the game he was playing. Maybe that was all this was to him, despite his claim otherwise. I didn't know what I wanted; to do everything I could to cure the Waste and save Mateo, of course. But preventing this Culling should've been burning inside me like an inferno. This was for my family, my people. Yet a part of me hesitated.

I caught a wisp of a familiar voice as I galloped up the stairs to class. It might have been my imagination—he'd been on my mind. Then I heard it again and I knew it was him. It came from the track level. I had just enough time to indulge my curiosity. I wanted to know if I'd see something different in Alexander, knowing what I now knew.

He was in the hallway, just off the staircase, dressed in his Tuck skin, his hair wet. Opposite him was the swan-like form of his elder sister. I had barely peeked around the corner, but she filled my vision like an oncoming train. Even just standing as she was, I could feel her presence. It was hard to peel my eyes away. I imagined her walking into a dingy warehouse on the fringe of Manhattan, appearing like a prophet risen anew, and taking what she desired by sheer force of will. It was a fanciful story—to someone who hadn't met Kristolan.

"That is not who I am. If you knew everything, you would understand. Have faith in me, Alexander…" she was saying, her voice far colder than the silken tone to which I was accustomed.

I ducked back. I didn't think she saw me. But she sensed me the way I sensed others, the way something inside warned me of imminent danger. We were alike, she and I. Both of us highborn—DN10-191 highborn.

"You'd better get to class," I heard her say to Alexander, but I had the feeling she was speaking to me as well.

I hurried to the stairs, taking pains to keep my steps quiet. I got to my seat a minute before Alexander arrived.

"Good run?" I asked when he sat down.

His mouth opened slightly, before running a hand through the damp lion's mane on top of his head. His face relaxed. "I had a lot to think about. Speed helps."

"I know what you mean. Growing up, it was the only thing that could get the world to stop." I thought about the contradiction in my words. "I guess that sounds strange."

"No, it doesn't. I get it, Daniela." His mouth twitched, but nothing more came out.

"Ready for the test?"

"We don't need to worry, as long as we know the materials. The analysis won't be a problem," said the arrogant Alexander.

He must've noticed my lips turn down. "It's okay to believe in yourself, Daniela."

"I prefer to come up from behind at the finish."

Mr. Lynder waltzed into the room. Conversation stopped. He held the battered notebook. My eyes fixed on it. I wondered where Drake was right now, what he was thinking—if he had been involved in the drone attack. I stole a glance at Alexander as Mr. Lynder lectured on some point about dramatic prose. The worst part of all this was I had no idea who my friends were.

After class Alexander caught up to me in the hall.

"Daniela, do you have a minute?" he asked, coming up from behind me. "I wanted to talk to you about Saturday."

I froze. *He's changed his mind.* I couldn't decide if the prospect made me feel elated or disappointed. We needed that DNA. But I dreaded doing what I needed to do to get it.

"I'd like to come and pick you up for the party, with your permission, of course."

I missed a breath. "You want to come to Bronx City?"

Alexander shrugged. "I want to come to wherever you are. If you're in Bronx City, I'll go there."

For a fleeting moment, I imagined Alexander explaining to Aba who he was, or shadow boxing with Kortilla's brothers. I'd never hear the end of it. He'd probably arrive with security.

"I'll be at Alissa's, actually. The logistics are a lot easier. I'll ping you the details. Is that okay?"

I watched him for any sign of relief, but he didn't show me any. "Of course."

I brushed Alexander's arm with a gentle hand as I left to go to my next class. He didn't feel like one of the bad guys. But he had been genetically engineered to be attractive, to be someone others would trust and follow. He might even be able to trill. I couldn't be sure what was real where he was concerned. In any case, I was going to drug him this weekend, then I was going to break into his father's company and steal their precious secrets. That was bigger than anything else. Whether Alexander was playing a game with me or not, it was going to end the same way between us: badly.

———✦✦✦———

The remainder of the week was perhaps the strangest I'd had at Tuck, perhaps the strangest of my life. I spent part of each evening reviewing the schematics of the Foster-Rose-Harts' massive city residence with Nythan, then the rest of the night cramming for Lynder's exam by myself, because Alissa had the answers somewhere in her subconscious and I didn't want any hint of them. Administration made me fork over a painful portion of my academic stipend for a replacement digiBook, but I devoted hours to selecting an evening dress from Alissa's extensive collection that had cost her parents a hundred times as much. All so I had something presentable to wear to a party that I was going to so I could steal a toothbrush. Ms. Gonzales did the dress alterations, even though Kortilla told me I shouldn't be going. I ran alongside Alexander at practice every day, enjoying it far too much given what I had to do. I thought about Mateo, but made no effort to find him. I didn't have anything to offer him yet.

When the day of Lynder's infamous test arrived, I was ready. Alexander's words had been conceited but prophetic. I knew the materials, so the analysis wasn't a problem. I actually enjoyed writing the essay. Lynder's questions challenged me to think, to make arguments and support them. In the end, he asked us about outsiders, a theme that bound together many of the disparate characters of Shelley, Huxley, and Vonnegut. I finished flicking out my essay before anyone else in the class.

I wrote that outsiders were often lonely, but they needed to be to change the world around them. And they understood loyalty far better than those blessed by the embrace of society.

I came into Manhattan just after lunch on Saturday so Dr. Willis could install my new tooth in her lab. She made me eat two protein bars before she did it. I wouldn't be eating again until this was over. The procedure was quick, but not quite as painless as the doctor promised. The tooth felt strange in my mouth—too long and too large, compared to my other teeth.

"Be careful what you put in your mouth," she told me. "Remember to give a strong exhale after you bite down."

I got to Alissa's place a little after three in the afternoon. Lara and Nythan were already there. By the look of the empty pizza boxes, they'd been there for a while. They had paper architectural blueprints of the house that I hadn't seen before, as well as some maps and drawings, spread out across Alissa's bedroom. Her parents were both at work. Apparently, that was normal for families in Manhattan on a Saturday.

"What are those?" I pointed at the strange depictions sprawled over Alissa's bed.

Nythan answered. "Those are Plan B, my dear."

"There's a Plan B?"

"Not really a plan. It's more like a contingency plan to get you out if something goes wrong."

"I'm glad to hear that. How are you going to get me out?"

"He's not going to be able to, so don't screw up," Lara said.

Nythan cleared his throat with customary drama. "Look, Daniela. If things go to hell, send me a red ping with the word 'invalid' in it. It's true we can't exactly come in and face off with their frontline security and drones, but we can provide some help. For example, I've got two more of my flying familiars ready, directional EMPs included. We can cut the power, take down most of their security, and warp the brains of near-by drones."

"But I'm still on my own inside," I observed.

Nythan and Alissa exchanged looks.

"There is someone nearby," Alissa offered, reluctant. "Someone you haven't met yet—Dillion. He's not inside the house, but close enough to do something. Especially if the power is off."

"How many of you are there?"

Nythan shrugged. "No idea. We all know each other because we're at Tuck, and we work together. Only Havelock knows the rest, and maybe not even him. If you're taken, the less you know the better."

"What happens if they do arrest me? I know about Have-lock, about you…The Authority has drugs, they can make anyone talk."

"Don't get caught," Lara said. "We're taking a huge risk. You can't even trill. This whole thing has been rushed. It's sloppy."

"We won't get a better chance at this," Nythan declared. "Trilling doesn't work on highborn. This is way better. It's coming together right when we need it. Our path into the Zig-gurat will be lost in weeks, triller or not. We have to go now. It's destiny. Daniela can do it, can't you?"

"I'll get you what you need."

"You'd better," Lara cautioned.

I met the challenge in her eyes with a stare of my own. Her anger reminded me of Drake, just more controlled. "If I fail, is Havelock's man to rescue me, or silence me?"

Alissa near shouted. "Rescue you! Daniela, we're on the same side."

"I wonder if someone told that to Chris-Chris."

"Who?" Alissa asked.

"No one you know," I said, relieved at her question.

"We leave no man or woman behind," Nythan declared. "I didn't go through all this to abandon you, Daniela. You're going to get it, and get out. It shall be our greatest moment. Do you believe me?"

I searched Nythan's face. I saw no deception in him. "Yes."

Nythan smiled. "Excellent. I'll leave you gals to get ready for the big date. I've got some other arrangements to work on. Remember, Daniela, ping me if it falls apart. We'll do what we can—I promise."

THIRTY-THREE

Alexander arrived at precisely eight o'clock.

He stood at Alissa's doorway in a midnight shaded tailcoat cut to the exact proportions of his body and a pleated shirt of starched whiteness with a high collar wrapped by a wide cravat the same gold color as his hair. His eyes burned like twin stars. His feet were clad in low-rise boots of faded platinum, his black trousers reaching just above the tops of his ankles. He looked like a creature of legend. Damn.

I stepped into the hall on unsteady legs. My gown had originally been a soft chrome silk, spun by specially engineered worms in Shanghai. Ms. Gonzales had tailored it for my taller, lankier frame by adding a section of stretched cotton fibers dipped in fabricated silver glitter. It was the most beautiful thing I'd ever worn, but still Frankenstein-esque: a blend of Bronx City ingenuity and Manhattan wealth. It was a rag compared to the elegance beside me.

"That is an amazing dress. I've never seen anything like it," Alexander told me. He bowed his head. "I should have expected no less from you."

Alissa snapped a picture from her viser even though I'd specifically asked her not to. She wore a great smile on her face. The hypocrisy of it was lost in the moment. I was glad when the lift doors closed behind us. We rode down in an uneasy silence. I tried to ignore the weaponized tooth in my mouth, without much success.

"Is it okay if we walk?" Alexander asked. "It's a rather pleasant night, and not very far."

I filled my lungs with the cool evening air. "I'd like that."

The sky was vast. The glow of the city made all but the brightest stars invisible, but the black dome above us was no less magnificent for it. Alexander's familiar trailed behind us like a flying metal dog.

"Thank you for agreeing to come with me," he said.

"I'm surprised you asked me."

We walked half a block before he answered. A soft breeze pushed us along, making our steps light and easy.

"I misjudged you when we first met. Not just you, but especially you. You reminded me of lessons I learned as I child…about looking within a person. And within myself. You certainly shouldn't be surprised I asked you."

"I'm not sure I understand. Why did you ask me, exactly?"

"Many reasons. But one is that you didn't want to come."

"Good plan."

The street lights let me see the amused grin on his face. "Let me try to explain, if I can. I'm not as good with words as you are, and wary of giving offense." He took another half a block to muster his thoughts. "Among the families I grew up with, and within my own, there is always the game. This competition to be more, have more, to seek position, status. I grew up living it. My father is a master of game, my sister…she is beyond that. In such a world, it is easy to forget there is another way." I saw the moon in his irises. "It has been a very long time since I met someone who wanted nothing from me."

I chewed on his words and my lip, focusing on what he omitted. "You mentioned your father and sister. What about your mother?"

"She was like you, I think. A mother first, a player of the game second. She is the one who taught me to try to be better, you might say. To have a purpose."

"Where is she now?"

"Gone," he said in a voice that said "ask no more." I didn't.

"I'm just a girl from across the river. You put too much faith in me." I had meant it to come out in jest, but my voice caught on something harder as I spoke. My tongue touched the hanging tooth in my mouth. I did want something.

"You're more than that, and we both know it."

Just how much do you know?

We were getting close to the Foster-Rose-Hart residence. I could see the drones hovering over the street from two blocks away.

"In my world, among the highborn, it can be easy..." Alexander's eyes became distant. "It can be easy to think you only need to look down. Even for me." He grimaced. "A mistake."

In that moment, under that sky, I could imagine a world better than the one we lived in. But my life had taught me a crueler wisdom. We turned the corner back to reality.

Twin lines of sedans stretched from one end of the block to the other. Giant lights, projected from a pair of dark winged drones overhead, cast a pallid glow over the complex at the center of the street. I could only see the spike-topped gate and a portion of the front lawn from where we stood. Private security clad in black suits with spiraling rose pins on their lapels scanned our visers as we walked onto the street.

"Very sorry, sir, I didn't recognize you in the dark. Welcome back," said the one that inspected Alexander, giving a slight bow as he waved us through. I wasn't quite sure what to make of the furtive stare he gave me when Alexander wasn't looking.

As we drew closer to the house I realized it was more of an estate than a typical Manhattan townhouse. The pictures failed to capture the reality of the place. The structure sat on a lot that would've been sufficient for four luxurious Manhattan residences. It stretched back so far that it reached the block behind it. The property was surrounded by an ornate metal gate on all sides, with high hedges and a trimmed green lawn between the house and the perimeter—an unimaginable luxury, even among the wealthy of Manhattan. The house itself was a garish thing, the entryway dominated by four great stone pillars forged in a modernist Greek style. A circular driveway led up to the front door from the street. A glass dome protruded from the house's fifth-story rooftop like a giant cye staring upwards. The folded wings of a V-copter leaned out from a landing pad on the far side of the roof.

"It's not much, but it's home," I muttered, not sure if I wanted Alexander to hear me or not. He did.

"It's all part of the game. It says: 'We have a lot to offer. Join us. Stay loyal. Or we have the power to crush you.'"

At the main gate leading to the driveway, twin pillars no wider than a flag pole projected beams of red and blue light at each other, creating a glowing curtain about four feet wide. A pair of Rose-Hart security minders scanned visers and requested that people pass through the detectors single file. Guests recognized Alexander as we drew close. The first couple greeted him with head bows, each nod slightly lower than the one Alexander returned. The boy looked vaguely familiar from school, although it was hard to tell amid his costume of glittering eye shadow and metal-beaded hair. His date was even more elaborately attired, in a gown of shifting colors, a tiara lodged in her silvery hair. Her neck was surrounded by a chain of rubies that appeared to grow from her skin. They might be students, but I felt a million miles from Tuck. The rules of conduct were different here.

"This is Daniela Machado," Alexander said to the couple by way of introduction. The chameleon dress girl eyed me like a wary mother. Her eyebrows hiked up her forehead at the pronouncement of my name. "Daniela, this is Trish Steam-Harris and Davis Palm-Giffords."

Head nods were offered—the latter considerably shallower than what Alexander had procured. I returned the gesture, uncomfortable and awkward.

Word of Alexander's location spread like a virus, drawing an overdressed swarm to us. I didn't bother trying to remember the litany of names offered. Their looks of disdain upon meeting me lingered longer. My mouth hurt from attempting fake smiles, so I stopped trying. These people—all of them highborn, and in the worst way, reminded me of why I was here. These were the people who made the Culling. If not them personally, then their families and the beliefs their world fostered. I wrapped my arm around Alexander's, nudging him steadily towards the door scanner. Not that I expected a respite from the aristocratic niceties inside. I just wanted to make some progress on my mission.

We reached the security station. I passed through the scanning tunnel first, forcing a nonchalance into my step that I didn't feel. There was a brilliant light, but no pain. No tingling. No alarm. Nythan was cocky, but for good reason. I hoped the rest of his plan would go as smoothly.

Alexander and I walked towards the house with our hands joined, joining a small procession of young couples draped in clothes and jewels. I gazed up at the sprawling mansion. The uppermost floors appeared dark.

"Isn't this disturbing your father?" I asked, trying to sound as if I was being polite, rather than a lying spy. A wince of annoyance flashed on Alexander's face.

"He is recovering in the HRZ. He's too tough to kill with a mere missile." Alexander's voice was not quite his own when he spoke about his father—something bitter hovered at its edge. "Only the neighbors are disturbed, and we pay them an honorarium for the inconvenience."

"Sorry, HRZ?"

"Hamptons Restricted Zone. Safe and quiet out there. No visitors, lots of security." Someone up ahead called out Alexander's name; he offered a regal-ish wave back.

"Restricted means no nopes allowed?"

"Of course not. Restricted means property owners only, and employed staff or properly invited guests. No transit traffic, no strangers. It's a zero-crime zone."

"Except the crime of its existence," I mumbled, but I'm sure he heard as well.

The arrival of more supplicants helped us avoid further discussion. It was for the best. Getting him upstairs was going to be hard if I started a fight before we made it to the front door. My blood was heating as I rallied my strength for another session of lip stretching.

"You two are track friends, right?" asked a copper-skinned girl with multiple names and a smile so sharp she could've used it to perform surgery.

"We'll see you inside," Alexander replied evenly. I missed Kortilla and we hadn't even made it into the house yet.

We passed under a great overhang that shielded the front door from the drone's artificial light. A pair of imposing cathedral-sized doors stood open before us. Glittered bodies glided past the portal like shooting stars. Alexander's hand squeezed mine and we entered the residence of the Foster-Rose-Harts.

I stepped into grandeur. The entry foyer soared three stories high, with interior balconies overlooking the sprawling marble floor. A pair of matching helix staircases on opposite sides of the expansive chamber twirled towards the higher levels. A great chandelier hung above, extending its crystal arms in eight directions. Attendants offered to take my coat or bag, despite the fact that I carried neither. The room and balconies overflowed with genetically enhanced bodies competing to be the brightest star in the night. The beauty in the room taunted that I had lived my entire life among the ordinary.

"Let's try to make our way towards the back if we can," Alexander said into my ear.

I nodded, lacking anything substantive to say. Groups of highborn clustered in the halls like nests of roaches. Waiters attired in pristine white suits adorned with golden buttons circulated with silver trays, offering food I barely knew existed: shining red claws from sea crabs, slices of raw fish laid upon polished rice with such artistry that it didn't look real, shrimp larger than two of my fingers.

"I thought crabs were endangered, and real fish too laced with pollutants to eat raw," I said.

"It's from our family's private stocks. The regulations don't apply to stuff not sold commercially," Alexander told me, his attention focused on navigating through the halls of his house. "You should try the crab. You might object to the ideology of having them, but not the taste."

That wasn't going to work with my special tooth. I declined the food, preferring to think I was sticking to my principles.

We passed into a windowed hallway that looked out onto a huge interior courtyard topped by the enormous glass dome that had been visible from the street. Circular tables with fire-lit candles dotted the space. Holographic birds fluttered through the air above them. A concentration of shining highborn mingled amid the flames and the finery, their hands filled with food and drink. At the center of them all, I saw her: Kristolan Foster-Rose-Hart. She glided through the crowd of fawners, smiling, touching, speaking to each one, but never quite stopping. Her smile flashed as she shared jokes, while her eyes reassured each person of their importance to her. Drake's hulky form hovered in her shadow, looking anxious. I remembered what Nythan had said about Drake's family being in debt to the Foster-Rose Harts—and Alexander's warning that his sister was not one to miss an opportunity that could be exploited.

Even as Kristolan reigned among the masses, she somehow noticed me. Those piercing orbs cut a path through the packed bodies to lock onto me. My throat clenched, and my mind tingled with alarm. I wondered why Alexander had really brought me here. This was not my place, my people. I wanted to do what I had to do and get out. My teeth clenched.

I expected Alexander to lead me out to the courtyard to join his sister, but he didn't. Instead, we skirted around the central area, down a cramped hall, passing through a sliding panel door into a more intimate salon. A gray-haired gentleman in a tuxedo played soft, graceful music on a silky black piano in one corner. Its top had been raised, and its crisp notes flowed like water over falls. A sofa and several soft-armed chairs furnished the space. Besides us, there was only one other couple present.

"I thought you might be a bit more comfortable in here," Alexander told me. "And it's quiet enough to talk. Can I get you something to drink?"

"Let me guess, inebriation age rules don't apply?"

"Correct, it's private property. I suspect you're more interested in sparring about the politics of alcohol than drinking it, but perhaps we should do both before you judge?"

"Why not? I'll let you be my guide."

Alexander motioned to a waiter standing at attention. "Klos d'Ambonnay," he ordered. The man gave a deep nod and scurried off. I hadn't even noticed the waiter when I came in. Very highborn of me.

"He's getting you the good stuff," said a voice behind me. I turned to find Anise standing there, a flute of clear bubbling liquid held in one hand. She wore a flowing gown of silver scales that contrasted with the onyx of her eyes. Alexander caught the waiter's attention with a grunt of his throat and flashed three fingers at the server.

"I've never seen anything quite like that dress. Or you, either, I suppose," Anise told me.

"All of us got here via Bronx City," I replied, unsure if I'd been complimented or insulted.

"What do you think so far?" she asked.

"A lot of very attractive people, wearing very expensive clothes, in a giant house, eating threatened species. None of whom seem particularly glad to have me among them."

"I'm glad to have you here, Daniela," Alexander proclaimed. "And Anise, so nice to have you with us, and…who is it tonight?"

"Gillal, of the Masford-Jayson clan." She looked around absently. "He wandered off to pay court to your sister and her cronies. Our families insisted we attend together." She made a gagging face. "Lucky me."

"If you don't like him, why…"

Anise smiled indulgently. "It's part of the game. This may seem a little ridiculous to you, from the outside. As you said, it looks like pretty people dressed in pretty clothes. But part of it is quite serious, I assure you. Families live or die based on the relationships forged in this house. And everyone wants Kristolan's favor"

"Why?" I wondered. "We're kids. Even Kris is just eighteen."

Anise glanced at Alexander, who wore a heavy frown. She turned back to me. "Take my family. We specialize in surface research—projected yields, disease progression, mineral depletion, weather analysis, water tables...blah, blah, but the Masford-Jayson family has over a trillion dollars in capital to allocate, and they buy our services to help them in their business. They, in turn, are salivating to get closer to the Foster-Rose-Harts, but Gillal couldn't score an invitation to this party to save his life."

"But you have one," I concluded.

"Alexander and I go way back," Anise said, a bit too proud.

The white-gloved waiter arrived with three sparkling glasses balanced on a tiny tray. "Klos d'Ambonnay," he pronounced, as if the name spoke for itself.

"Pulling out all the stops, Alexander," Anise remarked as we took our glasses. She placed her original depleted drink on the tray. "You've never offered *me* champagne from the last of the protected French estates."

"Cheers," Alexander said as if he hadn't heard her.

I tapped glasses with these two highborn, the sound blending with the piano's music. I raised the bubbling liquid to my lips. The taste was like the music: smooth, flowing, elegant. I wanted not to like it, but that was impossible. The memory of my first sip lingered; my mouth demanded more.

Anise watched me drink, a half-grin on her face. To Alexander, she said, "She'll do." She raised her glass again, draining the remaining contents in a single gulp. "I'll see you both around." She put a too-familiar hand on Alexander's arm before letting it slide away as she departed.

Anise slid the door closed as she left. We were alone with the piano player, the alcohol, and each other.

"Why does everyone defer to your sister? What is so special about her?" *Does her power go even beyond trilling?*

Alexander shut his eyes for a moment, as if weary. "Kris just has a way about her. She gets what she wants without seeming to have ever wanted it. Those who fall afoul of her, they seem to find mysterious misfortune. People sense there may be a new order coming."

"You don't approve?"

Alexander scanned the room. The waiter seemed too far away to overhear us, the pianist was occupied with his music. "I know her better than anyone. She was my protector for many years." He let go of a laden breath. "I miss the person she was." Those shining eyes dimmed.

"What happened?"

Alexander searched my face with cautious eyes. Then he shook his head. I didn't press further.

"I've listened to Mozart, and Bach, but I've never heard a piano played live before," I said. "It's lovely—as is the champagne."

"But?"

"But this isn't my world. And it's dangerous to forget that." I put my glass down on a nearby table.

"Dangerous for whom?"

"Both of us," I said, my voice only a bit above a whisper.

"Daniela, that is what…I want to speak of. Although I don't quite know how." He motioned to the sofa. I gladly rested my legs. My feet ached. "I believe that, as different as we are, there is something inside…" He stopped speaking, swallowed, then began again. "At the track the other day, you spoke of what you felt inside, when you run…"

The door slid open. Kristolan glided in like a swan swimming through a pond. The barely translucent fabric of her dress shimmered like sunlight on the water. I looked for Drake.

Somehow, Kris had given him the slip. But in his place was Mona Lisa Reves-Wyatt, lumbering along with something akin to menace. Alexander and I both stood.

"Alexander, people have been wondering where you were hiding," Kris chimed. "And Daniela, I'm so happy to have you with us tonight. I'm pleased you took our conversation to heart."

"Our conversation?"

That smile flashed at me, dazzling and warm, steel hidden underneath. "We spoke about not giving up on Tuck, about giving the place a chance. And now you're on the track team, and here, with Alexander."

She laid a hand on mine. Her skin was hot; its warmth ran through my body.

"I remember that. Thank you for all you said and did," I heard myself say.

Kris kept her hand on me as she turned to Alexander. "A brilliant choice, brother. I'm so pleased."

"Pleased?" I managed.

Kris leaned close to me, as if we were the most intimate of friends. It was like standing next to the sun after a night in the cold wilderness. "The great game is on display tonight. Alliances are signaled by the companions of the heirs. The future leadership of corporations assessed, and the amount of capital allocations negotiated. All desire a turn to feed at my family's trough, of course. You should know that most of the women here would slit their date's throat, and yours, to exchange places with you. It's rather brilliant of Alexander to bring a neutral party. He offends no one, keeps everyone guessing. A fine move indeed."

My blood went cold. I turned to Alexander, whose face remained statuesque, unreadable. *Was he part of this?* Kris radiated something that felt like benevolence, but wasn't. My head cleared, as if waking from a dream. I pulled my arm away from her touch, letting the ice flow through my veins. I remembered my mission: the DNA and the cure.

"Some people just come to listen to music, dance, and enjoy themselves," Alexander said.

"A few," his sister replied, batting her eyelashes as the door to the salon slid open and streams of people began to flow in. The laws of social gravity commanded no less. Her minions soon surrounded us.

I exchanged unpleasant pleasantries with at least two dozen highborn with a hundred names I didn't care to remember. They spoke of me without regard to my presence, much as a rancher might evaluate cattle: "a prize," "unexpected," and "unique specimen," were among the memorable turns of phrase. Alexander made several polite attempts to leave, each of which was thwarted by his sister insisting on someone else we simply must meet. I barely stopped myself from gnawing my teeth and releasing the clorodrine. Instead, I squeezed my fists near bloody. My blood burned. I wanted these people to pay. They would not be my masters.

My glazed eyes barely noticed as yet another stranger came before me. His countenance jerked me back to the present: the new arrival's face was as white as Nythan's, his eyes nearly as pale but for the ruby-tinted rings around his irises. He wore his hair long and as black as night, and had donned a suit to match, save for the silvery cravat at his neck. I felt Alexander stiffen beside me.

"Arik…We are so…fortunate that you can join us," Alexander said.

"Your sister invited me, Alexander." His voice was deep, slow, and hard. "A taunt, I imagine. Still, I thought it might be nice to see my father's house. It has been five years, after all."

"Kris does not taunt, as you well know," Alexander said. "It's always something deeper."

Arik's lips pulled slightly toward each side. "May I meet the lady beside you?"

"Of course," Alexander said, though his eyes stayed locked ahead. "This is Daniela Machado."

Arik gave the deepest bow of any person that evening. "I heard that Alexander had gone to the slum for his escort this year, but I see my sources had it reversed."

Alexander was in Arik's face before I had a chance to plant my knee in the young man's groin. The damn gown slowed me down. Alexander's hands became fists at his sides.

"I'm afraid I must ask you to leave," Alexander said.

Kris appeared again, as if out of nowhere, her voice silk, her soul ash. "Is our half-brother misbehaving?" she purred.

"I'm merely speaking what others only dare to whisper behind closed doors, as always," Arik said. He showed no fear of Alexander, nor any remorse for his words. If anything, he was enjoying himself.

Kris slid between the feuding pair.

"If an apology is required…" Kris began sweetly.

I didn't hear the rest. I left the room, rage pounding in my ears. My hands were tight balls. My anger was senseless. What did I care what a bunch of richies thought about me? I'd been labeled things a hundred times worse. And I was only there with one purpose. Storming off was a mistake. I willed my hands to unclench as I strode down the passage, unsure where I was headed, other than away from Kris, Arik and Alexander. Why the hell had he brought me here? Some kind of sick training, perhaps. It wasn't enough to see how tough I was on the track. He wanted to see how much highborn abuse I could take. I'd had enough of highborn niceties. I was ready to show Bronx City manners to these pups.

Alexander caught up with me in a room filled with billiard tables and several highborn smoking antique cigarettes as they jostled with long wooden sticks.

"Daniela, please, wait a moment," he said, coming up in a hurry from behind.

A pair of elegantly clad guests turned from their game, smoldering weeds in hand. "Alexander!" one exclaimed, his arms held wide, stick in one hand, cigarette in the other. I kept walking, and Alexander followed.

"Hey, what in all the good names…" I heard the player remark. I felt a familiar hand on my arm. He was careful not to squeeze.

I stopped and turned. Alexander wore a new expression, his face a shade of crimson that I hadn't thought possible.

"I'm sorry about that, and for how tonight has gone."

Another couple approached us, hands held up in greeting. Alexander looked at them, then at me.

"We need a conditioned run—now," he said. "You ready?"

I flashed my teeth. "It's your course. You lead."

Alexander took off at something like a fast walk, but the maneuvering was impressive. Anytime a guest appeared who wasn't deeply engrossed in an alternative conversation, Alexander turned, swerved, or backtracked. When confronted, he offered his deepest apologies while breaking into something close to an actual run. At the corner of a long, crowded hallway, I caught a glimpse of Drake, clad in gold but with gun sights for eyes. Alexander saw him as well. He rerouted us through the kitchen and catering prep areas. We took a dark, creaking stairway downward, then a shiny lift upwards.

"Not bad," I said, between breaths.

"It's the least I could do."

It wasn't until the lift doors opened that I fully appreciated where I was: the family floor. I had made it. Lights turned on as we stepped off the lift. I heard a high-pitched hum, something at the very edge of my hearing. Alexander flicked his fingers with well-practiced rapidity. *Security codes*, I guessed. The noise vanished.

I looked around, trying to match my surroundings with the drawings Nythan had showed me. We'd come off the lift into a long, bi-level living room, with screens and couches scattered about. Animated images of dark ocean waves rolled across the walls. *The fourth floor.* Alexander and Kris had their rooms up here. Landrew's rooms were on the level above, but there wasn't any additional security on the interlinking staircase. Or so Nythan believed. He'd been worried about the automated security on this floor, which Alexander had just disabled. If Landrew was truly away, there was nothing between me and success. Except Alexander.

After the constant din of the party, this floor was disconcertingly quiet. Unlike the rest of the house, it resembled an actual home. A digiBook lay on one of the tables, a Tuck skin hung over the back of a chair. Frozen frame images of Olympic runners were clustered on one section of wall. I recognized my hero, Moko Die, among them.

I walked over to the pictures. "I saw her on the net, when I was very young. At the Armory, when she qualified for the Olympics. The look on her face then—it's the same as in this image. As if she could find no peace anywhere but on the track. It stayed with me."

Alexander came up beside me, standing close. I felt the heat radiating off his arm. "I used to stare at them all, trying to capture the thought in their eyes. To know what was in their mind at that moment, when they needed everything they had to win."

I turned my head towards him. "Why?"

Alexander's eyes met mine. "I wanted to know if they were like us."

I looked down, afraid to betray my secrets. "What do you mean—like us?"

He waited for me to raise my head again. I didn't.

"I will be the first to trust then. As my mother would've wanted." He took a small step away from me. "I have something inside. It's more than just being highborn. It's something that makes me different. Faster on the track. And more. It is a power that can control."

I could barely breathe. *He can trill.* He had laid his secret at my feet. *Why?*

"What is it you expect me to say?" I managed. I had a mission. Mateo was counting on me.

"I did not bring you here for any of the reasons my sister suggested. Her words are poisoned fruit, as always. So I lay this secret at your feet. I will trust you. You don't need to say anything, if that trust is not returned."

My tongue was heavy. I didn't have any words to offer. Alexander had put his faith in me. But I had more to lose. Nythan's clorodrine tooth throbbed inside my mouth.

I forced myself to face him. "Why does it matter to you?"

"If you had been told you were chosen…unique among people, would you not want to know if that was lie? If you were really just one of many."

"Is that what your sister told you?"

Alexander's eyes narrowed. *He knows what I am. He knows that I know about his sister.*

"Yes," he admitted. "She has grown…dark. She was always ambitious, but not like this. These past years…I no longer recognize her." He shook his head.

The silence lingered as my mind raced. "Is this the real reason you brought me here tonight? To find out if I'm like you and your sister?" It shouldn't have surprised me. It shouldn't have hurt. But it did. Of course he wanted something from me. He was highborn.

Alexander glanced away, then back at me. "I lack Kris's grace or knack for this game of families. I didn't think they'd be so cruel." He sounded angry. "I'm sorry. And for Arik, who is my half-brother but a full jack-A. He was some scheme of Kris's, I suppose. I asked you here because I wanted to spend the evening with you. Because I'm drawn to your strength. Please believe that."

I stared into his eyes. "Why do you think I'm strong?"

"I sense what is inside you. A rage, untainted and pure. Free from the corruption of highborn games. I felt it tonight. You took all they had to offer, and stood your ground." He moved closer. His face, chiseled by a master, filled my vision. I could taste his breath.

Time slowed as the ice raced into my blood. I looked as hard as I could into the endless azure of his eyes, trying desperately to reach his soul and read what was inside him. I felt the power within him, akin to my own. That better world I had imagined on the walk over here seemed so close, so real. I ached to trust him. But I was no fool.

I bit down hard on the tooth.

THIRTY-FOUR

I handed the ivory comb holding Landrew Foster-Rose-Hart's hair and skin particles to a triumphantly grinning Nythan, while Alissa and Lara looked on. Even Lara seemed a little less dour at the delivery.

"I didn't think you had it in you," she told me. "Finally. If anyone deserves it, it's the Foster-Rose-Harts." There was venom in her words.

Nythan fingered the salt-colored strands as if he could read the molecular structure with his eyes. "Took you long enough to get out of there. It'll take at least half the week to grow the cells we need," he said. "But there is plenty to do while that is happening. Everything is set up at the safe house to begin breaking you out. We'll start early tomorrow."

"Monday," I told him. "I'm taking tomorrow off. Don't ping me. I'm not going to answer."

"This isn't a part-time gig," Lara said, anger sparking in her eyes. I wondered why this mattered so much to her. "We are all risking our lives. We only get one shot at this, and time is running out. You better do your part."

"I bled for the cause tonight," I told them. "I'll be there Monday after practice, Nythan. Kortilla will cover for me to stay out Monday night. I'll find my own way home. See you."

I walked out of the apartment without looking back.

I did my best to avoid everyone at school on Monday. Alexander was next to me in Lit, but we didn't say a word to each other. Even if he wanted to speak to me, Tuck wasn't the place for it. I took lunch in my lab room and gave a half-hearted effort in track practice. I caught Alexander watching me several times, but we kept our silence. Anise tried to get a few words out of him but failed.

Nythan met me outside the school and led me to a waiting corporate sedan with dark windows. Its interior was gloomy and inundated with artificially cooled air.

"Ready to get back to work, princess?" he asked, his tone petulant.

"How about I press the buttons and you get a shot full of drugs and have your mind manipulated by some experimental machine devised by a sixteen-year-old loon and a glorified medical intern?"

"Touché," Nythan said, his mocking grin returning. "What happened at the party?"

"I got your DNA sample."

"You seem angry. Missing Alexander boy?"

I let him see the determination burning inside me, the anger in my eyes. "I'm ready to get into the Ziggurat, and do whatever I have to do to save those people, and my brother. Don't doubt it. But if I'm going to risk my mind, my honor, and my life, I want to be a full partner. I want to know what's going on."

"Your honor?" Nythan asked with a skeptical chuckle.

"Don't evade."

Nythan sighed like a parent with a pesky child. I started grinding my teeth. The new one I bought yesterday in BC to replace Nythan's clorodrine one was too rough. Typical street tooth. "What is it you want to know?"

"The whole plan. How are you using the transit system to get inside? What do you expect me to do in there besides handle a guard?"

He strummed his fingers on his leg. "I'm not the operational guy. I do the science and computer hacking. They'll run us through the details this week, once we're sure the breaking out has been successful. Otherwise, there's no point in exposing the other members of the group. I don't even know everyone."

"So you don't plan on telling me what I'm supposed to do, or even who will be going with me? It sounds like we might need to stop this vehicle."

"If it makes you feel any better, I'm going with you. So are Alissa and Lara. We're in this together."

"Four Tuck students to break into one of the most secret and secure corporate facilities in the country? How does that make any sense?"

"We are probably the only people in the world who could manage it." He wasn't boasting. If anything, he seemed nervous. "Let's break you out. I'll get you the answers you want then. Trust me."

I didn't answer him.

The sedan's lights switched off as we approached the safe house. Nythan fiddled with a terminal next to his seat. Some kind of counter-measure, I guessed.

"Who's paying for all this? Havelock?"

Nythan rubbed his chin, considering. "What I've seen isn't big bucks. My equipment is top notch, but it belongs to the life center. That includes most of the stuff in the safe house,

which we, ahem—borrowed. The surveillance in the apartment is low tech stuff available to any hobbyist." He stopped
talking but kept thinking. "Getting the Fart house blueprints
took some doing…as did the work to access the magnetic transit tunnel. A few other items…yeah, they cost. You don't think
this is Havelock's show then?"

"I thought you would know who you've been working for."

"'With,' my dear. I don't work 'for' anyone," Nythan wore a
frown. "Havelock has done everything he promised so far, and
it's been fun. We're winning, in case you haven't noticed."

The sedan pulled into the parking garage. Nythan led me
upstairs with enough confidence that I knew he had been a fre-
quent visitor to this place. There was more light on this trip
than my last. I absorbed everything I could. Nythan used his
viser to flick open the door to the safe house. I stole a quick
glance at my own device, to make sure it was still working as
it should. Everything inside the apartment was how I remembered it, except Mateo was gone. Doc Willis sat at the table
reviewing brain images on a portable screen.

"Is that my head?"

She drummed four fingers on her visered hand. The screen
image projected into three dimensions before me. It looked
like an aquatic creature with a multi-colored flashlight inside.

"Cripes, a guild navigator is among us!" Nythan quipped.

Dr. Willis and I both ignored him.

"This is you, Daniela. The colors represent regions of activity. Notice the red flashes in the cerebrum. It denotes activity not present in most subjects." Another of Doc's fingers
twitched. A new image appeared next to the first one. "This
one is Marie-Ann's, before her breakout. Watch the cerebrum.
What do you see?"

"No red."

Another finger twitch. The projection changed slightly.

"This is after the breakout."

"It's red." But still less than mine. "What does that tell you?"

Dr. Willis stared at her screen again. "By itself…maybe nothing. Maybe something."

More finger motion. A gelatinous blob appeared before my eyes, its outer membrane shimmying like the surface of the ocean on a calm day. Inside the blob, something like a tiny heartbeat pulsed.

"Wow, is that from the scans of Daniela?" Nythan asked, pushing his face to within a couple of inches of the image. "I didn't have a chance to review the extracted cells."

"Behold a DN10-191-enabled cell. These little guys are clustered in your larynx and vocal cords, as well as your brain, and a few other places. They have a veil which makes them appear like ordinary cells, which I stripped away for this image."

"What is the light inside?"

"We're not really sure," Dr. Willis said. "There's a lot we don't understand about how DN10-191 manifests itself. We figured out a way to image them with special equipment. We trick them into showing themselves. But they seem to self-destruct if we try to remove or otherwise tamper with them. To tell the truth, we don't completely understand trilling, or how it works."

"What's the point in showing me this, then?"

"Because those readings shouldn't be there," Dr. Willis said. "Not yet. We didn't detect the presence of these cells in Marie-Ann until three days after she had broken out. They gradually increased in number over the following weeks. You seem to have more than she possessed already, and they are active in more areas."

"She's already broken out," Nythan proclaimed, his gaze still fixed on the pulsing mass floating above Dr. Willis's screen. "You're like Kris—a natural."

"Maybe," the doctor said. "We still don't know enough about the process to be sure. These are the markers we developed working with Marie-Ann. There may be others. You can't trill as far as we know. Therefore, something is missing. We should go ahead with the process anyway."

"Why not just test me? See what I can do?"

"It'll take an hour to prep the monitoring equipment...and anyway, Havelock expects the process to be run. Even if you do have the cells, we want a complete breakout—we want your full potential. It takes strong emotions to free the mind. We know that part works, let's keep to the procedure." Dr. Willis said.

I shook my head. "No way."

Nythan's head whipped towards me. "You said you were ready to do whatever you had to do."

"I'm not going to take a batch of home-brewed drugs if I don't have to, Nythan."

"Daniela, there is more to breaking-out than just the drugs. It's about unlocking the barriers in your mind that prevent you from controlling the ability. The drugs facilitate that. The cells are a necessary condition, but not sufficient. The process is the only way we know how to do it."

"Let's try it without the drugs."

"It won't work," Nythan said. "We tried it that way with Marie-Ann at first. The effect isn't strong enough with just the images. The subject needs to have complete focus, and believe what they are seeing is real."

"As you said, I'm not Marie-Ann," I challenged.

"Daniela, we don't have time to screw around. Havelock wants a demonstration tomorrow morning. Once we start preparations to go inside the Ziggurat, they can't be stopped. One chance only. If the breakout process doesn't work, we won't be able to reset and try again for twenty-four hours. We're cutting it tight as it is."

"Nythan, I told you I'm ready to do what needs to be done. That doesn't mean I trust you people." I looked over at Dr. Willis, then back at Nythan. "This is the way it's going to happen, or not at all. As you said, I'm your last chance. You want a triller, you'll do it this way."

"Jack me," Nythan cursed. "Have a seat in the bedroom. I'll fire up the equipment."

It took Dr. Willis and Nythan about fifteen minutes to get their contraptions ready. They squabbled like a couple of kids—each confident of his or her own genius. Neither did well at delegating. Nythan wanted to do all the prep, while Dr. Willis disagreed with some of his adjustments to the scenes I was to experience.

"That makes no sense," I heard him declare. Nythan's voice took on a high, almost feminine pitch when he was agitated. I just wanted to get it over with.

When the great minds were satisfied, they brought in a sensory pod, unrolling it onto the bed. After a quick diagnostic, Nythan pronounced that it was ready.

"Slide inside like it's a sleeping bag," he told me. "Which it is, more or less. The sensory gel will feel a bit cold at first. Maybe even slimy. Once it gets going, it'll feel like whatever we need it to."

I climbed inside. It was just as cold and slimy as predicted. Nythan zipped me up, while Dr. Willis brought over a bulky VR helmet.

"Don't try to fight the virtual-reality environment or you'll get sick. Keep looking forward as I lower it onto your head. Try not to think of this room, us, or anything else. Submit to the illusion or you'll get sick. The effect is powerful, but that's the journey you need to go on to unlock your potential," Dr. Willis told me.

She didn't wait for my consent. She slipped the thing over my head. It was like being lowered into a coffin. Everything went dark. The sensory pod must've activated as well, because I could no longer feel the bed, or the weight of my body. I was floating in the void.

I heard something in the distance: a bird's song, only it wasn't. I strained to make it out. The sound disappeared, then came again. I began to move. At first, it was like being a leaf carried on a soft gust of wind. Then the breeze became constant. My speed increased and I was flying, soaring. The sun broke through the darkness and I raced towards it, the wind in my face. Faster and faster. The circular splash of bloody light drew closer, larger. As I neared, I noticed the dark spots on its surface. They appeared and disappeared each time I blinked. Initially, the patterns appeared random. But they weren't. Shapes appeared. More circles, more blemishes on the surface of the star, linking themselves together. I recognized the shape: my mother's face. But not just a face. It was her.

I saw the night she disappeared. I watched her leaving the hospital where she worked, where she made me what I was. She walked quickly, her gait long, like mine. She followed a route she had walked countless times before, even in the depth of night. It was Manhattan. It was safe. But something lurked in the shadows—a predator. He wore a glove that could kill with a touch. In his heart was a dark mission. She had done wrong. Discovered a project that didn't exist. She had told others, so she would die. They didn't know what else she had done, about her theft, but the telling was enough to condemn her. The knowing would've been enough. The shadow moved closer to her, his feet silent. Faster. I yelled for her to run. To turn. She didn't hear. *Mommy!* I urged myself to fly to her, to save her. I kicked, and scraped, but I was an impotent angel, not of that world. The hand moved closer. It grabbed her, a rough jerk on her shoulder. My mother crumpled to the ground. She was gone. I screamed, a cry rumbling through my body. The terrible memory of that first night she didn't come home rushed through me; the endless worry, resurrected and relived. Then came the pain of the second night without her—the dread in my stomach, so awful that tears leaked from my eyes. It all came back to me, as fresh as a knife newly plunged into my heart. I didn't want this.

Then she was gone, and the pain with it. I flew towards that burning star again. The dots appeared. This time I dreaded them. I didn't want to keep going. The sensation of flying, the wind, the light, it was so powerful. I struggled to tear my thoughts away from what I saw and felt. Another image appeared on the star. Another person. Younger. A boy: Mateo. *No.* I closed my eyes, but I still saw him. *Where was I?* I wasn't really here. I fought to remember. I tried to focus on my body, on what was inside, not the sensations bombarding me. Mateo walked on the street, a different one than our mother. It wasn't late, but I feared for him. Mateo stared at me. His lips moved. *Don't trust these people.*

The sensory pod. I remembered. The damn sensory pod. The VR helmet. They were bombarding me with sensation. That jack-A doctor had told me only part of the truth. *Strong emotions.* That's what she said they needed to trigger the mind, to break out. My mind was conjuring all this though the machine. I tried to shut my eyes, my real eyes. It didn't work. The image was still there—Mateo running. Chased by men and machines. I reached inside myself for the cold. But I had no sense of the true me. I was flying somewhere else, every sense occupied by the machine that engulfed me. I focused on what it had felt like when I slid into the pod: the cold, slimy sleep-ing bag. That's where the real me was. That's what I should be feeling. My arms and legs were encased in gel that transmit-ted sensations to my body. My eyes were trapped in front of a screen. None of this was real. It was a bunch of Nythan's tricks, to cajole forth a power I already commanded. I remembered where my body was. I felt the cold. I didn't need these lies. I closed my real eyes, and drew myself inside, grateful I hadn't taken the drug. Then there would've been no escape.

The so-called breaking-out process kept running, perhaps for another hour. It was hard to tell. I kept my eyes shut. The artificially generated sensations prickled my body, but without the visual images to synergize with, they were slight things. I used the power in my cold place to remain numb. Safe in my internal cocoon, I let Nythan's house of horrors expend itself. I knew the machine was done when light—real light, appeared on the other side of my closed eyelids.

"Daniela, can you hear us?" asked Dr. Willis. "Do you know where you are?"

I knew, but I shook my head, my eyes still shut. "What's going on?" I asked in my best groggy voice.

"How do you feel?"

Like stabbing a knife in your heart. "My head…the pain," I mumbled.

"It will pass," Nythan said.

"Did it work?" I asked.

I imagined them looking at each other. "Your patterns were remarkably flat. Very different from Marie-Ann's," Dr. Willis said. "I don't know. You didn't have the drug. It's hard to know."

"Either way, you need to rest," Nythan told me. "Dr. Willis and I will take shifts keeping an eye on you. Get some sleep. Havelock will be here in the morning to observe the testing.

Marie-Ann took a lot longer, but I have a feeling you'll be fine."

"Nythan, I need to get back to Lenox," Dr. Willis said. "I can return here when my shift ends. That's going to be sometime around three in the morning though."

"No problem. I'll keep an eye on her. I'll send my mom a ping. No worries, I got this."

I listened to Dr. Willis's footsteps fading away. "See you in the morning, Daniela. I sure hope this worked. Everyone is counting on you."

I heard the door shut. She was gone. Just Nythan remained.

"I'll be next door if you need anything," he said. My face didn't even twitch.

I started a slow count in my head, imagining seconds elapsing, each number in sequential order. I got to twenty thousand before I heard the rhythmic sounds of a sleeping person's breathing from the other room. I flicked my finger beneath the covers, activating my own set of jamming countermeasures. Nythan wasn't the only one who could play that game. Once I got the confirmation that the room wasn't being monitored, I swung myself out of bed, checking my viser.

Time to get to work.

THIRTY-FIVE

Headmaster Havelock arrived before dawn. I was already awake, sharing a fabricated coffee with Dr. Willis and Nythan on the rickety table. Havelock wore a charcoal-shaded trench coat over his usual antique suit. He didn't arrive alone.

The man beside Havelock had an athlete's build and posture. His suit hugged his well-cut form, the thick cheekbones of his carved face pushed at the taut skin covering them. He had round leather eyes, and large, formidable hands. Chrome streaked the edges of his flaxen hair. Not an athlete, I decided. A fighter.

"This is Dillion Macleod," Havelock told us.

I recognized the name. The man watching me at Alexander's house. My so-called backup.

"Are you ready, Daniela?" Havelock asked, taking off his coat. "As you no doubt have been told, we have precious few days left. The Allocators' Ball approaches, but it's all for nothing without a triller. We can scrub the mission, but our access route will never work again. It may be years, or never, before we find another way into the Rose-Hart Ziggurat."

"I'm ready," I assured him.

"Doctor Willis told us you refused the drug," Dillion said. It was an accusation.

"I'm ready," I said, meeting his cold eyes.

"Doctor Willis, please proceed," Havelock said.

"Certainly," the doctor said. "I've got the equipment ready. I think we can start simple. Nythan, please stay at the table with Daniela. I'll take your drinks."

She positioned us facing each other. Nythan was amused. I tapped my foot softly under the table. Dr. Willis placed a metal disk, no bigger than a quarter, on my temple. It was heavier than it looked. She did the same to Nythan. With a few taps of her finger, a nearby screen began streaming data.

"All right, Daniela. Marie-Ann told us that trilling wasn't like talking. We wasted a lot of time before we got that right. The cells on the larynx threw us off. We thought that was where she should've focused. But it wasn't until we let her explore that her power manifested itself. According to Marie-Ann, the power was accessed through meditation, not raw effort. You have to relax, become aware of your body. She spoke of a sensation, a chill that she felt when her focus was at its best. When she felt that slight cold, she pushed it out through her throat, at the other person, trying to feel their mind. You should think of the command as you push outward, while you speak what you want the other person to do."

"What should I try to make Nythan do?"

"Tell him to scratch his nose—anything you like. The real test is on my screens," Dr. Willis said. "But let's take it slow. Start by closing your eyes. Listen to my voice. I'll try to guide you the way I guided Marie-Ann."

I tuned her out. She sounded like a self-important preacher. Instead, I dwelled on my anger. That was easy. I didn't know exactly what the people in this room wanted from me, but I was certain it was more than they had told me. They thought they could control me. They wanted me as their little bird who would sing. I offered them a taste of my power to get what I wanted.

I opened my eyes. I heard the breathing of four anxious people around me. My heart beat with anger, and power. I pushed the chill of my essence towards Nythan. It was a stream of frigid water flowing toward him. There was a stone wall between him and me, shielding him, but my essence flooded over it easily, washing over the mind hiding behind it.

"Nythan, there's a fly on your nose."

He smacked his face, nose and all. "Missed." He looked at his empty hand.

I smiled at the ease of my success.

Dr. Willis laughed. "Holy crap. Readings spiked on both of them." She looked at him. "Nythan, there wasn't any fly."

"Ridiculous," he insisted.

The doctor laughed again. "Damn, that worked. Nythan, you've been trilled."

"Huh? I think you are mistaken and confused, my dear doctor."

Dr. Willis looked up at Havelock and Dillion. "She altered his senses. She did it."

"We need something more concrete," Dillion said, his voice too flat to be pleasant. "Daniela, tell Doctor Willis she has her viser on her left arm instead of her right. She needs to send me a red ping."

I focused my eyes on Dr. Willis. I wondered at the real reason she had helped Mateo. I pushed the cold at her. She had a wall as well; it was steel, and taller and wider than Nythan's. She was ready for me. Nythan hadn't believed, but Dr. Willis knew what I could do. My power struck her defenses. My cold essence—the power of my mind—split, flowing upwards and to each side, looking for a way around her mental barrier. Dr. Willis's wall expanded, climbing higher and growing wider.

Her mind was quick. Her defenses held. My essence couldn't get through. But she hadn't protected underneath. I tunneled under her defenses while she was occupied by the feints travelling in other directions. I had her.

"Your viser is on your left arm," I told her. "Get a message to Dillion."

"What are the readings telling you, doctor?" Dillion asked.

Dr. Willis flicked several fingers on her left hand. She stared at her arm, and flicked again. Then she noticed the viser on her right arm. Her eyes grew wide. "I think...I put my viser on the wrong arm...How...?" She placed both hands on her head, pressing inward.

"Disorientation," Havelock said as he watched Dr. Willis struggle. "I felt it too, when I finally realized what Kristolan had done to me. When your mind discovers it's been tricked, it struggles to right itself. Nythan, how long will the effect last?"

"Depends on the mind, and how unnatural the change. Trilling doesn't change your thoughts as best as we can tell. It creates barriers and detours in the mind. Once the subject realizes he or she has been tricked, it's just a matter of time before the mind rights itself. But if you didn't know...Months is my best guess, based on the information we have. Maybe never if the triller is subtle enough."

"Let's be certain," Dillion said. "Please try me next, Daniela. Anything you like."

I inhaled, assessing my next target as I gathered my strength. Dillion didn't think I could make him do anything. He looked forward to testing his strength against the world. I jabbed the cold toward him. The wall facing me was forged of wood, and no bigger than Dr. Willis's. My essence split: left, right, over and under, coming at him like an avalanche. The top stream of my essence moved faster than the wall he built.

"Your hair is on fire," I told him.

He laughed. A haughty sound.

I realized there was another barrier behind the first. Not just a wall, but an impregnable shell of fire protecting him from my power. I approached it tentatively. I sensed its power. Dillion's mind pushed against mine. I recoiled, knives stabbing at my head.

"You're highborn," I accused.

He nodded his head. "It seems we have our triller."

THIRTY-SIX

T he school news feed on Tuesday morning announced that there would be a special delegation sent to Boston to assist with a charter school initiative, jointly backed by the Robin Hood Foundation and Tuck. Daniela Machado, Lara Rae, Nythan Royce and Alissa Stein had been selected to participate by the faculty. Parents were informed, apologies made for the last-minute nature of the assignment, and the benefits of such a prestigious posting were highlighted. Only we never left the city. Instead, a sedan took us to the Vision Quad, back to the dilapidated building that hosted the safe house.

There were two large cargo transports parked across from the building. They had RocketDyn markings, but something wasn't quite right about them. The exteriors were too clean; both had human drivers, and they looked very alert for men doing nothing. It had begun. Our chance. But I still didn't have the details I wanted. Only empty promises that the answers were coming.

Dillion met us inside the underground entrance and escorted us upstairs. There were paper schematics of the Ziggurat, or at least part of it, waiting for us on a new, larger table.

"How accurate is this?" Nythan asked. "I see a lot of manual corrections on these papers."

"I'm certain that it's the most accurate blueprint in existence outside of Rose-Hart Industries, and I'm equally sure it isn't perfect," Dillion told us. "But it will help."

I ran my hand over the cloth-like paper, studying the lines and proportions. I pictured the distances in my mind. The complex was massive. A city within a city. Handwritten notations had been added to the drawing at various locations. Havelock and Dillion had to have someone inside, someone with partial access, but not to the levels we needed to reach. There were a lot of areas drawn with dotted lines marked "estimated."

"What are these red circles?" I asked.

"Guard stations with human security officers," Dillion said. "These aren't rent-a-cops. They are Rose-Hart elite security, probably third generation employees. They're nopes, but dedicated partisans. Incorruptible."

"Not many on our route," I noted.

"Two guard stations, we think. Both staffed by a single security officer, according to our information," Dillion said. "The advantage of our plan, and our route, is that Rose-Hart doesn't trust their own employees with the knowledge of what happens on level eleven. Human security is less prevalent at the sub-level access lift, and on level eleven itself. Think you can handle two guards, Daniela?"

His tone hinted towards mocking.

"As long as they aren't highborn. What about others on the floor? Researchers, company employees?"

"We're going in after hours. We'll have minimal contact with regular staff. Also, the arrangements on level eleven are unique. You'll be briefed on that later. You might need to improvise with a scientist in an emergency. You ready?"

"I already answered that."

"We'll get you some more practice over the next few days," Dillion said. "You may need to work quickly, or at a distance. You need to know exactly what you are going to command, and what we need those guards to do."

"How are we going to get in there?" I asked. "I see a nice route to the lift, then up to the designated level. But how do we reach the sub-level to begin with?"

"We still need to keep operational secrecy on this mission," Dillion told me with an air of self-importance. "We'll get you there, believe it."

I glared at him. "This place is blanketed with countermeasures. No one is leaving. We go inside in days. It would be helpful to know the entire plan."

"Your role isn't to get us in," Dillion said. "That's up to the logistics team, and they are working on it. They'll be ready. You need to spend the next few days proving you aren't going to get everyone killed because you panic in front of the guards. Or flake out at the last minute."

"I'm not going anywhere unless I know how I'm getting there, and that someone has my back," I answered.

"Don't be an ass, Dillion," Alissa said. "Daniela's with us. She might be a highborn jack like you, but she got us the DNA. She's proved she's with us."

Dillion sighed. "Flip the paper."

I turned the blueprint over. On the other side was a series of drawings showing transit tunnels, including several under construction.

"The Magnetic Transit System supposedly being built by RocketDyn, is a partial truth. The initial system has been operational for a decade. This is just an expansion. The existing line runs along this route." He pointed to the edge of Manhattan island. "This is a port and transshipment facility owned by Rose-Hart Industries. They move sensitive cargo they don't trust to third parties through it. Some are things they don't want on surface roads, so they use the MTS. It has a stop at a secure facility here." He pointed to a multilevel subterranean structure with no interior details filled in. "Then it continues on to a special sub-floor beneath the Ziggurat. That's where we'll enter."

"How do we get access to a transit car?" I asked. "Traffic is bound to be closely monitored by remote operators. The cars probably have internal video feeds."

"We know what we're doing, Daniela," Dillion assured me, not hiding his annoyance at being questioned. "We've hacked the transit control system. The scheduled transit car will get stuck in the tunnel. We managed to finish the tracks of one of the new tunnels that link up with the operating line. They don't know it's active, but it'll be fully operational by Saturday. We'll steal one of the cars that have been put into place for the new line. It will pull into the Ziggurat sub-level precisely on time. The guard station will assume we are the scheduled arrival. Then you need to work your magic. We've got Landrew's DNA, which we used to create finger sheaths for the scanners. But the guard needs to think he's seeing Landrew Foster-Rose-Hart. That's the human fail-safe in their security. Can you do that?"

"I can do it."

"As you pointed out, we'll be watched remotely the whole time, including in the lift. So it has to look like we passed security normally. It has to look like we belong. The feeds are video, not audio. Once past the guard station, we ride up to eleven. No external monitoring inside the labs on that level. We don't know exactly what to expect, but, based on payroll records, we think there is one, perhaps two, security personnel on the floor. Most of the security is DNA coded, and we've got that covered. The controlColonies are in there. All of them.

And so is access to the closed-network computers with all the data we want. Nythan just has to hack it."

"You need me for the guards and any surprises," I said. "Nythan knows the computers and understands the Waste…Why are Alissa and Lara going? They're hardly fighters. Aren't we going to attract attention? I'm guessing we're a little young to be Rose-Hart employees, particularly in their most restricted areas."

I got a face of stone from Dillion. "Every one of you has a special talent. That's all you need to know. This briefing is over. Get to work. Show me you can do what you say. Let me worry about the rest."

I spent the next two days memorizing floor plans and improving my trilling abilities. Alissa, Lara, and Nythan acted as test subjects. The practice confirmed something I already knew: I had been able to trill for most of my life. I'd broken out when I was five years old, when I lost my mom. That was all the emotional turmoil a five-year-old needed. Maybe an adult needed Nythan's drugs and virtual reality process. But I didn't. Kris probably had a similar experience somewhere in her past.

My special place—the essence of cold that I drew upon when running and in times of stress—was the same reservoir of power I used to trill. It required total control over my body, the ability to marshal and direct the entirety of my will. I had been training for that my whole life on the track. It never occurred to me to use that power to impose my will upon others. But once I had been shown the way, I adapted my technique. A distance runner could also do sprints.

I could breach any of my companions' defenses, at least for the harmless commands I was implanting for practice. After the first day of trilling them I realized I should be more cautious about using my power on the same person. The more my companions worked with me, the better they got at fighting me off. I noticed it with Nythan first. His wall quickly became higher, stronger. It switched from stone to duraglass. His reaction time to my attacks became faster. I beat him with my tunneling trick, but the next time I tried it, his wall extended underground. With Lara, I deliberately flubbed most of my attempts to trill her, except when Dillion was watching. She crooned in pleasure each time she fought me off. I smiled inside.

Dillion came and went several times a day. He worked with each of the others on mission details they kept from me. I could've tried to trill it out of them, but Dillion was always checking in on our practice sessions. We were all beginning to get cabin fever. I stood by the boarded window, peeking out whenever I got the chance. There were small gaps where light could enter and leave.

"You should keep away from the windows," Dillion warned me. "There aren't any drones around here, but you never know who's looking."

I kept going to the windows, but only when he left the room.

On Thursday, just as we were all going crazy in that cramped, confined space, Dillion led us out of the safe house to a second, larger set of rooms one floor above. It was an all-interior space—no windows or other source of natural light. The floor was bare sheetrock, the walls mostly stripped to their girders. Cheap portable sodium lights provided the only illumination, except for the screens, of which there were at least a dozen scattered on walls and tables. A singular square machine, no larger than a fabricator, stood alone in another corner of the room, some type of communication array protruding from its mirror-like surface. It looked expensive. A stack of bedrolls had been shoved into another corner.

Havelock was already there, along with two other new faces. One was a tall, dark-skinned man with short clipped obsidian hair, who I guessed to be around Mateo's age. He had the same tall, nearly gaunt build as Havelock, but without the urbane mannerisms. I wondered if he was a fellow Rwandan. His companion was a woman, around the same age, deeply tanned, with bulb cut platinum hair on top of a rounded face. Her hair might have even been natural.

"You know them?" I whispered into Nythan's ear.

"Strangers to me," he said. "Check out the visers."

The devices around their wrists resembled Alissa's bioengineered Rose-Hart model, but several generations more advanced. I saw no metal or other hard surface. It was if their skin had been bleached to form a screen on their lower palm, while the rest of the device had been grafted onto their arm.

"Welcome everyone," Dillion announced to the room. "Please gather around. It's finally time for the operational team and the Tuck team to meet. You've been working towards the same goal, but have been kept apart for your mutual protection. With only days left, it's time to bring the two hands together. At least in part. So, Brice and Helena, please meet Nythan, Lara, Alissa, and Daniela."

There was wariness and arrogance in the new faces, but not warmth. These were not students. I doubted they were idealists. They looked like professionals with a job to do. I wondered if they were highborn like Dillion. Probably. More people immune to my power. My throat tightened looking at them, at their visers, and the strange communication equipment.

"The Tuck team will be going in with me," Dillion told everyone. "Helena will coordinate the hack of the MTS controls. We've arranged for an emergency shutdown of the transit car at eight thirty-five tomorrow evening. Brice will remotely pilot the hijacked transit car onto the regular track using our new access tunnel. Our phantom train will return to retrieve the team at nine fifteen. That leaves us thirty-five minutes inside. If we do this right, we'll get in and out, and they won't even know we were there."

"What happens if the trains aren't working? If Rose-Hart regains control of their transit system, how do we get out?" I asked.

Helena cleared her throat. "It'll happen the way Dillion says. Their systems are pretty good, but not closely watched. They're complacent. They don't think anyone knows about their underground railroad. We're already in their network. Their own secrecy helps us. They probably have limited personnel to handle emergencies. They won't be able to call their regular tech staff without violating their security protocols."

"Humor my hypothetical disaster scenario," I insisted. "What is Plan B?"

"The MTS trains move at two hundred miles per hour. The magnets beneath are super-cooled with liquid nitrogen. I don't suggest you enter the tunnels except via the train. If that isn't to your liking, there are three other entrances on the main level. Security staff of about fifty humans, and several dozen drones. And that's just within the building. The grounds have additional countermeasures. Trill to your heart's content, you won't make it out that way. It's our way or not at all."

I didn't hide my scowl. One way in or out. We were at the mercy of a bunch of people we barely knew. I doubted they were here to cure the Waste either. I glanced at Nythan, wondering at his thoughts. His face showed me nothing. His eyes just watched—a kid listening to the rules of the next game.

"Timing and movement will be crucial. We will be watched every second, from the tunnel until we get to level eleven, then again on the way out. It has to look authentic. First, that means we'll be using company-issued visers only—your own will stay here. Your new ones will not be able to transmit externally, which would trip the alarm anyway."

That news was like a lead weight in my stomach. I figured I'd be cut off, but now I wouldn't even have a viser I could rely on.

"Even Picasso needed decent brushes," Nythan said.

"We received your work requirements, Mr. Royce, and anticipated your needs. You'll be issued an organic model like I have, suitable for your needs. You can download whatever programs and tools you need to your new viser. These don't show on conventional scanners. We'll use facades over them so they appear to be standard-issue company models."

They don't show up on conventional scanners. Just like my repulse spray. As far as I knew, only California had biotech like that.

Dillion wasn't done. "Also, those of us going inside need to suit up and practice marching. We need to look the part for their remote security cameras. We'll be watched almost all the way in and out. Only the laboratories will be without remote monitoring."

For a moment I thought he was joking, but he wasn't. Dillion retrieved a large duffle bag filled with the strange skins I'd seen in the closet when Mateo had been in the safe house, the ones with Korean lettering. We took turns changing in the closets. The high collar clawed at the back of my neck. The suits lacked temperature controls or fit-to-wearer features like our Tuck skins, but they were noticeably thicker. The users needed to be insulated against external environmental conditions of some kind. The outfit was stiff and uncomfortable compared to a Tuck skin, but the extra padding allowed me to conceal my repulse spray within the long sleeve of my non-visered arm.

Dillion placed us in a line, and we marched as if we were soldiers in the army. He monitored spacing, pace, cadence, and eye movement. Again and again, back and forth, until we had it perfect. Then came turns. Then standing at attention, eyes forward. We simulated marching time from the MTS train to the guard station, practiced our exiting formation and walking speed. We did that drill a dozen times, with Brice and Helena calling out times. Dillion led us, acting in the role of drill sergeant.

"Why?" I asked, able to stand no more of the monotony. "Rose-Hart has kids marching in jumpsuits made in corporate Korea in their top secret research facility?"

"If you want to stay alive in there, you'll practice until you've got it exactly right," Dillion warned. "Let's go again."

We wasted our remaining days marching. Nythan looked bored but went along without audible complaint. Alissa seemed as frustrated as I was. Only Lara seemed focused. Indeed, she almost looked happy—a first for her.

We ate fabricated protein bars for our meals and slept in cushioned bags on the floor. Dillion, Brice, or Helena were always around. I wanted to speak to Nythan, but there wasn't an opportunity. Our visers were being jammed. Mission security, Dillion said. He kept a close watch on me.

Saturday arrived. Mission Day. I kept rubbing my hands on my suit to keep them dry. I fought down the urge to pace about. I thought I had this figured out. Nythan, Alissa, Lara, even Havelock were all people I understood. I hadn't counted on Dillion. I hadn't counted on highborn being part of the team, or the second interior room.

We reviewed the schematics and practiced the marching drills during our last morning and afternoon. Brice and Helena established themselves at desks, surrounded by terminals. I overheard enough to know they were communicating with others. Most likely in the tunnels. Havelock paced, but kept his exterior of aplomb.

He came up next to me as I fiddled with the foreign viser on my arm, towering like an ancient tree. "This is our chance, Daniela. The opportunity to change the world. To remake the fate of this nation, perhaps of all people."

"Why does it matter to you?" I asked.

"People will do what they need to do to survive; right or wrong, they will do it. That's what happened in my home, in Rwanda. One people nearly annihilated another." I heard the rare tinge of emotion in his voice. It reminded me of that flash of rage I had witnessed back at his house. "The same will happen here soon. Those who think they are superior will destroy those they think are less. This plague the highborn have developed will spread and become the ultimate weapon of silent genocide. Unless we stop it—completely. Unless *you* stop it. Remember that when you're inside."

THIRTY-SEVEN

We set out into the night, each of us attired in a dark Korean-made skin, except Dillion, who wore a dapper silver-and-black suit typical of a Rose-Hart executive. We crossed the street to the nearby construction site. Great mounds of dirt had been piled in seemingly random patterns, heavy earthmoving equipment had been parked, and portable toilet silos erected. Dillion led us to the second of the four free-standing toilets, unlocked the door with a sweep of his hand and stepped inside.

"Keep a steady grip on the way down."

I heard Nythan chuckle. "Classic."

I stepped inside the tiny cubicle to find that instead of a toilet seat, there was a hole and a ladder leading down into darkness. The odor of chemical disinfectant assailed me. I hoped it was coming from the nearby facilities rather than the hole I was lowering myself into.

"Now we're in it," Nythan whispered as I climbed downward.

The ladder led us to a machine carved access tunnel with still, fetid air and minimal lighting. We had just enough room to walk upright, single file. That passage led to a far larger underground transit tunnel. Portable work lights, strung from the top of the fifteen-foot-high ceilings, lit the underground passage. Walls of machine-cut rock surrounded us. Switches, sensors, and track supports were laid out at various intervals. An inert boring machine was parked in the center of the tunnel. I fought the urge to rub the unfamiliar gold tinged viser scratching my arm. It reminded me of how alone I was on this mission.

After a ten-minute walk, we came to a translucent curtain that extended from the tunnel ceiling to the floor, completely separating one side of the passage from the other. A zippered doorway was located in the middle of the barrier. A sign told onlookers that the door was for "Authorized Personnel Only." Dillion unzipped the doorway, led us through, then closed the zipper behind us.

A shining three-car transit train waited atop a freshly laid monorail track. A head popped out of one of the cars as we approached. The rest of the man's body followed a moment later. He wore a white RocketDyn uniform, but had a black-handled force pistol holstered on his waist.

"Six minutes till go," the man said. He wore one of the California visers.

"Everyone inside, in their assigned positions," Dillion told us.

We entered the MTS car, which closely resembled a Manhattan subway car, except that every surface gleamed. There was no place for a driver. A small control cubicle, about the same size as the portable bathroom we'd used to access the underground network, was located in the middle car, for the rare emergency when direct human intervention was required. We stood, holding the handles that dangled from the ceiling, keeping to our rehearsed order: Lara, myself, Nythan, then Alissa. Dillion followed us inside, the car doors closing behind him.

"Three minutes," he told us.

"Now is it safe to tell me why we're dressed in Korean skins?" I asked.

"Two minutes and forty-five seconds," Dillion said, acting like something that had come down the dark hole of a porta-toilet. "Follow the protocols we discussed."

Lara turned to me. "We're going in as chipped slaves."

My chin dropped. "Chipped slaves...here? In the US? In the laboratories of Rose-Hart? But why? They're thoughtless drones, what possible use..."

"Not ordinary chipped slaves. *Juche* workers. They're a new generation of chipped humans, developed by the Corporate Council of Korea." Lara trembled with an anger I'd seen in her only once before: that day at Alissa's house when she'd mentioned slavery,

"I thought Korea banned chipped slaves on pain of death..."

"There's nothing noble about that law. Korea has no need for them." The heat of her rage subsided, but her voice still wobbled. "Disciplinary education is so strict among the population that there is little dissent to any directive, and the Council has a surplus of mentally compromised workers from the old north to perform manual tasks that are suitable for the chipped elsewhere. But *Juche's* are something else. Their chips are implanted at birth, rather than later in life. Their specialization is determined by the highborn of the Corporate Council by the age of one, based on the projected desire of the client. Skills are downloaded into the child's developing brain. Their knowledge acquisition is far more rapid than any non-chipped human, even a highborn. Of course, complete obedience is input as well. By the time the subject has reached sixteen, he or she is ready for delivery. Or, in the case of the slaves ordered by Rose-Hart, they are ready for *export*. A ready-made scientist, one with no conscience, no morals, no family obligations, and absolutely loyal. Ready to work without wages for the rest of his or her life. And they are produced at least ten years faster than a traditional worker. Cheap and efficient."

"That's monstrous," I croaked. "Even for the high-born…But it makes sense. Who else could they rely on to develop their weapons of genocide? That explains how they kept it all a secret."

"They house them in an underground dormitory on the MTS line you saw on the map," Lara added. "No one even suspects they are in this country."

"'What shall it profit a man if he gains the world—and loses his soul,'" Nythan recited. "Oh, *Metropolis*, you saw it coming."

"When my father…" Lara closed her eyes, sucking in air. "When my father fell out of favor, my mother was pregnant with my brother." She turned away from me. I couldn't see her face.

"Remember that in there," Dillion said, his eyes locked on me. "Remember what these people are—what they are capable of."

Fire and ice flowed within me. There seemed no end to the madness of the world. I understood what drove Lara now: The hate for the people that had devised these creatures—and used her brother to make their human golems.

More pieces fell into place. The uniforms with Korean letters. Alissa and Lara's ancestry. I, with my dark hair and eyes. We would look like *juche* workers on the security videos. Alissa's hearing implants were too small to show up on video, and they were *organic*, like my repulse spray.

"How will Nythan fit in with the rest of us?" I asked.

Dillion answered. "They used Russian refugees for the initial trials. There are a few among the *products* delivered. Our pale pal won't cause a stir." He looked at his viser as the train began to hum softly. "Go time, people."

I heard Nythan mumbling to himself. "Like the mad woman said, 'may the odds be ever in our favor.'"

The ride was smooth and quick, the train nearly silent as it glided over the track below. I concentrated on my breathing, trying to steady myself. I had a mission to perform. Today was not the day to right every wrong. But it would be the day to strike a blow against the worst of the highborn. I hoped.

The doors swung open, as did a set of security gates along the edge of the tracks that shielded the facility from unauthorized access via the tunnel. Dillion shot me a final look that said "do your job," then exited. Lara led our line of faux human drones out behind him, our pacing steady, our steps quiet, our heads locked forward. I passed under the weapons scanner located above the first security gate without incident. My height allowed me to see over Lara's shoulder as we marched toward the security station.

The guard wore a vest of black, twin helix-shaped roses emblazoned on it like the arms of an ancient knight. The outfit matched the silver streaking through his slick black hair. He sat within a square of four transparent floor-to-ceiling walls, which I presumed were duraglass security screens, their data visible only to the person on the appropriate side of the wall. A metal door, large enough to drive two sedans through, had been built into the wall behind the security station.

"Requesting level eleven access," Dillion said as he stepped forward to place his hand sheathed in the cloned fingertips of Landrew Foster-Rose-Hart against the security screen. A retinal graft covered both eyes. Nythan had assured us it would fool the machines. The guard had no control of the doors—that was automated. But he would know that Dillion wasn't Landrew. That was where I came in.

I unleashed the force of my will against him. A flood of icy energy surged forth. My power didn't care about the nearly impregnable transparent alloy of the security station. It came fast and furious towards the guard—driving at what my mind pictured as a lonely wall of stone, no more than shoulder height. The guard didn't expect the onslaught. The sheer power of my cold will poured over his humble defenses, flooding the man's mind with my commands.

"The name on your screen matches the security identification data," I told him. "This is just another routine entry."

The guard gave no indication of having heard me. He glanced absently at Dillion and began tapping the wall. One tap. Two. Three. Enough time for ten beats of my heart.

"All clear," the guard said.

Some of the tension fell out of me. The giant portal rumbled open. Dillion led us through a wall as thick as three of us, into a white anteroom adjacent to the lift door. Dillion summoned the elevator with a touch of his false fingertips. The metal tomb closed behind us. We kept silent; we kept still. Cameras watched us, feeding our images to a control room in a distant part of the Ziggurat. But they didn't have cross-reference data from the MTS control room. We were the regularly scheduled *juche* shift change.

The lift doors opened without noise or prior warning. Dillion led us inside. We filed in, taking our pre-arranged locations. The lift was as silent as the train. I imagined us rising upwards from the ground into the great Ziggurat. To Landrew and his minions I wanted to shout: "*We are coming for you.* Go eat your prosperity through order."

The lift arrived at eleven, and Dillion led us out. His steps were slow, deliberate. He wanted to put the guard at ease. But he also wanted to give me time to assess the tactical situation.

Our information on level eleven was poor—educated guesses based on the design of other floors. Trouble came quickly.

A guard station was located ten feet from the elevator exit. It was the same transparent square as on the sub-level—an impenetrable shell that only a triller could overcome. We expected that. We didn't expect the additional guard standing at the end of the corridor behind the security station. He was at least fifty feet away from me. The farther security officer wore a black armored vest, force pistol at his side. But it wasn't the sidearm I feared. One flick of his visered hand and the alarm would go off, the floor would be sealed, and we were all dead. If we were lucky.

Dillion saw the danger as well. He placed each foot in front of the other almost reluctantly, giving me as much time as possible to assess the situation. I guessed that his mysterious California viser was weaponized in some way. But using it would be a last resort; weapons fire would trip the alarm. It was up to me.

I looked inside, sucking in as much of my life's essence as I dared. I thought of infants with silicon implanted in the back of their skulls. I thought of the men who dreamed up such horrors. I thought of those who made the Waste, who conjured the nightmare of trilling. I would not fail. I hurled forth my power, my soul, everything I had. The cold force of will left me in two streams. Each was a laser of determination, two tight beams rather than a flood.

Each guard had a wall protecting his mind. The first barrier was of brick, its mortar brittle. I made as if to scale it. The blocks multiplied with the speed of ten thousand craftsmen at work. It didn't matter. My concentrated will hit the first guard's mental masonry like a stone on glass. The fortification crumbled and his mind was mine for the taking.

The second barrier was steel, cold and high. It belonged to the more distant of the guards—a wary man. I came at it fast, but not as fast as I could have. The beam that was my will streaked to the right. The wall grew, extending its perimeter. We raced, my will versus the guard's innate mental defenses. But just as I did on the track, I held something back, while he gave it all he had. We raced down an infinite lane. I let the wall edge out ahead of me, extending its lead. All the time, my beam of will drifted up its face, ever so slightly. Just as the guard began to grow complacent, I turned on my remaining will, the beam surging upwards, moving faster than it had before. I was over the wall before his defenses could react. Another mind had fallen.

"Freeze," I commanded them both, my lips barely moving but my trill—that power that was more mind than sound—was no less potent for it.

Both men immobilized themselves. I realized that even their breathing had stopped. "Breathe," I commanded them both.

We were still being watched by unseen eyes. "We have approved access. This is another routine shift change," I told the guards.

Dillion led us past the security station, down the long, sterile corridor beyond. The door ahead was an airlock. Dillion kept his pace steady, but beads of sweat had gathered on the back of his neck. He used his fake fingertips to lead us inside.

We entered the airlock chamber, the door sealing ominously behind us. The too-bright lights above us dimmed slightly. I felt a wave of dizziness. My ears popped from a pressure change. The door ahead opened. We walked inside. Before us was the nerve center of level eleven.

I walked into the chamber of nightmares, where my greatest fears became real. The air temperature was just above freezing.

The primary laboratory consisted of two concentric rings. The first ring resembled the labs of the Lenox Life Center: tables, screens, machinery of all kinds. I caught an escaping gasp as I noticed the chipped slaves, attired in uniforms identical to my own, working like bees at several of the stations. They paid us no mind, their attention on their designated assignments: monitoring, analyzing, programming, splicing. They would keep at their tasks until directed otherwise.

The inner ring lay within a wall of thick transparent alloy—the same advanced duraglass used in the security stations. Inside was a controlled, sealed atmosphere. At its center was a shallow pool, no bigger than the bathtub in Alissa's apartment. Four glass rods, each the length of my forearm, stood in the pool, the bottom third of their length submerged in the thick liquid. Robot arms were positioned on all sides of the pool, available to manipulate or retrieve the precious control-Colonies within.

A man attired in an executive suit like Dillion's noticed us. He flicked his fingers and looked at his viser, not really paying attention as he walked towards us.

"I'm having trouble syncing the shift change log with you," he said.

The supervisor was distracted, his defenses weak. I got him with a quick jab of will through a white picket fence. "Freeze, but breathe," I commanded.

The chipped slaves still ignored us. There were no other humans in the lab. We were safe, for now. There were no security personnel trusted enough to gaze upon the horrors done here. We stood inside the eye of the hurricane.

Dillion scanned the room like a hawk, searching the ground for its prey. His lips twitched. I followed his gaze. He locked in on a pair of elaborate consoles attached to the inner ring wall.

"Watch the company suit," Dillion told me. "Make sure he doesn't break the trill. Don't move from that spot in case we need you."

He left me in his wake, hungry for whatever prize those consoles offered. It had to be something California wanted badly, to expend these resources. A weapon perhaps. I didn't like it. But I'd go along with it in exchange for the cure. Lara followed him, stopping beside a *juche* worker. The human drone paid no attention to her. Not even when she pulled the back of his high collar and placed her California viser over a bulge in the back of the man's neck. Lara's lips moved rapidly. She was speaking Korean. Hacking the *juche* worker, perhaps. Her special talent.

Nythan was spinning in circles, also searching for something.

"Over there," he said triumphantly. "A direct access terminal. It's sealed up, old style, just like we thought. Let's go, Alissa."

They walked over to a gray, rectangular box extending from the floor; it was a bit smaller than a fabricator. Its only surface feature was a manual black dial with numbers on it. It reminded me of an old-fashioned safe. No electronics; not hackable by conventional means. Alissa placed her right ear next to the door and started turning, her implant letting her hear what we could not. Nythan gazed at his viser intently as she worked. In less than a minute the door swung open. Nythan flicked his fingers on his visered arm even before he got to the interface embedded inside. Alissa hung over his shoulder.

"Just hack through and get the data, Nythan," she urged. "Don't get carried away. We don't have much time."

I watched Nythan working furiously, completely focused on the screens before him. He was in the near-trance state I'd seen on Tuck's rooftop. His fingers and eyes moved at an almost violent speed. I watched his lips tense. His face grew taut. Something unexpected was happening.

My spider-sense rang in my head. I felt my hands go numb. Havelock's face popped into my mind. His last words rang like a bell inside my head. The genocide will spread. *Unless we stop it—completely.*

I looked over at Dillion—he and Lara had activated the robotic arms with the help of the hacked *juche* worker. They were absorbed in whatever they were doing. I whispered into the ear of the frozen Rose-Hart supervisor next to me.

"Tell me where to find the cure for the Waste—for the Culling," I ordered.

He looked at me, his eyes sky blue. They were too innocent for a place such as this. "There is no cure," he told me.

Time stopped. My heart stopped. My breathing stopped. I was falling down a black chasm that went on forever. I couldn't feel my body; I couldn't see anything. *A fool.* That's all I had ever been. A blind fool. *Don't trust these people.* The memory of Matco's face yanked me back to the present.

"Status report of cure-development research," I ordered.

"All research into the reversal of the Culling was discontinued seven months after the initiation of Project Wool. No viable solution to halt the process has been identified."

They knew. Havelock, Dillion…maybe the others as well. They knew there was no cure from the start. I hadn't trusted them, not fully. I knew they wanted more than just a cure. But I hadn't suspected the cure itself was a lie. I thought I was clever. Instead, I was a pup among the wolves.

It all made sense now. They brought in an angry girl. A poor girl. Someone who hated the highborn. They watched me to make sure I was who they wanted. Alissa's job was to keep me close, groom me. Havelock dangled the track team in front of me with a special tryout, knowing Nessmier would snatch it away. That was why he'd been furious when Alexander got me in, why they all reacted with horror when I told them Alexander had invited me to his house. They wanted someone who hated the highborn as much as they did. They used Mateo; dangling the cure in front of me. All to make sure I didn't say no to this mission. Like the last girl who could trill must have. The one who had supposedly killed herself.

I walked over to Alissa and Nythan. He was still working furiously, his hair damp from sweat.

"It's not here," Nythan said, his voice near panic. "I've got every file. There's no cure. No Project Wool." He looked up at Alissa, his eyes as wide as I'd ever seen them. "We were wrong. How could we be wrong?"

"Just get the data you can, Nythan," Alissa said soothingly. "Now isn't the time to analyze. We'll figure it out."

I gazed cold hate at Alissa, my betrayer. My will was a sledgehammer. She had practiced fighting me off using her wall of polished marble, the stones high and precise. But it wasn't enough. My fury had no bounds, no limit. I punched at her with my mind. Her wall shattered into a ruined heap.

"Tell me what happened to Marie-Ann," I commanded.

Alissa turned to me. The muscles of her face twitched. The command was inside, but something within her still fought. She didn't want to answer. But she had no choice.

"Lara," she croaked. "She pushed her over the edge."

Nythan made a choking sound. "What? Alissa, what the hell are you talking about?"

"Why did Lara push her? Tell me."

Alissa's mouth twitched. "I told Marie-Ann about the true mission. She wouldn't agree to it. We'd seen her…talking to Kristolan…We…couldn't take the chance."

"Jacks of hell, Alissa. She was your friend—our friend," Nythan gasped, his mouth not quite closed. He gazed at me, his eyes pleading. He spoke with as much passion as I'd ever heard him muster. "I didn't know, Daniela. I swear it. I didn't know."

"Why didn't you tell Nythan about the true objective?" I asked Alissa.

"Havelock's orders," Alissa said. "Nythan's psychological profile suggested that the prospect of mass casualties would make him reevaluate his participation, and we needed his expertise."

Nythan's hands balled themselves into fists. He was trembling.

"What mass casualties? What does Havelock really want?" I asked.

"Modify the controlColonies. Introduce the Culling DNA to the highborn parent strand. Infect an entire generation of highborn, as they sought to infect us. If we can keep our operation secret, if we can get out of here without them noticing, it could be months, or years, before they detect the change. Hundreds of thousands, perhaps millions, will be infected. Their evil will be exposed beyond any ability to conceal it. They'll search frantically for a cure, even as their children die around them. The system will become tainted, untrusted. The highborn will end. Or at least, suffer devastating damage."

That was what Havelock meant by genocide. It was the highborn or the nopes, and he chose the highborn to die.

"They struck first, Daniela," Dillion said from behind me, his voice grave. "We are protecting ourselves." He stood no more than a foot away, his viser pointed at my head. His weaponized, Californian viser.

"What does California get out of this?" I asked. "Havelock couldn't have gotten here without you. He wouldn't have had the resources. Getting that train working took expertise."

"The embargo is killing us. People are in the streets, hungry and angry. Most of the world is against us. They want us to fail. We need to reunify, make this country whole again. But that's not going to happen as long as the Orderists are in power. This will bring them down. It will make people rethink everything."

"Did you try to kill Landrew Foster-Rose-Hart? Did you plan to attack the Allocators' Ball?"

"None of that is us. Landrew's faction wants to invade Cali, the President's supporters want to keep the embargo. Landrew planned the attack on the allocators. He wanted to provoke the allocators, get them all on his side, all those taxes and votes. He was betrayed by some of his own people. We don't know why. It wasn't us."

"It's the same stupid game," I said. "Killing each other. You're just as bad. Not every highborn is evil. If you condemn children to die at twenty, inscribing their fate into their genes before they are even born, how is that any better than what the Corporate Council has done in Korea?"

"You can't be this naive," Dillion spat. "Not where you come from. I know. I grew up someplace not so different. We are highborn in our genes, but our minds are free. We can make the choices that need to be made. I'm sorry we had to lie to you. We couldn't take the chance. Not after Marie-Ann. Not after you cozied up to that highborn jack-A. But you've shown you are a fighter. Join us, Daniela, and we'll develop the cure. We've got the computer data."

"We should take the controlColonies," Nythan said. "I've been looking at the Waste for years, without finding the solution. We'll need the actual strains to make quick progress."

Dillion shook his head. "If they know we were here, this all falls apart. The rods stay. That's the highest priority. I'm sorry, but this world requires hard choices."

My eyes narrowed. They had told me trilling a highborn was impossible. But Nythan had never counted on someone like me. I'd been practicing since I was five.

"Don't do it, Daniela," Dillion warned, his fingers flexing anxiously. "It can't be done. And I'm not about to let you try. Your mouth even twitches and I'll put you down. You can't get out of here without me. My men control the train. You're dead if you try to leave here and I'm not with you."

His reflexes were probably as quick as mine. He expected an attack. And he was highborn. It wouldn't work. But I didn't see any other way.

Dillion's eyes darted to his left as a screen hurtled towards him. He was quick, batting it away with his non-visered hand. But Nythan's desperate gambit had given me the opening I needed. I plowed into Dillion with my right shoulder, putting everything I had into it. He was bigger, but I was fast. I heard the wind escape his lungs as he toppled onto the floor. I shoved a fist into his gut. I had my repulse spray in my hand a moment later. But he'd been trained to fight. His instincts took over. He rolled away even as I sprayed. The liquid caught the back of his neck but missed his face. Dillion gritted his teeth in agony even as he scrambled out of the way of my next shot. I chased him, spraying. I hit one of his hands with another burst. He cried out in pain. My spider-sense screamed. I twisted backwards as a projectile shot from Dillion's viser, racing past my chin and striking the armored wall of the chamber's inner ring. I waited for the alarm. Nothing. This room was invisible to the rest of the Ziggurat.

Lara crashed into me from behind. I staggered forward as she shoved me, more angry than strong. But she'd surprised me. I barely kept a grip on the repulse spray as I dropped to my knees. I thrust an elbow behind me, catching Lara on the mouth. I heard a satisfying crunch. I grabbed her head with both of my hands, pulling her close to me, her face pressed next to mine.

"Enough," Dillion spat. "Put your hands on your head, you stupid bitch."

He was standing above me, his viser aimed at my head. I showed him both my hands, empty. Slowly, I stood, my eyes never leaving his. He was in pain. The room smelled like burned flesh. His gaze said that he intended to kill me. I smiled. That got him. He had enough time for a split second of panic before Lara emptied the repulse spray onto his face, just as I had commanded.

Dillion cupped his hands over his eyes. He screamed, clawing at his face. But he was highborn. He yanked his hands down from his bubbling skin. Both eyelids were shut. He couldn't see. Yet he still managed to spread his arms and leap towards the last spot I'd been standing in. I tried to twirl away, but he caught my hair with one of his hands. He pulled me down with him, thrashing at me even as his agony ate away at him. I jammed my knee into his gut, but he didn't flinch. His nails dug into my arms. I felt my suit tear. The next moment his entire body jerked in a single sudden spasm, as if administered by an electric shock. He was completely still for a moment. Then he slumped down, his powerful fingers limp. A bioScalpel protruded from his back, Nythan's trembling hand on the handle. Blood began to pool beneath him.

"Is he dead?" Nythan asked.

"As good as, I think," I said, pulling myself back to my feet.

"Now what?" he asked.

I looked at the inner glass, at the controlColonies within. "Can you cure the Waste? Really cure it?"

"By myself? No. But with some help, and facilities and resources, perhaps. But I lack all of those, since I doubt Headmaster Havelock will be in a generous mood if we ever meet him again. But if we're to have any chance of saving your brother, we need those rods. I've already got the computer data." He raised his viser.

"Can you trash this place? Wipe out their work? You said it's a closed system—not a network. We take the rods, destroy the data, and they can't replicate the Waste. They can't replicate the trilling gene. Not for many years, at least."

Nythan rubbed his eyes. "You're mostly correct. They might have a backup somewhere. But I'll leave a nice little Trojan virus to deal with that. Way better than what I unleashed at Tuck. That was a baby compared to what I'll leave here. I tucked it into this crazy viser they gave me, just in case things went bad. We just might be able to get it all." He grinned. The game was back on for him.

"Get started," I told him. "I'll fish out those rods."

"The consoles control the arms. The *juche* has already unlocked the system. Shouldn't be too hard to finish the work. There'll be a small door with an airlock somewhere inside the room. Bring the rods through there one at a time. Try not to drop them. They shouldn't weigh more than three pounds each."

I looked at my viser. It was one minute past nine. Not much time. We both got to work. The mechanized arms weren't difficult to operate, but neither were they fast.

"We've got five minutes," I told Nythan as I finished retrieving the rods.

"I'm ready," he said, still flicking his fingers as he stood up from the terminal. "How do we get out?"

"Same way we got in," I said. "That fancy-suited supervisor I trilled is easy enough to control. His hands can operate the security detectors. I'll tell him he's taking us out on the next scheduled tram. I'll get Alissa and Lara to think the mission has been completed and they are following Dillion out."

"Time is ticking," Nythan pointed out. "On the way out, tell the security guards to receive a data confirmation from our supervisor friend, then feed it into their network. It's another virus I'll implant. Hopefully it'll erase their security feeds, so they don't know who we are. It's set to blow in about fifteen minutes."

"Got it."

He shoved the rods inside his skin and adjusted the supervisor's viser while I performed the necessary commands for our companions. Even with the bulk of the suit, I could see the outline of the rods, but only if I looked carefully. The original mission required secrecy, ours didn't—we didn't care about never being discovered. We only needed a few minutes to get to the train.

I commanded the Rose-Hart executive to lead us out of the airlock. The rest of us followed him. The temperature and pressure returned to normal. The exterior door swung open, revealing the long, white corridor with the guard station at the end. The moment I stepped out of the airlock behind Lara, the guard I had frozen on the way in turned sharply towards me. He wore a confused look on his face, like a man abruptly woken from a deep slumber.

I attacked before he got his wits back. My mind formed into a spray of small circular pellets. I came at him like the blast of a shotgun, portions of my will assaulting his sluggish defenses from all directions. His wall grew upwards and sideways. He caught almost everything I sent in the first wave. But three pellets got through. That was enough to wreak havoc. I saw his eyes flutter. I came again with a flood of cold will. This time he was too slow to stop me.

"Freeze. Breathe," I ordered.

The other security guard looked at us from his tiny fortress. He squinted, perhaps not quite sure what he heard.

"Hallis, did you say something?" he asked the supervisor leading our line.

I took that guard down as easily as I had the first time. A hard, straight spear of will was all it took. I commanded him to download Nythan's virus into the Rose-Hart security system, then freeze himself. I stole a surreptitious glance at my viser. We had two minutes left. The lift arrived and carried us downstairs, back to the sub-level. The enormous vault door groaned open, ignorant of my impatience. The opening became man-sized. Then bigger. Finally, the portal was fully opened. The suited executive started walking again, his pace measured and unhurried. I held my breath as we stepped through. No train.

I froze the final security officer. We were two minutes late. All this way, and we had missed it. Or had it never even come? I could feel Nythan grow anxious behind me. I stared at the tracks.

Out of the corner of my eye, I saw light. The blur of something. I blinked twice more and an MTS train appeared, new and beautiful. My heart grew inside me. I fought to keep the smile off my face. The train door slid open.

The supervisor led us on board. The doors shut behind us. The emergency override chamber was occupied. A head peeked out.

"Need a ride?" Alexander asked me.

THIRTY-EIGHT

"What is that jack-a-jock doing here?" Nythan demanded. He sounded more upset than he should've considering we'd otherwise have been stranded inside the Ziggurat.

"Well met, Nythan Royce." Alexander said it as if Nythan had offered him a hug rather than an insult. He went back to the emergency controls. The train glided out of the station.

"He's saving our tails, Nythan. Or would you rather find another way out?" I grabbed a handhold close to where Alexander worked the manual train controls. He was clad in dark enameled body armor, a force pistol holstered at his waist. The sight was jarring—like seeing Aba walking around with a machete. But hadn't I just broken into Rose-Hart Industries? Hadn't I been a part of killing Dillion?

"Save us? Him and what army?" Nythan asked.

"The only one I could think of to help us," I said, my voice quiet with worry.

I hadn't anticipated California and their professional soldiers being involved. I hadn't realized the danger when I had brought those most dear into my scheme. But I had been right to trust Alexander. I had doubted him for a time inside the Ziggurat, but here he was.

"You told him about us? Are you insane?" Nythan's voice trembled with outrage. "Why didn't you floor him with my magic tooth like you were supposed to?"

I closed my eyes for a fleeting moment. That night at Alexander's house seemed an eternity ago, the agony of my decisions a mere echo of their former power. But I hadn't forgotten the image of Alexander drawing close to me. That was seared into my soul. Something inside me had cried out as I bit down on that tooth. Instead of exhaling the foul gas at Alexander, I had whipped my head towards the wall, away from him.

"I decided on something more difficult, Nythan." Alexander turned from the control panel as I spoke. "I decided I could trust him."

Nythan's eyes widened. "Jack me, but why would you of all people do that? He's as highborn as a person can be. Two rounds of gene sifting to make that mighty specimen."

My gaze locked with Alexander's as I answered. "I realized that if we're going to make a better world, the people who live in this one need to change." I swallowed hard. "I need to change."

Nythan shook his head. "I never figured you for an idealist, Daniela. Or a fool."

"It's only foolish if she was wrong," Alexander said, his voice a deep rumble. "She's not. I've not been blind to what is going on. Quite the opposite."

"He can trill, Nythan. He trusted me enough to share his secret. He did it before he knew about any of this."

"Does he know what his family is? What they've done?" Nythan demanded, looking at me, but he was really speaking to Alexander.

Alexander nodded solemnly. "My father is a man comfortable in the darkness. My mother told me that, a long time ago. I knew he sought…unconventional solutions to the disorder around him. I had not thought he would go so far as genocide. I am sorry for that blindness. It…it is hard to accept such evil, even when it is right in front of you."

"And your sister?" Nythan pressed.

"She told me what she was, four years ago. She showed me how to tap into what was inside me. But she also told me we were the only ones—chosen in some way. A lie, of course, to serve her own ends, her thirst for power. She is like my father, a master of the game. But something happened between them, my father and Kris. A rift between the aging king and his impatient pupil. Something bad enough that I suspect she may have been responsible for the attempt on his life. His security has been instructed to keep everyone away from the HRZ, where he is ailing. Kris is corrupted by the darkness. Only her outside shines. Inside there is a cancer."

"If she's so bad, why did she break you out?" Nythan challenged. "What did you promise her?"

Alexander's back stiffened. "I promised her *nothing*. Of course she had plans for me, some scheme that required bringing me into this secret. She's two years older than me, and I once looked up to her. Loved her. Before she became what she is now. She sought to control me with lies, to have another minion to do her bidding. For a time it worked." His chin lifted. "I know better than anyone how dangerous she is. You think it is my father who is the greatest danger. You are *wrong*. It is Kristolan you should fear. For there is nothing she would not do to feed her own hunger to control…everything. The school, the company, that won't be enough. I finally realize that. And she has the power to do it."

I shivered, but Nythan's face was still twisted with disbelief.

"You are willing to turn your back on your highborn family to help us?" Skepticism dripped from his lips.

Alexander was silent for a few moments, his face unreadable. When he spoke, the words came slowly, reluctantly. "I had a mother. She's gone now. But when I was seven, shortly before she left, she told me...things about my father. Things not meant for a child, but if she didn't tell me then, there would never have been another chance. Her words live inside me, as she does. She told me that I could choose to be better than the world around me. I've spent my life trying to give meaning to those words. She was my family. Not the man who supposedly was my father. Not my sister, not anymore. So I'm turning my back on nothing, Nythan Royce. Rather, I am choosing the path I had always chosen: that of honor."

Nythan snorted. Blood rushed to my face, anger laced my words.

"Nythan, he just risked his life to save yours. Since the day I met him, he's done everything he said he would. And he *never* lied to me." My glare bored into Nythan. He flushed. "I made the choice to trust him. It wasn't easy for me, with the life I've lived. I know what's inside him. I can sense it. If I can trust Alexander, why can't you?"

Nythan's strangely pale eyes darkened for a moment. He studied Alexander's face, then mine. "Seeing as he's at the controls, I don't have much of a choice, do I?"

"No," I said.

"In that case, I suppose I'll give your boy a chance. At least till we're safely out of here."

Alexander acknowledged the sentiment with a deep nod.

Nythan grinned. "Thanks for saving our rears, by the way."

THIRTY-NINE

The train slowed, then jerked to a stop, bringing us all back to the urgency of the present. We had made it back to the access tunnel, but Rose-Hart's security wouldn't be far behind.

The door opened and Mateo's lieutenant, Inky, stepped inside, dressed in barrio rags, an old projectile pistol in his hand. I recognized Kross as well. He followed in a similar outfit, with a similar weapon, but had a blood-stained bandage on his left shoulder. Seeing it made my throat tighten. *Did you really expect no one would get hurt?* I'd told Alexander that my brother could help. We'd all planned it. But I hadn't truly considered the cost until now. I hadn't counted on the depth of Havelock's betrayal.

"What's up Dee?" Inky said, as if we had just met on the street. He raised the barrel of his pistol to the left temple of the Rose-Hart supervisor. "Who's this turd?"

"I got it," I told him. "Put the gun down."

He didn't. I walked over to the suited Rose-Hart executive. He was babbling to himself—his mind struggling to rid itself of the artificial pathways I had forced upon it. His forehead was bathed in moisture. His eyes darted about.

"Sleep," I ordered. He lay down in the middle of the floor. "Forget everything you saw today."

"Nice trick," Inky said as he watched the man lie down like an obedient puppy. "What else can you make him do? Bark?"

"I'll tell you about it another time."

"What about the rest of these jokers?" Inky asked, waving his gun at Nythan, Alissa, and Lara as if it were a finger.

I put a hand on Nythan's shoulder. "Nythan is on our team. The other two…" I looked at them. Lara's jaw was grinding. She had a strong will. Her surroundings were no longer consistent with the lie I had placed in her mind. Leaving them here meant they'd be captured. Interrogated. Probably murdered. I turned my attention to Alissa. She had almost been a friend. Almost. Even if it was based on a lie. But she had been part of Marie-Ann's murder. I couldn't trust her, or forgive her.

"Alissa and Lara, head back to the safe house. Get some rest, then go home. Good work today," I said. Lara continued to look around even as my command took root in her mind.

"Is this our team?" Alissa asked, uncertain.

"You accomplished your objective. Get some rest," I assured her.

"What is up with them, Dee?" Inky asked. "Those girls look wacked. I always enjoy jacking up some highborn, but this is getting weird. Mateo said this was big, and he's the boss, but still—"

"Later. Is anyone hurt besides Kross?" I asked. "Where's Mateo?"

"I'm here," my brother answered, sticking his head inside the train. He had a bit of blood on the corner of his lip, but otherwise appeared unharmed. "Kross took a grazing shot from one of those damn visers. A few other scrapes. But we got the drop on them. There were only five, including the one who went with you."

I wrapped my arms around Mateo. "Thanks for coming through. I owe you one."

"I'll remember you said that." My brother flashed a little boy's smile. He carried a bag of visers from the safe house. Nythan and I grabbed our familiar devices gratefully.

I turned to Alexander. "How did you find us? Or the access to the train? They transferred us to an interior room I didn't know about. I couldn't get back to the window to send a message."

"Your brother improvised."

I looked expectantly at Mateo.

"When you went a whole day without signaling, we knew something had happened. Those California tough guys, they wouldn't last ten minutes in the barrio. They had every fancy tech gadget you could think of and some you couldn't imagine. Seriously, they had stuff to block sensor sweeps, jam comm channels, hide power sources. They had stealth radio links…but they never bothered to worry about some damn simple snoopin'."

"Snoopin'?" Nythan asked.

"Yeah, smart guy," Inky said. "It's when you like…wait till it's night, then sneak upstairs on your own two legs with your own two ears and a little bitty flashlight. You see one room is empty, but hey, there's like tracks on the really dirty floor. And the footprints go upstairs. And then, you go next door and stick your little ear up to the wall and listen. No visers, no gadgets, no richie tricks."

Mateo laughed. "Once we saw you climb into the toilet—loved that by the way—we got the drop on them. They split up and got to work. They were all so focused on their silly screens and visers it was almost easy."

"Where are they?" I asked.

"What's left of 'em, they in the garage," Inky declared proudly.

"You killed them?" I said to Mateo, feeling like I'd been punched in the gut.

"What else we goin' to do with 'em, Dee?" Inky asked. "The one I tried to reason with gave Kross that thing on his shoulder. Little Jim shot the bastard in the eye."

"Didn't really have a choice," Mateo told me, his eyes serious. "I told you this was for keeps when you and the rich boy asked for help. You said you understood."

I nodded, knowing this was on me. It was them or us. California would be looking for blood if they ever found out who did this. But I didn't think they would. Rose-Hart would take the blame.

"What about Havelock?" I asked.

"Not here," Alexander said. "Lucky or smart, or both. But he's gone."

He wouldn't give up, I knew. And I'd added myself to his list of enemies. But that was a problem for another day. "You got transport?" I asked Mateo. "Nythan's got the rods and the data. We gotta' get out of here before Rose-Hart figures out they've been hit and turns out the troops."

"Cars are in the underground garage with the rest of the boys," he said. "Barrio's going to be the safest place for a while. No one's getting into Manhattan because of the jack-A's Ball, but they don't really care about anyone leaving. Once the corp reviews their security feeds, they'll come looking for you, though, even in BC. Corps have got a long memory and a nasty temper."

Nythan shrugged. "Maybe. Maybe not. I put a Trojan virus into their security system. A nasty one. Might not be anything for them to see. But let's not take any chances. Laying low in BC sounds like a good idea. The sooner the better."

We hurried out of the train, back through the narrow access corridor, then up the ladder that led to the toilet. Mateo led the way. I ran between Alexander and Nythan. The night was cool, the sky clear. No drones. At least, none in the Vision Quad. We jogged across the street, then down the garage ramp on the far side of the beat-up apartment building. My spider-sense started tingling. I grabbed hold of Nythan with one hand, Alexander with the other.

"Something's wrong," I called out.

Too late.

FORTY

A pair of blazing headlights clicked on directly in front of us. For several moments I saw only white as my eyes adjusted to the glare. My instinct told me to run. But I knew it was too late for that. Men in body armor, carrying force rifles, ran out from the light. Two circled around our group. The light made it hard to tell how many more there were.

"Inside, inside, inside," the men behind us ordered. "Hands on your head. Keep walking, down into the garage."

I reached for the cold power inside me. I knew Alexander was doing the same. The bastards would have to deal with two trillers. But first we had to know how many we faced. And if any were highborn.

They brought us inside the old parking lot, out of easy view. They kept a distance from us, their weapons poised. The light dimmed to a more comfortable intensity. Little Jim was lying on the ground in a pool of his own blood just in front of a row of sedans. Alissa, Lara, and four more of the *Corazones* were sitting on the floor not far away, their hands bound in front of them with Authority-grade wires. Their expressions were grim, except for Alissa, who had a bruise on her face, her eyes wide with terror.

"Hands on top of your heads," ordered a female voice, hard and strong. She had pupils nearly as black as her body armor, her arms thick and toned. "Any of you even flinch and I'll put a hole in your skull." She scanned the group, not blinking as her companions came forward to disarm Alexander and the *Corazones*. They moved with caution and confidence, like panthers on the prowl. I probed their minds with my will. Power radiated back at me. They were highborn.

"Lindra," Alexander said to the woman. "You're supposed to be protecting my father. And Nero...Blane. What are you doing here?"

"Welcome, little people," said another voice. One I recognized. A chill passed through me.

Drake walked out from the shadows, a sadistic grin on his face. He looked like a parody of an Authority stormtrooper in his black getup, a wicked-looking force rifle clutched uneasily in both hands. More of the brave new world. The kids had guns now, even if Drake looked ridiculous with it. Alone, I wouldn't have been afraid of him. But he wasn't by himself. The others were professional fighters. Killers.

"Daddy finally bit it, Alexander," Drake said with mocking delight. "You might say your father's former employees are looking to the future."

"Keep a distance, Drake," Lindra cautioned. "Let us handle this. We don't know how many of them are highborn."

"Relax, Lindra," Drake said. "Only Alexander and the girl are our kind, and I'm faster than either of them. You've got your orders and I've got mine. Stick to the brawn." He tapped his head. "I've got the juice in here to do what needs to be done."

"What do you mean looking to the future?" Alexander asked. But I already knew what was coming. There was only one reason Drake would be here.

"Your sister sends her regards. We're going to deliver you and your lady to her intact. Along with the controlColonies held by that runty ghost over there, and the data you stole. Your sister will have it all: the most valuable asset of Rose-Hart Industries, as well as sole possession of the trilling gene and the Culling data."

"Powerful leverage against any other contenders for control of the family voting shares—Arik included," Alexander said.

Drake gave him a pat on the cheek. "You are so smart. Alexander the Great. And you don't even know the half of it. Your sister has got big plans." Alexander's eyes flashed with alarm. Drake turned to me. "Little miss street trash. But hell of a job in there, trasher. Got the rods, and took care of the California cops. But you aren't really trash, are you? You're a highborn slumming it." He laughed. It sounded maniacal. I recalled what Alissa had said about Marie-Ann coming un-hinged. Listening to Drake, I believed it. "Kris wants to talk to you as well. She'd like to know how you figured out how to trill."

"Why would I talk to someone who is going to hurt my friends? Whose goon sent a drone to kill me. And who will probably finish the job once she gets what she wants."

Drake gave a terrifying chomp of his teeth. They looked like fangs. "I can't believe you and the ghost boy dodged my drone. You deserved it after what you did to me on the track. But if you play nice, who knows what Kris'll do for you? She's the only person with any hope of developing a cure now...And if you don't...well, Kris thinks of everything. She's got your blood sister with her too. Kortilla, yeah? So you better be on your best behavior."

"Kortilla has nothing to do with this." I struggled to keep the panic from my voice.

Drake's lips curled in a feral snarl. "Kris is always extra care-ful. Had a hard time getting that one. You told her to hide out with her bro, huh? Good idea. Except I can trill too. And it's easy to find out what you want that way. Just like I'm going to do to your motley crew here."

Rage flooded through my body; my limbs felt like magma. I felt my will struggling to explode out of me. To strike out at Drake. But he was highborn. I gritted my teeth, trying to hold the angry beast inside.

"How did you find us?" Alexander asked.

Drake flashed googly eyes at Alexander, then me. He was definitely off his rocker. Lindra saw it as well. Her finger rested uneasily on the trigger of her force rifle. She could mow us down with it in seconds. Landrew's other ex-security officers stood to my left and right, a good ten feet away. I might be able to reach Lindra, but there was no way to get to the others before they fried me.

"You love birds have got to be more careful where you do your chatting. Did you really think Kris wasn't going to no-tice her brother wandering off with the Latina temptress? Or that she didn't have means to monitor her own home?" Drake chuckled again. "Okay, play time's over. Give me the rods and your viser, runty. Play nice and I'll deliver your thumbs to your daddy so he has something to remind him of you."

Drake grabbed Nythan by the neck. I didn't doubt that he would kill him, or any of us. The scent of madness lingered on him.

Our enemy had superior weaponry, and they had us in their power. Worse, all four were highborn. Kris had been careful. She understood the power of trilling. She had been doing it longer than anyone else. But she wasn't a runner. Competition wasn't in her blood. She hadn't been calling on the power day after day, race after race, using everything to get ahead.

I knew what Alexander was thinking, and he knew that I was ready. I felt him gathering his power. I extended my hand and Alexander took it. Together, we attacked a highborn.

In my mind, I stood above a lake—a pool of my own life force. It represented every bit of strength I possessed, and I called it to me. It came into my lungs in a flood. I drew it up into my fingers, and through the bottoms of my feet. It swirled around me like a tornado. My head felt as if it would burst. I felt a tinge of madness, a place where the power would become my master rather than the other way around. I thought of Drake: he who had done nothing but ill to my friends and me. A person who reeked of hate.

My will came at him as a storm—a wall of thick, angry clouds advancing on the flaming sphere around Drake's mind. Thunder announced my presence. Alexander was there as well: a great eagle of light, talons the size of a car and a wingspan wider than the East River. We charged towards the sphere of blazing fire shielding Drake's mind. Blue flames crackled amid the crimson surface of the star. The power of the barrier pressed against my mind as I neared.

I sent a curtain of rain at Drake, tiny droplets of will that contacted the sphere in a flashing explosion of light. The wall of fire surged as I drew closer. Alexander's eagle soared ahead of me, its talons extended, coming in to strafe the inferno. The silvery bird cried in pain as flares of boiling crimson erupted towards it. The eagle swept around, circling away from the scorching power of Drake's defenses.

This was nothing like the other minds I had faced. With non-highborn, I could evade a mind's defenses, find an opening in the wall and slip a punch inside like a nimble boxer. There was no opening in Drake's mind. He was shielded by genetic manipulation. The only way through was to fight. But that wasn't the greatest danger. When I pushed my will at

Drake, his trilling ability responded in kind. We were joined by the power of our minds. This was to be a battle of wills. Either I would shatter his defenses and impose my dominance upon him, or my mind would break in the attempt. Drake's sphere pulsed at the challenge. I met its call.

My storm spread out, as if opening its arms for an embrace. Clouds rolled forth in every direction, creating a blanket of storm. My tempest spread far enough that it could wrap around the entirety of the star before it. I came at Drake, an unstoppable sheet to smother the flames of his inferno.

The agony of a thousand knives met me. The crackling thunder of the storm gave expression to my agony. I had placed myself atop a boiling cauldron, and it hungered to consume me. Drake's sphere shook and thrashed as I squeezed it. It was like the correction I had endured at the hands of the Authority, except more painful by an unimaginable margin. This was the moment of torment when soldiers cried out for their mothers, when they knew with certainty that death had come to claim them. But I had survived correction. And this time I was not alone.

Alexander's eagle flew into my cloud of will, passing his power to me as it did so. A surge of energy swept through me like a tidal wave. For an instant I was within that place of chaotic power, delirious with energy. If a human could be a god, I was one in that moment. Drake's fire collapsed as I smothered it with the force of two wills. What had been burning iron became glass. I pushed harder, driven by need, and by hate. The sphere shattered—a star that burned no more. The highborn who had been Drake Pillis-Smith became my puppet.

"The Rose-Hart men are your enemies. They will betray you. Kill them before they kill you. Kill them all," I told Drake.

A force rifle flashed. Its deadly pulse fired almost too quickly for the human eye to see. I blinked and one of the Rose-Hart men had a hole through the center of his chest, his face frozen in mute horror. Drake spun at the second rifleman. Two highborn reflexes were matched against each other. Drake had surprise, but Landrew's former guard had instinct drilled into him from years of service. They fired simultaneously. Drake shot at the other man's head—in a flash, everything above the rifleman's neck had simply been erased. But the dead can still exact vengeance. A blast from the headless shooter's weapon cut through Drake's left rib. Drake dropped to his knees, his weapon falling, both hands clutching the gash in his side.

I crashed into Lindra, shoulder first. I put all my strength into the jump, shoving off the ground and hurling myself headfirst against her unprotected side. I expected her to go down on impact. She didn't. She staggered backwards, but stayed on her feet. I was trapped in an awkward bear hug position, struggling to keep her arms and the force rifle she held pinned against her chest. She thrashed like a bronco trying to throw its rider. I flew to the left, then the right, but I held on, my hands ghost white from the effort. What the hell was everyone else doing?

A hammer smashed into my forehead. No, not a hammer. Lindra's skull. Blackness invaded my vision, like wet paint dripping from a canvas. Everything faded out. I fell backwards. Someone caught me before I hit the ground.

I woke up to find Mateo and Alexander looking down at me. Mateo had my head cradled in his lap. Lindra sat bloody and unconscious a short distance away. The wound looked bad. She wouldn't make it.

"How do you feel?" Alexander asked.

"Same way you'd feel if someone had slammed a rock-filled head into your skull." I rubbed my head. "How long was I out?"

"A couple of minutes," Mateo told me. "We need to get out of here. We'll carry you into the car."

I forced myself up. A mistake. The world rushed at me, then spun in circles. I held out my arms for balance, biting my lip till I tasted blood. My vision steadied. I saw Mateo shaking his head. Drake was lying on the ground, bleeding badly. Inky had a force rifle pointed at the highborn's face.

"Where's Kortilla?" I demanded.

Drake's eyes shut, then opened again. His stare was blank. It might have been his injury, or what Alexander and I had done to his mind. We hadn't influenced him, or tricked him—we had broken him.

I got down on my knees. "I own you," I whispered in his ear, pushing the burning cold of my will into him. "Tell me where Kris has taken Kortilla."

Drake's eyes moved, trying to focus. Streaks of blood ran through his pupils. Drool leaked from his mouth. "HRZ…" he croaked. His eyes shut. I felt for a pulse. Irregular, but still going.

"Why did she kill her father?"

Drake didn't stir. I pushed my will deeper into him, looking for any consciousness still hiding within him. I found nothing. His heart might be beating, but the man was just a shell. He wouldn't last much longer.

"What else does Kris want the controlColonies for?" Alexander demanded.

Nothing.

I stood, looking down at Drake. For him I felt no pity. Justice had found him, even if I was a flawed messenger.

"How do we get to the HRZ?" I asked Alexander. "The Authority will have patrols all over the sky."

"We could wait till the morning—" Alexander said.

"No way," I answered. "If Drake doesn't return, Kris will know something went wrong. We'll never get to her then. She'll use Kortilla against me, she'll do anything to get the controlColonies. She wants control of Rose-Hart and the trilling gene. You told us how dangerous she is, how ruthless. We must go now."

Alexander looked at me, his lips tight. After a moment, he nodded. "Lindra and the others worked security for my father. They were out at the estate in the HRZ with him. Which means they came into Manhattan today, which also means they had a way of getting back there." Alexander rubbed his chin. "They must have used one of the Rose-Hart V-copters. Its transponder signal allows it to enter HRZ airspace without being shot down. Kris must have gotten flight plan approval from the Authority to enter Manhattan. She probably said the aircraft was carrying my father to the Allocators' Ball. She must have secured approval for a route out of the city as well."

My hopes rose. "Where would they have landed the aircraft?"

"All the commercial landing ports are closed for the Ball. The roof of my house is the logical place."

FORTY-ONE

We had four vehicles, but two were gas-powered jalopies banned below One Hundred and Tenth Street. A violation of Manhattan vehicle emission standards would ordinarily result in a fine, but tonight, with the Authority out in such force, we couldn't risk a traffic stop. Alexander, Mateo, Inky, and I piled into the sleek sedan that belonged to Alexander's family. Its tinted windows gave us full privacy, as long as we weren't pulled over by an Authority patrol—unlikely in Rose-Hart's vehicle. We each carried force rifles taken from Drake and his men, and had piled several more in the back. I was used to hating the people who held these things. It felt cold and ugly in my hand.

"I'll take the other car with Kross and the rest of Mateo's goons. I need to stop at my place," Nythan said. "I've got some equipment we'll need. And I want to secure the control-Colonies and data."

"What about Alissa and Lara?" Alexander asked.

I hesitated, conflicting emotions raging inside me. Alexander's eyes were on me, assessing. "Drop them near the subway station, Nythan. I'll tell them they need to find their own way home. There's no sense in leaving them here for Rose-Hart."

Nythan seemed relieved. "No problem."

"We've got to hurry, Nythan," I said. "Kortilla…"

"I hear you. Trust me, you'll want my familiars in case of trouble," Nythan said. "It's important Kortilla realizes I'm the hero here. Don't worry, it's not far from my condo to Alexander's place. It'll take you some time to warm up the V-copter. I'll be there ten minutes after you."

We piled into the vehicles. Surface traffic was light, but drone patrols were heavy outside the Vision Quad. Alexander directed the sedan through the gate surrounding his estate, then into an underground garage. An aged attendant greeted us at the interior door leading to the house. His face turned ghost-like when he saw the force rifles.

"Not a word, Gibbs," Alexander said. "No questions, and keep this quiet."

"Of course," he managed, wiping the shock from his face and restoring its original mask—the facade of someone in life-long service.

"How do you know he's not with Kris?" I asked Alexander once we were inside. "Or one of the others."

"Gibbs? I've known him my whole life. He's just—"

"A servant?" Mateo finished for him, contempt edging into his voice.

"Kris arranged for the V-copter to land on the roof of your house, for Drake and a bunch of goons to use it, and presumably take off again with us on board," I pointed out.

Realization crept onto Alexander's face.

"How many people in the house?"

"Three. The rest are out in the HRZ."

"Keep them occupied. Tell them how important they are to you. Just keep them together till Nythan gets here."

"What can he do?" Alexander asked.

"He's the master of computer viruses. He spreads them the way Inky spreads germs. He can take out the house communications and power. And their visers."

"They could still leave and find a way to contact her," Mateo pointed out. "I'll leave Kross here to keep an eye on them. He's hurt anyway."

"Kross? In charge of this place?" Inky said. "Oh yeah. He'll take good care of it, don't worry, rich boy." His rotten teeth somehow managed to sparkle.

Nythan, Kross, and the rest of the *Corazones* arrived eight minutes after we did. Alexander wore a troubled frown but did what I asked. I didn't imagine the staff liked having a street punk like Kross in here, much less being locked in a room with him. But Alexander gave the order. And Kross had a force rifle. Nythan duly released one of his viruses into the house network.

"I can't believe you are actually asking me to do this." He had a huge smile on his face. "To think, it's a favor to trash the Foster-Rose-Hart private network."

Alexander, Mateo, Nythan, and I headed to the roof, trailed by Inky and the rest of Mateo's gang. There were two aircraft on the rooftop landing pad, both surrounded by a glowing circle of lights, their twin propeller turrets rotated upwards. The aircraft looked like larger versions of the drones I saw in the sky above BC most days, except with a bigger fuselage and engines. Twin rose helix markings adorned the sides of both machines. I couldn't tell them apart. Alexander put his hand on each of the aircraft.

"This one is still warm," he said. "It must be our bird."

"You driving?" Nythan asked him. He had his Tuck bag slung over his shoulder. I presumed the familiars were inside.

"It's got autopilot, but I can fly her, if necessary."

I climbed into the co-pilot seat beside Alexander. Nythan, Mateo, and the *Corazones* occupied six of the ten plush loungers lining the rear of the aircraft. I fumbled with the seat belt, feeling foolish at my ineptitude.

"You've never flown before, have you?" Alexander asked me.

I clicked the safety harness into place. "Never had any place to go." I looked over at him. "I'm sorry about your father."

Alexander shook his head. "A father is something different than what I had. He provided material comfort, he expected a son he could display. He was a transactional man." I thought I saw some pain in his eyes, despite the cold words. "Still, I didn't think he would do something like the Culling. I cannot mourn him. Nor can I allow Kris to control Rose-Hart. Whatever her plans for the company, for those rods, she will not give it up. She does not accept defeat. Her desires cannot be sated."

"You said she wasn't always like this…"

His eyes tightened. "I've been thinking about that. Especially after what I witnessed tonight. It might be the power, Daniela. It started with that, I think, as I look back. That madness…Drake seemed to have been affected as well."

I remembered what I'd experienced as I drew upon my will to defeat Drake. That intoxicating feeling. I hadn't wanted to release it. My hands shook. People were not meant to have power such as we possessed. Perhaps there was a cost.

"If there is a way…to save her, I must do so," Alexander told me. "She is my sister."

I turned away from him. I understood that blood takes care of blood. I'd do the same for Mateo. But if I had to trade Kris for Kortilla, I would do it, regardless of what Alexander wanted. I hoped it didn't come to that.

"Let's go," I said.

He turned his attention to the controls. Data scrolled across a virtual screen projected onto the front window. He flicked his fingers, syncing his viser with the aircraft.

"It's got a pre-programmed flight path out of the city. Routing us due north, then east to the HRZ. Computers show about eighteen minutes of flying time." The engines were making purring sounds as Alexander spoke. "Three minutes until takeoff. I'm signaling Manhattan control to let them know we'll be airborne shortly."

"What happens if your sister figures out it's not Drake returning?" I asked.

"The house is equipped with defensive capabilities in case of a terrorist attack. Armed drones, as well as anti-aircraft countermeasures. If Kris wanted to shoot us down, she could. This is a transit model, not a fighter. It doesn't have any weapons."

"We need a better plan than that."

"Then we've got about eighteen minutes to come up with one."

CHAPTER

FORTY-TWO

Alexander let the autopilot have control. I watched the lights of Manhattan fade into the distance through the V-copter's window. The city glittered within the outline of my likeness as we pulled away from the ground. I wore a face I barely recognized, one beset with fatigue and worry. It was a somber picture, despite the quiet beauty of the lights below.

Alexander sent schematics of the estate to our visers. It made his city house look like a backyard tent. A main house, two separate guest houses, a servants' residence, two pools, tennis courts, and separate outdoor and indoor track facilities sprawled across a walled estate on a private oceanfront. I studied Alexander's face when I should've been memorizing the building interiors. What did growing up with such luxury do to a person? I wondered what he'd think of Aba's place.

A klaxon rang when we entered the restricted airspace of the HRZ. I gazed downward. Lights were sparse. But even without being able to see the details, I knew the homes below were luxurious, spacious, and used only occasionally by their owners. This was the countryside playground of the elite.

"We should just bomb the place," Mateo said.

It was an emotional and stupid thing to say. Typical of Mateo. But I knew exactly how he felt. I doubted Alexander did.

"Four minutes till we reach estate airspace," Alexander announced as he checked gauges and screens. Simulated images of the structures below appeared on the window in front of me: great expanses of watered grass, soil-planted trees, giant climate-regulated homes that could've housed the entirety of my Bronx City tenement.

"You ready, Nythan?" Alexander called out.

"Just keep flying," Nythan replied. "I'll be ready."

Alexander restored the aircraft to manual flight mode. He pointed the control stick downward. The klaxon sounded.

"PLEASE BE ADVISED THAT YOU HAVE DEVIATED FROM YOUR PRE-PLANNED FLIGHT PATH," said the U-cab lady's twin sister.

The ground leaped upwards as Alexander pressed down on the controls. The aircraft began to jump like a bicycle over rocky ground. The engines took on an unruly tone.

"Air turbulence," Alexander told us unnecessarily. "Can your little boys handle this, Nythan?"

"You do your job, I'll do mine."

The plane plunged violently, as if a giant hand had slapped it from above. If I'd had anything left in my stomach, I would've shared it with the floor.

"YOU HAVE DROPPED BELOW THE RECOMMENDED CRUISING ALTITUDE FOR THIS AIRCRAFT. SAFETY PROTOCOLS WILL ENGAGE IN THREE, TWO..."

"Override," Alexander barked.

Even in the darkness, I could feel how close we were to the ground. The lights were no more than twenty feet below us. The aircraft jerked up, down, then to the side. The unhappy groaning of the engines was near deafening as they strained to deal with the wind conditions. Alexander gripped the control stick with both hands, eyes focused on the engine readouts.

"Almost there," Alexander yelled.

The aircraft yelled back. An angry alarm sounded, piercing and urgent. The cockpit lights flashed an ugly red.

"FOREIGN OBJECTS ON A COLLISION COURSE WITH THIS AIRCRAFT. YOU ARE ADVISED TO ALTER COURSE IMMEDIATELY."

"Missiles incoming, Nythan," Alexander shouted.

"Open the frakkin' door, then!" Nythan called back.

Alexander flicked the fingers on his visered hand even as he continued to wrestle with the control stick. Frigid wind swept into the aircraft like an avalanche down a mountain. The noise was deafening. My lungs burned as the icy air filled them.

A radar image appeared on the window in front of me, an infrared visual beside it. On the screen, the missiles looked like black spears, the heat of their engine fire flashing red behind them. The distance between us and the projectiles dwindled. Two thousand, one thousand, five hundred. Alexander yanked the stick; the aircraft banked hard to the left. The missiles veered right, following the floating familiar Nythan had hurled out the door. The smaller machine's phantom transmission tempted the missiles like red meat for a hound.

Alexander pulled hard on the control. The engines raged in agony. I was hurled forward, the restraints saving me from an unpleasant meeting with the panel in front of me. The aircraft slowed far quicker than I would've thought possible. I heard the engines rotate into a vertical position. Then an explosion erupted to my right—a cascade of angry color. The aircraft shook again. Debris struck our hull, the sound like hail on a flimsy roof.

"That should foul up their infrared for a bit," Nythan said. "Take us down."

The engines were in vertical landing mode. Alexander eased us down onto the lush grass of the Foster-Rose-Hart estate. The aircraft gave a final jolt, then was still. The silence that followed was disconcerting. I could hear ocean waves crashing on a nearby beach.

"They might think they got us, at least for a couple of minutes," Alexander said. "But Nythan, you better get little drone number two moving."

"Already on his way, big boy."

Alexander and I slid out of our seats, heading for the exits. Mateo and I clasped hands as I stood at the door.

"Careful, sis'," he told me. "You only think you're indestructible."

"You too. Bail me out if I get into trouble."

Alexander swung himself out the exit, down the ladder, disappearing into the night. I followed. I heard Mateo barking at his men as my feet touched the ground. Alexander and I had left our rifles behind. There was no choice given Nythan's plan.

"Make sure Kortilla knows it was my drones, my idea," he called out to us.

I could see the lights of the main house about a thousand meters away. The engines of Nythan's familiar hovered behind us, emitting a steady hum. Salty gusts whipped across my face.

"Let's go," I said, taking off at a full sprint. Alexander did the same.

We ran parallel for the first one hundred meters. Running beside Alexander was like running beside a train. Perfect rhythm, perfect strides. It was also a stupid risk. I swerved away, heading right. He banked left. We lost each other in the darkness.

I forced myself to keep swerving as I ran. The cut grass was soft and slightly damp. I took my speed down a notch, worried about my footing as I dashed in random directions. Five hundred meters left. I imagined infrared scopes searching through the darkness, gunmen on the house's balcony hungry for a kill. I wasn't wrong. My spider-sense jolted a warning just in time for me to dive to the ground, sliding forward on the grass. The area behind me flashed and sizzled as if struck by lightning. Another volley of force blasts erupted, these coming from at least one hundred meters behind me as Mateo, Nythan, and the others opened fire. They didn't have night-vision scopes, but they could shoot at the flashes. I heard Nythan's drone flying past me. I rolled to my left, then hurried to my feet, pouring on the speed. I swerved left some more, then to the right again. More rifle flashes. Two blazes pulsed to my left. Probably at Alexander. More lightning crackled towards the darkness behind me, trying to quiet our covering fire. Two hundred meters left. I was an easy target this close. Floodlights clicked on, turning the night into day. I hit the ground, rolling as quickly as I could. My spider-sense rang in my head like a hundred church bells. A force rifle discharge roasted the grass six inches to my left. More covering fire rang out, blast after blast. The weapons' impact had punched several gaping holes in the walls of the house. A small fire burned inside. The walls were flame resistant, but not the interior furnishings. The rich did like their expensive antiques. Another explosion to my left targeted Alexander. They had us. But darkness surged forth to save us.

Nythan's familiar had gotten close enough to work its magic. The wave it unleashed was silent, but magnificently potent. No more lights, no more computers, no more visers, no more force rifles. It was all dead. Anything with a power core in the path of the pulse wave was extinguished. Eat that, Kristolan—bet you didn't see a directional EMP blast coming.

I got to my feet, dashing the remaining distance to the house. Alexander met me at one of the breaches. I squeezed his shoulder in darkness. I smelled smoke. The fire-suppression system would have been knocked out too. I clenched and unclenched my fists, impatient for Mateo to arrive. The ten seconds it took felt like an hour before my brother and the *Corazones* emerged from the darkness.

"Keep a perimeter—at least twenty feet back. Spread out, keep away from the house," I reminded them. "Smart and stubborn doesn't mean you can't be trilled. Kris is powerful. Give us the light sticks and two functional pulse rifles."

"Dee, let me go in. There is no way some highborn is controlling my mind," Mateo insisted. "Kortilla is my blood too."

I wrapped a hand around the back of my brother's neck. "I know you're family with her, Mateo. But please, listen to me, like you have never done before, *hermano*. Kristolan will own you if you come near her. The way I owned Drake in the garage. I can handle anything in there, except losing you or Kortilla. You and your boys cover the exits. Make sure she doesn't try to get out with Kortilla. You hear me?"

"I hear," Mateo grumbled. I released him.

"Let's go get Kortilla," I said to Alexander.

"If there is a way, without harming Kris, we take it," he replied.

I nodded, but it was a lie. I wasn't any less determined to do whatever had to be done.

FORTY-THREE

We climbed into the blast hole, both of us with force rifles in hand, light sticks slung around our necks. The gun was heavy, strange. I knew how to pull a trigger, but I didn't have much faith in my aim. I'd never shot a gun before, much less a force rifle. Still, I was glad to have it, particularly since Kris didn't have one that worked anymore.

"Lifts will be out," Alexander whispered. "Which means the stairs are the only way in or out. The central staircase is straight ahead, then take your first right. There's back stairs as well. She might try to get out that way. I'll take it. The family suites are on the third floor. Kris likes grand spaces. She'll be up there, either in our father's room or her own."

"I'll see you up there," I told him, my words more confident than my legs.

I followed Alexander's directions, picking my way carefully through the near darkness, both hands on the rifle. I reached the main staircase and gazed upwards. It was a switch-back construction, with elaborate handrails and thick carpets covering the steps. I began to climb. There was smoke on the second floor. It wasn't critical yet, but time was running short.

I heard a force rifle blast in the distance. Then a second. Maybe some of Kris's men trying to leave. Kris probably paid well, but sticking around unarmed in a burning house that was under attack was a hard call to answer.

I kept climbing, step-by-step. Even with the light stick, I couldn't see more than a few feet ahead of me. The acrid air made my eyes water. A sound to my right made me spin. I raised the rifle. Someone was running through the dark, coming hard. My finger twitched on the trigger, my mind raced. *Kris would never come at me this way.* I hesitated. Kortilla exploded out of the night. She came right at me, arms out, her face crazed.

"K—wait!" I yelled. It was no use.

She grabbed the rifle. Her hands struggled with mine. I needed to calm her down. But if I took my mind off the fight, Kortilla was going to blow my head off. Her hand fought with mine at the trigger. We shoved each other, the rifle wedged between us. There was only one way to do this. I told myself Kortilla would understand. I took a step backwards, turning to my side as I did. Kortilla, in her agitated state, didn't anticipate the move. Her strength and momentum sent her flying past me toward the stairs. She missed the first step in the darkness, as I knew she would. I caught the back of her shirt as she fell forward, enough to slow her down. I needed a bit of space, but I didn't want her to end up with a broken neck. Once I saw Kortilla's hands were in front of her, I let go. She'd be on me again in a few moments, but that was all I needed.

I gathered my will. Smoke rose from the floor below. My spider-sense wanted me out of here. I felt dizzy, but managed to find the cold within. I drew the essence, preparing to strike at my friend, my sister. For her own good. Even if it drove me mad. That was when I felt the blade press against my neck. Kris dug the pointy tip through the Korean skin I wore, into the flesh of my collar bone—not too deep, just enough to draw blood. A message.

"Grab the gun," Kris ordered.

The strong hands emerged from the polluted mist around me and took my force rifle. Kris's goon had a shaved head, a swollen face, and nothing but hate in his eyes.

Kortilla emerged from the staircase, her face contorted like a hissing cat. She flexed her fingers as if they were claws.

"Easy, pet, I've got our enemy under control now," Kris crooned. "Keep an eye out for her wicked friends—and my brother."

Kortilla took a last, hungry look at me before disappearing into the darkness to do her master's bidding. I seethed in Kris's clutches. "What did you do to her?"

Kris giggled like a dinner bell, the sound light, and sickly merry. "The power can be used…creatively. It is so much more than you realize. How many are still out there?"

"Six, all armed with ranged weapons. Far away and hidden in the dark. I know the limits of your power. Every vehicle within ten miles has been fried by the EMP blast, except the V-copter. You're not getting out of here. Either you burn alive in this house or get roasted by force blasts outside."

"Not with you and Kortilla as my hostages," Kris said. "That's your blood out there, right? Your brother and his gang. Oh, I know them well. They aren't going to risk you two precious things getting hurt."

I spat, defying the blade at my throat. "They won't let you escape. And there are too many out there for you to trill. Mateo defied your power before, in the Manhattan safe house when you tried to arrange the assassination of your father."

She scoffed at my accusation, but it was half-hearted. I wondered if Alexander was nearby. It was too dark in here for him to fire, even if he was close. Even if he was willing to shoot his sister.

"Why kill Landrew now? So public—not like you at all," I goaded.

"I was saving myself. The bastard found out I could trill. You didn't know my father. He could never allow a power like that to exist out of his control. He was planning to chip me. My own father. He had some experimental device developed by the Koreans to use on me. He would've done the same to you, once he found out what you are. You should be thanking me."

"And what do you plan to do with the controlColonies?" I sneered, although she couldn't see it. "I sense your hunger. You are no better than your father."

She answered by pressing her blade harder. "I just need to walk out of here, and you're going to help me."

She shoved me towards the stairs. I took a single step then pushed back. The smoke was spreading upwards.

"You richies don't get the barrio. Never will. Mateo isn't going to let you take me anywhere, nor Kortilla. I might die when Mateo and his boys take you down, but you're not leaving this place alive. Those are their orders."

I sensed the power within her. Her mind probed mine. I opened myself to her as much as I dared, the power within our minds drawing us together, as it had with Drake. "You know I'm telling the truth."

"Then we'll die together," Kris told me. "It is too bad it ends like this. We could have helped each other. I could have been your teacher." She let a hint of fanaticism creep into her voice. She sounded convincing.

But I knew she lied. Her mind was so close to mine. Emotion raged within her. I sensed her. She was a great actress. She could shape her words into any form, making them as hard or bitter or sweet as she chose. But she did not want to die. She feared leaving this world, the way a child fears relinquishing a precious toy.

"A bargain," I offered to her, letting her hear fear as I spoke.

"What bargain?" Kris spat her wariness.

"Kortilla, Mateo, and Alexander go free, no harm comes to the rest of the *Corazones*. In exchange, you get everything you want."

Her blade pressed at me again. "I thought you were an AT genius. Are you an idiot, or do you think I'm one? How do you have anything I want?"

"You want to be the singular voice in the night. To have this world for yourself, gazing down on all you survey. Nothing less will satisfy you, and I can deliver it. I will give myself to you. My mind becomes yours, a slave to your will. No chip required."

Kris's breathing stopped. "How?"

"I'll lower my defenses. Highborn can be trilled. Alexander and I did it, with Drake. That's how we got here. Even genetically enhanced mental defenses can be breached by multiple powerful minds. Or if the subject is willing. I'll lower my barrier and give my mind to you. In exchange for my brother's life, and my sister Kortilla's, and the others I care about. And for your promise to use the controlColonies to find a cure for the Waste. Its location is in my mind. Stop the Culling. You don't need it. You will be the master triller, the only person in the world to develop the power. And you will have the control-Colonies. There will never be another like you." I reached out with my mind, trying to sense Alexander. I hoped he would understand what I had to do. He had to be there, but I could feel nothing except Kristolan's twisted desires.

"You lie," Kris accused, but her declaration was laced with suppressed longing. I offered the fruit of Eden. "Why would

you willingly become a slave? You are like Alexander—a fighter, a creature of honor, a fool."

"There can only be one chosen, one queen. So I am already
dead, one way or another." I sucked at the foul air, letting desperation inundate my voice. "I choose to give my life for those
it has always belonged to: Mateo, Kortilla, my blood. You feel
the truth of my words: I have lived only for Mateo. Everything
I have ever done, coming to Tuck, helping Havelock, it was to
save my brother. And I failed. This is my last chance." I opened
more of my mind to her, letting her sense this part of me, the
deepest core of my being.

Kris ached for my promise to be true. But she was also a
master of deception—wary of others who might try to wield
lies against her. "You speak the truth about your brother, but
that is not the same as being willing to become a slave."

"I open myself to you now. There is nothing more for you
to believe or disbelieve. My mind is yours. You need only take
the briefest glance and it is done. The truth is before you."

I opened my mind to Kristolan. My body shook as I did it.
I was opening myself to something worse than death. I hid my
last bit of hope in a tiny corner of myself, a place that I thought
she would not see.

Around me was a sphere, the barrier of ice that engulfed
me. It was not a single piece, but hundreds of layers of varying
density and temperature, each rotating to form a single, impenetrable wall of impossible strength. Steam rose from its
crystalline surface. I had lived my life within its protective
shell. Now, I commanded it to open. It was like stepping outside in a blizzard naked. In that moment, I was alone as I'd ever
been.

A tiny hole formed on one side of the ice. A tunnel to
my mind. Reluctantly, it grew, widening like a sinkhole in the
earth, swallowing the hard-forged defenses of my being. What

began as a mere pinprick became a crack, then a portal so massive that it made a slicing arc through the shell surrounding me. The gaping hole begged Kristolan to come collar me.

Her cold will appeared at the fringe of my consciousness, a pair of eyes in the distance. In her mind, she saw what I had done. She recognized the opening that led to my innermost mind. It shocked her. Once inside, she could impose her whims upon me.

The temptation was too great. Her calculations were simple: the reward near incalculable, and she knew of no risk. At worst, the hole would close and she would kill me with the knife. Kristolan's probing eyes soon became the whole of her will.

A magnificent beast of legend appeared within my consciousness and flew hard at the passage into my mind—a dragon born of dreams. The creature had eyes the same color as Kristolan's set within its massive, tapered head. Its wings were like emerald glass, its scales gleaming like amethysts set out in the sun. The beast soared with the agility of a hawk and the grace of a swan. But for all its beauty, there was no mistaking its hunger. It was a creature with greed in its heart. It was Kristolan's will sent to claim me, but it carried the essence of her mind within its phantom form.

The way to my mind remained opened. The dragon's eyes darted about, searching for danger, for deception. It came to the precipice. Somewhere, Kris hesitated. Then the beast flapped its great wings, thrusting itself within the barrier, seeking to evade whatever trap I might spring at the last moment. It passed completely through the immense sphere that had defended me, a roar of delight escaping its lips. Victory. Until the dragon slammed into the unyielding power of Alexander's mind, waiting unseen within my own.

His will lashed out at Kristolan. She recoiled with agonizing fury. I sensed her confusion, which quickly turned to fear. She had never dared face a highborn mind. She did not understand the implications of attempting to impose her dominance on a highborn triller. The will she had sent was linked with her own mind, her essence. A highborn triller did not merely defend a mind; a triller could attack through the link. Kris had ventured out of the castle that was her own self, and placed herself in a battle against two trillers. I shut the icy sphere surrounding my being, sealing her in. There would be no escape. I closed in on Kristolan like an unstoppable glacier. She struck at Alexander, then me, with the desperate madness of a cornered beast. Waves of anger pushed against me. My mind held. But Alexander buckled. He stopped attacking her. *He doesn't want to hurt her*, I realized.

Kris and her dragon knew no mercy. Free from her brother's attack, she came at me. A blade sank into my mind. Somewhere, I screamed. White-hot pain cut through me. She was so much stronger than me; I was a mere leaf in the wind. She pounded my will. Without Alexander's help, she would destroy my mind. Pressure built around me. My cold sphere trembled. It walls drew inward. I was afraid. I glimpsed a void worse than death. *Never trust a highborn.*

A storm of cold swept over me, its power enveloping me. At once, I grew stronger. A familiar presence returned. Alexander's strength blended with my own. Kris's onslaught faltered. I hammered my will against hers. Alexander did the same. There was no hesitation this time. We attacked, our wills and minds linked. The strength, the madness, the desire that made up Kristolan fell before us. Together, we ground her mind to dust.

The hand at my throat went limp. I snatched the knife from Kris and slashed at her minion beside me. The blade sank into his throat. A geyser of blood erupted upwards. Alexander exploded through the darkness, his shoulder striking the dying man, sending him toppling down the stairwell with an ugly thud.

Kortilla remained nearby, in the darkness. I prepared to meet her assault with a trill. But somehow she came at me with tears rather than hate. Alexander tried to jump between us, not trusting what he saw, but I held him aside with an outstretched arm. I knew Kortilla's soul as well as my own. She had vanquished whatever ills Kris had put into her head. I grabbed my friend in my arms, my sister. I didn't want to let go.

FORTY-FOUR

We set down on the landing pad of Alexander's Manhattan home just as dawn broke above the eastern horizon. Mateo and his *Corazones* exited first, each dirty, exhausted, and elated. The bonuses Alexander had promised them were enough that they might count themselves rich—by Bronx City standards. For the next few months, at least.

Mateo stayed behind on the roof to wait for me. He looked at me with a face far less innocent than I had seen before. He was even more haggard than his men, and I feared it wasn't just from the long days and nights he had endured. My throat went stiff at the sight. A reminder of my failure.

I didn't say what I felt. I held him, for just a brief moment, then let him go.

"Go see Aba," I told him.

"I'll put in a good word for you," Mateo said.

"It won't do any good, but thanks."

He left to join the others. Those he considered his blood.

Kortilla and Nythan exited next. I had put in the best word I could for Nythan with Kortilla. He had come through for me in the end, and Kortilla could do worse than to spend some time with our resident genius. I certainly needed Nythan if I was to going to find a cure.

My vouching might have done a bit of good. He'd kept Kortilla's attention for a few hours, which was no easy thing to manage. I pulled her beside me. Nythan stopped as well, not quite willing to relinquish her company.

"Sorry for dragging you into this," I told her.

"We've been in this together since we were five, *hermana*. Blood takes care of blood."

Alexander exited just as the engines finished powering down. The rooftop became quiet without their constant hum.

"What will happen to Kris?" I asked him.

"The latest update is that she is still unresponsive to stimuli. Her organs are functioning, but brain activity is minimal. Our doctors have moved her to a private facility. They'll keep a close eye on her and report any change to me."

"Can you cure this thing?" I asked and pleaded. "Once Nythan gets you the controlColonies and the data, can we actually save Mateo?"

"There are treatments," Alexander assured me. "You told me Dr. Willis mentioned some of that to you. I have access to some very fine medical personnel. Get him there. It gives him time, at least. That's all I can promise for now."

"That's good for one person. What about the rest of Bronx City? And all the other places the Waste may be lurking."

"I'll make arrangements to set Nythan up at a new facility in Bronx City. I'll get him as many resources as I can. Perhaps we can track down Dr. Willis, or her research, at least."

"I know everything she knows and more," Nythan boasted, his chest puffed. I knew without looking that Kortilla was rolling her eyes. "We've got the data and rods."

I shook my head. "Nythan, you may be almost as brilliant as you think you are. But you are but one sixteen-year-old mind. We need Rose-Hart scientists, the company's money, its labs."

Alexander hesitated. "I'll try."

"But Kris is...you're Landrew's heir now, right?"

"As I mentioned before, it's more complicated than that. Arik is actually the oldest. That's why Kris needed the control-Colonies. For leverage."

"But you have some unique advantages, don't you, big guy?" Nythan pointed out. "Like being able to trill for instance."

Alexander looked at Nythan as if the smaller boy had struck him. "I'm not my sister, nor my father. I will not manipulate minds for such a purpose."

"That's why the bad guys usually win," Nythan replied.

My life had often shown me that Nythan was right. I remembered Kristolan's words about Alexander: *A fighter, a creature of honor, a fool.* She'd named me as being the same. She was wrong. I hadn't forgotten where I came from: the bottom of the iceberg. I would not abandon my people. Alexander's wealth allowed him to afford such a thing as honor. I would fight, however I must.

A fresh blaze of light from the east caught hold of us, the rays shining through a corridor of soaring towers lined up like soldiers at attention. It was a fiery passage that could lead anywhere. I looked around at the people who stood beside me now. Trust was a rare thing. Loyalty even rarer. I wrapped one arm around Kortilla, and the other around Alexander. Nythan dared to nudge in next to Kortilla.

"As a wise captain once said: 'We have done the impossible, and that makes us mighty,'" Nythan proclaimed.

I smiled at him, and the rest of my friends around me. We still had battles to fight. But in that moment, this world seemed just fine.

THE END

Join my mailing list at juliannorth.com and receive a free short story set in the same world as *Age of Order* (albeit with a very different narrator). I am a new author. If you enjoyed *Age of Order*, please help others find it by leaving a review on Amazon.

T hank you for going on this journey with me. And it has been a journey. *Age of Order* was inspired by my experiences dealing with school admissions for my young sons in my adopted home of New York City—truly a dystopian experience. While this book takes place in a distant future, elements of the society reflected within these pages are all too real. The story grew from this seed, then took on a life of its own. Writing in the dim hours after my kids went to sleep, the story came together remarkably quickly, as if aching to be told. I hope you found something that you enjoyed within these pages.

I must also offer a reminder and some apologies. First, let me remind everyone that this is a *story*. Those of you familiar with New York City may recognize certain locations, words and sentiments. Please remember that all of this is fiction. Next, to those of you who participate in track and field: I am sorry. I used plenty of artistic license. It was all for the story. Finally, readers familiar with naming customs in many Spanish-speaking countries will have recognized that I made some compromises for the story in this area as well. Daniela Machado should really be Daniela Machado Avila. Kortilla's proper name should be Kortilla Gonzales Menendez. During editing and beta reading it became clear that some English-speaking readers unaccustomed to the different naming conventions kept thinking they were spotting errors in the text. The hyphenated highborn names were causing additional confusion. My solution was to strip Daniela and Kortilla of their maternal names. The compromise still itches.

Writing *Age of Order* has been a privilege. That you have taken the time to read it is an honor. I offer my thanks and a deep highborn-style bow.

Blood takes care of blood.

CPSIA information can be obtained
at www.ICGtesting.com
Printed in the USA
LVOW13s1452180318
570238LV00009B/359/P